Seduced at Sea

MICHELLE CONDER
SCARLET WILSON
ANDREA LAURENCE

MILLS & BOON

First Published in Great Britain 2019
by Mills & Boon, an imprint of HarperCollins*Publishers*
1 London Bridge Street, London, SE1 9GF

SEDUCED AT SEA © 2019 Harlequin Books S. A.

His Last Chance at Redemption © 2012 Michelle Conder
Holiday with the Millionaire © 2016 Scarlet Wilson
More Than He Expected © 2012 Andrea Laurence

ISBN: 978-0-263-27745-6

0919

MIX
Paper from
responsible sources
FSC
www.fsc.org
FSC C007454

This book is produced from independently certified FSC™
paper to ensure responsible forest management.

For more information visit: www.harpercollins.co.uk/green

Printed and bound in Spain
by CPI, Barcelona

HIS LAST CHANCE AT REDEMPTION

MICHELLE CONDER

For Finn, Pia and Reif.

CHAPTER ONE

COULD a man really die of boredom?

Leonid Aleksandrov stared down at his plate of—what had he ordered? Beef? Lamb?—and tried to blank out the blonde actress prattling away at him across the table as if he was one of her girlfriends.

To be fair it was most likely nervous chatter because, he had the good grace to acknowledge, he was a man on the edge. At the end of his tether, his executive assistant, Danny Butler, would say, and even a blind Russian boar could sense that.

But how could he be anything else? The tragedy that had occurred this week was newsworthy all over the world and the press were once again snapping at his heels to get a piece of him. Questioning who he was and sniffing into his past. Looking for Mafia connections one minute and then calling him a hero the next. But a true hero didn't have things in his life he regretted, did he?

Not that anyone would find anything on him. Seventeen years ago Leo had created a new identity for himself and thanks to Mother Russia being a country of smoke and mirrors he'd been able to bury the misery of his real childhood and reinvent a whole new one.

A much more palatable one.

So far no one knew any better. The press surmised that he was a dangerous man and, somewhat ironically, they didn't know the half of it.

But what on earth had possessed him—on his first day back in London—to take the latest 'it girl' to lunch at this high-end, nosey London eatery? On her birthday of all days.

Ah, yes, sex. Respite. A moment's relaxation. The gym had failed this week and he'd been looking for another outlet.

But no doubt Danny had thought no-frills sex in a hotel room was a bit cold-blooded on the actress's special day; hence the lunch date.

Leo shook his head. Danny had been with him for eight years now and even though he was as close to a friend as Leo had ever had, he was still a bit too modern and senti-mental for Leo's liking. And he'd blast him for suggesting the actress meet him in the hotel *restaurant* instead of the hotel *penthouse*.

What he had wanted was to get laid and get back to work, not sit down to a three course luncheon. Now, however, after forty minutes of polite chitchat about nothing more interest-ing than hairstyles and movie shoots, his libido had hit rock bottom.

Thank you, Danny boy.

'Leo, I swear, if I didn't know any better I'd think you hadn't listened to a word I've said.'

So not entirely without a brain then. That was something at least. A month ago they'd met at a party and she'd been texting on and off with innocent little invitations for Leo to attend this and that ever since. Well, 'this and that' was nigh and he couldn't have been less interested in taking things fur-ther if he was standing next to her wax look-alike at Madame Tussauds. In fact, right now, that would be preferable. Quieter, at least.

Leo pushed his half-eaten lunch aside and dropped his napkin onto his plate.

'Tiffany, it's been *enthralling*, but I have to go. Finish up. Have dessert—' he hesitated as he glanced at her emaciated figure '—or not.' He pushed back his chair and paused when he saw her overly plump bottom lip quiver; which may have been a trick of the light because a moment later her composure was flawless.

'Just like that?' She waved her hand insouciantly, her actor's face firmly in place. 'And to think people said you were dynamic. Fascinating. *Exciting*.'

Leo's eyes narrowed. 'We're in the wrong place for me to show you exciting, *dorogusha*, and now I'm all out of time.'

And interest.

'They also said you were heartless.' That last was delivered without even a hint of bitterness and his eyes narrowed on the challenging tilt of her head, his senses homing in on the purr in her voice.

So that was it. He was a challenge to her. A mountain she wanted to conquer. He could understand that even though he wasn't a man driven by challenges. He'd learned early on that rising to a challenge usually led to mistakes, pain. Leo didn't do that. He wanted something; he got it. No challenge required.

And Tiffany Tait had definitely overplayed her hand with that comment. Smarter women than her had tried to get their hooks into him without success. He was considered the consummate commitment-phobe and it was a reputation he had carefully cultivated for years.

He stood and buttoned his single-breasted suit jacket. '*They* are right. I am without a heart and no woman will ever change that. Something to remember next time you want to play games.'

With that he walked out. Leaving her and the Cartier bracelet Danny had kindly procured for her as a birthday gift at the last minute. No doubt Leo would hear about his unchivalrous behaviour in some gossip rag at some stage. Not that he cared. Today he'd been looking for a few moments of oblivion to push aside the memory of five of his men being buried alive in an accident on one of his construction sites, and the agony of lifting mountains of cement and steel alongside rescue crews all week to get to them.

They'd reached two in time; the other three were gone. Just like his uncle seventeen years earlier.

Leo's mouth pulled tight as he wound his way through the 'beautiful people' who cast covert glances from behind their crystal glasses.

Usually he loved his life. Proclaimed the richest man in Russia, with enough super toys to fill any action flick, a surfeit of women clamouring to warm his bed and a business he loved—he was understandably riding high. Today he'd almost welcome being back at the end of his father's belt than return to work.

And really he shouldn't have been rude to Tiffany Tait. It wasn't her fault she bored him. He chose that type of woman for a reason—physical gratification and lack of emotional connection. If he was getting bored with eye candy he'd just have to get over himself.

Thirty minutes later and feeling marginally better now that the restaurant ordeal was over he stalked through his outer office and told his new secretary to get Danny—immediately.

Still nervous of him, she cleared her throat before speaking. 'He's already waiting for you, Mr Aleksandrov.'

'Leo,' he corrected her, pushing open his office door and striding inside.

'If you ever send me to a poncy restaurant again instead of a private suite when I tell you I want to get laid I'll fire you.'

'It's her birthday,' Danny replied smoothly.

Leo dropped into his leather-and-chrome chair and surveyed the mountain of paperwork that had accumulated on his desk in his absence.

'I don't care if it's her last day on earth. We both would have had a better time in a bed. Send her another something from somewhere, would you?' He picked up a stock market report and scowled. Bloody volatile fear-driven markets.

When would people learn not to react to every flicker of the sun's rays as if it was about to go out?

'You were rude, then?'

Leo didn't look up. 'It's possible.'

He heard Danny sigh. 'I was about to call you back anyway. You have bigger problems to contend with right now.'

Leo went still at his EA's ominous tone. *Bohze*, not another site problem.

He didn't ask, just waited for Danny to continue. But instead of saying anything, Danny handed him a pink sheet of paper with tiny coloured flowers dotted along the top.

Leo read the brief message and his foul mood plummeted.

'You're not serious?'

'It seems so. I haven't been able to reach her by phone.'

'Have you had Security try to track her down?'

'They're on it but no luck so far. She says she's heading to Spain.'

'I can read.'

A heavy silence fell between them and Leo scanned the note once again to make sure he hadn't been mistaken.

Then he leaned back in his chair and rubbed the back of his neck, feeling his muscles bunch but not release. He crumpled the pink paper in his fist and lobbed it across the room. 'How many hours do we have?'

'Two. The childcare centre closes at five.'

Leo swore under his breath and jerked to his feet.

'It's only for the long weekend. She'll be back on Monday,' Danny added, highlighting the only positive in the message.

Leo stared out of his office window and watched the London Eye do a lazy circuit in the glittering summer sunshine. The wharf was a hive of teeming tourists probably spending more money than they had and he'd gladly hand over half of his vast fortune to any one of them if they could solve his current problem.

Four years ago he'd met a young model at Brussels Airport

when all flights had been grounded due to inclement weather. Leo hadn't even thought twice about it. Beautiful, more-than-willing woman, long night. It made sense.

Her wanting to get pregnant to a rich stranger still didn't. The woman in question had been on the hunt for a rich husband instead of a rich career and had deliberately used a tampered condom. Three months later she'd come to him and told him the 'good' news.

She'd been hoping for a ring. What she'd got was a house and a monthly allowance once paternity had been confirmed.

Leo wasn't father material. He had blood running through his veins he had never intended to pass on. The fact that this model—Amanda Weston—had duped him had made him crazy. After the fog had cleared and logic had returned he'd done the honourable thing. He'd covered all her financial expenses and made her promise to keep the boy as far away from him as possible. He might have inadvertently given someone life but he wasn't about to completely stuff it up by being part of the child's life as well.

Recollections of his own childhood danced at the edges of his mind like circus performers wielding brightly coloured batons with which to prod him. First the death of three of his men had reminded him of the horrendous circumstances surrounding his beloved uncle's death and now the prospect of having to care for his three-year-old son was bringing up even worse memories. His mother. His father. His *brother*.

With ruthless determination Leo banished his memories and refocused on the one thing he could trust. Work.

He turned back to Danny. 'What's happening with the Thessaly ethanol plant?'

'So, you still haven't said. Are you going to Paris this weekend with Simon, or not?'

Lexi stopped trying to put the wheel back on a broken toy

truck and looked over at her best friend and business partner, Aimee Madigan.

Aimee had one eye on the group of kids enjoying free play at the Little Angels childcare centre they had started together two years ago and the other on the yarn she was carefully winding back into a ball. 'And please don't tell me you have to work,' her friend added with a sense of resigned certainty.

Lexi grimaced. She was supposed to be heading to Paris for the long weekend with a guy she'd been seeing casually for two months. And no doubt Simon would expect their relationship to advance to the next stage—sex—but Lexi wasn't convinced that was such a good idea.

She had let herself be worn down by a man's pursuit once before and the experience still left a bitter taste in her mouth. Only she didn't really want to be worn down. The truth was, her life was wonderful as it was; she'd let herself be weakened once before by a man's pursuit and the experience still left a bitter taste in her mouth. 'You know the second centre is at a crucial stage of the planning. If I don't get the loan approved in the next week or so, we won't have one.'

'I take it things didn't go so well then with Darth Vader this morning?'

Lexi grinned at Aimee's use of the pet moniker they had attributed to their hard-nosed bank manager and tried not to feel despondent. 'He's still got some concerns about how much the renovations are costing and some aspects of the business plan.'

'I wish I could help you.'

Lexi shook her head. 'This is my area of the business and you do enough around here. I'll sort it somehow.'

Aimee stopped winding her wool and looked at Lexi as if she'd just had a great idea. 'I know, maybe you could do that somewhere between the Arc de Triomphe and the Louvre,' she suggested, only half tongue-in-cheek.

'Oh, yeah, I'm sure Simon would *really* love that!' Lexi laughed.

'Well, he *is* shelling out for The Ritz so it seems a shame to miss it altogether. And he does seem very nice.'

'He is,' Lexi replied, wishing Aimee would let the topic drop.

'Lex, you're still using work as an excuse to avoid having a proper relationship with a man,' Aimee reproved.

Lexi scraped her finger on the toy car. 'Ow, damn.' She sucked the scratch and tried to keep her answer light and simple. 'Maybe I just haven't met the love of my life yet.'

'And you won't with the amount of hours you spend here.'

'I'm happy.'

'Not every man is an immature skunk like Brandon, Lex, and it has been four years.'

Lexi pulled a face. She'd been best friends with Aimee since high school and she knew her friend had her best interests at heart. And she also knew Aimee was right, but Brandon's betrayal had echoed that of her father's just a little too closely and Lexi wasn't at all sure she was willing to risk her heart again any time soon.

'I know that,' she said on a sigh. And she did. But even thinking about having a relationship brought up all her old insecurities and the truth, which she was far too embarrassed to ever admit to anyone—including Aimee—was that she wasn't great at sex. Wasn't overly sexual at all. Which, if she was being completely honest, was the main reason she didn't want to go to Paris. That and the fact that she didn't actually *want* to have sex with Simon. But admitting that made her feel as if there was something wrong with her.

And maybe there was… Wasn't that what Brandon had implied?

She walked over to give the truck back to the three-year-old who had broken it. 'Here you go, Jake. Just be a bit more careful when you play with it this time.' She scanned the group and didn't even hear the high-pitched sounds of kids digging to China in the sandpit and chasing each other around the various climbing frames during their free play session. It was getting towards the end of the day and half the kids had already been collected. Her eyes fell on Ty Weston playing quietly by himself hammering at the small wooden table, and her heart gripped a little.

Professionally, Lexi would never admit to having a favourite at the centre, but personally she and Ty had clicked. Had done from the moment he'd joined the centre as a runty one-year-old. Small for his age back then, he was now veering on the taller end of the scale for three.

'You know,' Aimee began almost tentatively when Lexi picked up another tangled ball of wool and started winding it, 'we could always ditch the idea of the second childcare centre.'

'What?' Lexi was genuinely shocked by Aimee's suggestion. This was their dream and the area of London they were planning to open their new centre was in desperate need of decent childcare. 'I can't believe you would say that after all we've put into it. And I have no intention of quitting just because my love life is suffering and because we've had a few setbacks.'

'Lex, you *don't* have a love life and we're paying rent on an empty building that's nowhere near finished. Maybe you need to give up on the idea of us becoming the saviour of the childcare world.'

Fortunately for Aimee, Lexi didn't get a chance to respond to that because one of their co-workers interrupted them.

'Excuse me, Lexi.'

Lexi turned as Tina stepped through the double glass doorway leading into the main room.

'What is it, Tina?'

Tina grinned. 'There's a hot guy wanting to pick up Ty Weston but I don't know who he is.'

Hot guy? Probably a model, Lexi thought dismissively.

'His mother is supposed to be collecting him tonight,' Lexi said. But she wouldn't be surprised if the flaky Amanda Weston had forgotten. The woman didn't seem to care about her son and ever since her mother, Ty's grandmother and main carer, had passed away two weeks ago, Amanda had become even worse. 'What's his name?'

'Didn't say.' Tina waggled her eyebrows. 'But I think he might be a movie star.'

Lexi laughed at Tina's stage whisper.

'I'll be sure to get his autograph for you,' she whispered back.

'Forget the autograph. Just let him know I'm single.'

'How do you know *he* is?' Lexi countered.

Tina raised her left hand. 'No rings.'

'Maybe I should go,' Aimee interrupted gravely. 'This sounds serious.'

Lexi rolled her eyes and swiped her hands down her grubby peasant skirt. 'Yeah, I'm sure Todd would *love* that! Watch Ty for me, can you? He's been a bit fragile lately.'

She stepped inside the softly lit main room and noticed the outline of a tall, broad-shouldered man just visible through the window into her office. A sense of trepidation settled in her stomach at the very stillness he seemed to project through the glass.

Telling herself not to be dramatic, Lexi straightened her shoulders and opened the door to her office, stopping short when possibly the most divine-looking man she had ever seen turned to face her.

Hot guy?

The man was scorching. Tall and leanly muscled in a beautifully cut grey suit and black open-necked shirt. He had a chiselled jaw sporting a five o'clock shadow, heart-stopping blue eyes framed by jet-black lashes, close-cropped dirty blond hair and enough sexual confidence to make a courtesan blush.

Various film star names ran through her head but none of them seemed to match. No star she could recall had that air of controlled menace about them. Not that she'd met that many…or any, in fact. Her gaze rose back up over his superb physique and her breath stalled somewhere between her throat and her lungs as their eyes met. His gaze was that of a predatory animal sizing up its prey. Or maybe an army general contemplating war. Whoever he was, he was no ordinary movie star.

Lexi curved suddenly dry lips into a professional smile and ignored the way her stomach seemed to have bottomed out. 'Good afternoon. My name is Lexi Somers. How may I help you?'

Those dangerous blue eyes raked her from head to toe and made the strange feeling in the pit of her stomach slide lower.

'I'm here to collect Ty Weston.' His voice was dark, accented. Russian? Something East European anyway. Which explained the slashing cheekbones and strong jaw. Against her better judgement, she looked into his eyes again and was surprised not just because of her unexpected physical reaction, but because he also seemed familiar.

She had seen him before.

No. She shook her head and then masked the unconscious movement by stepping past him to the relative safety of the other side of her oak desk. She would definitely remember him if she'd seen him before. *And* his smell. Clean, citrusy with a hint of wood. She would *definitely* have remembered *that*.

Lexi thought about sitting down, but immediately discounted the idea. Even in her three-inch heels he towered over her and instinct warned her not to concede one of those inches to him or he'd steamroll right over top of her. She'd been cursing the shoes all day, having dressed formally for her meeting at the bank this morning and only realising she'd left her comfortable flats at home when she'd changed out of her business suit. Now she was glad for the extra height.

'And you are?' She kept her voice courteous, calling on years of defusing difficult situations in an attempt to lighten the tension in the room.

'Here to collect Ty Weston.' He looked down his slightly crooked nose at her and Lexi felt the first stirrings of irritation she usually had no trouble keeping in check.

'Yes. You said that. But I'll need a little more information before I can release him into your care.' Even saying that last word felt like a misnomer given his steely demeanour.

He folded his arms across his chest and the room seemed to shrink. 'What kind of information?'

'Your name for one.'

Despite her better judgement, Lexi dropped into her comfortable chair. Her feet were killing her and she hoped it would induce him to do the same; anything to make him seem a little less imposing. 'Please, take a seat,' she offered with forced equanimity.

He didn't answer, nor did he take up her suggestion. Just scanned the room like some sort of secret service operative and Lexi felt her pang of unease turn into a shiver of real dread. Should she be calling the police right now? Did the man have a gun thrust into the back of that expensive-looking suit?

Lexi gave herself a mental head slap. It wasn't like her to overdramatise situations. Still… 'I have to say you're making me feel distinctly nervous.'

His eyes found hers again and a jolt of something other than fear shimmied through her. 'I am Leo Aleksandrov.' His tone told her she should recognise who he was but she didn't. Her life was far too busy to read gossip magazines.

'I can tell that's supposed to mean something to me, but I'm sorry, it doesn't.'

He shrugged. His first human movement. 'That is of no consequence to me. Now, please—' he inclined his head in what Lexi imagined was supposed to be a demonstration of politeness but just came across as an incredibly superior gesture '—I am short on time.'

She frowned. 'What is your relationship to Ty Weston?'

'Not your concern,' he said, his nostrils flaring slightly as if the question was beneath him.

'Actually, it's very much my concern—' Lexi barely controlled her growing annoyance '—if you're serious about taking him with you.'

'Did I not say I was short on time?'

Lexi's eyebrows hit her hairline at his condescending tone. Just who did this guy think he was? 'And did I not say I required more information from you? We don't usually allow the children in our care to just go off with anyone who happens in off the street. There are procedures to follow. Forms to sign.'

He looked as if he hadn't considered that. Then his eyes raked over her again and Lexi wished she was still wearing her professional suit from earlier. 'I'd like to speak to the manager.'

She smiled, never more pleased at being able to utter her next words. 'I am the manager.'

He stared at her and Lexi couldn't drag her eyes from his intense blue eyes.

'I apologise,' he said finally, a mocking lilt in his voice that suggested otherwise. 'It seems we are at loggerheads, Ms Somers—'

'Miss.'

Now why had she said that? She preferred Ms!

'*Miss* Somers,' he intoned. 'And while I appreciate your concern for Ty Weston's welfare, I have permission from the boy's mother to collect him this evening as she is apparently out of town.'

Lexi frowned at his use of the word 'apparently.' 'I'm sorry, but it doesn't seem as if she has informed the centre of this change. Do you have proof of this permission?'

He paused and his mouth quirked slightly upwards. 'Alas, I left it back in my office.'

Lexi nodded, not at all convinced by what he was saying.

'Well, alas, Mr—' Damn, what was his last name again? '—you'll just have to come back when you have your proof.' She stood up. 'Now, if you'll excuse me—'

'You're dismissing me!' The shocked outrage on his ruggedly handsome face would have made her laugh any other time but right now butterflies were tap dancing in her stomach and making her feel strange.

'Yes, I do believe I am.'

He planted his hands on top of the paperwork on her desk and leaned towards her. 'Listen, Miss Somers, I've had just about as much as I can take of your obstinacy.'

'*My* obstinacy?' Lexi leaned back in her chair and tried to stare him down. Which wasn't easy. In his anger his eyes had taken on a cold precision that could cut through lead. 'That's rich.'

Maybe she *should* call the police.

Some of her nervousness must have shown because his eyes narrowed. 'I can assure you this is all completely aboveboard.'

'Then you won't mind if I contact Amanda.'

He straightened up and pulled at his cuffs. 'Please do. And if you get through pass the phone this way.'

Frowning even harder Lexi collected Ty's file from the corner cabinet, conscious of his eyes on her the whole time. Ignoring him she returned to her seat and dialled Amanda Weston's mobile number.

After a minute the phone clicked over onto voicemail and Lexi left a brief message asking her to call and hung up.

'She's not available,' she said a little unnecessarily, given he had heard her message.

The man, Leo Alek-someone, didn't seem surprised.

Just then another parent arrived at the gate to be buzzed into the centre and Lexi rose to her feet. 'If you'll excuse me, I need to attend to someone else and while I do I'll double check with my colleagues as to whether Amanda passed on a message about you.'

She headed towards the door and felt his body move infinitesimally, as if he planned to follow her.

'I wouldn't,' she warned him coolly, heart pounding a mile a minute. 'We have panic buttons carefully placed throughout the centre and if you follow me I'll set one off.'

He stared at her for a long moment and then smiled.

Lexi's breath caught at the dazzling effect of that smile. Then it turned lazy as he noted her reaction. 'You're bluffing, Miss Somers.'

Yes, she was. They had one panic button in the centre and she had no doubt he'd be on her before she could even instruct someone to activate it.

'Follow me and find out,' she dared, wondering at the husky challenge in her voice. Something about this man's inherent sense of authority, that came with being super rich, or super famous, rubbed her up the wrong way.

He cocked his head, his eyes running over her as if she was a delicacy he wouldn't mind nibbling. Heat constricted her throat and when his gaze dropped to her chest her breasts seemed to expand and tighten in a completely visceral response that was as shocking as it was unexpected.

His eyes, no longer icy, met hers and lust, the like she had never experienced before, exploded deep in her belly as she registered the inherent interest he didn't have the good manners to hide. 'Don't be long.'

Don't be... Lexi stalked out of the room.

Had she ever met a ruder, more charismatic man in her life?

CHAPTER TWO

LEO watched the petite brunette sweep out of her office as if the hounds of hell were after her, her ponytail bobbing behind her head like an overwound pendulum.

Run, angel, run.

He smiled to himself, unable to take his eyes off her trim figure.

He shouldn't have goaded her like that but he couldn't resist the way her exotic golden eyes had sparkled at him crossly and the way her creamy skin had flushed pink.

She'd had the strangest effect on him the minute she'd come striding through the door like some field marshal about to do battle. Her heart-shaped face tipped at an angle that said she could easily take on Alexander the Great and win.

Okay, maybe it wasn't the *strangest* effect. Maybe it was a purely sexual one, but it had hit him from left field because she wasn't his usual type. Too uptight—despite the Snow White attire—and too small. Delicate even. Her waist appearing so slender he could wrap his hands around her without any trouble at all. He liked his women a little taller, a little more sophisticated and a *lot* more accommodating.

He cupped his hands behind his head and spied the contents of her desk. Papers, brightly coloured pens, cotton dolls and a computer keyboard, all neatly arranged. Soft pink curtains hung from the single window and various child related paraphernalia lined the walls.

And some New-Agey smell had got up his nose and he had yet to locate the source. He wondered how Lexi Somers smelled and whether her neat figure would live up to the promise outlined in her prim blouse and red skirt. Then he told himself to quit it—he wasn't here for that.

Only his mind had already conjured up a pleasurable image of the hint of puckered nipples beneath the lacy bra she wore and his mouth watered as he wondered at their colour. Their taste. He'd noticed her response to his perusal of her body earlier and as much as she might be trying to appear cool and calm—he could tell she was a fireball of nerves inside.

What would she be like in bed? Coolly efficient, or hot and abandoned?

The thought hadn't fully formed in his mind before the annoying bell over her office door tinkled. His senses stood to attention at the sound of her determined footsteps crossing the linoleum flooring in shoes more befitting a party-girl than a childcare manager. And what was up with that? Clearly she was a woman who played on her sexuality.

Definitely hot and abandoned, he decided, and unconsciously breathed deep as she skirted past him. Just the hint of vanilla and…musk? Seductive, whatever it was, he thought, slightly bemused at his one-track mind.

'I'm sorry you've wasted your time, Mr…'

'Aleksandrov.' He said his surname more slowly, amused despite himself that she might really not know who he was. It happened so rarely nowadays.

'Aleksandrov.' She smiled, her hands folded primly together on her desk as if the matter was resolved.

Leo twisted his mouth into a smile and slouched back in the wooden chair built for a doll. 'And why is that, *Miss* Somers?' he asked casually, unwilling to refute her mistaken belief that she was in control of this situation just yet.

'I've checked with my colleagues and there has been no

message about a change in pick up arrangements so I cannot release Ty Weston into your care.'

Leo felt an itch attack his left eyebrow and ignored it. Just as he ignored her statement. Instead he folded his arms across his chest and stared her down, waiting for her to break. Surprisingly, she held his gaze longer than he had expected. Then she sat straighter. 'I think it's time you left.'

If only he could.

'What are you going to do when nobody comes to collect Ty?'

A flicker of doubt clouded her eyes and she let out a pent-up breath. 'Look, I've had a lousy day so far and you're not making it any better. I have no idea who you— Oh! You're—'

'Ty's father.'

He spoke at the same time as she had deduced the information and he raised a mocking brow at her cleverness.

'The eyes. You have his eyes.'

Leo didn't know that. He'd never once looked at the photos his security team provided in their regular updates on his son.

A sheen of sweat broke out across his brow at the thought of meeting him now. Already emotions and guilt he'd had no trouble keeping at bay for years were swelling inside him like heavy rain filling a river, and he mentally cursed Amanda Weston and her conniving ways.

Leo stood up, ignoring the heat of Lexi Somers' gaze as it raked over his chest, pulling his stomach muscles tight.

Perhaps he should have told her his relationship to Ty from the outset, but the last thing he wanted was word to get out that he had a son. If it did he'd have to supply Ty with a security detail for the rest of his childhood and he had wanted to avoid that at all costs. 'Fine. Now you can go get him. I'll wait here.'

The surprise that had softened her full lips disappeared and she shook her head. 'I'm sorry; I can't do that.'

Leo felt the return of his earlier annoyance at her stubbornness. 'Why not?'

'You're not on his list of appointed people permitted to collect him.'

Chort vozmi! 'What a load of rubbish,' he rasped.

She stood up to face him and gripped the edges of her desk. 'It's not rubbish. We have procedures in the centre to ensure the children's safety and—'

'If you knew who I was you wouldn't be arguing with me.'

He blew out a breath. He sounded like a self-important ass and the look on the brunette's face said she'd come to the same conclusion.

'Why? Because you're above the law?' The imperious question didn't require an answer but he wanted to give her one. He wanted to take the line his Cossack ancestors would have done: press her up against the wall and take what her wide-spaced golden eyes had been offering since she'd first marched into the room. Then he'd take his son and get the hell out of there.

Pity a couple of centuries had spoiled that option.

'I'm his father,' he ground out, the words sounding strange to his ears.

'A father whose name is not on any of our forms,' she reminded him. 'And why is that?'

Leo reined in surging guilt that threatened to spiral into rage and paced two steps to the back of the room.

He sucked in a deep breath, knowing that logically she had a point even though her question was way out of line.

He turned back to face her. 'Look, Miss Somers—' he unclenched his jaw '—I want to be here about as much as you want me here but I don't have a choice. Amanda delivered a note to my office advising me that there was no one else to take care of Ty. Otherwise I wouldn't be here.'

'Are you having custody issues?'

Leo felt his eyes harden. 'I am not about to discuss my personal business with you.'

She stood firm. 'And I'm not about to release a child into the care of a man I've never met before and who is not on his list of trusted carers.'

Leo rubbed his neck. 'Try his mother again.'

She looked as if she wouldn't but then picked up the phone and hit redial.

'Still no answer.'

Leo swore and saw her eyes widen in silent reprimand. Too bad. The angel didn't like his language.

Then he returned to the doll's chair and sprawled in front of her. 'So what do we do now?'

For the first time since she returned she looked unsure and swivelled around to check the clock behind her.

'Half an hour to go, angel. Maybe we should find something else to do other than argue to make the time go quicker.'

Her eyes took on the size of the dinner plates his lunch had been served on and he cursed his rampaging libido. What was he doing thinking about sex with this woman at a time like this? 'Forget I said that.'

'I most certainly will. It was tacky in the extreme.'

Leo's eyes wandered over her with insolent abandon. 'Don't pretend you haven't thought about it, angel.'

She gasped and he smiled at her outrage. 'I most certainly have not! And do not call me angel.'

He smiled. She had. And so had he.

'I'll call you whatever I want and you're a liar.'

'And you're incredibly rude.'

He shrugged and checked the clock. 'Are you seriously going to make me wait until six o'clock before I can take him?' He'd never come up against such resistance from a woman before.

'No. I'm going to call the police.' She reached for the phone and he leaned across the desk and covered her hand with one of his. Sensation shot up his arm at the contact and for a moment all he could do was stare at her.

Time seemed suspended between them and then she wrenched her hand out from under his. 'Get your hands off me.'

'Settle down, Miss Somers, before you get hysterical.'

'I do not get *hysterical*. But you are crossing the line Mr Aleksandrov, and I want you to leave.'

Leo scrubbed his face. At least she remembered his name this time. 'I apologise. Call the police if it makes you feel better but it won't change anything. Amanda Weston has done a runner for the weekend and I'm all the kid's got.'

The angel rubbed the back of her hand as if she could still feel his touch and Leo's fingers flexed involuntarily because he could definitely still feel the silk of her skin. 'That remains to be seen.'

He glanced at the clock. 'Five minutes to go. Surely Amanda would be here by now if she was coming.'

'Not necessarily. She's often late, sometimes even forgetting to turn up at all.'

'What?' He was genuinely shocked by her comment and he saw the moment she knew she'd said too much. 'How many times?'

'Pardon?'

'How many times has she forgotten?'

'I can't remember.' She tucked a strand of hair behind her ear and he knew she was lying. He stared at her until she grew uncomfortable. 'A few since her mother passed away.'

He frowned. 'Her mother died?'

'She fell and broke her hip two weeks ago. I understand there was a complication with the surgery.'

He shook his head. 'I didn't know.'

'Why am I not surprised.'

It was a statement, not a question, and he scowled, deciding to ignore her disparaging tone. 'Why should that affect when Amanda picks the boy up?'

'Because she doesn't normally do it. As I understand it her mother was Ty's main carer.'

Leo frowned. Ty's grandmother had taken care of him? Maybe he should have read those reports after all.

'You didn't know that either, did you?' The angel didn't look impressed and he wanted to tell her she had no right to judge him.

'So it would seem,' he snapped, getting up and stalking the short distance to the rear of the room and back.

Leo noticed that she watched him as if she was trying to read him and he felt uncomfortable under her close scrutiny. He instinctively knew that if he told her he'd never even met his son she'd take umbrage and probably call in the army to deal with him and the truth was—he was a little worried. Danny was organising a nanny to meet him at his apartment to take over from him but…what would he do with a three-year-old until then?

Long suppressed memories of his baby brother spiked in his head—that soft little body, his cheeky grin, the way he had called him 'Layo.' Leo swallowed past the bile in his throat and refixed his gaze on Lexi Somers. His eyes dropped to the row of pearl buttons on her blouse and he imagined grabbing the collar and ripping them off. Imagined baring her to his hungry gaze and lifting her onto the desk and burying himself deep inside her. His body hardened, but sex wouldn't change the inevitable, only delay it, and he knew that was the reason it was on his mind so much since he'd arrived here. He was trying to distract himself. It had nothing to do with the brunette with the tiny waist and golden eyes.

'Mr Aleksandrov, are you okay?' He blanked his expression and told himself to stop being an ass and figure out this problem. Give him a stock market crash or a potential hotel site to assess and he'd have the situation under control in minutes. Dealing with the needs of a young child was so far removed from his reality he was struggling to be one step ahead of the issues.

Then it hit him. He'd forgotten to treat this situation like a business transaction. And hadn't he learned that everything came down to one thing?

'How much do you need to hand Ty over?'

'Excuse me?'

His eyes grew flinty. 'You heard. I'm a wealthy man.' He raked her with cool eyes. 'I'm sure your wardrobe could do with an update.'

Her mouth fell open and she stared at him as if he'd just asked her how to build a pipe bomb. 'Are you seriously trying to bribe me?'

Leo closed his eyes and then glanced at the ceiling before bringing his gaze back to her. He stood up. 'I already told you I'm short on time and you've wasted enough of it. I'm the boy's father; even you recognised that, so just—'

The phone ringing interrupted him and they both stared at it as if it were a snake. Then the angel leaned over to pick it up. He could tell straight away it was Amanda by the way her eyes flew to his. 'I see,' she murmured, before turning her back on him.

Leo's anger spiked and he lunged for the phone and yanked it out of her hands. 'Amanda, what do you—' *think you're doing?* he finished silently as the call was disconnected. He stared at the phone and swore viciously before tossing it onto Ty's file.

He felt confined and edgy in the tiny room. Then the annoying tinkle above the door sounded and a blonde poked her head through and eyed him as one would a dangerous animal. Which was exactly how he felt.

'Everything okay in here, Lex?'

Lexi's eyes flashed to his and he waited for her to say no.

'I think so. But can you hang around for another couple of minutes?'

'Sure. Ty is the only one left and Tina's gone.' The woman glanced in his direction and then dropped her eyes.

'Okay. I'll have this sorted in a jiffy,' Lexi said.

Leo looked at her. 'What's a jiffy?'

She seemed momentarily confused and then shook her head. 'I have no idea. It's a figure of speech. You're Russian?'

'*Da.* Yes. And you are English?'

'Yes.'

Something indefinable passed between them and then, thankfully, she shook her head and broke the connection. 'Okay. It seems that Amanda *has* gone away for the week-end and she just had enough time to tell me that you are Ty's father before you wrenched the phone from my hand like a Neanderthal.'

Leo didn't flinch at the criticism. 'Good. Then I can go.'

He stood and heard her release a noisy breath before she too rose to her feet.

'What now?' he growled, desperate to put this woman with her accusing golden-green eyes behind him.

'Why are you not on any of his forms?'

'Amanda has sole custody.'

'Why?'

'At the risk of sounding rude, Miss Somers, that's none of your business.'

'You're wrong.' She rounded her desk and stood in front of him. 'Ty is in my care and as I don't have written author-ity to hand him over to you I could still lose my licence as a childcare provider if I released him to you and something happened to him.'

'I appreciate your predicament but that is not my fault. Amanda should have made the proper arrangements.'

She considered him for a moment. 'Promise me you're not

some maniac of a father who is going to do something terrible the moment you have him alone.'

The skin on Leo's face pulled tight and his mouth went dry as she inadvertently tore a strip off one of the bandages concealing his childhood wounds. He was aware that his breathing had become shallow and that his blood was roaring in his ears.

He couldn't seem to tear his eyes away from hers and yet looking into her innocently questioning gaze was searing him with pain. 'I would never intentionally hurt my son,' he said hoarsely, his accent thicker as he fought to contain memories from the past.

He waited for her to contradict him. To say that she could see the blackness inside him, but she didn't. Instead she nodded curtly. 'Follow me.'

He released a harsh breath and followed her out into the main area of the centre, which was eerily neat and quiet. The blonde from before stepped through the opposite doorway. 'Ty is in the sandpit.'

'Thanks, Aimee. You go ahead. I'll be home shortly.'

'I'll probably be at Todd's.'

Lexi smiled and Leo's stomach did a somersault. 'I'll see you next week then.'

'Have a fun time away if you decide to go.' She raised her eyebrows and Leo wondered where Lexi Somers was going this weekend and why he cared. Then he forgot about it as the blonde walked away and he was confronted with an empty doorway.

His heart felt like a dead weight in his chest as he stepped through it and gazed at the blond-haired toddler happily making truck sounds as he scooped sand into the digger.

Chort vozmi. God damn it. He couldn't do this.

He turned to the woman behind him and gripped her arms as a fear he hadn't felt in years assailed him.

* * *

'You can't do what?' Lexi asked, her eyes racing across Leo Aleksandrov's suddenly pale face. He looked as if he were facing a smoking gun and she had no idea what to do. Her heart hammered in her chest. This close, she could see the blue of his eyes was shot through with silver and the stubble lining his jaw made his face impossibly handsome. 'Mr Aleksandrov?'

Her soft tone seemed to bring his eyes back into focus because he let her go and stepped backwards as he turned to stare at his son.

She rubbed her arms and glanced at Ty, who was regarding them curiously, no hint of recognition on his face at all. She tried to remember what Amanda Weston had said about Ty's father when she had first enrolled Ty at the centre but her memory was hazy. Something about him not being interested in Ty and a request that they not ask Ty about him. Obviously, whatever had happened between Amanda and Leo, it had not ended well and Ty had borne the brunt of that.

Lexi felt sick. She hated men who didn't take responsibility for their actions, who didn't care enough about their children to spend time with them.

Trying to quell her rising anger for Ty's sake, Lexi stepped forward. 'Ty, come on. Your da— Oh!'

Strong fingers bit into her upper arms as the man behind her grabbed her and hauled her back against him. Lexi stumbled in her high heels and fell back against a chest as rock-solid as granite. The breath left her lungs as one of his powerful arms banded her torso just below her breasts to keep her upright.

She instantly caught fire at his touch, unbidden lust tightening her breasts and sending a spiral of heat straight to her pelvis. Shocked by her instant sexual response—a response she'd been trying to deny since she'd first seen him—Lexi turned in the circle of his arms with every intention of pushing him away. Only once her hands flattened against the brick wall of his chest, his heat and his scent had a paralysing effect on her senses. Now she didn't want to push him away. Now she wanted to rise up onto her toes and kiss him. As if reading her thoughts, his eyes darkened to navy and took on a fierce quality that sent her senses into overdrive.

The faint buzzing of the airconditioning and the gentle sound of the wind chimes receded and Lexi was completely captivated as his head slowly lowered to hers. His hands at her waist tightened, pulling her inexorably closer, and her startled gaze flew to his as she felt the unmistakable edge of his erection brush against her belly.

His eyes held hers, his mouth hovering just out of reach, their breaths mingling, and Lexi couldn't move. Then his gaze clouded over, registering the shock she felt, and before she could suck in another breath he shoved her back from him and stalked inside.

Lexi followed him to the doorway as if in a daze, her body sending all sorts of mixed messages to her brain. One of which was to follow him inside and press herself up against him and never let go. Which was just crazy! She never behaved like that. Not even with Brandon!

'He doesn't know I'm his father.'

The harsh words broke into her personal thoughts and when she realised what he had said she couldn't hide her horror. 'How—'

'We've never met.'

What?

Lexi gripped the door frame, shaking her head. 'That's not possible.'

Leo's face as he looked at her was grim, all signs of his earlier arousal gone, while her own body still felt soft and jittery from the shock of all that maleness pressed so intimately against her own. She'd been right in her premonition before. The man was lethal—just not in the way she had expected.

His mouth tightened and she realised she was staring at it,

wondering how it would have felt if he hadn't stopped him-self before. If she'd taken matters into her own hands and... *whoa, girl, hold the fort. You do not want to kiss this man.*

'I assure you it is,' he rasped raggedly.

Lexi's mind retraced their conversation and a thousand questions winged into it. But uppermost in her thinking was Ty's welfare. He hadn't been the same since his grandmother had passed away and now, to be taken by a strange man for three days—even if he was his father—could have a huge psychological impact on him.

And could she trust that this dangerous Russian was tell-ing the truth about why he wanted Ty?

She forced herself to meet Leo's guarded eyes and willed her mind to concentrate on what was important. 'If that's true, he's not going to feel comfortable going with you,' she informed him shortly.

He rubbed the back of his neck and glanced away. 'I know I should have thought of that earlier and organised the nanny to meet me here instead of my apartment.'

'Nanny?' Lexi frowned and glanced behind her to make sure Ty was still playing happily. 'Has Ty met this person before?'

'No.'

'Then he won't be happy with her either.'

'She'll know what to do.'

'Not necessarily. Do you even have a proper car seat fitted?'

'I have a limousine.'

'That doesn't answer my question. Listen, if Ty doesn't know you and you're taking him to an unfamiliar place, that will be scary for a three-year-old. Not to mention potentially damaging to his psyche.'

'You let me worry about his psyche,' he growled impa-tiently and Lexi could see from the arrogant tilt of his head that his momentary panic from before was over and that he was firmly back in control.

'It doesn't seem that you've been worried about much at all where your son is concerned,' she said tartly.

His gaze sharpened. 'Who do you think pays for this fancy establishment?'

'I meant emotionally.'

He looked at her as if she were speaking a foreign language and she huffed out a breath. Arguing was not going to solve this situation. 'He needs something familiar. Do you have his favourite toy? Blanket?'

For a minute he looked utterly lost and despite the fact that she despised his type, her heart went out to him.

He paced away from her and it seemed an age before he answered. Then he turned and her breath stalled at the sight of the bold smile that tilted the corners of his sexy mouth. 'I have something better.'

She was almost afraid to ask. 'Like what?'

'Like you.'

CHAPTER THREE

'WHY is he crying?' Leo asked, tugging loose another button on his shirt, which felt suddenly too tight. Ty had been crying on and off for half an hour and the sobs were twisting his gut to the point where he couldn't concentrate on work.

Lexi Somers, who had reluctantly accompanied him to his apartment two hours ago, reached across and took the distressed toddler from the matronly arms of the nanny, Mrs Parsons, whom Danny had organised. Instantly the boy cuddled into her and started sucking his thumb, huge teardrops clinging to his lower lashes.

Leo was aware that his pulse was racing just looking at his son and turned his attention to the woman holding him. Which wasn't much better because his mind instantly recalled the feel of her soft body against his and the moment he'd almost kissed her. As if he needed that complication right now. Today, at lunchtime, he would have welcomed the way she made him feel. Now, with his world unravelling at the seams, the last thing he needed to think about was sex. Especially sex with a cute woman who was utterly furious with him.

'He's not comfortable with Mrs Parsons yet, but that's to be expected,' she answered him briskly, one of her hands rubbing Ty's back soothingly. 'This is all very traumatic for him.' The reproach in her voice was unmistakable.

Not just for him, Leo thought.

'He seems very comfortable with you,' he said.

'I've looked after him almost every weekday for two years. It's only natural he feels comfortable with me.'

Leo felt movement behind him and turned to see Danny standing in the door of his home office. 'Dmitri is on the phone.'

'Right.' Due to the delay in collecting Ty, Leo still had work to wrap up. But first he needed to sort the problem of Ty and the nanny. 'You take him to bed,' he instructed Lexi. 'And then—'

'Please.'

Leo blinked at her quiet reprimand.

He thought about telling her that if she interrupted him one more time with that gorgeous mouth he'd do something they'd both regret but found himself in the unique position of needing somebody else more than they needed him. A situation he did not like at all. He had to get rid of her and the sooner the better. 'Please, Miss Somers, would you be so kind as to take my son to his bed?'

He could tell she wasn't fooled by his mocking tone, but that was okay. He knew she'd do it. Ever since she had told Ty that this 'nice' man was taking them on an adventure and had made it sound as if it could rival Disney World he knew she was a soft touch under her no-nonsense exterior—a weakness he was ruthless enough to exploit.

'Which room is his?' she muttered.

'This way.' Leo hadn't thought about which of his spare rooms to give Ty, but they were both the same so he chose the first one he came to.

He opened the door and inhaled vanilla as Lexi moved past him and looked around the room, a frown marring her smooth forehead.

King-sized bed, bedside tables, French windows leading to an outside balcony, private bathroom. What was there to frown about? Except maybe the absence of a cot. *Chort vozmi.* He hadn't thought of that.

'Are they locked?' She nodded towards the French windows and spoke softly as the toddler was almost asleep in her arms, something Leo was glad about because he couldn't look at Ty without remembering his brother, Sasha.

'Of course,' he said, but he walked over and rattled the handles anyway.

'He really has never been here before has he?' she said, almost to herself.

'I told you that.'

'Yes, but I don't think I wanted to believe you.'

'I don't lie.'

She cast him a fathomless look. 'Can I have some more pillows?'

'Why?'

'Because he'll feel more secure if he's surrounded by pillows. This bed is too big for him.'

Leo opened the inbuilt wardrobe and pulled out three spare pillows and placed them on the end of the bed. 'Anything else?'

'Pyjamas.'

He glanced at Ty's jeans and T-shirt. 'Can't he sleep in what he's got on?'

'Do you sleep in jeans?'

Her sharp rebuke both surprised and irritated him.

'Are you trying to find out what I sleep in, Miss Somers?' he asked, wondering if her eyes flashed golden when she was aroused as they did when she was angered.

He expected her to snap at him but instead she smiled sweetly. 'I already know. It's called a coffin.'

Leo blinked, astounded at her unexpected sassiness and then she surprised him again by shushing him. 'Just go.' She waved him away with her free hand as if he were an annoying insect. 'I'll take care of this.'

Leo left, not sure whether to be bemused or outraged at her temerity.

* * *

Lexi fixed the bed so that Ty wouldn't fall out of it and then sat beside him while he fell into a deep sleep.

Then she picked up her phone and called Aimee in case she hadn't left for her boyfriend's house and was worried as to why she hadn't returned to their shared apartment. When Lexi told her who Ty's father was she could almost see Aimee slap her forehead.

'I knew I recognised him. Oh, my God. I didn't know he had a son.'

'What do you know about him?' Lexi found herself asking without actually meaning to. Because really she already knew any information Aimee could impart would just be more nails in the coffin she had accused him of sleeping in. Her lips twitched now at the remembered surprise on his face when she'd said that. Clearly people didn't tell him when he was being overbearing and arrogant often enough.

'He's mega wealthy. And I mean *mega*.' Aimee added with emphasis. 'Russian. Has been in the papers all week because he helped rescue two of his workers from a massive construction accident in Dubai. Remember, I told you about it.'

'Mmm,' Lexi said noncommittally. She had a vague recollection but the problems with their second centre had been taking up a lot of her head space lately.

'He also changes his girlfriends as often as he changes his underwear and is supposed to be fantastic in bed. *Hubba hubba.*'

'And which magazine did that little titbit come out of?' Lexi asked, thinking that it was most likely true.

'I can't remember. Anyway, what's he like?'

'Arrogant, rude, obnoxious.' Chiselled, gorgeous and utterly male, a little voice taunted.

Which she promptly ignored. She'd met Leo Aleksandrov's type before. Oh, not with the mega-wealthy tag, but arrogant men who viewed permanent relationships the way they

viewed dental hygiene—sometimes required, but not necessarily so.

Her father had been one of those: a professional golfer who
had never married her mother despite having two children
with her, and who had then left them all to take up with his
mistress. And Brandon had been no better. At the time they'd
met he'd been a charismatic, well-connected university jock
who had pursued her and convinced her he was falling for
her, all in the name of sport.

Finding out that she had been played like so many other
girls he had gone after had made her feel ill, as had his complaint that she had not only been too serious, but that she had
been below average in bed. Of course she hadn't *believed*
him, but it hadn't stopped her confidence from taking a heavy
knock. So heavy, in fact, she hadn't dated seriously since.

Suddenly an image of Simon popped into her mind and she
groaned. She couldn't do it. She wasn't ready to get serious
with anyone yet. Maybe she never would be and that might not
be a bad thing. She had good friends, a growing business…

Lexi realised Aimee was still talking about Leo and felt
rude for being so caught up in her own thoughts she hadn't
been paying attention. 'I'm sorry, Aim, I haven't been listening but I don't want to talk about this man any more. He's too
irritating for words.'

'Irritating or irresistible?' her friend joked.

'I'm not going to dignify that with an answer,' she said,
ignoring her brain's contradictory messages about him. 'But
don't tell anyone about Ty being his son. I'm not sure what's
going on yet, but I would hate Ty to get hurt in any way.'

She rang off and let herself out of the room, leaving the
bedroom door slightly ajar in order to listen out for Ty.

She walked down the wide carpeted hallway, taking in
the astounding dimensions of the sleekly designed penthouse
apartment she was in. So this was how the other half lived!

It was like being in another world. The whole apartment

looked as if it had come straight out of some modern architecture magazine, with not a rumpled doily in sight. She smirked as she thought about what Leo Aleksandrov would make of her and Aimee's shabby little two-room apartment, with throw rugs and papers and half completed sewing projects hanging around on the dining room table. If she were to put down anything half completed here it would likely get up and run away. And while the place was undoubtedly beautiful, it lacked soul. It lacked that special quality that made a house a home.

Not that it mattered, she thought, as she stopped in the doorway of the main sitting room, when the exterior walls were made up almost entirely of glass and showcased a view of London Lexi would normally have to buy a ticket to see.

And in front of that impressive wall of glass was the impressive sight of a brooding Leo Aleksandrov, pacing up and down like a tiger trapped in a too small cage.

As if sensing her presence, he stopped, and Lexi felt every one of her senses go on high alert as his eyes swept over her.

She normally had to buy a ticket to see a man like him as well. Usually on a movie screen. His virility was not at all adversely affected by the slightly crumpled shirt that clung to his wide shoulders. He'd rolled his shirtsleeves to reveal powerful, hair-roughened forearms; Lexi already knew the leashed power behind those arms and she shivered.

He broke her train of thought by shoving his hands into his pockets and she felt a flood of colour swamp her face as she realised that she'd been caught staring.

Pretending she wasn't at all flustered by his presence—and wishing it was the truth—she smiled briefly and then turned away to search the room for her bag. 'Ty is asleep and I'm leaving.'

'You can't.'

She stopped in the middle of the room and looked at him. 'Excuse me?'

'I've dismissed Mrs Parsons.'

'Why would you do that? She was perfect.'

He regarded her levelly. 'She doesn't have a passport.'

Lexi didn't hide her shock. 'You dismissed a woman on the grounds that she's not well traveled? That's a bit narrow-minded isn't it?'

'I didn't dismiss her because of that,' he flashed at her, rubbing the back of his neck as if this whole conversation was terribly unnecessary. 'Look, perhaps you should sit down.'

'I don't want to sit down,' she flashed right back.

'I'm just as unhappy about this turn of events as you are but, realistically, it would have taken Ty too long to get used to her anyway.'

Lexi raised an eyebrow. He'd become an expert on his son now had he? 'So who are you going to get to help you out?' she asked, knowing before she'd even finished her question what his answer would be. 'No.' She shook her head and spoke before he'd even opened his mouth. 'That's not possible.'

'I will, of course, pay you for your time.'

'No!'

His lack of any response to her vehemence made her nervous. 'Anyway, I'm busy this weekend,' she said, hating that she felt as if she had to explain herself to this man. She moistened her lips and watched his eyes follow the movement. His gaze lingered and once again she wondered how his lips would feel against her own. Aimee's words about his sexual prowess popped into her head and her lips were once again bone-dry.

Oh, Lord, she had to get out of here.

His eyes returned to hers and she expelled a breath in a rush.

'Doing?'

'I'm going to Paris,' she declared. Deciding there and then that she'd give Simon a chance. It was time. Past time. And Simon was a saint compared to this man.

'Your friend seemed to think you hadn't yet made up your mind.'

Lexi frowned, wondering how he knew that. 'Aimee doesn't know everything,' she said, slightly flustered.

'And whom are you going to the city of light with, hmmm?'

Lexi felt her jaw clench at his supercilious tone. Simon would never have asked that question! He was well-mannered, polite, civilised, boring...

No. He was perfect.

Frustrated with her erratic thoughts, Lexi glanced towards the entrance foyer and wondered if she shouldn't just head for the door and be done with Leo Aleksandrov.

As if sensing her intention, his body tensed, his eyes fixed on her as if he would spring if she made the slightest movement to flee.

'You haven't answered my question.'

'Because it's none of your business!' she exclaimed hotly.

His penetrating gaze held hers but his body relaxed as if her answer had been predictable. Then he made her teeth clench even harder when he smiled knowingly. 'I'll send you and your lover first class next weekend.'

Lexi's eyebrows hit her hairline. 'You'll send?' she repeated indignantly. Just who did this man think he was?

'Pay. Organise.' He blew out a frustrated breath. 'Stop getting caught up on semantics.'

'Mr Aleksandrov, I—'

'I have to go to Greece for the weekend. I need somebody I can trust to take care of Ty.'

'You want me to go to Greece with you? For the long weekend?'

Lexi wasn't even prepared to go into the next room with him, let alone another country!

'No. I was taking Mrs Parsons to Greece because she is an unknown entity for both myself and Ty, and I felt it was better to have her close by. You, on the other hand, are not an unknown entity. You have looked after my son for two years and you will be perfectly fine to take care of him here, in London. And, as I said—' he paused, regarding her calmly '—I'll pay you. Well.'

'Is money your answer to everything?' Lexi snapped.

'Not *everything*, no.'

Her lips compressed at his sensually mocking smile.

'How much?' he asked with quiet confidence.

Lexi tried not to be intimidated by his size and understated force of will. Hadn't he realised that she wasn't the type of person who could be bought? Or was he the type of person who paid off everyone in order to get his own way? She wouldn't be at all surprised to find out that he was. 'You mean I can name my price?' she asked sweetly, as if she might actually be considering his offer.

'What's the number?' he demanded curtly, his smile flattening as if her answer had displeased him, though why that should be the case she hadn't a clue.

Lexi paused. Would he pay any figure? For a minute she was tempted to find out but she didn't play these types of games and it would give her more satisfaction to put him—and his open bank account—in their rightful place.

'The number is that there is no number. You don't deserve my help. Goodbye.'

Lexi didn't look at him as she picked up her bag and dropped her mobile phone inside. She was about to stride out of the door with her head held high when Leo's quiet voice stopped her.

'I might not. But Ty does.'

Lexi turned and stared at him incredulously. 'Are you trying to *emotionally* blackmail me now?'

'If it means you'll stay, yes.'

Lexi couldn't believe the gall of the man. Had he no shame?

'You get a girl pregnant and then don't even have the decency to get to know your own flesh and blood and now you'll do whatever it takes to have someone you don't even know take care of him. What kind of a man are you?'

He jammed his hands onto his hips and glared at her. 'Don't pass judgement on things you don't understand.'

'Oh, I understand all right,' Lexi fumed. 'I understand that your lifestyle is so precious you rejected an innocent child. Well, that's something you should have thought about *before* you got Amanda Weston pregnant, not *after*.'

'This has nothing to do with my lifestyle and everything to do with Ty's well-being.'

'And just how do you figure that?'

A muscle ticked in his jaw. 'I don't have to explain myself to you but I did not reject my son.'

'Oh? What would you call it?'

'Since he was born I have paid for every single thing he needs and I have six monthly reports carried out to ensure that he is safe and well cared for.'

'Reports that failed to inform you that his mother travels so often that his grandmother was his main carer until her death a fortnight ago.'

He had the grace to look uncomfortable, pulling at the collar on his shirt in a telling movement.

'And,' he continued, as if she hadn't spoken, 'I fully intend to have a relationship with him when he's older.'

Of all the...

'Older and less work?' she scoffed. 'He needs you now. A boy looks to his father as he grows up to figure out what it means to be a man. What kind of a man will he grow up to be with an absent father who never cared enough to spend time with him?' Lexi stopped, aware that her impassioned speech was about to get out of hand. But damn it, that was exactly what had happened to her brother, Joe, who had become lost and angry in his teenage years, even though Lexi and her mother had done their best to shield him from feeling rejected by his father.

'By all means say what you think, Miss Somers.'

Lexi shook her head. 'I don't believe in wasting time on empty words.'

'Rare for your sex, I have to say.'

'Oh—' Lexi shook her head '—I'll add chauvinist to your list of personal attributes, shall I?'

'I meant it as a compliment.'

'That's even worse!'

He leaned his hip against the edge of the sofa and cocked his head. 'Will I like any of the other things on your list?'

Lexi shot him a fulminating glare, feeling a little spent after her tirade. 'What do you think?'

He laughed and Lexi felt a tug of awareness low in her pelvis as he studied her, his casual stance and insolent regard making her aware of her femininity—her womanliness—in a way she hated. Making her think of sex—of all things!

She swallowed heavily and his eyes dropped to her throat and Lexi nearly raised her hand to cover it. What was he thinking about? Heat crept up her neck and she was afraid she might know.

'I think you're a woman with exacting standards that not many men manage to live up to.'

Lexi blinked. 'I think you'd fail to live up to most people's standards,' she retorted, stung a little by his assessment of her.

'You'd be surprised.'

'I'm not talking about the hundreds of women you go through like disposable razors.'

He smiled at that. 'Neither was I. And for your information, I use an electric.'

'Well, you didn't use it today,' she said hotly and then wished she hadn't when a sexy smile crossed his face. Damn. Now he probably thought she liked his stubble. Wanted to touch it, even. Huh! As if.

She tightened her hold on her bag, aware that the conversation was taking a dangerous turn. 'This is irrelevant.'

'I agree.' He pushed off from the sofa and sat down on it, his arms spread wide along the back like a sultan surveying his kingdom. 'So tell me, what is it going to take to get you to agree to take care of Ty this weekend?'

'Surely you have someone else who can help you out. A girlfriend, perhaps?'

'Is that your way of asking if I'm available, Miss Somers?'

Lexi glared at him. 'That's my way of asking if you have someone else to help you out. I would ask if you had a mother but I'm not sure you weren't hatched from an egg.'

Leo laughed, a deep, husky sound that sent tingles tracking down her spine. 'I'm single. But, even if I wasn't, bringing a girlfriend in at this late stage isn't really the answer, is it?'

It wasn't really a question and, worst of all, she knew he was right. Lexi glanced outside at the endless view of the night sky and felt oddly cornered. 'I can't just drop everything in my life to help you.'

'Think of it as helping Ty. You might find that more palatable,' he drawled.

Lexi made a derisive sound in the back of her throat and thought that if she wasn't such a nice person—and the thought of touching him didn't scare her so much—she'd smack him. 'Oh, you're good.'

'Thank you.'

'It wasn't a compliment.'

'I know.'

Just as he knew she was about to capitulate.

Lexi ground her teeth together and turned back and focused on the elegant dome of St Paul's Cathedral in the distance. Anything was better than looking at Leo sprawled on the sofa with arrogant nonchalance. No doubt he would be attending parties in Greece and having a lovely time. A lovely time without his son. Lexi drummed her fingers against her arm. Just like her father.

'What are you waiting for, Miss Somers?' Leo drawled, his accent giving the words a sexy edge. 'The stars to align?'

Lexi fumed. Arrogant so-and-so... And then an idea sprouted. What if he took Ty to Greece and had a chance to get to know his son? Would that change his attitude towards Ty? She didn't know, but it was worth a try and it was better than staying in London where there was no chance at all of that happening. Lexi didn't trust that Amanda could look after Ty without her mother around and, although Leo Aleksandrov didn't appear to be much better, she had to find out.

She turned back to consider him and tried to ignore sensations she would rather not feel shimmy down her spine as he looked back at her with lazy insolence. 'I'll do it if you take Ty with you.'

His eyelids lowered and when he raised them his eyes were no longer lazy or insolent, but hard and flat. 'Never been to Greece, angel?'

'Your list just got longer.'

Knowing the type of man he was she hadn't expected to win this point without a fight but, instead of arguing with her, he slowly rose to his feet, his eyes on her the whole time. Then he smiled, a killer's smile, and Lexi felt the cold plate-glass window through her clothing and realised she'd backed up a step. 'Careful, angel, you might fall.'

Lexi stiffened her spine and gave him a look that had been known to stay the rowdiest of children. 'I'm not afraid of you Mr Aleksandrov.' Or the way he called her *angel*, with the tiniest hint of sexual promise behind it.

Much, anyway.

She lifted her chin just a fraction as he continued to stare at her and then finally—thankfully—he nodded his head and gestured towards the door.

'Let me show you to your room.'

Lexi nearly threw her hands up in the air as she realised that she'd just inadvertently agreed to go to Greece with him.

The *last* thing she wanted to do. But how could she say no, now? 'I must be mad,' she muttered under her breath, trailing him up the long corridor towards the bedrooms.

He stopped in front of the room next to the one Ty occupied.

Lexi folded her arms across her chest. 'Why do I have to stay here tonight if you're not leaving until the morning?'

'Insurance.'

'If I give my word then I keep it.'

'But you haven't given me your word.'

She very nearly stamped her foot at that. 'Are you always this argumentative?'

He leant against the door frame regarding her lazily. 'Funny, I was going to ask the same thing about you.' His voice held a husky quality she knew he'd probably used on a hundred other women and she hardened her resolve not to be affected by him.

Lexi took a deep breath. 'I give you my word I will return first thing in the morning.'

He shrugged. 'It doesn't matter. I need you here tonight in case Ty wakes up.'

Lexi wanted to argue with him but again he had a point. 'I don't have anything to wear to bed,' she mumbled, feeling utterly defeated and uncharacteristically irritable.

He held out his hand. 'Give me your address and keys and I'll send my driver to pick up whatever you need.'

'Why can't I go myself?'

'Because Ty might wake up.'

'I'll be an hour,' she said, completely exasperated.

'No.'

'Well, I'm not having someone I don't know go through my things.'

And she knew Aimee would be at Todd's by now so she couldn't very well call and get her to send her things over in a cab.

He looked down at her, his blue eyes twin pools of open sensuality. 'There's always your birthday suit.'

Lexi chose to ignore the dangerous gleam in his gaze and instead focused on the fact that this man was the worst type of playboy around. Then she remembered his suggestive comment in her office earlier. The man would probably have sex with a lamp post if it offered.

'I don't suppose one of your many girlfriends left a nightie I could borrow, did they?' she asked sweetly.

She was hoping he'd be a little embarrassed by her sarcasm, but instead the smile that curled the corners of his mouth was lethally sexy. 'I don't have *girlfriends*. But if you're referring to my many bed partners, I'll check.'

Lexi blew out a tank-load of air after he walked out and placed her bag on the embroidered silk bedspread and stood with her hands on her hips, wondering what she had got herself into. Then the hairs on the back of her neck rose and she didn't need to glance in the full-length mirror opposite to know he was back. She turned just in time to catch a wad of grey fabric he tossed at her. Holding it up, she saw it was a well-worn T-shirt someone might wear to the gym. 'This is yours,' she said huskily.

He looked at her through heavy-lidded eyes. 'And I'll dream about you in it all night, angel.'

'I don't find comments like that funny,' she reprimanded.

He smiled again and grabbed the door handle. 'Goodnight, Miss Somers. Oh—' he paused and Lexi felt her nerves, already jangling on a knife edge split down the middle '—in case I forget to tell you. I appreciate you staying. And tell lover boy I'm sorry for ruining his *plans*.' That last was spoken with not even a shred of sincerity. The louse.

She had fallen in with the devil and he was every bit as ruthless as myth suggested.

CHAPTER FOUR

LEXI didn't know what had woken her. The room was pitch-black so it wasn't yet morning and then she heard it again. A low, deep moaning sound.

'Ty.'

She stumbled out of bed and down the hall into his room, only to pull up short when she found him sound asleep, his face relaxed and peaceful in the soft glow of the bedside lamp.

Wondering if she had been so on edge with the whole 'sleeping at a billionaire's apartment' thing she had dreamt it, she was about to go back to bed when she heard it again.

'Leo.' She exhaled the word into the still night.

It was Leo, not Ty.

Lexi was momentarily paralysed in the middle of the dark-ened hallway, her heart thumping in her chest, indecision turning her into a statue. Then she heard him moan some-thing that sounded like 'No, Sasha' and her legs carried her forward. She had always been a sucker for anyone in need. Stopping by roadsides to tend to hurt animals, collecting birds and trying to nurse them back to health. Once she had even demanded her mother stop the car and had rescued a lamb from a tangle of barbed wire. That lamb had been the love of her eight-year-old life, following her around in the garden every day as if it had imprinted on her.

Lexi forgot all about the lamb as she cautiously pushed open the door to Leo's room and peered into the gloom. As her eyes adjusted, she could make out the richly furnished room, the curtains slightly parted, letting in a finger of light that fell across the end of an enormous bed.

The man in it moved restlessly and Lexi's eyes were drawn to the dark sheet that was tangled around his lower body. He lay on his back, one arm flung over his head, the other outstretched as if he was reaching for something. His chest was bare and utterly magnificent. Broad and lean with densely packed muscles beneath a light covering of chest hair that arrowed all the way down over his shadowed abdomen and beyond. And yes, it looked like he had a six-pack, she thought resentfully.

Lexi couldn't tear her eyes away as he shifted restlessly and remembered his question about whether she wanted to know what he slept in, hoping it was more than it looked like right now. He moaned again and rolled onto his side, fingers flexing and such a look of anguished despair on his face that Lexi's heart leapt and she automatically went to him. Whatever he was dreaming about, she felt sure he'd be better off awake than asleep.

Without even thinking, she reached down and placed her hand gently against the rounded ball of his shoulder.

Leo's reaction was instantaneous and, before she could draw breath, Lexi felt all the air whoosh out of her lungs as she found herself flat on her back beneath him. The expression on his face was so intense real fear rippled through her body.

'Mr Aleksandrov...Leo!' Lexi raised her hands to his naked chest and shoved against solid muscle that didn't give an inch. Heat spiked through her as her fingers slipped to the firm muscles of his shoulders, her lower body instantly clenching in reaction to the pressure of his hard, hair-roughened thighs pressed so intimately against her own. She tried to shift against him but she was literally pinned down and then she gasped, going stock-still as she felt the hardness of his erection pressed intimately between her thighs.

Oh, boy! Sensation the like she had never experienced arced through her body, turning it liquid, and she found herself involuntarily arching into him to assuage the ache that had sprung up deep in her pelvis.

She knew he felt her undeniably sexual response because the hand that gripped her arm moved to the nape of her neck and then fisted in her hair as he tilted her face up towards his. She wanted to tell him he was dreaming, but she lost all sense of reason as their eyes met in the dimly lit room and everything else faded. A breath shuddered through her and as his masculine scent acted like a drug on her senses she raised her face to receive the hard promise of his beautiful mouth.

It was as if all the tension of worrying about Ty and the second childcare centre, and Leo himself, coalesced into this moment and she gave herself over to the feel of him, moaning in pleasure as his lips crushed hers in a hard, possessive kiss.

Excitement barrelled through her and her hands slid up the smooth skin of his back, kneading and testing the muscles as she went. His skilful tongue demanded entrance to her mouth and when she gave it their muted groans mingled hotly in the otherwise silent room. Lexi felt as if she were on fire and when his hands started roaming over her body, learning her shape, it was all she could do not to tell him to hurry up as his hands moved closer and closer to her aching breasts. She shifted again, trying to make it easier for him, and then cried out as he sensed what she needed and shoved his hand up under her T-shirt and palmed her naked breast, the rough pad of his thumb drawing an animalistic sound from her throat as it swept across her painfully sensitive nipple.

'Oh!' Her legs scissored helplessly as she tried to lift her hips under the heavy weight of his, energy building inside of her and driving her towards a nirvana she'd never felt in a man's arms before.

'Easy,' his rough, sleep-laden voice whispered against her ear at the same time as one of his hands slid to her hips to stay her restless squirming.

But it was as if that one word had intruded on a magical, secret world and shattered it, reality returning with a sickening thud as she recalled where she was and who she was with.

Lexi pushed against his chest, her movements now frenzied for a different reason. 'Leo…Mr Aleksandrov. Get off. You've had a bad dream.'

He stilled instantly, hovering over her. Then his hand slipped from her bottom and he rolled onto his back.

Lexi jumped to her feet, her body feeling both hot and cold, her breathing ragged.

She didn't know what to say and wondered if he'd fallen back asleep and then she heard a young child's cry.

Ty.

Her thoughts a complete jumble Lexi did the only thing she could—she fled. Down the hall and straight into Ty's room.

Leo woke, feeling as if he had a hangover. He'd slept, fitfully and the recurring dream he'd had on and off since his brother's death had returned last night to haunt him. Of course he knew why, but he didn't want to think about that any more than he wanted to recall Sasha's death. A death he had inadvertently caused.

Leo turned his head to the side, as if that might dislodge the heavy guilt shrouding his heart, and caught the faintest trace of vanilla. Instantly another memory, a much more pleasurable one, slammed through his body and turned him as hard as stone.

Lexi Somers. She'd woken him and he'd momentarily thought it was his father attacking him. Had he hurt her? His mind sifted through the way he'd gripped her arms and brought her under him, the feel of her soft curves, the warm

V of her thighs as she'd cradled him intimately. Her taste... like the sweetest dessert...

Leo closed his eyes. There was something about her that had called to him since they'd met, so coming fully awake to find her under him had been too great a temptation to resist.

Chort vozmi.

He hadn't meant to kiss her but she'd said his name and lifted herself against him and what was a man supposed to do with that? The natural thing, of course.

Shafts of pleasure pulsed his groin as he recalled the feel of her mouth, the touch of her fingers.

He cursed again.

He couldn't remember ever being so turned on and if she hadn't stopped him he'd have buried himself inside her with no questions asked.

He pushed out of bed and padded into the bathroom. He didn't bother shaving and just rolled straight into the shower, welcoming the stinging bite of icy-cold water as it lashed his shoulders and overheated torso.

He leant his forehead against the wall and refocused his mind. He had a massive weekend planned. The maiden voyage of his new super-yacht, *Proteus*, which he had helped design and which he planned to use as a prototype to launch a new area of his business—building first-class environmentally powered yachts, ferries and ships. But first he had to convince the Greek environmental minister to sell him land in Thessaly for a new cutting-edge ethanol plant that could revolutionise the world's use of friendly fuel sources and one he needed to power his future ships.

Then there was Ty. For most of the night he'd tried to figure out how to handle things this weekend, Lexi's questions about why he didn't know him and her assertion of how much Ty needed him weighing heavily on his conscience. The trouble was he couldn't look at Ty without thinking of Sasha and he couldn't think of Sasha without getting emotional—

something that made his blood curdle. Emotions led to two things in his experience—weakness or violence—neither of which he wanted to let into his life. Which was why, despite his guilt, he'd stayed away from Ty. It would have been selfish to have done anything else and the last time he'd acted selfishly his brother had lost his life.

Sighing heavily, he quickly pulled on his usual work attire and paused outside Ty's partially opened doorway. Not hearing any sound, he pushed the door further open to check if he was up.

What greeted him was the sweet curve of Lexi Somers' backside in the pale pink panties he'd shoved his hand into not a few hours ago. She was asleep on her side, his T-shirt bunched around her waist, her magnificent hair like a dark flag streaming out behind her, her body curved like a protective bow around the small form of his son.

Leo felt a vice grip his heart and absently rubbed his chest. They both looked so innocent, so untouchable, and his mouth tightened as he forced himself to turn away and leave the room.

He should never have agreed to take them to Greece.

CHAPTER FIVE

A THOUGHT that had only grown stronger since his private plane had taken off from Heathrow an hour ago. Having worked with Danny for the past hour, he now cupped his hands behind his head and stretched his legs out in front of him.

His eyes cruised Lexi Somers' creamy complexion and lowered to her even white teeth as she smiled at something Ty said. They were sitting on the floor playing with toy cars Lexi had insisted he buy at the airport. She was wearing a plain T-shirt and denim jeans with her hair in a ponytail and should have looked like any other girl, but she didn't. She had an understated sexiness that she didn't seem to be aware of and while he appreciated that the scrubbed, girl-next door image turned some men on, he hadn't numbered among them before now.

He wondered how lover boy had taken the news that Paris was off and whether she had told him about the kisses they had shared the night before.

Probably not. Women were rarely honest about such things. And if she had, and lover boy was worth his salt, he would have come and laid Leo out cold. That was what he would have done if the situation had been reversed. If she was his and some guy had held her underneath him. But why was he thinking like this? She wasn't his. No woman was, or ever would be.

Leo scowled, annoyed with his thoughts and the way she had treated him with polite detachment since she had woken this morning. She hadn't mentioned what had transpired in his bed last night and he knew that was for the best. Why re-hash something he didn't care to explain, or repeat?

But he couldn't deny that her indifference rankled. They had stopped briefly at her apartment and, much to her chagrin, he had accompanied her inside. He'd wanted to appease some latent curiosity about who she really was and what her motivation was for wanting to accompany him to Greece. Initially he had wondered if a latent gold-digger hadn't been hiding beneath her down-to-earth demeanour but, if anything her home only confirmed that she was most likely a nice girl. Soft furnishings, family photos on the mantelpiece in the sitting room, personal knick-knacks carefully placed on well-worn surfaces. The opposite of the various homes he kept around the world, which were always pristine and well ordered. Like his life usually was.

And hell, she hadn't even known who he was when they'd first met!

He glanced at Ty and cursed Danny's lack of foresight in sending him a nanny without a passport, knowing as he did that it wasn't Danny's fault. None of it was. It was his. And only he could fix things. The key now was to keep Lexi and Ty as far away from him as possible, which shouldn't be too hard. Yes, they'd be trapped together on his yacht for three days but the thing was as big as two football fields and consisted of eight levels. How hard could it be?

Bracing himself, Leo looked at his son. A boy he didn't want and a boy who hadn't asked to be born. Some might call it fate that Amanda had conceived on that one time they had had sex. He knew Lexi Somers thought Ty was suffering from his absence but Leo didn't want to believe that. He had always believed he was doing the right thing, the honourable thing, in staying out of Ty's life. In leaving him with his mother. But it seemed he might have been wrong and he couldn't stomach that. Couldn't stomach the thought of making a mistake again, of being responsible for another person's future happiness.

But still Lexi's words nagged at him. Was she right in suggesting that Ty's emotional needs were suffering? She was the expert who had cared for him for two years. Why would she say it if it wasn't true? And why had Amanda's mother been looking after Ty? He needed to find out more information, that was clear.

'Do you want to come join us?' The soft query from the angel—on the floor—brought his attention back to the present. His eyes met hers and he saw a wealth of questions in her guarded expression. She was trying to figure him out and that wasn't going to happen.

He stood up and pierced her with a warning look that had been known to make grown men quake.

The plane dipped slightly and one of the small cars Ty was playing with rolled towards him. Leo automatically bent to pick it up and then his eyes met his son's. They *were* blue, like his. And he could see now how Lexi had made the connection between them so quickly. On top of the eye colour, his son had the slashing eyebrows and strong bone structure that indicated his Cossack ancestry. Leo held his breath as dark images of Sasha at that age rolled into his brain like thunderclouds.

Ty moved towards him, intent on getting his car, and Leo felt the urge to get as far away from him as possible. Then he felt the unmistakable shift of the aircraft as it hit an air pocket, the bottom seeming to fall out of the plane. As if in slow motion, Ty stumbled, his little arms instinctively thrown forward to break his fall, and Leo reacted purely on instinct—reaching down and lifting his son into his arms before bracing himself against the side of the plane. They staggered together and Ty flung his arms around Leo's neck and for the first time ever

Leo breathed in his clean, little boy scent. His eyes closed, his body tensed. Within seconds the turbulence had passed, the plane once again steady.

'Are you okay?' Lexi's worried voice broke his paralysis and he opened his eyes to find her standing in front of him. He released a breath and clenched his jaw. No, he was not okay.

'Here.' He thrust Ty at her. 'Make sure he's strapped in at all times while the plane is in the air,' he grated coldly.

'Mr Aleksandrov...' He didn't know what she had been about to say and he didn't wait around to hear, making his way to his private bedroom for the rest of the journey. He slumped down on the edge of the bed and held his unsteady hands in front of him. Ty had felt so small and fragile. He spread his fingers and turned them back and forth, no longer seeing his own hands but those of his father's. How had he hit them at such a young age?

Athens was a revelation to Lexi. Hot, dry, crumbly...ancient! She loved it. Loved the busyness of the streets and the organised chaos of locals, tourists and Vespas winging in and out of the traffic.

She pointed things out to Ty as their taxi fought its way through the gridlock to God only knew where. She hadn't seen Leo after the incident on the plane and again found herself wondering at the type of man he was. She hadn't missed the pain behind his eyes as he had looked at Ty on the plane. Almost as if he was looking at someone else. A ghost. And did that have anything to do with his nightmare last night?

She knew from reading his biography online that he was an only child to 'warm and loving parents' who had died in a tragic accident when he was twenty. From there he had bought a scaffolding company and turned it into a global entity before expanding into hotels and construction. According to Wikipedia he had become the richest man in Russia by his thirtieth birthday, a position he still held five years on.

But if he came from such a loving family, why had he never accepted Ty as his son? What had gone wrong between him and Amanda? She hadn't been able to find any information about his connection to either one of them online, which was strange for such a high-profile person—which she now realised he was.

Not to mention the most exciting male she had ever set eyes on. Not that she planned to do anything about that. She only wished she wasn't so physically aware of him.

Like now, with her thigh touching the length of his in the taxi they had been forced to take from the airport. They were supposed to have ridden in Leo's helicopter, but as soon as Ty had heard the whine of the rotors he'd started to cry and Lexi had been pleasantly surprised when Leo had ordered a taxi instead. Now she was unpleasantly hot pressed against him in the confines of the small car and, from what she could tell by the amount of tapping Leo was doing on his phone, he hadn't noticed at all.

Finally, they alighted from the taxi and Lexi stretched and looked around. The port of Piraeus was teeming with activity and various large ferries and boats were docked at the tiny, industrious harbour, Athens rising behind her in a tier of mostly grubby, worn, age-old buildings.

'Look, Ty—' she pointed up the hill, where a cluster of deep green trees circled below the rocky ledge that housed the Parthenon and other ancient ruins '—the Acropolis.'

The little boy looked, but of course showed none of the excitement that she felt.

'Hurry up, it's hot,' Leo demanded grumpily behind her.

She turned and spotted the four casually dressed bodyguards she was still not used to flanking them.

'Of course it's hot.' She smiled, determined not to let his dark mood, or her own awareness of him as a man, colour her enjoyment of her surroundings. He had forced her to come, but it was her natural inclination to try and find the best in every situation. 'It's summer in Greece. Have you been to the Acropolis before?'

Leo scowled down at her. 'No.'

'Is this your first time in Athens, then?' she asked interestedly, shading her eyes against the sun as she looked up at him.

'I come here to work, not play.' He glanced at Ty and then back. 'Is he heavy?'

'No.'

'Good. Danny will give you a tour of *Proteus* and see to anything that you need.'

'Oh, what will you be doing?'

Her question caught Leo off guard and he didn't know if it was the heat of the sun, or her annoying serenity, or the fact he'd just spent the better part of an hour pressed up against her in a stifling taxi, but his patience was paper-thin. 'If I wanted to answer to someone, Miss Somers, I'd have a wife.'

Her eyebrows shot up and her exotic eyes, which had sparkled before as she'd enjoyed her surroundings, turned frigid. 'A novel concept for you, to be sure,' she retorted, stalking off ahead of him as if she were a queen dismissing a minion.

No, angel, you're the novel concept.

Simmering with frustration, Leo found himself absently watching the provocative sway of her hips in jeans that were surely a size too small before indicating to two of his security detail to follow her.

He boarded his yacht and his captain and two engineers were waiting to give him a personal tour. When that was done, he headed to his private office to work.

Only his mind wouldn't focus and by nightfall he had given up. Tomorrow he would have up to thirty guests enjoying a weekend on-board and he would need to be in top form for the meetings he had planned.

Even though it was late, he decided to stop by the pool deck for a drink. It was empty, the bar closed and most of the sun loungers packed away for the night. He took a seat in a deck-chair under the awning, out of sight of the prying lens of any roving paparazzi that had got wind he was on-board, and enjoyed the peaceful sound of the sea slapping against the sides of the nearby vessels and the distant rumble of city traffic.

He heard a door behind him slide open and presumed it was a steward come to see if he wanted something to drink. Then he heard the soft sound of flip-flops crossing the deck and knew it wasn't a staff member. He watched Lexi Somers stroll to the railing and gaze out over the harbour and back towards Athens.

There wasn't anything overtly sexual about her in hot pink leggings and a jade-green oversized shirt but he couldn't take his eyes off her. She had been getting under his skin since the moment he had met her. But he couldn't for the life of him understand the attraction. She didn't appear to be like any other woman he'd met before. She was beautiful but didn't flaunt it, she seemed intelligent and switched on and yet she played children's games with ease and enthusiasm. And she spoke her mind—a quality he had never admired in a woman before.

In some ways she reminded him of the way his mother had been with Sasha—gentle and loving. Although Leo knew that his mother must have cared for him too, he knew that she had never approved of him. Where Sasha had been gentle, he had been rough. Where Sasha had been passive, he had been aggressive. He remembered that too often she had told him he was just like his father and she hadn't meant it as a compliment.

He returned his attention to Lexi Somers, who looked almost lost as she gazed out over the water, and he wondered if she was thinking about Paris. About her Parisian lover. Missing him, even.

'Unless your intention is to be on the cover of the morning paper tomorrow, I suggest you stand back from the railing.'

'Oh.' She jumped at the sound of his voice and squinted

to where he sat in the semi-darkness, the deck lit only by a few well-spaced down-lights.

'I didn't see you sitting back there in the dark.'

Leo crossed one foot over his opposite knee, his hands clasped behind his head as he slouched a little further into his deckchair. 'So it seems.'

'I was trying to see if I could see the Parthenon at night. I hear it's beautiful.'

'All you'll see is camera flashes going off if you're not careful. Or is that what you want?'

'Oh, yes, that would be great,' she scoffed. 'As you can see, I've dressed for the occasion.'

Leo reluctantly ran his eyes over her. She looked more than fine to him. 'They won't know who you are anyway. And since I wasn't standing beside you they're unlikely to dig. Most likely they'll assume you're staff. Except if you wander around in that red bikini you had on today. I don't usually let my staff dress like that when they're working.'

'Lucky I'm not staff.'

'Your choice,' he said, reminding her of her wish not to be paid for the weekend. Which still irked him. If he was paying her the lines of their relationship would be clearer and he wouldn't always be thinking of crossing them.

She narrowed her eyes as she walked towards him. 'I didn't see you by the pool earlier today.'

'I was on the bridge.'

'Spying?'

'Going over the itinerary with my captain,' he advised curtly.

'I was teasing,' she informed him and Leo felt his teeth gnash together at her amused expression.

She wandered over and stood beside his table. 'Ty loves the water. In summer we get out buckets and let the kids play with water in the sandpit and he's first in line. He also loves to run. I don't know if you noticed but when he gets going he's—'

'What's that you're holding?'

She glanced at the white plastic object in her hand. 'A monitor.'

Leo frowned, immediately suspicious. 'For what?'

'Ty. It was one of the things I requested on the list I put together this morning.'

'What's it for?'

'If he wakes up and cries out I'll hear him. It's a bit like a walkie-talkie but it only transmits signals one way.'

'You can't be available to him day and night,' he said somewhat churlishly.

'Somebody has to be.'

Leo ignored the shaft of guilt that speared his gut and made a mental note to ask his housekeeper to organise someone to assist her during Ty's sleep time.

Just then a steward came out and asked if they would like drinks and Lexi surprised him by ordering a chamomile tea.

'It's very calming. You should try some.'

'Are you suggesting I'm not calm?'

She tilted her head and her long hair spilled over one shoulder. 'I don't think I'll answer that lest we start an argument.'

'You're here. That's almost guaranteed to start one.'

She smiled. 'Now *you're* teasing.' Her eyes sparkled as she tried not to laugh at him again.

He wasn't, but he decided to let it ride. Sitting out on his deck on a moonlit night with a beautiful woman he did not want to be attracted to was not conducive to bringing out his sense of humour.

'I tried to find you earlier tonight.'

'Why?'

She gripped the back of the deckchair in front of her. 'I wanted to ask you if you would like to read Ty a bedtime story.'

'I was in a meeting,' he said, his voice sharper than he intended.

She tilted her head as she considered his answer. 'Would you have done it if you hadn't been in a meeting?'

He was shocked when she called his bluff.

'No.'

He could see that his curt reply had surprised her and he was glad. Don't ask questions, *moya milaya,* that you don't want answers to.

'Why not?' she asked softly.

Did the woman never give up? Did she somehow expect him to open up and spill his guts all because she had asked an insightful question in a nice voice?

Leo leaned forward, his elbows on his knees, annoyed with himself and her. 'You really want to know?'

She stepped forward, drawn in. 'If you want to tell me.'

'Take a seat.' He indicated the deckchair next to his, his voice low.

She looked from him to the chair and back, a shade warily, and Leo felt some primitive thrill of a bygone age rise up inside himself. The lure was set and she just had to take two more steps and then he'd trap her and tell her to mind her own business. That he would not discuss his relationship with his son with her or anyone else. He might even kiss her as well. Just to find out if she really did taste as good as his recall said she did.

She hesitated beside the chair, but he could tell she hadn't taken the bait. More was the pity. 'There's always tomorrow night.'

He raised a mocking eyebrow. 'To take a seat?'

Her eyes flashed. 'To read him a story.'

'Alas, I'm all out of fairy tales, angel.'

She pursed her lips at the pet name he'd given her and he cocked his head as he considered her. 'Is that why you became a childcare worker? You like fairy tales.'

'I like children. They're honest and pure.'

Like her? He leant back in his chair. 'Could it be that you prefer dealing with children more than adults?'

'Of course not.'

'Of course yes!' He gave an unrepentant grin at her fervent denial, enjoying himself all of a sudden.

Something her next sharp words ground into dust.

'Do you have any intention of spending time with your son this weekend?'

'I didn't think you wanted an argument,' he sneered.

'I don't. I just think it's important.'

'You're not here to orchestrate a family reunion, Miss Somers, so stop trying.'

Her eyes glittered angrily in the low light. 'You would have to be a family in the first place for me to be able to do that,' she blazed back at him.

Fortunately the steward arrived with their beverages and eased the tension that had hardened the air between them. He could feel Lexi watching him but he ignored her and picked up his bottle of mineral water, lamenting the fact that he had given up alcohol seventeen years ago and wishing it was a full bottle of Stolichnaya instead.

'I don't understand you,' she said, breaking the silence once the steward was safely out of earshot. 'You grew up in what sounds like a wonderful family and yet you treat Ty as if he doesn't exist.'

Leo observed her with a level of calmness he was far from feeling. 'I won't discuss my relationship with my son with you, Miss Somers,' he said through clenched teeth, 'so stop prying.' She pulled the chair out opposite him and Leo felt as if a rock had settled in his stomach. She had an uncanny knack of making him feel guilty about Ty but she didn't know the truth behind his decision. She didn't know what he was capable of and for a split second he considered telling her. Which was madness! He never talked about himself. Ever.

And he sure as hell wouldn't be telling Lexi Somers about it either.

He was just about to return to his suite when she bent one knee up and rested her chin on it. 'Do you ever do anything besides work?'

A myriad of answers formed in his head but they would be dangerous to play to. Because while intellectually he had already decided to ignore the chemistry between them, physically he had already started to respond to the hint of vanilla carried across to him on the warm evening air.

'Sometimes,' he said evenly.

'Like what?'

Like sex. His nostrils flared as the thought hardened his groin. *Right here and right now if she were willing.* He saw her eyes widen slightly and knew she had picked up on the direction of his thoughts. Maybe the fact that he was staring at her mouth wasn't very subtle.

'Looking for a demonstration, angel?'

The air between them became charged and he noticed her running her silver necklace between her fingers.

Oh, boy.

In trying to find out more about him and how best to influence him into spending time with Ty, Lexi had inadvertently jumped into a minefield with a man who knew where all the loaded mines were.

He wasn't trying to hide his sexual interest in her and she was shocked to see it. She had convinced herself that what had happened last night was because they had both been half asleep and that the chemistry she felt was entirely one-sided, but perhaps that wasn't the case. Or perhaps he was just bored and toying with her to avoid talking about himself. That would make more sense but, whatever it was, she was just glad he hadn't remembered his nightmare last night or what had followed.

It would also help if she could stop thinking about how well the man kissed and how hard his muscles had felt pressing her into the bed. God, he made her feel desperate for sex and already her body felt hotter, heavier. But she wasn't any good at sexual banter and her cup clattered as she put it down. 'I think I might go to bed,' she said, inwardly grimacing at her gaucheness.

'Scared, angel?'

'Of?' she asked carelessly, glancing everywhere but at him.

'The way I make you feel, for one.' His voice was a lazy purr.

'Excuse me?' She coughed out a laugh as if he'd just told her an implausible joke.

His smile said he didn't believe her for a second and his stunning eyes glittered in the low light, laughing at her.

'So tell me,' he said in a way that put her even more on edge, 'how did lover boy take your rejection last night?'

'It wasn't a rejection.' She bristled at his arrogant confidence. Well, it was, she supposed, but it had nothing to do with him. 'And his name is Simon.'

'That wasn't what I asked.'

'I'm not telling you,' she said, wishing now that she had headed for her room when the thought had first occurred to her.

'It's different when the boot's on the other foot, isn't it, angel?'

'Stop calling me angel,' Lexi fumed, feeling decidedly unsettled by his nettling. Especially when she conceded that *maybe* he had a point. If she wouldn't answer his questions, why should he answer hers? 'And of course he wasn't happy, but he understood.'

It was one of the qualities that had initially drawn her to Simon. Calm, methodical, rational, dependable.

'Understood what?' Leo's dark voice broke into her thoughts. 'That he came second to me?'

Oh, what an ego!

'That isn't what happened at all,' Lexi countered, uncomfortably aware that Simon would *always* come second to him if a woman had a choice.

'No?' He gave a wolfish smile.

'No.'

'So you told him what happened in my bed last night then?' he asked silkily.

Lexi's breath lodged in her throat. Damn it, he *had* remembered what had happened and had only been *toying* with her. How had she thought even for a second that a man like him would be interested in her as a woman?

'Your list just got longer,' she said smartly.

He disconcerted her by laughing. 'Admit it, angel, you're attracted to me.'

'You're wrong about that.' She cleared her throat and nearly spilt her cup of tea.. 'I would never be attracted to a man like you.' It was a lie, but oh, she wished it wasn't.

'Trying to insult me to deflect how you feel isn't very original,' he said softly.

'Neither is the size of your ego.'

Rather than be insulted, he laughed again. 'I liked you in my bed,' he said softly.

His lips curved into a lazy grin that made her stomach flip.

'I was *not* in your bed,' she insisted sharply, frustrated by her body's automatic reaction to his suggestive tone. She had yet to find anything positive about this man and yet her body responded to his every move as if he was master of it. How could that happen when she didn't even like him?

'No?' He scratched the sexy stubble on his jaw with well-shaped, capable fingers. 'Then my imagination is very vivid because I can still taste your sweet mouth under mine.'

Lexi stifled a gasp. 'You were having a nightmare.'

'Those kinds of dreams are never nightmares, angel.'

She forced herself to hold his sensual gaze and decided the best thing she could do was to ignore his sexual banter. 'Do you have them often?' she asked, trying to redirect the conversation.

'Erotic dreams? Not since I was a youth.'

'Nightmares.'

His eyes turned flinty. 'You were mistaken if you thought I was having a nightmare. Perhaps you're just looking for an excuse as to why you kissed me last night.'

'*You* kissed *me*.'

'That's not how I remember it.' He gazed at her through sleepy eyes.

It wasn't exactly how she remembered it either.

'You were asleep. I was… We were both half asleep,' she babbled stupidly.

'And it was a lovely way to be woken up. I won't be at all upset if you do it again.'

'I would never go into your room voluntarily. You called out in your sleep. Someone named Sasha.'

'You must have been mistaken. But now *I'm* going to bed.' He stood up abruptly and towered over her. 'Care to give me a goodnight kiss, angel?'

Lexi stiffened at the audacious invitation and the instaneous 'yes' that leapt into her mind.

'Just in case you're labouring under the misapprehension that I find you funny, Mr Aleksandrov, I don't.'

She held her breath as his smouldering gaze lingered on her mouth. 'Now there's a pity. We might have had some fun together if you should ever lighten up.'

If she…? Lexi's face paled as his offhanded comment bit deep and shattered her confidence.

Arrogant, stupid ass!

CHAPTER SIX

THE next morning Lexi didn't see Leo at all, which was a good thing, she told herself.

She was still frustrated at their conversation last night, realising too late that he'd used sexual innuendo to avoid talking about Ty and then had inadvertently hit on the same complaint Brandon had had with her. And if at times she appeared uptight it was because she'd learned to guard her feelings from a young age, her father's betrayal having sapped all the happiness from her home for a long time after he'd left.

She frowned. Maybe she should just give up on her goal to reunite father and son. Maybe it would be better if she avoided Leo at all costs. Ty wasn't her child and she knew better than to become too attached to a child who was in her temporary care. And maybe Ty was better off with Amanda. It certainly seemed that way with the little interest Leo continued to display towards his son.

Yes, she'd stop playing some modern version of Mary Poppins and keep well away from Leo Aleksandrov. Right after she spoke to him this morning about the young Greek girl, Carolina, he had apparently assigned to assist her. As if she needed an assistant!

She rounded a corner of the yacht and smiled politely as yet another group of uber-trendy individuals passed her in the corridor.

Leo's weekend guests had arrived throughout the morning, some joining her and Ty by the pool and slipping into holiday mode as if they'd been born to it. One woman in particular, the supermodel Katya—no last name required, which was so yesterday, Lexi thought churlishly—had immediately rubbed her up the wrong way. Though whether that was because she had clung to Leo like the last autumn leaf on a tree or because she had that air of practised superiority about her Lexi wasn't sure.

Oh, who was she kidding? She'd been put out because of the way *Leo* had looked at *her*. A woman who was tall, stunning and exactly his type. Lexi wondered if she was his current mistress and felt her mouth pinch together. If she was, he was more of a cad than she had given him credit for. Flirting outrageously with her—kissing her and touching her—while his girlfriend was in transit from America.

Lexi wandered from deck to deck and had no idea what level she was now on. She was almost out of breath and finally understood that the central glass elevator, beautifully inlaid with designer plants and flowers, was not just a showpiece for guests to appreciate as they wandered past!

This ship, which Leo called a yacht, had so many rooms it was more like a floating castle. A very sleek and richly furnished castle with more natural stone and marble than a Renaissance church.

She stopped in the doorway of an elegant sitting room and noticed the supermodel, Katya, at the far end, shaking her finger at a young staff member, who looked as if she was about to collapse.

Used to sorting out all kinds of problems Lexi didn't think twice before approaching to offer her assistance. The younger girl, whom she had met downstairs earlier, looked at her with open relief.

'Hi there; what seems to be the problem?' she asked pleasantly.

The supermodel swung around sharply at the sound of her

voice. She looked Lexi up and down as if she was considering whether or not she was worthy of an answer, and then waved her hand dismissively at the other girl.

'The *problem* is that laundry staff are not supposed to occupy the same room as a guest.'

'I was delivering t-t-towels to the second pool area,' the young girl stammered.

'Does this look like a swimming pool to you?' the model snapped.

'Again, I'm sorry ma'am. I got lost.'

Lexi threw the younger girl a sympathetic glance but Katya wasn't finished reprimanding her.

'You pass them onto the steward anyway, you imbecile. You shouldn't be above deck yourself.'

Not above deck in this glorious weather! Was that true? Lexi was flabbergasted and appalled at the model's attitude in equal measure. 'Excuse me, but that's no way to speak to anybody,' she reproved, not caring if this woman *was* Leo's latest mistress.

The model's eyes widened at her tone. 'And who are you to speak to me like that?' She regarded Lexi as if she were an ugly bug—which was exactly how she felt, standing beside the couture-clad model wearing a chain store white vest top and khaki shorts. 'Aren't you some sort of servant yourself? You shouldn't be up here either.'

Lexi ignored the comment and was about to offer to take the towels and leave the model to her own horrible company when Leo's deep voice cracked through the air like a whip.

'Katya.'

Lexi noticed the model curve her body into a provocative pose as Leo approached. He looked fit and utterly male in navy trousers and a crisp white dress shirt. 'If I ever catch you speaking to my staff like that again it will be your last time on one of my yachts.'

'Leo, darling,' the model cooed, 'I was just informing these girls of the rules and they got upset.'

'You were being a bitch. Leave us.'

'Leo!' She tried to hook her arm through his but he cast her a look that would have turned mortals into stone.

She sniffed and blinked a sexy glance from beneath her thickly coated lashes. 'I'll be by the pool.'

They all watched her saunter out of the room and Leo turned to the laundress. 'I apologise, Stella, for any offence my guest may have caused you. Here, let me take those.'

He knew the laundress's name? Lexi wouldn't have believed it if she hadn't heard it with her own ears. *And* he was going to carry towels?

'Thank you, Mr Aleksandrov.' Stella handed over her bundle and all but curtsied before scurrying out of the room.

'Nice company you keep,' Lexi said.

'Not everyone behaves like that.'

They stared at each other for a moment too long and then Lexi remembered that she'd been looking for him. 'I wanted to ask why you assigned Carolina to assist me.'

He hesitated before answering. 'You have a problem with my decision?'

How did he know she had a problem with it when she'd tried to keep her query light? 'No. Well, yes. I'm a qualified childcare provider. I can look after one child with my hands tied behind my back.'

'Ah, you think I'm questioning your professional integrity.'

'Aren't you?'

'No, Lexi. I've seen how good you are with Ty. But I don't expect you to be on call for him twenty-four seven. Carolina is to relieve you while he sleeps.' He looked down at the monitor in her hand and his brows drew together. 'Is that what he's doing now?'

'Yes. He usually has a midday nap at the centre and I thought the consistent rhythm would help him adjust.'

'Then shouldn't Carolina have this device?'

'Carolina is sitting in with him and I'll return once I hear him wake up.'

He nodded. 'Even better. Have you had lunch?'

Lexi paused, something in his expression when she had said Carolina was in with Ty sparking an instinctive knowledge deep inside her. 'You do care about him, don't you?'

Leo blinked slowly, his expression inscrutable. 'I repeat—have you had lunch?'

Lexi sighed, realising her comment had completely ruined the brief moment of accord between them.

'No, I haven't had lunch.'

'Come. It is being served on the pool deck today.'

Lexi shook her head. Having decided that she needed to keep her distance from him, the last thing she should do was sit down to lunch at his table. 'I can eat in the mess hall with the other staff.'

Leo was about to object when Danny walked into the room. 'Everyone is seated for lunch, Leo.'

Leo nodded but didn't take his eyes off Lexi. 'You will dine at my table.'

Again she shook her head. He was too virile, too male. And the way he towered over her made her too aware of her own femininity, her own *vulnerability* in his magnetic presence. 'You were the one who told me I was staff.'

'And you were the one who reminded me that you weren't,' he informed her silkily.

Lexi sighed. 'I'm hardly dressed for a proper luncheon.'

Leo slowly ran his sizzling gaze down over her casual clothing and down her bare legs and sandalled feet and all the way back up again.

'You look fine.' His voice was gruff, the tone sending frissons of sensation skittering into her belly. Given that she found it hard to keep her eyes off him she would really rather eat a hundred miles from where he was.

She was about to try some other excuse when her phone rang and she reached into her pocket and pulled it out. Recognising the number of her builder, Lexi smiled with relief. She'd been waiting for his call since yesterday and mentally crossed her fingers that he had good news about the renovations on the new centre. 'Excuse me,' she murmured, 'but I have to take this.'

Leo scowled as he watched Lexi Somers' toned legs take her to the other end of the room, wondering who was on the other end of the phone that had made her face light up with such obvious delight.

Her lover?

He felt his good mood at the progress he'd made in his meetings this morning evaporate into thin air.

His scowl deepened when he saw Lexi's expression turn worried. Was lover boy giving her a hard time? And why did it rankle so much to see her so affected by it?

'What's up?' Danny looked at him quizzically and Leo realised that Danny had picked up on his keen interest in the obstinate brunette.

'Nothing. Just see that Lexi Somers has lunch at my table,' he said curtly.

He stalked off but instead of his mood picking up when Lexi did eventually grace his table with her presence, it only worsened. She was too natural and friendly for his liking. A little *too* natural and *too* friendly with the American film-maker, Tom Shepherd. And he didn't like that he'd noticed and liked even less that it was bothering him so much. He couldn't concentrate on the lavish meal his world-class chef had prepared, or the conversation that was going on around him.

All he could hear were snippets of conversation as Tom charmed her with stories about the documentary film he was producing—the one Leo was bankrolling—and how interested she was in it, her smile generous and warm, her golden eyes sparkling as she sipped her Riesling and unself-consciously de-veined prawns before popping them into her mouth. He could see Tom was fascinated with her and it would appear that his interest was reciprocated. And where was her loyalty to her Parisian lover as she flirted with Tom Shepherd?

Leo snorted out a quiet breath. She was no different from any other female who saw a better meal ticket come along. But, if that was the case, why hadn't she latched onto him? Because he knew, without conceit, that he was the best meal ticket on this yacht, even with some of the world's most influential men currently dining at his lavishly set table.

Logically, Leo knew he was being ridiculous since he'd already decided not to pursue her, but for once logic and his libido were diametrically opposed to each other. He couldn't look away as Tom touched Lexi's arm and leant close to indicate for her to look at a flock of pelicans soaring overhead. The whole table seemed mesmerised by the majestic birds but all Leo could do was stare as Lexi's face lit up. Unbidden, an image of her pale figure in his bed the other night came to mind, her hair spread over his pillow just before he'd speared his fingers into it and crushed her mouth beneath his. The way she had met his demands with a hunger that had seemed to match his own. Her soft mews of pleasure as his hand had cupped her breast, the silky skin of her bottom—

'Did you say something?' Danny murmured.

'Only that I should have let her go to the mess hall,' Leo growled, turning away from the amused glint in his EA's eyes and striking up a conversation with the Greek minister about the reason they were even able to watch birds circling above his damned yacht this weekend.

'Jet skis?' Leo repeated blankly as he stared at Tom Shepherd.

'Yeah, you know? Motorbikes on water.' Tom smirked. 'You don't mind if we take them out for a spin, do you? Lexi's a jet ski virgin and I said I'd show her what she was missing.'

Leo's jaw clenched at Tom's provocative comment. The yacht was temporarily anchored between two small private islands and the water was deep enough so there wasn't any reason for him to say no. But he wanted to.

'I need to speak with Miss Somers.' He flashed his teeth in a tight smile. 'Take someone else.'

Before Tom could stage his protest, Danny stopped at his side. 'Leo, the men are waiting in the stateroom to resume the meeting, as you requested.'

Leo muttered a curse under his breath. If he'd been dealing with Australians or the English the negotiations would have been finished by now. No way would they have pulled up stumps to be wined and dined with a decadent lunch midway through an important meeting. No, they would have put up with soggy sandwiches and finger food at the conference table until the deal was signed, sealed and delivered. Then gone out and got drunk by way of celebrating.

'Well, that settles it.' Tom clasped Lexi's shoulder lightly and Leo was glad to see her eyes flicker to Tom's hand uncertainly as she shifted out from under his hold. 'Come on,' he said to Lexi. 'I promise you'll love it.'

'Where's Ty?' Leo found himself asking. 'Your charge.'

Lexi looked at him but he couldn't read her expression. 'He's still asleep. He probably will be for another forty minutes at least.'

With no other way to prevent her from going with Tom, Leo signalled a nearby steward. 'Have the jet skis organised for Mr Shepherd and any other interested guests.' Then he turned back to Tom. 'Be careful.'

Tom shook his head as if Leo was mad. 'I always am, man; don't sweat it.'

Leo shoved his hands into his pockets and watched as Tom cupped Lexi's elbow and led her towards the elevator, annoyed when she didn't shake him off the second time.

'I don't think he's realised she's off-limits yet,' Danny murmured.

Leo shot him a warning look. 'That's because she isn't.'

Leo stormed down to the conference room and ignored the irrational urge to go after Lexi and take her out on the thing himself.

Not that he wanted to go out on a damned jet ski. He wanted to focus on what he enjoyed most—business. He'd been working for two years on developing this ethanol plant and he wasn't about to jeopardise it to have fun in the sun.

What did he care about the sparkling blue waters of the Aegean, or the sandy islands surrounding him? To him, this location was just another venue to continue his business dealings. Relaxing was something he did after hours either at the gym or with a woman. Lazing around on a beach or riding a jet ski had never been on his list of things to do.

But half an hour later he was glad he'd insisted Danny stay in the meeting because he was the only one holding it all together. For some reason, Leo couldn't seem to get his brain into gear. Maybe he'd had too much sun upstairs because the state-of-the-art airconditioning wasn't doing anything to cool his blood. Nor was the buzzing of the jet skis and the delighted catcalls and squeals of his guests as they enjoyed themselves outside his window.

Leo paced around the airconditioned room and understood how a jungle cat felt locked up in a zoo.

He noticed the conversation had stopped and waved his hand absently. 'Carry on,' he said to the Greek minister's young and ambitious lawyer. 'I'm listening.'

He ignored Danny's concerned glances and stalked over to the window, watching as four jet skis were lined up ready to race.

One of the men yelled, 'Go' and they all gunned the engines, the skis lurching full speed over the water. Leo's eyes cut to Tom, who had Lexi on the back without a life jacket.

A cold sense of dread settled over his skin. He should have stopped her from going. Or, better yet, gone with her. His instincts had been on high alert and if she got hurt it would be his fault. He didn't question his need to protect her and nor did he ignore it. The last time he had, he'd lost his brother.

'Take five, gentlemen,' he threw over his shoulder as he marched out of the room.

CHAPTER SEVEN

HE MADE it to the lower deck just as Tom hit a rough patch of water and the ski lifted into the air and landed at a sharp angle. Leo's heart flew into his mouth as Lexi screamed and flew off the side of the machine and disappeared under the water. For a split second he was paralysed as the rider behind Tom rode dangerously close to the wake.

Then he moved. Jumped onto the lower ramp and grabbed the remaining jet ski from one of the attendants, flying out over the sparkling sea to where Lexi had gone under. The other riders hadn't realised what had happened and Tom had just got his machine under control when Leo reached the place Lexi had gone under.

Fortunately, her head broke the surface but Leo could see she had swallowed water and was having trouble breathing.

He cut the engine and leaned down over the side. 'Lexi, give me your hand,' he shouted. She looked disoriented and flailed around and Leo hooked his arm around her torso and hauled her up in front of him.

'Is she all right?' Tom called out as he pulled up alongside.

'You'd better hope so, Shepherd,' Leo snarled. He quickly ran his eyes over Lexi, but he couldn't get a good look at her as she curled over his arm retching violently.

Leo cursed, ordering Tom to go back and get the in-house doctor. He held Lexi against his chest as he yanked on the throttle and headed towards the nearby island. It was closer than the yacht and he wanted to get her horizontal as quickly as possible.

The small curved inlet was deserted and once he hit the shallow water he jumped down and swung Lexi up into his arms. He ran through the breakwater and dropped to his knees and gently laid her onto the sand. She was shaking with reaction, her clothes clinging to her like a second skin, but other than that she didn't appear injured.

'Did the ski hit you anywhere?' he asked hoarsely.

She shook her head and winced a little. 'No.' She raised a shaky hand to push her hair out of her eyes and he leaned forward and did it for her. 'I think I just got winded when I hit the water.'

She tried to sit up but Leo held her down with an unsteady hand on her shoulder. 'Lie back. Shepherd's getting the doctor.'

'I'm okay.' She moved her arms and legs carefully to make sure. Leo's heart was still lodged in his throat and adrenalin coursed through his blood.

'Just keep still,' he growled, the wealth of emotion in his voice raising her eyes to his. He couldn't look away and nor, it seemed, could she. The world receded; even the relentless heat from the sun in a cloudless blue sky faded into the background as Leo felt emotions he didn't want to name roll through him, searching for purchase.

Without conscious thought, he raised an unsteady hand to the side of her face. 'You could have been killed.' His voice was rough and heat arced between them as he gazed into golden eyes framed by long, wet, spiky lashes. His fingers stroked into her hair and she nestled her cheek into the curve of his palm.

Fascinated, Leo watched the gold of her eyes become eaten up by black, leaving only a ring of emerald-green, and his body caught fire at the implicit message her dilated pupils transmitted to him. Green. Her eyes turned green with passion.

As if somehow driven by the need to affirm that she was okay, Leo's eyes dropped to her parted lips seconds before his head followed.

He didn't know if she too was driven by the scare of her accident but her mouth flowered beneath his and her hands speared into his hair as she answered the urgent demand of his lips.

One of his arms banded around her lower back as he raised her to him and he felt the tips of her breasts nestle against his chest as she strained closer, the heat of her body burning through her flimsy vest top and his shirt as she caught fire in his arms.

Her urgency more than matched his and he revelled in the way she tried to take charge of the kiss, her thumbs gliding over his cheekbones as she held his face steady while she sipped and nipped at his mouth. He let her play for maybe a second before crushing her mouth beneath his. She moaned and he answered that sound of pleasure with a low groan of his own, pressing her back into the sand and taking control of the kiss.

This was total insanity but he couldn't deny how much his body ached to take her. His tongue curled around hers and his mouth turned hard as the same primitive hunger he'd felt with her the other night took hold and threatened to consume him, all sense of reason and caution flying into the air to be fried by the midafternoon sun.

He didn't know how it was possible for the sound of the approaching jet ski to be heard over the loud beating of his heart but fortunately it brought him to his senses and he wrenched his mouth from hers, his body throbbing with unslaked desire.

Her mouth was kiss-swollen and he knew the good doctor would know what had happened even if he hadn't seen them and Leo cursed his own stupidity. The woman had nearly died in an accident and he'd what—tried to ravish her?

Emotions exploded through him and landed with unerring accuracy on Tom Shepherd as he barrelled up the sand towards them. Rage the like he couldn't remember took over from lust and circuited his body. His muscles tensed and for a split second he contemplated meeting him halfway and putting his fist through his face.

Lexi must have sensed his intent because she placed her warm palm on his forearm. 'Don't.' That softly spoken plea brought him back to his senses and stopped him in his tracks. A bar room full of men hadn't been able to stop him after he'd located the man responsible for the death of his uncle in a work-related accident but this woman could contain him with the slightest touch. Of course he'd been irrational with pain at the time his uncle had died, but somehow the emotions he'd felt today when he'd watched Lexi go under hadn't been that much different. Which was absurd. He'd loved his uncle and didn't care a whit about Lexi Somers.

'Lexi, are you okay?' Tom's concern was palpable and Leo shook off his disconcerting thoughts and pierced him with a look. If he but knew it, Tom Shepherd was only standing because of the woman he'd nearly killed. He hadn't put a life jacket on Lexi and Leo knew why. And he knew why Tom had gone extra fast to make her cling to his back. Had she enjoyed it, pressed up against Tom's back as she'd held tight? Had she been thinking of *Tom* when she'd responded to *his* kisses moments ago? Leo inwardly cursed the direction of his thoughts. This sense of jealousy—because he recognised that was what it was even though he had never experienced it before—was so unlike him. Women were always easy to come by and easy to let go.

Unused to feeling so out of balance, Leo turned his anger on her. 'Why the hell didn't you insist on wearing a life jacket?' he snarled.

He could see his sudden attack had startled her and that she was floundering over how to answer him.

'That was my fault, Leo,' Tom answered like a protective beau. 'I said she wouldn't need one.'

'Excuse me. If I could just see the patient.' The doctor pushed the two men aside and crouched beside Lexi and Leo paced away from them before he did hit Tom. He hadn't been in a fist fight for seventeen years and he was disgusted with his loss of control that nearly saw him in one now. He didn't understand this possessive urge he felt towards Lexi Somers but it had to stop. She wasn't his and she never would be. He would never want her to be, despite his continued desire to take her to bed. That was just lust. Unusual in its intensity, yes, but still something he could control.

The doctor finished examining her and sat back on his haunches. 'You're fine. You've taken in a bit of water but your lungs sound clear enough. It doesn't appear you were hit and I expect you'll make a full recovery by this evening, but get some rest when you get back all the same.'

'I feel fine now,' Lexi said, hugging her knees close to her chest.

'Thanks, Gerard,' Leo murmured. 'Tom can return you to the yacht.'

Tom hesitated. 'I'm really sorry, Lexi.'

'That's okay, Tom. Accidents happen.'

'No, they don't,' Leo cut in. 'That was a stupid thing to do, Shepherd, and if I see you on one of my skis again without a life jacket I'll find someone else to do the East India project.'

Lexi's eyes flew to Leo as he squared off against Tom. The East India project was *his* idea? Lexi was shocked. The man worked tirelessly to save men he had probably never met after a building accident, knew the name of a staff member who ranked low down on the yacht's employment hierarchy, and now funded documentaries to bring the plight of children in the Third World to the attention of others—and these were just things she knew about. It didn't make sense that a man like that would not want to have a relationship with his son.

Unless he was still pining for the mother of that child?

Lexi's throat constricted at the unexpected thought that Leo might still be so in love with the beautiful Amanda Weston that he couldn't even stand to have their son in his orbit if he couldn't have her as well. Not that he'd said as much—but what other explanation could there be?

Lexi remembered how her own mother had been so deeply affected when her father's double life had come to light she had never risked her heart on another man again, turning instead to fostering children to fulfil the void his defection had left behind. Lexi had admired her mother for providing such a caring environment for other children, but she had always struggled when a child who had become part of their family had been returned to their own home.

'Okay, okay, my friend; I can see you're upset.' Tom held his hands up towards Leo in a conciliatory nature. 'We'll talk later by which time I hope your ire has cooled enough to accept my most humble apology.'

Lexi was surprised at Leo's aggressiveness and felt sorry for the retreating Tom. It had been remiss of him not to remind her to wear a life jacket but…

'Leo, really…it was an accident,' Lexi protested.

'It was avoidable.' Leo turned to face her, his blue eyes rapier sharp as he glared at her. 'If you had been wearing a life jacket you wouldn't have gone under,' he rasped forcefully.

'I didn't know I had to.' Was this really the same man who not twenty minutes ago had kissed her into a liquid puddle of need?

'I know that,' he snapped. 'And you know the reason Shepherd didn't tell you to put one on.'

His icy gaze raked down over her body and it took her a

second for his meaning to register. 'Are you suggesting...? That's ridiculous,' she said indignantly.

'It's the truth. He probably took his cue from your flirting with him during lunch. Probably earlier in the pool, for all I know.'

Lexi felt a blast of anger curl her hands into fists. 'And I suppose that kiss before on the sand was my fault as well? I encouraged you by lying back, unable to catch my breath.'

Leo rubbed the back of his neck. 'That kiss was the result of an extremely stressful situation,' he grated.

'Do tell.'

'Do tell what? As I recall, you weren't exactly reluctant a few minutes ago.'

Lexi shut up then. He was right; she'd been far from reluctant and she needed more time to reconcile her attraction to a man she didn't respect and who confused her mind and her senses in equal measure. She still felt light-headed from his kiss and the heat of his body pressing her so firmly into the sand.

'Yes, well, as you said, it was stress. And I think we should just forget it ever happened.'

'Fine with me.'

Lexi felt lost for words at his easy acceptance of her rebuttal and leant forward to brush the sugar-soft sand from her legs. What had she wanted him to say? That his kisses had been special? As if.

'We should get back,' he bit out tersely.

'Yes,' she agreed absently, too caught up in her own tumultuous response to this man to wonder at his irritation.

Leo led the way down to the water's edge and it wasn't until the hot sand gave way to the coolness of the water that she realised just *how* she would be getting back to the yacht.

'I'm not riding with you on that,' she protested a little too vehemently.

Leo waded towards the jet ski. 'What are you going to do—swim?'

He swung himself up onto the bobbing ski with envious athleticism, his leanly muscled torso rippling beneath his still damp shirt from where he'd held her wet body against him. 'It's not that far,' she said, trying to calculate the distance between the island and his yacht.

'It's over two kilometres and you've had a fall.'

'I was only winded,' she reminded him.

Leo gunned the engine and stretched out his hand. 'Get on,' he snarled, not bothering to hide his annoyance.

'You've ruined your trousers,' she commented inanely, noticing for the first time that he was still wearing suit trousers that were wet up to his knees and moulded to his muscular calves.

'My trousers are the least of my concerns,' he dismissed, beckoning to her. 'Come. You need to get out of this hot sun.'

Lexi eyed the jet ski dubiously. 'Can't you call the tender?'

'What with?' His lips curved into a mocking smile. 'My bat phone?'

Lexi didn't know if he was being humorous or not, she just knew that touching him was a bad idea. She fiddled with her necklace and his eyes narrowed on the movement.

'Don't make me have to come over there and get you,' he warned softly.

Lexi's heart skipped a beat, images of him lifting her up with those muscular arms and cradling her against his solid chest motivating her to wade through the warm water towards him. There was plenty of room behind him anyway and if he went slowly enough she wouldn't even have to hang onto him.

'Promise you won't go fast.'

'Whatever you want,' he drawled and Lexi's eyes cut to his. Whatever she wanted. She wanted him to kiss her like he had on the beach and never stop.

No.

She blinked away the unwelcome thoughts—that was so not what she wanted. Tomorrow she would be back in London and this weekend would be a distant dream. A one-night stand with a Russian playboy with questionable morals was not what the good doctor had ordered at all!

She reached out to take his hand and could have kicked herself for not grabbing the side of the ski instead when he effortlessly hauled her up in front of him, his strong thighs moulded to the outside of her own.

Lexi sucked in a quick breath. 'I can ride behind.'

'No,' his deep voice rumbled beside her ear and Lexi held herself completely still.

'And you dare to call me obstinate,' she fumed, so tense she felt ready to snap.

'Just sit still,' he growled as he expertly turned the machine towards the yacht and revved the engine.

Lexi ignored the way her insides clenched and turned molten with desire at his rough command. She held herself stiffly within the cage his arms made around her and only dared breathe again when he pulled up alongside the yacht's rear ramp.

A small welcoming committee was waiting to make sure she was okay and they clapped as Leo jumped easily onto the end of the yacht and held out his hand to help her up.

Lexi smiled up at everyone and then placed her hand in Leo's. The muscles in his forearms rippled as he effortlessly hauled her up and it was only as their eyes met that Lexi realised that she hadn't thanked him for rescuing her.

'Thank you,' she said, her voice husky and a little embarrassed.

She saw Leo's nostrils flare but other than that he didn't acknowledge her words and she turned her glazed eyes from his piercing gaze to focus on the others.

She reassured everyone that she was fine, mini drama over, and patted Tom's arm. 'Stop with the guilty look. I'm fine.'

'I can't help feeling bad. Let me take you up and get you a cool drink.'

She was about to say she'd like that when Leo interrupted, 'The doctor ordered rest.'

Lexi turned to find Leo glowering at Tom. 'I can—'

'Go to your room,' he said, his eyes on Tom.

Lexi felt her hackles rise at his proprietorial air. 'I'm fine,' she asserted.

He swung his blue eyes to hers and Lexi had to force herself not to feel intimidated. 'Good to know.' He stepped between her and Tom. 'One thing, angel.' He leaned close and lowered his tone so only she could hear and Lexi sucked in her breath to ensure that they didn't touch. 'If you're going to be having sex with anyone this weekend it won't be Tom Shepherd.'

Lexi blinked and before her befuddled brain could formulate any sort of decent response he had stalked past her and taken the curved staircase up to the next level, two steps at a time.

CHAPTER EIGHT

What on earth had he meant by that?

Lexi had asked herself the same question over and over all afternoon. She wasn't planning to have sex with anyone that weekend, let alone Tom Shepherd. And Leo's comment had been insulting in the extreme, implying that she was inviting attention, which she most definitely wasn't.

And if she wasn't going to have sex with Tom, then who was he thinking would take his place? Certainly not him if the way he'd jumped on her request that they forget all about those scorching kisses back on the beach was any indication.

Lexi leaned towards her bathroom mirror and swiped bronze eye shadow across her eyelids and then rubbed at the corner of her eye when she applied too much.

To say that Leo's behaviour confused her would be an understatement. Anyone would think that his behaviour towards her after the accident was possessive but, really, he was probably just concerned she was going to slap him with a law suit.

Deciding on a soft pink lip gloss, she stood back from the mirror and eyed herself critically. Her figure was neat and small and entirely unremarkable, although she did like the way her breasts looked in the halter-style amber maxi-dress she had bought in the sales last year and hadn't had a chance to wear yet. At least it made her look as if she had cleavage.

Shoving it into her weekend bag while Leo had prowled around her living room while she packed had been a spur of the moment decision but now she wondered if it wasn't a little risqué. Not that she had anything else suitable to wear to his soirée tonight. A soirée she didn't even want to attend but had been informed she was expected to. And why was that? And why was her heart beating faster at the thought?

She stretched the silky fabric of her dress over her breasts, which suddenly seemed heavy and overly sensitive as they chafed the soft fabric. She traced her hands along the outer swell of each breast, remembering how Leo's much larger ones had skimmed that exact place hours earlier and her nipples tightened into aching points. A light thrumming feeling took up residence between her thighs as she imagined his mouth at her breast, his tongue. She imagined him taking her flesh into his mouth, could almost see the back of his blond head as she gazed at herself in the mirror.

A small whimper escaped from her lips and Lexi dropped her hands, her eyes slightly dazed as she gazed at her reflection. This was ridiculous. The man turned on the entire female population. Was she really considering adding herself to their ranks? Knowing the type of man he was? And, worse, knowing he would undoubtedly be disappointed with her sexually—as Brandon had been?

Oh, why was she even thinking like this?

She viciously twisted her heavy mass of hair into a bun and started stabbing pins into it.

A man who could have anyone did not go for moderately pretty girls unless they threw themselves at him and that was about as likely to happen as her being asked to model in a Victoria's Secret parade!

Lexi glanced down and realised she had used up the whole board of hairpins. Disgusted at her distracted thoughts, she stepped into high-heeled sandals and went to check on Ty.

Once she'd done that, she arrived in a ballroom the size of a basketball court, dimly lit by crystal chandeliers and alive with the happy chatter of Leo's guests and a live jazz band set up in the corner beside a wooden dance floor.

She swept her gaze around the room and her heart stopped beating when she noticed that Katya had taken up residence by Leo's side and it would have taken a crowbar to prise her away from him.

And he didn't seem to mind at all. In fact he was welcoming her attentions, his hand laying across the small of her back whenever she leaned in to whisper something to him—which appeared to be every five seconds.

Lexi's breath caught as her eyes drifted over Leo in a sleekly tailored black tuxedo. The black bow tie—which she had always found a touch effeminate on other men—only served to enhance his dangerous appeal—drawing attention to the strong column of his tanned neck and square jaw. The jacket hugged wide shoulders and drew in around his lean, hard-packed waist.

The tall model, dressed in a tiny white dress that loved every one of her generous curves and set off her red-gold hair, which hung like a smooth sheet down her back, the perfect feminine foil for his masculine sensuality. The yin to his yang.

Lexi drew in a sharp breath and tried to convince herself that she wasn't upset. Because he really wasn't her type and yet she literally ached to have him touch her again. To touch him. She could explain it away when she had been half asleep, or half-drowned, but now, in a room full of party-goers, his effect on her was a little hard to fob off.

Not wanting to dwell on something she couldn't fully understand, she startled a waiter by whisking a glass of champagne off his tray as he walked past. Not that she knew why she bothered because she doubted she'd be able to get a millimetre of the delicious liquid past the boulder lodged in her throat.

She felt her breathing take on an uneven kilter and her

heart pound and for a minute she felt lost and completely humiliated. Because, even though she had taken umbrage with Leo's kisses, with his possessive behaviour in front of Tom, a small part of her had thought that…what? That he might actually want to be with her? That he might seriously find her attractive? That he might have invited her to his party to be with him?

She felt like a fool. A fool who had dressed up for nothing.

No, not nothing. She would have a good time if it killed her.

'Care to dance, *omorphe kopella*?'

Lexi turned at the sound of a deep Mediterranean voice beside her. The man who had spoken to her was tall, though not as tall as Leo, and clean-shaven, with raven black hair and a cleft in his chin.

'My name is Anton Pompidou. I am a lawyer with the Greek government.'

'I'm Lexi Somers. Childcare manager.'

He smiled and held out his hand. 'You forgot to say beautiful.' His smile wasn't exactly smarmy, but he was smooth and she could tell he was used to getting his way with women. Lexi was just about to decline his invitation when she noticed Leo place his hand in the small of Katya's back again as she leaned in to whisper some sweet nothing in his ear and found herself agreeing instead. 'I'd love to.'

Anton's smile widened and Lexi fervently hoped he didn't read too much into her overzealous acceptance.

Which, a short time later, after he offered to escort her outside for some 'fresh air', she realised he had.

'Look, I'm really sorry,' she informed him as he tried to take her into his arms, 'but I really did just come out here for air.'

'Is there a problem out here?'

Lexi made a small, pained noise as she recognised Leo's gravelly accented voice behind her just before he came into view.

'No problem, Mr Aleksandrov.' The tall Greek released her and all but bowed down to him. 'Miss Somers required some fresh air.'

'And now she requires some privacy,' Leo drawled, his eyes pinned to hers as he spoke to the lawyer.

Some small part of Lexi willed the man to defy him but it didn't happen. Leo had an air of command about him few men possessed and even fewer argued with.

'You should know that when a man offers to take a woman outside for air it's rarely what he's offering,' he said shortly.

Lexi turned back to the twinkling lights of the distant island she had been admiring earlier. 'Thanks for the tip.'

'That is Naxos,' he told her after a brief pause.

'I didn't ask.'

'You are angry with me.'

Lexi released a deep breath and turned her head to look at him. She thought how unfairly good-looking he was in the moonlight. 'He thinks we're together now.'

'So?'

'So…so you're overbearing and arrogant.'

'So?'

Lexi huffed out a breath. 'I don't know. Just go back to your supermodel accessory, would you. I'm too tired to argue with you tonight.' She turned back to look out over the inky sea that shone silver in the moonlight.

'Then don't.'

Lexi's eyes swung back to his and she shook her head as she clearly read the meaning behind that simple statement. 'You can't just waltz out here and treat me as if…as if…'

'As if I own you?'

His silky words stole the breath from her lungs and set her heart pumping madly behind her breastbone. 'What do you want, Leo?' she asked without really meaning to but now waiting with bated breath for his answer.

* * *

You.

The single word floated into the front of his brain like a neon sign and he didn't try to push it away as usual.

Why bother? He wanted her. She wanted him and he had already decided the best thing to do now was to give in to it.

He'd tried to ignore her all night. Had even used Katya as some sort of shield, but as soon as Anton Pompidou had laid his hands on Lexi he'd known the game was up.

Warning bells might be going off inside his head louder than a New Year's Eve countdown but he might as well have been in a kamikaze jet on autopilot for all the good they were doing him.

He looked at her now, her low-cut gown shimmering around her, and he knew that he wanted her more than he'd wanted to possess anything else in his life.

'You,' he said softly, the word falling between them like a sacred offering.

He heard her breath hitch and saw her body tense, her nipples tight as they pushed against the silky fabric of her dress. He knew the air was still too warm to have brought about that reaction and his groin hardened to painful proportions as it read the signals her body was sending out.

If he didn't touch her soon, if he didn't get her beneath him in his bed, he just might implode.

She wasn't looking at him but awareness vibrated between them and burned up some of the few remaining brain cells that were still functioning inside his head.

Then she turned her head, an errant curl falling over her forehead, the look in her eyes utterly disparaging.

'Why? Did your supermodel turn you down?'

He sucked in a steadying breath. 'I didn't offer her anything.'

'Really?' She arched a delicate brow and snagged the piece of hair behind her ear. 'Could have fooled me.'

'I think I hurt you tonight.'

'You confuse me,' she said with raw honesty, 'but if you're seriously offering me a night in your bed then I have to tell you I'm not interested in casual sex.'

Leo studied her, aware of the scent of the sea air and the loud thud of his own heart.

'There will be nothing casual about the sex we have, angel.'

Her eyes dropped away from his and he wondered at the flash of—uncertainty? Insecurity?—that crossed her face.

'Lexi?'

She shook her head at him. 'I've known men like you and… you have too many secrets, Leo. I couldn't be with someone I couldn't trust.'

Leo felt the skin on his face pull tight. 'Are you saying I'm dishonest?'

'I'm saying I don't know who you are. You give nothing away and…'

'Somebody hurt you?'

Lexi huffed out a breath and shrugged her shoulders but the movement was stilted. 'My father led a double life and when my mother found out it nearly killed her.' She tugged at the necklace nestled between her breasts agitatedly and then dropped it when she saw him looking. 'I don't know why I just told you that.'

'Because you want to sleep with me but you're torn.'

She shook her head. Oh, to be so confident. 'I've never met anyone like you but…like I said, you have secrets and they scare me.'

'Believe me, *moya milaya*, it would scare you more to know them.'

She shivered and wrapped her arms around her waist and Leo cursed himself for saying what he had. Then he cursed her for being the person she was. She was too genuine and almost innocent in her view of the world. She made his conscience spike and he knew that pursuing her after this would be selfish and he'd promised himself he'd never be selfish again after Sasha's death.

He heard a discreet cough behind him. 'Someone had better be dead, Danny,' he growled, not looking at his EA.

'You might wish that were the case in a minute.'

Leo turned at the serious note in Danny's voice. 'What is it?'

'You said to inform you immediately if we got word from Amanda.'

Leo's eyes narrowed. 'You found her, then.'

'Not exactly. I've been checking your emails all day and this came in.' He handed him a piece of paper and Leo took it, a sense of dread forming a knot in his belly.

He scanned the email and started sweating like a man trapped in a steel cage with a dozen hungry lions for company. 'Married?' He shook his head. 'She can't do this.'

Danny didn't say anything and Leo knew that his worst nightmare had come true. Amanda was demanding that he take full custody of Ty. She had remarried and Ty didn't fit into their lifestyle.

He felt the fist in his belly rise to his heart and emotion and pain clawed at him as memories of the past hurtled into his consciousness.

Air became choked in his lungs and Leo felt the panic he had experienced at the childcare centre when he'd first seen Ty take hold.

He needed space.

Time to think. Without looking at either occupant on the deck, he crumpled the piece of paper into his fist and stalked off.

CHAPTER NINE

LEXI wandered down the long walkways and spiral staircases until she came to her and Ty's suite of rooms. She checked on Ty and smoothed his hair off his forehead as she watched him sleeping peacefully. He looked so much like Leo and her mind automatically wondered where he had gone. What he was doing.

He had said 'married' in such a tortured voice Lexi could only surmise that Amanda had remarried and the news had clearly devastated him. Her heart clenched in reaction and her skin grew hot. Her earlier assumption that he still harboured strong feelings for Amanda Weston was clearly correct.

She straightened Ty's sheets and let herself out of his room and crossed to her own. She knew Carolina was asleep in the other room with the monitor on and that she would not be needed any more tonight.

She kicked off her heels and wandered out onto her private terrace. The air held a faint chill now that a soft breeze had picked up and she rubbed her bare arms. She turned back inside and poured herself a glass of water and sat down at the small writing desk, running her fingers over the edge of her laptop before jumping up again. She was too wired to sleep and too restless to work.

Again her mind drifted to Leo and she wondered if he would want someone to be there for him when he was feeling terrible. Instinctively, she knew that he wouldn't but sometimes people didn't know what they needed until they had it. She knew he wasn't a talker but maybe he'd never had anyone offer a listening ear before. She might question his morals and his life choices, but he was a human being in pain and everyone needed someone at a time like this.

Not questioning her motives too closely, Lexi donned her heels and decided that the only way to put her mind at rest was to find him, make sure he was okay and then return to her room.

Pleased with her plan, she took the elevator up to his level and tapped lightly on his door. After a minute she knocked harder and then, still hearing nothing, turned the door knob and opened the door.

She hadn't really expected it to be unlocked and now she was faced with the dilemma of whether to just close it and leave or…close it definitely!

'Remind me to station security outside my door.' Leo's gruff words carried across the room and nearly gave her a heart attack and Lexi let the door swing further open, just in time to see Leo disappearing into the opposite doorway.

Okay, so he wasn't dead… Lexi let her gaze drift over the room in front of her and gasped at the size and understated opulence that greeted her eyes.

It was a living room with a huge cream sofa and matching chairs that looked comfortable enough to sleep on. Large domed lamps flanked the sofa and gave the room an intimate, golden glow that set off the smooth polished cabinetry around the room to perfection. A flat-screen TV lined one entire wall and opposite that an open doorway led into what Lexi assumed was the bedroom Leo had just disappeared through.

Before she could stop herself she crossed the carpeted floor, trying not to think about the last time she had entered Leo's bedroom in his London apartment, and peeked inside. It *was* his bedroom and it was dominated by a huge bed facing curved floor-to-ceiling windows that looked onto a private deck. Clearly the man liked his views.

Lexi saw him sprawled on one of the sun loungers outside and wandered to the open doorway; the light of the moon casting him in shadows.

'What do you want?'

He didn't turn and Lexi hovered there, uncertain as to whether she should stay or go, some inner instinct telling her that he needed her right now. 'I wanted to make sure you were okay.'

Stars twinkled overhead in the navy sky and the only sound was that of water slapping as it broke against the side of the yacht. 'Still trying to solve the problems of the world, angel?'

Lexi returned her gaze back to him. He wasn't looking at her, but lay with his eyes closed and his hands folded behind his head. 'No. I thought you might like company.'

He opened his eyes, his gaze raking her from head to toe before closing them again. 'You're wearing too many clothes for the company I need right now.'

'It might help if you talked about what's wrong.'

'Really.' His voice was snide and Lexi questioned her decision to interrupt him. 'Let's give it a try, shall we. I don't want Amanda to be married and to leave me in charge of the care of my son.' He bared his teeth in a parody of a smile. '*Net.* Still married. What a surprise.'

Lexi moved out onto the balcony and shivered as she felt the chill in the air descend on her bare skin. Or was that just the frost coming off the brooding man with his eyes now fixed on some dark spot in the distance? She perched on the matching chair beside his. 'I know you're upset at the news.'

'Upset? I'm not upset, angel. I'm furious.'

'Because you love her?' she acknowledged ruefully.

'You think that's what's going on here? You think that I *love* Amanda Weston?'

'You seemed devastated by the email she sent and—'

His sneer stopped the rest of her words. 'And you thought it was a love gone wrong. I don't do love, angel.'

'If it's not love you feel for Amanda, then…I'm confused. Why do you act as if Ty doesn't exist?'

'Because to me he doesn't.'

Lexi's breath caught in her throat. She wouldn't believe that. She *couldn't*. 'I don't believe you.'

He paused and she didn't think he was going to answer her.

'You want to know what happened with Amanda, I'll tell you. She came onto me at the Brussels Airport when all flights were grounded and we had sex. It was never going to be anything more than one night but she was looking for a rich husband and we used her condom—which I later found out she had already tampered with. It was a one-night fluke but she hit the jackpot.'

'That's terrible.'

Leo looked at Lexi's shocked face. Why had he told her that? He'd never told anyone before. Was it because he was sick of her thinking that he'd abandoned Ty for nothing? 'Poor Lexi. Doesn't that fit in with your ideal world where two parents love their children beyond measure?' He shook his head dourly and turned back to the ocean.

'I don't live in a fantasy world, Leo, if that's what you're suggesting. I know that sometimes one loving parent is better than two who can't get along.'

Leo glanced back at her averted face. Her chin was angled defiantly, her spine rigid. He knew instantly that whatever had gone on in her own childhood had affected her deeply and, despite his never having been interested in a woman's past before, he couldn't hold back his curiosity. 'You're talking about your father's double life, I take it.'

She stared at her hands for a minute and then her eyes met his. 'Yes. My father was a mildly successful golfer who travelled the world and my mother accepted that as part and parcel of loving him. She was a very understanding person and she never pushed to travel with him—mainly, I think, because she would have found it hard with Joe and I—but nor did she push to marry him. Then one night her world fell apart when the daughter he had fathered with his long-time mistress had an accident and his mistress gave him an ultimatum. Mum or her.'

Leo looked over and saw that Lexi's jaw was tight. 'And he chose the other woman.'

'He did try to visit Joe and I but…somehow he never seemed to make it.' She gave a forced laugh. 'For years we would dutifully dress in our best clothes once a month in the hope that today would be the day he would keep to his promise. Only it rarely was and soon Joe stopped dressing up altogether.'

'And you?' he asked. 'Did you stop dressing up?'

She fingered the necklace, a move he had noticed her do countless times before when she was nervous, and wondered who had given it to her. 'I'm a bit of an optimist.' She laughed a little self-consciously. 'I might have given him more of a chance than Joe.'

'A bit of a dreamer, you mean,' he said, but there was no harshness behind the words. Just resignation that he could never be as forgiving. 'Who gave you that?'

His eyes dropped to the necklace she was drawing back and forth across her bottom lip and wished it was his tongue.

'My father gave it to me on my tenth birthday.'

'And you've never taken it off since,' he guessed.

She let it drop back down between her breasts and when she spoke her voice was choked. 'You make me sound pathetic.'

'Not pathetic. Just someone who believes in happy ever afters.'

'Is that such a bad thing?'

Leo wasn't particularly comfortable with the turn of the

conversation and contemplated telling her to leave. If only he didn't want her so damned much. 'Only if it means you don't see things for what they really are,' he said, raising a mocking eyebrow, willing her to deny that she didn't.

'What makes you think that I don't?'

His eyebrow climbed higher. 'You wear a necklace to keep a connection with a man who deserted you and you need to ask that?'

Lexi's hand rose to her neck. 'I just… I never…'

'You never wanted to accept that he chose the other family?'

Her hand dropped and she pushed off the lounger and walked to the railing, gripping it firmly and leaning slightly forward as she gazed down at the sea. 'You're very astute.'

Leo didn't respond. He could see that she was deep in thought and he was struggling with his own desire to go to her. Comfort her. Then she glanced back over her shoulder and the delicate muscles around her shoulder blades shifted alluringly.

'Children are innocent. They don't ask to be born. They deserve proper care. And…' she paused and he watched her throat work as she swallowed '…I guess I always hoped he'd come back. I hated that his selfishness caused my mother to have to work two jobs, because that was hard on us all.' She paused. 'I don't know why I still wear the necklace.'

'So you became a childcare worker to provide care for kids whose parents have to go to work?'

She looked surprised, as if she hadn't made that connection before. But it explained why she was so keen for him to have a relationship with Ty and why she was so wary of him. A wariness she was right to feel.

'What's your relationship with your father like now?' he asked softly.

'We don't have one.' Her eyes connected earnestly with his. 'It's what I've been trying to tell you. Now is the time to get to know Ty. I haven't seen my father in ten years and Joe even longer than that.'

Leo looked away as she came to sit back down opposite him. He had more than just Amanda's subterfuge keeping him away from Ty.

'You should be thankful he left, angel. Sometimes a man who is forced to marry because he gets a woman pregnant makes everyone's life hell.'

She looked at him curiously. 'That sounds like you're speaking from experience.'

Leo didn't know if it was the lateness of the hour, the shock of Amanda's defection or Lexi Somers soft compassion but he found himself wanting to tell her things he'd never told another living soul.

He sighed. Maybe if he did tell her some of it she would understand why Ty was better off without him. 'My father married my mother because she was pregnant with me and he spent the first ten years of my life making it a living hell.'

Lexi looked at the taut lines of Leo's neck and knew he was speaking the truth, but it was a long way from what she'd read about him. 'I thought you had a happy childhood?'

'Ah, my bio. Nice story, isn't it.'

'What's the real story?' she asked quietly.

'Why do you want to know? Hoping to earn a few extra dollars by selling an exposé?'

'Of course not. I just want to help.'

'Like I said. You have too many clothes on for that. Not that I don't love that dress. You know what it makes me want to do?' He swung his legs to the side and twisted in his seat so that he was facing her, his knees wide, his feet firmly planted either side of her legs. 'It makes me want to grab those two triangles of fabric barely covering your gorgeous breasts and rip it straight down the middle. Does that shock you, little

Lexi?' He paused and all Lexi could hear was the sound of her own heart beating too fast. 'Or excite you?'

She knew he was trying to distract her. That he didn't want to talk about his life story. She also knew that she wanted him to tell her. She wanted to know him. Know the real Leo Aleksandrov. As if seeking to put distance between them, he moved abruptly to stand at the railing, staring off into the balmy distance.

Lexi moistened her lips before asking, 'What's the real story, Leo?'

He turned his head and looked down at her. 'Like horror stories do you?' His voice was a low growl and Lexi sensed the pain he was trying desperately to hold at bay.

He had the look of a lost child about him and Lexi was reminded of Ty the first time she had met him, mistrust stamped all over his beautiful face. But she wouldn't push Leo any further. It would be beyond arrogant of her to assume that just because she found it better to talk through her issues, he would too.

He rubbed a hand over the back of his neck and for a minute she didn't think he was going to say anything. Then he flopped back down on the chair and stared at the starry sky. 'I grew up in the Tundra—a hellhole of a place where nothing grows and it's so bitterly cold in winter you feel like your bones are freezing. My father was a miner with Mafioso connections and my mother was a shop girl who let love turn her blind. When my father drank he turned violent and my mother bore the brunt of his loss of control. At times I tried to stop him but I could never protect her from his brute strength.'

'How could you—you were just a child?' she cried.

'No child wants to see their mother hurt. Of course every time I tried to help he thought it was a great joke and tried to challenge me. Taunted me until I gave in.'

Lexi felt sick and it took a great deal of effort to control the emotion in her voice. 'How old were you when this started?'

'Six, seven. I don't remember.' He gave a telling shrug.

He remembered all right. Too well, Lexi guessed.

'I do remember his favourite modus operandi was a sly backhand just when you thought the jibes and beltings had finished.'

Lexi swallowed and made an inarticulate sound of distress. 'Do you still see him?' she asked, her breathing ragged and uneven where his was almost meditatively calm.

'No.' His eyes when they fixed on hers were empty. 'He died in prison.'

'Was that when you were ten?'

He looked at her warily.

'You said the first ten years were awful. I just wondered if that was when your father went to jail.'

'Got a sharp brain, haven't you, angel?'

'So…things got better after that?'

'Things did get better. My father went to prison and I went to live with my uncle.'

'Where was your mother?'

'She couldn't look after me. I was too wild. Used to get into fights all the time. Very bad news.'

Lexi was still trying to comprehend that his mother had sent him away when she noticed that his tone had darkened. 'Your mother sent you away?'

'Oh, Lexi, with the bleeding heart. Don't be so outraged.' He touched her face briefly and then stood up and paced across the balcony, unable to keep still. 'She had her reasons and it was the best decision she could have made. My uncle wasn't at all like my father. He was gruff and proud, but he controlled his emotions. Until I came to stay, he had lived his adult life alone. He taught me how to contain my rage.'

Lexi wondered if Leo realised that he had made himself over in his uncle's image. A man facing the world alone. Her heart went out to him. 'Do you still see him?'

'He died. A work-related accident.'

'On a building site,' Lexi guessed.

'*Da*. And now you know.' He spread his arms wide. 'All the dirty details of who I really am and why I can't be a father to Ty.'

'No—' Lexi shook her head '—I don't know that at all.'

He huffed out a laugh. 'Then you're not as smart as I thought you were. I'm not a good bet, Lexi. I can't be responsible for Ty.'

Was that it? Was that why he was so determined that Ty was better off without him? Not because he was afraid of losing his lifestyle, but because he was afraid of becoming his father. Afraid of hurting those who relied on him.

'Leo, that's fear talking. It's not who you are,' she said, catching her breath at his fierce expression as he swung around to face her again.

'Haven't you heard anything I've said? I'm a violent man.'

'You think you'd hurt Ty?' Lexi shook her head. 'I don't.'

'My father couldn't help it. Who's to say I'll be any different?'

'Your father *could* help it. He *chose* not to.'

Lexi's heart went out to Leo trapped as a young child in a world with such a damaged adult, but she forced herself to focus on what still needed to be said.

'Leo, I don't know who your parents were but I'd say they were two people who shouldn't have been together. They brought out the worst in each other and maybe didn't have the maturity to see the error of their ways. But whatever their story is—it doesn't have to be yours.'

'It doesn't matter, Lexi. I'm empty inside. I have nothing to give.'

Lexi frowned. 'You think you can't love?' How much this man had suffered!

'Not think. I don't.'

'What about your uncle?'

'Yes, maybe. I cared for him. But...' His voice trailed away and he rubbed the back of his neck. 'There's no point talking about this.'

'Because it hurts too much?'

'Because I am what I am.'

Leo gripped the railing more tightly and Lexi went to him and laid her hand on his arm. 'Spend time with Ty. Just the two of you. I haven't seen you take any time off since we got here.'

'No.' He moved his hand out from under hers and flopped down on the sun lounger, his hands dangling between his wide-spread knees.

Lexi could feel him closing off and she didn't know what else to say to him. 'He needs you, Leo.'

'He needs a decent father.'

Lexi placed her hands on her hips, determined to get through to him on this point. 'Yes. You. And you need him.'

He shook his head slowly and the look in his eyes as they swept over her changed, became heated. 'What I need is for you to go to bed.'

'I—'

He shook his head, his eyes becoming guarded. 'No more. There's only so much happy reminiscing a man can take. Especially when the woman he's reminiscing with is only half dressed.' His lips twisted into a wry smile.

'I'm not half dressed.'

'Tell me you're wearing a bra beneath that dress.'

'Well, no, but—'

'Like I said. Half dressed.'

She sensed the air thicken between them and couldn't look away. It was like being on the beach again, just before he'd kissed her. His blue eyes dark, his features taut, but not with pain now—with something her body instantly recognised. And wanted.

'I think you're trying to change the subject.'

'Smart *and* quick.'

He stared at her. Lexi became aware that the only sound on the balcony was the beating of her own frantic heart. She couldn't have moved even if she'd wanted to and he recognised her hesitation for what it was.

He shook his head slowly. 'You don't do casual sex.' His voice was heavy, low, laden with sensual restraint.

Lexi swallowed. Kissing him had shaken her to her core. As had his revelations. He was right. She didn't do casual sex. Or at least she never had before, but would indulging in it once be so wrong? She wasn't deluding herself that sex with Leo would be more than that. But he made her feel things she'd never felt before. She couldn't help wanting more of that. But could she risk her self-esteem on it?

She stared at him. He looked predatory. Hungry. For her?

Her nipples tingled and a hollow aching feeling made her lower body clench. With sudden alarm Lexi realised that her body was already readying itself to make love with him. Just the thought made the throbbing worse and her heart kicked up. It seemed, from her body's point of view, she couldn't *not* risk it. 'You said the sex wouldn't be casual.' Was that breathless, seductive voice really hers?

He didn't respond immediately and she was momentarily struck with the horrible sense that maybe he had been trying to let her down gently.

Like a helpless mouse that had backed itself into a corner, Lexi's stomach pitched and then he held out his hand.

'Come here.'

CHAPTER TEN

LEXI noted the way his chest moved in time with his deep even breaths and that the skin on his face seemed to be pulled tight. His eyes tracked over her with such sexual purpose there was no mistaking his intention and her arousal returned on a rush of liquid heat.

He wanted her and she wanted him and nothing else seemed to matter right now.

As if in a dream state, she moved towards him.

When she reached him he widened his legs and drew her closer between his thighs, his large hands light as they enveloped her waist.

Then he breathed deeply and rested his forehead on her chest.

Lexi could feel the warmth of his breath through the thin fabric of her dress and gave in to the urge to stroke her fingers through his short hair. The strands felt crisp and soft at the same time. Her fingers flexed and clung and she wondered if the hair on his chest would feel the same way.

He raised his head and her hands stilled at the intensity of the desire she could see banked behind his eyes.

'Do you know how beautiful you are?'

No, but he made her *feel* beautiful. Lexi felt a shiver race through her whole body and she knew he felt it because his fingers tightened around her waist. And thank God they did because her bones melted and her legs nearly gave out.

Her hands moved of their own accord down the side of his face and cupped his square jaw, her fingertips scraping over the stubble on his face. 'I imagined this would be hard,' she murmured. 'But it's soft.'

She saw him take a deep breath. One of the hands at her waist rose to the nape of her neck as he gently guided her face down to his. 'I want you,' he said gruffly and another spasm of need weakened her knees even more and brought her closer to the heat of his big body.

She wanted him too. She couldn't deny it. Couldn't even remember why she should. Nothing seemed to matter except this man and this moment and then his lips finally touched hers and her brain closed down completely.

Leo's mouth already knew the shape and texture of her sweet mouth but still, kissing her now, was like the first time and his groin jerked with pleasure as her mouth opened over his. He tried to be gentle, but he was already hard and aching with desire for her. His tongue circling inside her mouth as he tasted her. Hers following his lead and tasting him right back.

He smoothed his hands up over her naked back and then he wrapped them around her and stood up, taking her with him.

She gasped and wrapped her arms around his neck as he carried her inside and he felt like a warrior who had just won a great prize.

He set her down beside his bed and stood her before him as he sat on the edge of it. His eyes drifted over her gorgeous body and, wanting to see all of her at once, he gripped the silky fabric covering her breasts and would have ripped the dress in two if she hadn't put her hands over his to stop him. 'I love this dress.'

He smiled into her passion-drugged eyes. 'I don't have time for zips. And I promise I'll buy twenty more for you to replace it.' Then he ripped it—straight down the middle.

Her breath hitched in her throat and her hands immediately came up to cover her breasts.

Leo felt her shocked hesitation and glanced into her eyes. 'What is it, angel?'

Her mouth pulled down at the corners. 'I'm afraid I'm not what you're used to.'

She was self-conscious! The realisation floored him and reminded him of her hesitation on the upstairs deck. Uncertainty wasn't what he had expected from this woman who was verbally able to go toe to toe with him when no other woman had ever tried before.

Leo ran a finger along the defined bones of her clavicle and felt something reverent pass through him. He couldn't remember ever wanting a woman as much as he wanted Lexi Somers and his body was vibrating with the tension of holding himself in check.

He leaned back slowly so that he could take his fill of her. She stood before him like an elegant courtesan—her petite frame ghosted in the faint light from his bedside lamps, her hands covering her small, perfect breasts, her hair still up, but slightly messy, and a delicate lace bikini brief that rode low on her hips.

He breathed deeply and smoothed his hand up her neck and over the smooth skin of her jaw. 'You're the most beautiful woman I've ever seen,' he said huskily, realising how true that was, his hands not quite steady as he tunnelled them into her hair to hold her still to receive his deep kiss. His fingers met resistance and he tore his mouth from hers and started pulling hair pins from her hair. Within seconds his hands were filled with small brown pieces of looped metal and he leaned back and stared up at her. 'Remind me to take out shares in carbon steel the next time you shop for hair products.'

She laughed, a soft, sultry sound that curled inside him. 'My hair isn't that easy to work with,' she said, slowly raising her arms to loosen it so that it fell past her shoulders like a dark cloud.

Leo meant to dump the small pins on the bedside table beside her but, with her arms raised above her head and her body almost naked before him, he quite forgot to breathe, the pins falling to the carpet.

He reached out and measured the span of her waist with both hands. Then he smiled. 'So small, so feminine.' He leaned forward and planted open-mouth kisses on the outside of each rounded breast. Her body quivered and waited as he slowly made his way closer and closer to the tight pink buds that awaited his lips. She moaned softly and he felt her nails bite into his shoulders as she shifted slightly so that his mouth skated across her nipple. He blew gently and her hands moved to cradle his skull to guide him to her.

'Please, Leo,' she begged, arching closer.

'Please what?' he whispered against her. 'Please this?' He laved her nipple with the tip of his tongue and when she whimpered and sagged against him he held her up easily and suckled her more fully into his mouth. Her fingernails dug into his shoulder blades and gave him a heady feeling that made his erection throb.

'Take off my shirt,' he growled against her flesh, tearing the buttons as he helped her get it off him so that she could touch him in return.

His nostrils flared as her hands found his chest and her hungry caresses sent his self-control skittering into the ether.

She almost sobbed with pleasure as he tortured each breast in turn and he felt a primitive thrill at the feel of her pressing into him. She was every bit as responsive as he had imagined she would be and she was his. All his.

She made a moue of protest as he released her nipple. 'It only gets better from here, angel,' he promised throatily, not exactly gentle as he wrapped one arm around her waist and, bringing his mouth to hers, turned her and deposited her on the middle of the bed. He moved her legs apart with his knee, his aching body looming over hers as he continued to ravage her mouth.

He kept his weight on his arms as her hands swept over his biceps, his shoulders, and down the hard planes of his chest, setting him on fire wherever she touched him.

'Leo, it's too much.' Her lower body writhed against his knee and he could no longer wait to test the wet heat of her arousal. He trailed his hand down her flat belly and skimmed across the top of her panties, a rough sound escaping his throat as he palmed her and found her damp. Her hips came up off the bed and he released her breast to tug her panties off. He sat back on his haunches and gazed down at her femininity. Her splayed thighs, moist breasts and dark hair that was wild against the cream bedspread.

He settled his hand against her abdomen as he'd imagined doing many times before and moved one of her legs further apart.

'You're not naked yet,' she murmured and he could hear the embarrassment in her voice.

His eyes met hers. 'If I get naked I'll climb inside you and I want to make it last.' His thumbs pressed gently against the soft skin of her inner thighs.

'Leo…' His name was more a groan than a word. 'Come back up here.'

He glanced up at her. 'You don't like what I'm about to do?'

Her chest rose unsteadily as she drew in a deep breath. 'I don't know,' she muttered, shielding her eyes with her arm.

He paused. No man had done this for her? He felt a primitive thrill race through him at the thought of introducing her to such intimate pleasure.

'Look at me,' he commanded roughly, waiting for her to move her arm and then watching her face as he trailed a finger lightly through her silky moist curls, barely restraining himself as he gently parted her. Her breath hitched and his heart beat erratically.

'Beautiful,' he whispered, sliding a finger inside her. He had imagined her like this from the moment he'd laid eyes on her and the reality far outweighed his fantasy. He watched the way her eyes widened and her mouth went lax as he drove her higher and higher towards her climax. He was completely wild for her but, more than that, he wanted to watch her come. Wanted to taste her while she did. He'd never experienced such an intense desire to give a woman pleasure.

He watched her eyes open even wider as he lowered his head towards her body, his brain closing down as he slid his hands beneath her buttocks and raised her to his mouth for the first time.

Lexi's fingers tangled in Leo's short hair and she nearly screamed as she felt his tongue and his lips doing the most delicious things to her body. Brandon had never touched her like this and the pleasure was beyond her realm of comprehension. Her body felt as if it were a puppet moving closer and closer to something just outside of her reach. Then she heard Leo's voice from far away telling her to relax and when she did, she screamed, her body shattering into a million tiny pieces and emotions she'd never experienced spiralled through her.

For all she knew she could have lost hours as her body continued to shoot jolts of pleasure through her system and a satisfied smile curved her lips as she felt Leo rise up over her in a purely dominating posture.

'There were stars,' she murmured dazedly, her arms looping lethargically around his neck. 'And I don't think I'll ever move again.'

'Good. Because you're exactly where you need to be. And this time I might throw in the moon as well.' Leo's accent was rougher than ever.

'Promises, promises,' she teased, lying still as she felt him sheath himself with a condom.

Leo laughed and planted his palms either side of her face to protect her from his full weight and she could feel his hair-roughened thighs lying solidly between her own.

She felt the hard length of him probe her entrance and his biceps shook as he held himself in check. 'Open wider angel, and let me in.' She did as he commanded and his control seemed to give out because he surged into her in one power-ful thrust of his hips.

Lexi gasped and tensed as her body felt stretched like never before.

Leo stilled and dragged his lips from hers, his hands cra-dling her face. 'Lexi, are you okay?'

She sucked in a breath and nodded, her fingernails easing out of the dents she'd made in his hips.

'You're so tight, *moya milaya*. Just relax for me and we'll fit together perfectly.'

His words made Lexi's pelvis soften even more and when he felt her muscles release he sank all the way inside her. He held still for another moment but Lexi's body had already adjusted and he was hitting a spot that sent gushes of plea-sure cascading through her lower body. She raised one of her legs up over his hips and felt him smile against her mouth.

'That's better.' His mouth left a moist trail over her jawline and Lexi's body arched under his as he began to move inside her in a masterful rhythm. 'Now come for me again, angel, while I'm inside you,' he ordered in a voice that sounded as unsteady as she felt. Lexi couldn't resist the build-up of plea-sure any more than the tide could resist the pull of the moon. She couldn't think as her body shattered once more in an even deeper climax. Her body clamped down around his and drew a sound from his throat that was almost subhuman as he surged forward twice more before finding his own release.

* * *

Leo woke, slightly disoriented, and shifted under the weight of the warm, naked female who had wound herself around him like tinsel on a Christmas tree, one leg thrown over his thighs, her head nestled in the crook of his arm, her small breasts flattened against his side and her slender fingers spread wide over his chest. He didn't remember falling asleep but a glance at the faint grey dawn outside the windows told him he must have. The yacht was still moving so he knew they hadn't yet reached Athens.

He gently flexed his stiff shoulder muscles and Lexi adjusted herself like a contented cat, snuggling in closer and sighing in her sleep.

His fist clenched at the sound and he had the instant urge to break free from her hold and run for his life. He wasn't used to sleeping next to someone, that was the problem. It had nothing to do with the deep sense of well-being enveloping him in a warm, peaceful cocoon. A concept he hadn't felt in…forever.

It wasn't that he had a lot of one-night stands; it was more that he liked his space. Needed his space. And he didn't want any woman to get the wrong idea and start mentally rearranging his furniture.

His fingers drifted through the silk of Lexi's hair as he recalled in minute detail how he had taken that warm, tight body with his own. He felt his groin stir at the memory and knew that the smart thing to do would be to get out of bed and go for an early morning swim. Grab a coffee and start work.

Some of his tension must have leached out of him because Lexi whimpered and caressed his shoulder with her smooth cheek. Leo's hand immediately flexed against her hip and slid down around the soft curve of her lower back, his fingers stroking her soft skin. She must have liked it because the leg she had thrown over his thigh rubbed his and now he was fully erect and, instead of following his saner instincts and climbing out of bed, he found himself shifting again and urging her small, compact body to lie over his. Her thighs automatically splayed to accommodate his hardness while his two hands caressed her curvaceous bottom.

He shouldn't be doing this.

Taking advantage of her while she slept. He might have stopped but then she widened her thighs even more and whispered, 'Don't stop,' into his ear. Leo turned his head and caught her mouth with his in a kiss that went from soft to carnal faster than his Maserati hit a hundred clicks. She pushed up sleepily, her hands on his shoulders, her mane of hair falling around her and resting just above her pert breasts, which had taken on a luminescent quality in the pre-dawn light. Leo groaned and reached for one at the same time as he delved into his side drawer for protection. She arched into his caress and lifted her lower body against his but he stayed her with a hand on her hip.

'Wait,' he whispered gruffly.

He protected them both and nearly came on the spot as she reached down and guided him into her body.

Her moan precipitated his own and he'd never felt such overpowering pleasure as he did at that moment. If he'd been at all capable of thinking he might have been concerned but she moved her hips experimentally against his and he pushed her hair back off her breasts and cupped her in his large hands, watching as she rode him into the sweetest orgasm of his life.

While he was still coming down from a place he didn't think he'd ever been before he stroked a lazy line up and down her spine.

She made a low murmur of pleasure and slipped off him to snuggle into the crook of his arm again.

'I'm all sweaty.'

'You feel fantastic.' He traced a finger over her hip and the gentle swell of her belly without really realising he was doing it. Then she shifted her top leg more comfortably over his and his heart caught.

'You know, when I first saw you I thought you were heartless and unapproachable,' she murmured sleepily. 'But that's just what you want people to think, isn't it?'

No. He *was* heartless and unapproachable.

Normally.

Normally, when his brain was operating at one hundred per cent capacity. Normally, when he was with any other woman but her. He felt a frisson of unease slither through him as her fingers once again threaded through the hair on his chest.

Now he should get her up. Send her back to her room. Give her every indication of how this situation was going to play out.

Her breathing became choppy and he knew she'd sensed the subtle sense of dread that had overcome him.

'Did I just ruin everything with my big mouth?' She lifted her head, uncertainty threaded through her voice just as her fingers had been lightly threading through the hair on his chest before he'd ruined it.

'No,' he said gruffly. He moved a hand into her hair and gently urged her head back down onto his shoulder. 'Sleep.'

She let out a sigh that whispered across his skin like the sea breeze.

Leave. He'd meant to say *leave.*

CHAPTER ELEVEN

Lexi woke the next morning and the first thing she registered was that she was smiling. The second, as she moved her legs and rolled over, was that her body felt different.

Languid. Replete. Achy.

Her eyes flew to the empty pillow beside her and then around the masculine bedroom. Empty, both. She breathed out and let the sense of happiness glide over her again.

Leo. Last night.

And then another emotion took hold.

Panic. What had she done?

She rolled back onto her stomach and groaned into the pillow. She'd come to his room last night because she'd been worried about his state of mind. She'd stayed because… because…he was just so male. So commanding. When he'd said, 'Come here,' in his rough, accented voice she had felt powerless to resist. Hadn't wanted to resist. Some part of her knowing that to do so was pointless. This thing between them had been building since the moment she'd first walked into her office and seen him standing there like a modern day terminator, about to take her room apart if he didn't get what he wanted.

After her initial uncertainty last night she had felt so uninhibited. So free! Her insides started to melt at just the thought of all the things they had done together.

It was everything she had ever fantasised sex could be

and more. So much more. When he had moved over her and his body had first joined with hers something inside her had shifted and she remembered thinking that she would be forever changed after that. That no other man could ever possibly make her feel the way he did.

But that was absurd…and unnecessarily sombre.

Feeling silly at the thought she lay still, straining to hear any signs of life in the outer rooms of Leo's private suite. Almost relieved when she didn't hear anything but seagulls circling overhead and the low, intermittent murmur of distant voices through the open balcony doors.

Relaxing slightly, her mind flashed back to his childhood revelations. She felt warm knowing that he had trusted her with such sensitive information and wondered if he'd told anyone else. He wasn't at all what she had expected after meeting him in her office. He wasn't the privileged, shallow bigot she had first thought.

Like her, he was damaged. He truly believed he had nothing to offer his son but the pain he had experienced as a boy. She thought that if his father was in the room right then she would smack him. How anybody could hit a child she didn't know and her own childhood upset at having an absent father faded into the background compared to the agony Leo had suffered.

Lexi instinctively felt that there was no way Leo was like his father. There was no way a person who hurt others cared about his staff the way Leo did and nor would they care that their son might feel afraid spending a weekend in a strange apartment with a nanny he had never met before. Nor, she felt sure, would they get six monthly checks carried out on a son they supposedly didn't care about to ensure his safety.

Ty!

She'd forgotten all about him!

Was he okay? She knew that he liked Carolina but Carolina wouldn't know where to find her if Ty should need her.

Jumping out of bed, she quickly scrambled around for her dress and felt a blush flood across her cheeks as she remembered that Leo had torn it down the middle.

At least her knickers were still in one piece. She found them on the carpet and wriggled into them, berating her memory for reminding her how he had peeled them slowly down her legs last night. Shaking off the effects of those memories she walked into Leo's wardrobe, her eyes growing bigger than balloons as she took in the rows of beautifully crafted male clothing on offer. All of it formal, or semi-formal. She felt a bit awkward riffling through his shelves in search of a T-shirt and a pang of regret that he had not stayed to wake her this morning punctured the small bubble of bliss she had been feeling.

Last night he had said she was beautiful, feminine—and she had felt as if he adored her. Only that was silly. He didn't adore her. He wasn't even here.

And why wasn't he here? Had last night not been as good for him as it had been for her? She swallowed hard and pushed those unwanted thoughts aside. He was just busy. He had things to do. He wouldn't have had time to wait around for her to wake up and wasn't it more considerate that he'd left her to sleep?

Yes. No. Maybe. It would have been nice to have been kissed awake by him. Had he wanted to do that? Had he even stopped for a moment beside the bed and watched her sleep? No, of course he hadn't and wanting the opposite to be true was a one way ticket to heartache and misery. She knew that better than anyone.

Finally locating maybe the only casual item of clothing in his wardrobe, Lexi donned a long-sleeved black T-shirt that dangled way down over her hands and covered her almost to her knees. Feeling decently covered, she grabbed her sling back heels and rolled her dress into a tight ball. She considered fixing her hair and straightening the bed but thought maybe it was best to get out of there before the maid showed up to make it.

Or, worse—Leo himself. Because she wasn't sure how she was going to face him now. Cool sophisticate who entered into one-night stands whenever the desire took her, or…actually there was no 'or.' The 'or' was a clinging, love-struck fool. She'd played that role once before with Brandon and it hadn't been any fun then either.

Hearing a clamour of raised voices outside, Lexi walked to the floor-to-ceiling windows that faced port-side and realised that they were docked in Athens.

The yacht must have sailed through the night and it was time to go home. In a couple of hours, last night would be nothing but a pleasant memory. She leant her forehead against the cool glass. Why did that thought make her feel so hollow? Surely she wasn't silly enough to want more from a man like Leo Aleksandrov… A man who had turned short term relationships into an art form.

Last night she had said that she didn't live in a fantasy world and she didn't. Not any more. When she was younger she'd always dreamed of her father coming home, of her parents being reunited, and she hadn't realised how affected she was by her father's abandonment. Oh, she knew the thought of finding love made her nervous and she didn't need to see a shrink to tell her that that was because of her father's inconsistent role in her life and Brandon's treachery. But she hadn't realised until last night how much she had shelved the idea of having a family of her own.

She pushed away from the glass, the revelation strangely unsettling.

And really, it was a good thing that Leo hadn't waited around this morning. This was more honest. This told her exactly where she stood in his life.

Yes, Lexi smiled to herself, it was a very good thing he had left.

* * *

She was lying to herself. It wasn't a good thing.

Slowly, over the course of the morning that had now turned into afternoon, Lexi's insecurities had taken such a stranglehold that she felt as if she were choking.

She hadn't expected him to come chasing after her as if she were the love of his life, but nor had she expected to be totally ignored. His continued absence told her more clearly than words that last night had meant nothing to him.

And she didn't want that to make her feel empty. Sad. She didn't want it to make her wonder if she had actually been terrible in bed. She hadn't seized up as she had done with Brandon but…that didn't make her a femme fatale either, did it? She shook her head. Just the thought was laughable.

Home. She needed to go home. Off this yacht and away from Leo so she could lick her wounds in peace and forget that she'd most likely just made a bigger mistake than she had with Brandon.

She watched Ty splashing around in the pool with Carolina and felt anger start to take hold. She didn't know if it was directed more at Leo or herself, and she didn't much care—it just felt a lot better than self-pity.

Leo had to get off this yacht and the sooner the better. He'd woken up with a horrible sense of well-being that had set his heart beating so fast he wouldn't have been surprised if he'd had a heart attack. He'd been wrapped around Lexi Somers as if his life depended on it. Then he'd remembered everything he'd told her the night before and could have cut out his own tongue. Thank God, he'd had meetings to finish up and guests to see off his yacht all morning to keep him busy.

But now that he was alone in his office his mind turned to Amanda Weston and what he was going to do about Ty. He didn't want the responsibility that came with relationships, knew he wouldn't be any good at them. And despite Lexi's assertions last night that he wasn't like his father, he knew he couldn't be a parent to Ty. He controlled his aggression nowadays but that didn't mean he wouldn't hurt Ty one day. And he'd rather die than do that.

Ty deserved more than he could give. He deserved a man who knew how to be a father. A man who knew how to love.

A crisp knock on his office door brought his mind back and he called out, 'Enter,' with a little more relish than he was actually feeling.

Lexi stood framed in the doorway, wearing a white strapless sundress that was partially transparent where the red triangles of her bikini had dampened the fabric. Her glorious sable hair, also damp from the pool, hung down her back and her chin was angled, her eyes glittering bright gold.

'I'm sorry to bother you, but I wanted to know what time we were due to leave for London,' she said, standing before him as if she had a steel pole for a backbone.

No prizes for guessing her mood, he thought, somewhat humourlessly.

He leaned back in his admiral's chair and wondered what had set her off. 'And good morning to you too, angel.'

'Actually, you're a little late with that particular greeting—it's afternoon.'

Ah, so that was it. She was upset because he hadn't seen her all day. Women always wanted the post-sex cuddle and conversation and naturally she wouldn't be any different. But he'd known that and hadn't that been one of the drivers in keeping him so busy all day? That and the fact that she was so damned nice and that last night had been so damned good.

But was that her fault? And was it anything to truly be worried about?

So he had slept with her and it had been possibly the best sex of his life.

Nyevazhno. Unimportant.

That just proved that his instincts were on the money. He'd known sex with her would be dynamite and it was. And that made the fact that he still burned for her completely normal. What man wouldn't want to repeat an experience like that? He felt his body stir predictably as memories of last night sifted into his consciousness.

And it also wasn't her fault that his life had been turned upside down and punishing her for Amanda's deception was not going to accomplish anything.

'I apologise,' he said in a perfunctory fashion that did nothing to lessen the grim set of her pretty mouth.

'For?' She stared down her nose at him and he realised she wasn't going to make this easy. He could hardly blame her. Last night had been beyond sensational and he'd treated her like a one-night stand. Maybe worse.

He spread his hands out over his desk, choosing his words carefully. 'I should have been there when you woke up this morning. In my defence, I wanted to let you sleep and I had guests to see off. Meetings to finish up.'

'I only asked what time we were leaving, Mr Aleksandrov,' she said dismissively. 'I don't need a breakdown of your whole day.'

Mr Aleksandrov? She was seriously peeved and he felt irrationally annoyed with her. What did she think last night had been about, anyway? He'd made no promises to her.

'I've apologised for my behaviour and I'm sorry I hurt you.'

She arched a brow. 'You didn't hurt me, but it's clear you regret last night and I'm happy to forget it as well.'

'I regret a lot of things about last night, angel, but the sex isn't one of them.'

'Well, that's the part I do regret!' she cried and then clamped her mouth shut as if she'd said too much. Which she had.

He relaxed back in his chair. 'Last night was phenomenal.'

'Whatever.'

'You don't agree?'

'I'd just like to go home.'

Leo tapped his fingers on some papers on his desk. He wasn't used to women wanting to forget a night in his bed. Quite the opposite, in fact. He glanced down at the folder he was absently tapping and noticed it was the prospectus for a hotel in Santorini his investment team were planning to visit at the end of the week. It was old and barely standing but, still, the proprietor would no doubt pretend he had the upper hand. It was the way business was done here.

But why would his busy team need to travel out here when he was already in Greece? It would be no skin off his nose if he detoured to view the property before leaving the country. It would take half a day at the most and would give him more time to figure out what to do about Ty if his security team failed to locate Amanda any time soon.

'That's not possible, *moya milaya*.' She blinked at him, looking as surprised as he felt at coming to such a rushed decision.

'Excuse me?'

Committed, he continued. 'Unfortunately, I have further business to attend to in Greece and have decided to stay on a bit longer.'

'So why do you need me?'

'I would have thought that was obvious.' Let her interpret that as she would.

'Ty has bonded with Carolina and she's great with him.'

'Maybe so,' he said, recognising that what she said was most likely true, but not ready to have her leave him just yet. 'But yesterday when he hurt himself no one could comfort him but you.' She looked frustrated. 'And last night did you not suggest I should stay on?' he reminded her.

'I suggested you take a holiday with Ty. Not work.'

'And so I will.'

He hadn't planned to do that at all but there was a saying in his country: 'One who sits between two chairs may easily fall down.' Once he found Amanda and worked things out with her he'd hand Ty back, but in the meantime maybe it wouldn't hurt to get to know him a little.

An image of Lexi and Ty lying on the carpeted floor of his private library drawing and laughing together the afternoon before came into his mind. At the time he'd been reminded of images of his own dysfunctional childhood but what had stuck the most was that, rather than feeling awash with the cold sweat of fear he'd felt when he'd first seen Ty at the childcare centre, he'd felt something else. Something calmer. And for the first time he hadn't seen Sasha when he had looked at his son.

Yes, maybe it was time to sit on the chair—at least for an hour here and there between work.

'I can't stay. I have to work tomorrow.' Lexi's words sounded loud in the loaded silence and he frowned. What she had to do was to get back into his bed, but right now he didn't think she'd be too amenable to that suggestion.

She couldn't stay. Not when all he wanted was for her to help him out with Ty. Already her heart was racing at the thought of spending more time with Leo, her mind telling her all sorts of fanciful things. That she cared for him—more than cared for him. Which she didn't, of course. She just wasn't the type to have casual sex and her mind automatically wanted to attach meaning to what they'd done last night. It was what had happened with Brandon. Back then she had ignored her instincts that had warned her he was a player and convinced herself she was in love with him. Thankfully, she was mature enough to see the potential for that now, but still…staying in this man's orbit would be like putting Ty in a chocolate shop and telling him he couldn't eat anything.

'Don't you have someone else who can take care of the centre in your absence?' he asked.

'Sure. I'll call up one of my many minions, shall I?' she tried to joke, but it fell flat.

'You must have other staff who can take over in case of emergencies.'

'I do. But this isn't an emergency and I also have a business proposal I need to write.' A proposal she had planned to work on this weekend and hadn't touched!

'A proposal for what?'

Lexi was so tense at being this close to him and not letting on how much he affected her she nearly stormed out. Only he would likely follow and answering him was undoubtedly quicker.

'A new childcare centre Aimee and I want to open.'

'You're expanding?'

His surprise was obvious and she didn't know whether to feel pleased or insulted!

'Not if I don't get the current building problems ironed out.'

He regarded her thoughtfully and the room grew hotter. 'I will help you.'

'What? How?' She shook her head. That was the last thing she had expected him to say.

He looked at her with benign patience. 'Lexi, I run a global company. I think I might be qualified to help you with a business proposal.'

She hadn't thought of that.

'It's what I believe you English call a no-brainer,' he continued. 'You help me, I help you. And it will make up for your refusal to let me pay you for the past three days.'

Lexi mulled this over. She wanted her new childcare centre more than anything else and Leo was supposed to be an incredibly savvy businessman, but...could she really stay on with last night still lying heavily between them? She squirmed a little and told herself if it meant getting her new business up and running, of course she could.

Maybe...

'What time frame are we talking about?' she asked, standing behind the chair facing his desk.

Leo smiled as if she had already agreed and her lips pinched together. 'I don't expect what I need to do to take more than a couple of days.'

'I'll need my proposal completed by Friday,' she told him smartly.

'We'll do it tonight.'

Lexi sucked in a breath. 'And it's just business, right?' The question was out of her mouth before she'd fully thought it through and it landed between them like a dead weight.

His smile hardened. 'Are you asking me or telling me?'

Lexi could feel her heart galloping behind her breastbone and she just hoped he couldn't see it. Because what had happened between them last night—the way he had treated her this morning—made her feel too raw, too vulnerable for her to risk sleeping with him again.

'Telling you.'

He nodded stiffly. 'Then I will, of course, respect your wishes.'

'Thank you.'

'Sudovolstviyem, moya milaya.'

Lexi didn't know what he'd just said and didn't ask for a translation, just watched as he walked out of the room with the lithe grace of a world class athlete and took all the oxygen in the room with him. Then she flopped onto the chair she'd been gripping like a life buoy.

Well, that was easy. But what had she expected? That he would put up an argument? Insist on sleeping with her?

She felt flat and heavy and strangely deflated and yet she should be happy. Leo was taking his responsibilities as a father seriously and he was going to lend her his vast experience in business to help make one of her dreams come true. What more did she want?

CHAPTER TWELVE

'I THOUGHT the plan was for you to look over my proposal.'

Leo looked across at the frosty woman holding onto the railing on the pool deck as if it were the only thing keeping her alive.

'And we will. But first there is a magnificent sunset to enjoy and an even better dinner to eat.'

'I'm not very hungry.'

'You didn't eat lunch.'

'How do you know that?'

'My chef makes it his mission to inspect each plate that is returned. He pays particular attention to the full ones.'

'I wasn't hungry then either.'

'And the sunset?'

'What about it?'

'You haven't disparaged the sunset yet.'

Her lips twitched at his attempt at humour. 'I'm working up to it.'

Leo smiled. After their tense meeting in his office earlier he'd decided there was no way she would be sleeping alone while she was on his yacht but that perhaps he needed to make up for his earlier behaviour and woo her a little. Not that she was making it easy in a fitted blouse and short summer skirt that drew his eyes to her shapely legs and made him want to lay her across the elegantly set table beside the pool and have his wicked way with her. Frankly, polite conversation was the last thing he felt like right now!

'Work up to it while we eat,' he suggested, gesturing for her to take a seat at the table. She eyed it as if it were a guillotine and he hid a smile. She was a definite challenge and one he was surprised to find he didn't mind rising to.

'I think someone must have misinterpreted your intentions when they set this table,' she murmured almost to herself.

Leo glanced at the gleaming silverware, crystal glasses and a centre candle waiting to be lit. It was a romantic setting and just as he'd ordered.

'It's not to your liking?' he asked as he held out her chair.

She sat, but was careful not to brush up against him. 'It's a touch intimate.'

'Not for what I have in mind.'

She met his eyes sharply as he sat down opposite her. 'Which is?'

'Let's eat first. I always find I argue better on a full stomach.'

Lexi laughed despite herself and told her heart to stop its unruly fluttering.

'Would you care for wine tonight?'

She needed something to ward off the charming man opposite her and nodded up at the waiter holding two bottles in his hand.

'Red or white, ma'am?'

'White. Thank you.' She watched as her glass was filled with sparkling wine and realised she was finding excuses not to look at Leo lest he see how affected she was by the sight of him, the golden rays of the dying sun turning him into a bronzed god. His blue eyes were brilliant in his tanned face, his muscular legs accentuated by the low-riding denim jeans, the sexy casual top... Jeans? Since when did he wear jeans? And why, oh, why, did he have to look so good in them?

'You're wearing jeans!' She knew she sounded accusing and took a fortifying gulp of wine to hide the gauche comment.

He looked down at himself. 'You don't like them?'

No, she didn't *like* them—she *loved* them.

'You don't normally wear them to a business meeting.'

He smiled. 'How's the wine?'

Lexi recognised that he was changing the topic—again—and noticed his own glass had been taken away.

'You're not drinking?'

'I don't drink alcohol.'

She gazed at him and wondered if he recognised that his decision to abstain from alcohol was just another way he was different from his father and scolded herself for still trying to find things about him she liked.

The waiter returned with a plate of tempting seafood and, despite her misgivings, Lexi found the whole dinner to be sublime. The chef delivered a six course *menu degustation* of light seafood and vegetarian dishes that couldn't help but imbue a sense that all was well with the world.

Lexi flopped back in her chair and eyed the man opposite her in the flickering candlelight, the quiet evening only broken periodically by the slap of a fish as it broke the surface of the sea, and the soft lilt of jazz music that played through the yacht's complex sound system.

Leo seemed relaxed as well and surprisingly the conversation had flowed easily. He'd told her a little about his travels and his business and had asked her plenty about her own, getting her to explain some of her ideas about where she wanted her business to go. She'd felt a little self-conscious at first but he'd proven an avid listener and was one of the few people whose eyes didn't glaze over when she went on and on and on about her passion. Whenever she was out with Aimee and this happened her friend would slice her hand dramatically across her throat to let her know when she was boring the pants off her listener.

'I don't think I told you that you look extremely beautiful tonight. I like your hair down.'

Lexi's heart lurched in her chest and she told herself to calm down. He was paying her a compliment, nothing more.

She stared at him and did her best to feel composed but he was like a sublime male animal relaxed back in his chair, his eyes intent on her face, making her think about how he had looked as he'd risen above her last night and entered her body. How he had felt in her hand. Big…almost impossibly big.

'Nothing to say, angel, *moy*?'

My angel, he said. But she wasn't his and never would be and maybe that tiny hint of wishing it otherwise meant that she'd had just a little too much wine.

'Maybe—' she cleared her throat '—we should just get on and look at my proposal.' She made to get up and collect her laptop from the sofa she had dropped it onto when she'd first come out on deck but he waylaid her with his hand on her forearm.

Lexi stilled as his thumb brushed across the underside of her wrist, tingling sensations causing goose bumps to rise up on her skin and a shiver to ripple all the way down her spine.

'What's the rush?'

The rush was that she was becoming seduced by the balmy night, the candlelit table, the soft music, the wine, the man… Oh, boy, the man!

'Come. Dance with me.'

'Leo, I can't do this.'

'Sure you can. You stand in the circle of my arms, put your hand in mine, and then you let me lead.'

He smiled wolfishly and she gave a short laugh. 'Very funny.'

He stood up and came around the table towards her. 'Let me show you.'

He grabbed her hand and pulled her to her feet. 'Leo, don't. I can't think straight when you touch me.'

His smile was one of pure male satisfaction. 'You know the secret to a man's heart.'

'I don't think it's your heart that's affected by that comment.'

His arm came around to the small of her back and he started moving her in time with the music. 'Maybe not my heart, but another major organ is definitely involved.'

'Only a man considers his *ego* a major organ,' she said loftily.

He laughed and Lexi felt as if some foreign being had invaded her body and switched off her brain. What was she doing flirting with him like this? He didn't want her. And, even if he did, could she sleep with him again without being swamped by her insecurities? And did she want to? No...

'Leo, please...don't play games with me.'

His eyes narrowed and she looked away. 'Someone hurt you. Someone other than your father.' His quiet concern made her stumble and he gathered her even closer against him, her heart pounding out a litany that was totally out of time with the music.

She felt ridiculously safe in his arms—which was like saying a bunny was safe with a wolf—but did she feel safe enough to talk about Brandon?

She hesitated and remembered all that he had told her the night before. 'I was younger and he was immature—I was too, I guess. We met at university, in the library, and he was persistent. It wasn't till later that I found out a couple of his friends had made a bet that he couldn't get me into bed... We were intimate a couple of times but...sex has never been my forte and he soon found someone else.'

Someone else to take her place before he'd even told her their time together was over!

Leo swore. 'He was your first lover.'

Brandon had been her *only* lover besides him. Not that she was going to tell him that.

'Lexi?' He stopped moving and took her chin between his finger and thumb and forced her eyes to his. 'He was your only lover.' The statement was made with quiet conviction and she cringed.

Oh, God, was it so obvious? 'I never knew nights on the Aegean could be so balmy,' she announced cheerfully as she tried to pull her chin away to look out over the sea.

He tightened his grip, his eyes boring into hers. 'He made you feel inadequate?'

Finally the man asked a question. And if she could be more embarrassed she didn't know how. 'Can we *please* talk about something else?'

'Lexi, you are the most beautiful, sensual woman I've known and last night was...' He hesitated. '*Moy bohze*, I get hard just thinking about last night.' He swore softly. 'I get hard just *thinking* about *you*!'

Lexi was shocked by the vehemence in his tone. 'Is that unusual?'

Leo groaned. 'Angel, that's unheard of for me. But I can see you're having trouble believing that and I'm sorry for my contribution in making you feel that way. Whatever that jerk said to you, I can guarantee he was speaking of his own inadequacies, not yours. This morning I was an ass and... Angel, you take my breath away. I thought that was obvious.'

His voice resounded with raw emotion and Lexi felt years of angst and uncertainty fade into the atmosphere. 'Not to me,' she said huskily.

Leo made a growling sound low in his throat and a thrill of excitement shot through her blood. 'Then it's time I did something about that.'

He drew her slowly back into his arms and tilted her chin up so that she was looking at him. 'I want to make love with you, Lexi. I want to pleasure you and banish whatever negative memories your first lover erroneously planted in your beautiful head once and for all.' He swallowed heavily. 'Tell me you want that too.'

Lexi's breath caught and she stared at him. Emotions bubbled up inside her and her mouth went dry. How did someone resist an invitation like that, knowing what was likely to happen next?

They couldn't.

At least she couldn't. Maybe it was time to stop thinking so hard about the future and to just live in the present. She knew he still had secrets but she wasn't looking to marry the guy. This was just…well, she didn't know what this was other than another night in the arms of a man who made her feel fantastic about herself.

Banishing her doubts and deciding to take a chance, she raised her eyes to his. 'Yes.'

He expelled a rough breath as she placed her hand in his and let him lead her to the corner of the deck to a white sofa, wide enough to encompass ten people with room to spare. He moved back from her and leaned against the side of the boat, his arms folded across his chest, his eyes enigmatic in the light cast by the moon and a few well-spaced down lights. 'Take off your blouse.'

Lexi stood before him and let out a ragged breath of her own, self-doubt tightening her throat. But then she saw the fierce hunger shining in his eyes and it just seemed to melt away. It was time to reclaim her femininity and she realised that was what Leo was helping her to do.

And rather than feeling inadequate, she felt excited. Sensual. Thrilled.

Lexi stepped back and held Leo's gaze as her fumbling fingers worked the buttons down the centre of her blouse. When she was done, she slowly shrugged out of it and goose bumps rose up over her skin as Leo's gaze dropped to her breasts. The night was cool, but she knew her nipples were pointed because of the way this man was looking at her more than the temperature of the air.

'Now the bra.' His voice was thick and as slumberous as his eyelids.

Lexi reached behind her and unhooked her bra. She crossed one arm over her breasts and let one strap fall to her elbows and then the other before cupping her hands over both breasts, feeling even more empowered as she saw his nostrils flare. She held her hands in front of her like some practised courtesan and his eyes cut to hers. 'Drop it.' She held her breath and did as he asked, not sure what to do with her hands as he stared at her.

So maybe not such a great courtesan after all...

He was so still as he looked his fill of her it was almost unnatural and, as if she'd done this a thousand times before, she arched her torso slightly in his direction in silent supplication. Last night she had worried that he would find her too small, now she felt as if she was without equal.

His eyes dropped to her legs. 'Lose the skirt.'

Lexi's lower body flooded with warmth at his rough command. She didn't know how it was that he turned her on so completely but her body was ready for his, even though he hadn't touched her yet—this striptease seducing her as much as it was him. Feeling sexually charged, she ignored her skirt and bent forward instead, hooking her fingers around the edge of her black silk knickers and, making sure that her skirt didn't ride up, she let them slide to the floor. Then she slowly straightened, running her hands up her legs as she did so. Enjoying the way his breath hitched at her provocative movements.

She tilted her face up and studied the fierce intensity lighting his eyes, which looked almost black in the dim light. She didn't think she'd ever wanted anything more than she wanted to make love with this man right now and she stepped forward into his personal space.

'Your turn.'

She watched him take a deep shuddering breath and then he ripped his beautiful top up over his head, one of the seams tearing loudly in the still night.

'You really need to have more respect for clothing,' Lexi teased, releasing a shuddering breath as his hot hands reached out and spanned her waist. He tugged her forward one more step until there was barely a breath separating them and then his eyes connected with hers. 'I'm not in the mood to be gentle.'

She trembled and her own hands rose to spread out over his impressive pectoral muscles, her gaze drinking in the bronzed perfection of his chest and the sexy line of fuzz that bisected his abdomen. 'Neither am I,' she said on a rushed breath.

Her words seemed to release him from some dream state because he groaned and pulled her roughly in to him, her breasts scraping pleasurably against the hair on his chest as he lifted her to his mouth. She let out a long, low sound as he found her peaked nipple and suckled her firmly, her arms winding around his neck to clasp his head.

'Put your legs around my waist,' he growled against her aching flesh.

She did as he asked and Leo bunched her short skirt higher, his fingers digging into the soft globes of her bottom. She was the most exciting woman he had ever known and he couldn't get enough of her.

He delved into her wet heat and he nearly came apart in his jeans as she writhed against him and opened readily to his intimate touch.

'*Bohze*, Lexi, you're so wet.'

'For you. Only for you,' she murmured against the side of his neck.

Groaning, he laid her on the soft sofa behind them with one hand and released the zip on his jeans with the other. She clung to him, her hands on his face, in his hair, her voice one soft continuous moan against his lips. He positioned himself at her entrance and was about to surge deep when her hands stopped their urgent exploration and he felt her stiffen.

'Leo. Protection.' Her voice was a breathless whisper close to his ear and it took him a moment to focus enough to digest what she had said.

Then he cursed. 'Damn. Are you on the Pill?'

She shook her head and a lick of unease spiked in his brain when he realised just how close he was to losing control. He never trusted women with contraception.

Cursing again, he fumbled around in the sagging back pocket of his jeans for the condom he'd put there for just this purpose.

'Hurry up, it's getting cold down here.'

Leo smiled down at her. 'Now we wouldn't want that happening, would we?' He sheathed himself and shifted between her splayed thighs and leaned over her. 'Lie back,' he ordered gruffly, running his hands over her creamy torso and tweaking her nipples as she reclined fully, her dark hair rippling on the pale cushions.

Leo held her gaze as he moved into position and then, unable to extend the anticipation any longer he pushed into her in one slow, powerful thrust.

She made a low keening sound and closed her eyes and so did he. She felt like heaven. Her body so tight. So slick. So soft.

'Leo, oh, God.' Her torso arched off the sofa as he plunged in and out and set up a fierce rhythm.

He felt his climax building too quickly and tried to contain it but for once he couldn't. The erotic image of Lexi splayed out before him, her breathy moans of pleasure…

'Lexi.' It felt as if her name was wrenched from some place deep inside him. 'Come for me, angel, I can't…' He grimaced, sweat beading his brow as he concentrated on giving her pleasure and, just when he thought he couldn't hold back any longer, he felt the telltale contractions as her orgasm hit and he let go in a rush, throwing his head back and practically baying to the moon in ecstasy.

It took forever to come back to earth and steady his heartbeat, the aftershocks of what they'd shared weakening his whole body till he could barely lift himself off her.

He rose up onto his elbow and looked down at her, spread out under him, sated, replete and as comatose as he felt, and he felt his chest constrict. Unnamed emotions rolled through him, seeking purchase, and he buried his face in the side of her neck, not wanting her to see just how much their lovemaking had affected him. Like last time, the instinct to flee gripped him and then her soft hands drifted over the sweat cooling on his back and he felt instantly calm. 'I think I like it rough,' she murmured, planting soft kisses along his hairline.

Bohze, she slayed him. He slid his hands along the length of her torso until he reached her chin and then he turned her face towards his so that his mouth could capture hers. It was a sweet kiss, almost tender after the wild sex. She wrapped her arms around his neck with such gleeful abandon he felt the knot in his chest tighten and chose to ignore it. For tonight, anyway.

'Still cold, angel *moy*?'

'Mmm…cold? I feel like I just flew into the sun.'

'The feeling is mutual, I assure you.'

He moved off her, dealt with the condom and pulled his jeans up to cover himself before scooping her up into his arms.

'Where are we going?'

'My bed. That was just the first course.'

'Well, if you're half as good as your chef, I can't wait for the next five.'

'You realise you just signed the man's termination papers,' he muttered half seriously.

She punched his arm lightly. 'I did not.'

Leo very nearly stumbled; it felt so nice to actually have someone play with him like this and he realised that he felt happy. The only times he'd ever felt like this had been during those rare times when his mother had been happy and Sasha had been alive.

He knew Lexi Somers was dangerous. Unfortunately, she was also addictive and he was nowhere near finished with her yet.

But after a week he would be. He didn't doubt that for a second.

CHAPTER THIRTEEN

'STOP hovering. Go join Ty in the pool.'

Lexi released her tense shoulders and scowled down at Leo's bent head, which was still damp from where he'd been playing with Ty in the water earlier. 'You've been looking at the proposal for half an hour. Haven't you finished yet?'

'You're going to dent my ego, angel, if you think I can rewrite a whole business proposal in half an hour.'

Lexi's face fell and she tried not to cringe. 'Is it that bad?'

'Relax. It's not bad at all. In fact, if you should ever find yourself out of a job I'd hire you in a heartbeat.'

'Really?'

'I don't say things I don't mean. From what I can see you've done your homework and there's a definite need in the market. But explain this.' He pointed to a row of figures in a graph. 'It looks like you're charging less than your current business, which seems fine while you build up your clientele, but it never evens out. Even taking into account the different demographic of the new centre, it seems low.'

'The people using the childcare centre can't really afford to pay more and there's a lack of government funding in that zone, which would normally subsidise our income and which we're hoping will change some way down the track.'

'You can't run a business on hope and if you're not careful you'll have to prop up this centre with your first, which will jeopardise both.'

'I know, but if we put our prices up it defeats the purpose of what we're offering.'

'Can you cut back on staff?'

Lexi shook her head. 'I won't compromise quality of care for economic gain.'

Leo sighed. 'I always knew you were a soft touch—I just didn't realise how soft.'

Lexi glanced over at Ty and Carolina, splashing each other in the pool. They had all been playing similarly an hour earlier and Lexi's heart still felt light at the memory of Leo interacting with his son. He still hadn't told Ty he was his father and Lexi wondered when he intended to do that, but she had no doubt he would. Not that she should be thinking about that when she should be focused on work.

'Is it so hopeless, then?' she said, turning her mind back to business and trying to keep the despondency out of her voice.

Leo glanced at her, his eyes lingering on her mouth for so long she thought he might kiss her and her body started to tingle. Last night had been even more phenomenal than the first and now, even when she thought of Brandon, she couldn't conjure up one ounce of insecurity.

'You keep looking at me like that, I'll drag you back to my lair and not let you out all day,' he growled softly.

Her look at *him*!

Lexi's eyes lifted from his mouth and the world receded. Then Ty squealed and the world returned with a thud.

'Right.' He cleared his throat. 'Pull up a seat. You need a contingency plan.'

Lexi sat down and for the next hour became more and more overawed as he took her through one cost-saving idea after another.

'Wow, I'm impressed. If I was a bank, I'd lend you a million dollars.'

His smile was wolfish. 'How do you think I bought my first scaffolding company?'

'Why scaffolding?'

'Honestly, I wanted to avenge my uncle by closing down the company that had been responsible for his senseless death. Then one night, after I got into yet another fight I was sitting in the hospital waiting room nursing a broken nose when the richest man in Russia came on the news. There was something about the way he stood and the way others treated him... I wanted to be him. So I changed tack. Bought the company, sacked the incompetent management team and the rest, as they say, is history.'

'How old were you?'

'Eighteen.'

'Eighteen!' She frowned. 'So you never went to university either?'

Leo looked up from the laptop and realised what he'd just said. He couldn't remember ever suffering from a loose tongue before but, ever since he'd told her his 'charming' childhood story, he could feel that he had become less guarded around her. Which wasn't great because he didn't want to slip up and tell her about Sasha and the selfish part he had played in his death.

He thought about the email from Amanda and wondered why it no longer angered him as much as it had last night. The circumstances were still the same and yet he felt different. Tossing the ball with Ty and Lexi in the pool this morning hadn't been as hard as he had thought it would be. In fact it hadn't been a hardship at all.

Lexi's conviction that he wasn't like his father—that he had a choice—played over in his head. Was she right? Logically it made sense, and he certainly didn't *feel* like he could physically hurt Ty, but could he take that risk and look after him full time on his own? No. It was too great a responsibility and if he got it wrong—the outcome could be fatal.

With past memories forcibly tamping down on his previous enjoyment of working alongside Lexi, he closed the lid of her laptop.

'No,' he said curtly. 'And now I have a hotel to view on Santorini.' He stood up. 'I think you'll find what we did this morning helpful.'

He was about to walk off when he made the mistake of glancing down at her. She wasn't looking at him but he could see that his churlishness had hurt her and something twisted in his gut. It was because of last night. It was because some bastard had hurt her and he didn't want to add to the damage he had done to her self-confidence. In fact last night he'd gone out of his way to make her feel cherished. Hardly a hardship, given how turned on she made him feel. But she also made him feel other things he'd rather not name, let alone face.

'Why don't you come with me?' The words were out of his mouth before he'd fully formed the thought and she looked at him with surprise.

'Seriously?' The smile she shot at him was beyond beautiful.

'I don't see why not. It's a tourist destination. You've never been. You can look around while I work.' He made it sound like a no-brainer but he was questioning his own sanity in making the offer.

'Okay. Great.'

'Meet me at the tender in twenty minutes,' he said sharply.

Fifteen minutes later, Leo marched towards the lower deck, snapping instructions into his phone, and stopped dead as he saw Ty bouncing up and down on the white leather seat of the tender. His eyes flew to Lexi's and he blanked out his moment of disquiet. When he'd extended the invitation he had meant it to be just for her.

'I hope it's okay if Ty comes along,' she said.

'Of course.' He inclined his head, remembering at the last minute that his agreement was to spend time with his son.

But he'd already put in an hour today.

The skin on his forehead pulled tight. If he wasn't careful he'd be spending every minute of every day with both of them. And why didn't that thought fill him with as much dread as it would have a week ago?

'No. Absolutely not.'

'But why not?' Lexi persisted. 'You've finished looking at the hotel and the beach is straight down that path. Have you ever been to a black sand beach?'

'No, and I don't want to.'

Lexi put her hands on her hips and stared straight into Leo's aviator glasses. She knew he didn't want to go to the beach and she hadn't missed the look on his face when he'd approached the tender earlier and spotted Ty seated beside her. She knew he didn't really want him here either but he'd made a promise to her yesterday that he would spend time with his son and she didn't want to think that his promises were as hollow as her father's.

Leo's phone rang and he turned away to answer it and Lexi rolled her eyes.

'Look, Lexi—horsies.'

Lexi followed Ty's line of vision to a row of sturdy grey donkeys, resplendent in their multicoloured rugs and faded leather saddlery. Ty started towards them and Lexi grabbed his hand.

'They're donkeys, sweets, and we can't go that way. Have a look at these colourful rocks instead.'

She didn't think he was going to cooperate but then he acquiesced and moved towards the various-sized volcanic rocks lining the ancient path. She watched him squat down on the side of the path and saw one of Leo's security team move into place nearby. The four men who seemed to follow Leo everywhere were so discreet she actually forgot they were even there.

Lexi cast her eyes around the arid landscape that was so

unlike anything she had ever seen before. Tiny cobbled streets full of chatty tourists, incredibly beautiful views of a pristine blue sea from the various rocky outcrops and the quaint white cubed buildings, some with brilliant blue trim, tripping down the cliff faces.

But, as riveting as the scenery was Lexi still found her eyes drawn to Leo in his familiar crisp white shirt and suit trousers. Her eyes stripped away those clothes and she could so easily picture his wide shoulders and lean torso, his long, muscular legs. She knew he swam as a form of exercise but the cut of his body also came from centuries of strong alpha males who had fought the land, and each other, for their very survival.

To stop herself staring at him like an adoring fan she walked to the edge of the path and glanced down the winding red-dirt track to the beach below. It would be a shame to come all this way and not see the black sand but—

'Ten minutes.'

'Sorry?' Lexi turned as Leo came up behind her.

'Ten minutes and not a minute longer.'

Lexi beamed a smile at him when she realised he was relenting about going to the beach. 'And, angel, don't make me regret it.' The words were gruff, but a smile tugged at the corners of his mouth and she felt gloriously happy.

'Okay. But can we ride the donkey down?'

He shook his head as if she were a lost cause and set off down the path.

As they breasted the row of little donkeys Ty's face lit up and she saw a resigned expression flicker across Leo's. When he stopped to converse with the elderly white-haired guide with a bandanna tied around his neck and a blue beret shielding his head she hid her smile beneath the wide brim of her own hat.

She watched as he picked Ty up and perched him atop his chosen steed and felt as light as a bubble as he then proceeded to walk protectively beside him as the donkey set off at a snail's pace down the hill.

He might not realise it, but he was slowly starting to build a connection with Ty and, once he did, she felt sure he wouldn't be able to help falling in love with him. In fact, she sensed that he already was. The only thing she was really having trouble sensing was what was happening between the two of them.

She knew why she had slept with him last night of course. She had felt emboldened by his obvious desire for her and empowered by her renewed sense of self. He had made her feel sexy. Sensual. And it was proving a hard thing to give up, even though she knew he wasn't interested in anything permanent. But that was okay, she reminded herself. Hadn't she decided last night to stop worrying so much about the future and just live in the here and now?

And the here and now was scorching. Both the sun above her straw hat and the man walking alongside a donkey with his son balanced precariously on top.

To stop herself daydreaming, she let her eyes wander to the family of four ahead. The husband had his arm slung over his wife's shoulders while their two girls giggled exuberantly and clung to their donkeys, the leather saddles creaking at each ungainly step the donkeys took.

The couple looked so relaxed and happy—comfortable in each other's space—that it pierced Lexi to the core. This was what she had wanted for her own parents.

This was what she wanted for herself.

She glanced at Leo and realised he was watching the family as well. Then he turned, his eyes snagging with hers. Lexi felt as if she had her heart in her mouth and forced a nonchalant smile to her lips.

Yes, she might want this for herself one day but she wasn't silly enough to think she would get it with him even if she wished it otherwise.

So much for not daydreaming.

* * *

Surprisingly, Leo found he was enjoying himself. He had walked the stinking donkey all the way down the hillside and was now standing on the pebbled black beach holding a fistful of colourful shells and rocks that Lexi and Ty had insisted on collecting along the shoreline. Lexi had rolled up her lightweight trousers, which clung like a second skin to her sexy bottom, and was holding Ty's hand as the waves gently lapped at her ankles.

He thought of the couple he had seen walking their two girls on donkeys ahead of Ty's and brooded. For a minute he had wanted to sling his arm over Lexi's shoulders and draw her close but her cool smile told him he would be way off base in doing so and it had brought him to his senses. He might be still flummoxed with what it was about this woman that attracted him so much but he wasn't going to be an idiot about it. And while he'd presumed that the attraction would start to wane after he'd had her, it was still early days yet. Give him a week with her in his bed and he'd see things differently.

'Take your shoes off and come in,' Lexi called out to him from the shoreline. 'The water is amazingly warm and silky.'

Like her skin.

'No.' He cleared his throat. 'I'm good.'

The bright smile she'd worn ever since he'd given in and agreed to take them to the beach dimmed a little and he felt like the world's biggest spoilsport. He could enjoy a beach as much as the next person, damn it.

With that in mind, he pulled out his phone and called the tender to come and pick them up directly from the beach. If she wanted to enjoy a beach he'd take her to a real one that wasn't crowded with noisy holidaymakers like this one.

Lexi closed her eyes and turned her face up to the sun and let another fistful of sugar-soft sand sift through her fingers as she lay on the beach chair Leo had organised to be delivered from the nearby yacht. The beach was privately owned and, since they were the only ones on it, it almost felt as if they were shipwrecked. Shipwrecked with an icebox full of treats and drinks, a beach umbrella to ward off the sun's rays, since there were no actual trees on the island to speak of, and a mega-yacht anchored a little way out at sea with every conceivable luxury known to mankind. She smiled and nearly pinched herself to make sure she wasn't dreaming.

The only sound around her was the sound of Ty and Leo building a sandcastle by the water's edge and the whisper of the gentle waves as they rolled on and off the beach.

This was so far removed from her real life it was like entering a fantastic dream. She just had to keep reminding herself of that every time her mind started trying to build its own sandcastles in the air!

'So what do you think of *this* beach?' Leo's deep voice rumbled from somewhere overhead and interrupted her happy thoughts.

Lexi squinted up at his dark outline and smiled. 'It's okay if you like this sort of thing,' she mused as if she wasn't sure if she did.

His eyes trailed over her and her nipples peaked. 'It seems to me this is exactly the sort of thing you like.'

'Well, the sand is very soft.'

'And hot. Like you. And now me.'

'You could always take a dip in the ocean to cool off.'

'I do plan to take a dip,' he said suggestively, 'but it's not in the ocean. Have you had enough of this beach for one day?'

Lexi felt a zing of excitement deep inside her as his brilliant blue eyes lingered on her lips. She had now. 'Yes. You?'

'No need to ask, angel.'

Leo quickly organised the tender to head over and pick them up and, after a shower and a light dinner, Lexi returned to her room and wrapped herself in an oversized cotton cardigan before wandering outside to her private balcony. She had thought about heading up onto one of the main decks for a relaxing drink but she was tired from all the sun and lack of sleep the night before, and didn't want to appear as if she was deliberately seeking Leo out. Their relationship had shifted gear in a big way today and she didn't know what to make of it or how to ask what he was thinking without appearing needy and insecure.

She knew he still had secrets and she didn't feel as if she could truly let herself relax with him until she found out more about him. She was desperate to know who Sasha was for one, and why Leo's dreams were so tormented. She'd been wrong about how he felt about Amanda and she didn't want to make up stories in her head about Sasha either, but that seemed impossible for her *not* to do.

'Is Ty asleep?'

Lexi felt Leo's presence just before he spoke and looked over her shoulder, her heart skipping a beat at the sight of him, fresh from the shower in T-shirt and jeans. There was something about seeing him in casual gear that reached out to her. He looked like someone who was accessible and not the out of reach Russian oligarch that he really was. 'Yes. He went out like a light half an hour ago.'

She turned back to stare out over the water and felt him come up behind her. 'And you? How are you feeling?'

Confused.

'Tired. It was a wonderful day. Thank you for taking us.'

He reached out and wrapped his arms around her waist, pulling her back into his chest. 'The day's not over yet,' he murmured against the top of her head.

Lexi let herself lean her full weight into him and soaked up his manly smell, which now seemed so familiar to her.

Gathering her courage in hand, she decided she had nothing to lose by asking the question uppermost in her mind. 'Can I ask you something?'

'You know that always makes a man want to say no.'

'Who's Sasha?'

He stiffened for a moment before fanning his hands out over her belly and bending his knees a little so he could nuzzle the side of her neck. 'Sasha is no one you need to worry about.'

Lexi felt *herself* stiffen this time and gripped the wooden railing more tightly. 'You're not still seeing her, are you?'

He stopped nuzzling her and spun her abruptly towards him, grasping her chin between his thumb and finger and forcing her eyes to his, his expression fierce. 'I'm not your father or your ex, Lexi. I don't play around on a woman if I'm sleeping with her.'

Lexi swallowed, not doubting him for a second but remembering an earlier comment he had made about not having girlfriends, only bed partners. 'That's good to know.'

'Anything else?' His voice was clipped and her heart sank a little when she realised that he wasn't going to answer her question.

'You won't tell me, will you?'

He let out an exasperated breath and released her chin. 'Sasha is not relevant to you and me.'

No, whoever Sasha was, she was relevant to him, otherwise he wouldn't mind talking about her.

Lexi folded her arms and looked down at the tiny space between their bodies. She felt raw and exposed and she could feel the tension coming off him in waves. She glanced up at him and almost raised her hand to smooth the frown line marring his perfect brow. 'And what *is* you and me, Leo?' she asked the other question that had been milling around the outskirts of her mind all day, holding her breath as she waited for his answer, remembering too late her new-found intent to live in the moment.

He rubbed the back of his neck in that telltale sign that said he was stressed. Lexi wondered if her question was the death knell of whatever it was that was going on between them, the thought making her stomach clench painfully.

'I don't know.' He reached out and his hands curved around her hips, the familiar warmth of his touch flooding her lower body. 'But I want you more than I've ever wanted any other woman. Is that enough for you?'

Lexi held her breath. Was it? She knew that if she said no he would walk away from her without a backward glance and deep down in her heart she knew she didn't want that. Not yet. Maybe not ever.

Swallowing hard against that thought, she raised her arms and ran her hands over the taut muscles and sinews of his arms until she reached his shoulders. She felt his body quiver under her touch and heard the whistle of air as he released a pent-up breath between his teeth.

He held himself absolutely still as he waited for her to continue and Lexi made up her mind. She didn't know if his answer *was* enough but she wouldn't worry about the future. And what was there to worry about, anyway, if she made sure her heart stayed clearly out of whatever this thing was between them?

An affair?

A fling?

'I don't know.' She gave him the same answer he had given her because it was the most honest. 'But I know I've never felt like this with any other man and I'm not ready to let it go,' she breathed, raising herself onto her tiptoes and kissing him at the same time as he wrapped his arms around her body and crushed her to him.

CHAPTER FOURTEEN

BUT old habits died hard and three days later, as she sat in Leo's library and hit the send button to email her revamped business proposal to her bank manager, Lexi knew she was getting in too deep.

Apart from one afternoon when Leo had flown to Athens to finalise the business deals that had instigated this trip, he had kept his word and spent almost every minute of each day with her and Ty and it had been lovely. Too lovely. But too often Lexi had caught her runaway heart drumming up stories of a future between them that her practical side had scoffed at.

It was like having a split personality. Or having the puppets Punch and Judy in her head. Punch would start daydreaming and going off on a completely inappropriate tangent and Judy would return and bop him on the head.

Lexi pushed her computer aside and stretched the kinks in her neck and tried to go easy on herself. Because who wouldn't dream of a future with a man like Leo Aleksandrov?

Yes, he was arrogant and demanding and always wanted things his way, but he was also gentle and tender and never ran roughshod over her wishes. In fact, this week, he had almost gone out of his way to *fulfil* her wishes. And not just in the bedroom.

And he had completely eradicated her feelings of insecurity, at least with him. She couldn't imagine ever making love with another man with such joyful abandon and was now gladder than ever that she had been honest with Simon about how she felt. It just pained her that she couldn't be as honest with Leo.

But then how did she feel about him?

She liked him, of course, but…that was all she could ever let it be. Because, as tender as he had been with her, as insatiable as he was in bed, he didn't let himself do emotion. And of course there was still the mysterious Sasha floating around in the background.

'There you are, *moya milaya*.' Lexi looked up, startled by the sound of Leo's voice. 'Come—' he held out his hand to her '—I have a surprise for you.'

'What is it?'

'If I tell you, it won't be a surprise.'

Lexi smiled and pushed her gloomy thoughts aside. They were leaving in two days. Plenty of time to feel gloomy after that. 'Okay.'

He dropped a searing kiss on her lips and almost dragged her out of the library and down to her bedroom. There, in front of her full-length mirror, was a metal rack stacked with what looked like couture evening dresses.

She turned to him, slightly bemused. 'I don't understand.'

'It's very simple. I tore your dress the other night and now I'm replacing it.'

Lexi raised her eyebrows. 'With fifty new ones!'

'You never know when the urge might take me over again,' Leo drawled, the wicked grin on his face sending her pulse rate soaring. 'They are all in your size. Choose one to wear tonight and do what you want with the others.'

Lexi ran her hand over the beautiful gowns. If she sold them she imagined she might just make enough money to pay for the renovations to the building for her new childcare centre! 'This is too much, Leo.'

'Enough.' He waved his hand at her imperiously. 'We are going to dinner. You have nothing to wear. Ordinarily, I wouldn't mind—but tonight there will be other diners around and I am nothing if not possessive with what is mine.'

Oh, if only she was.

Lexi cleared her throat. 'Where are we going?'

'Get dressed and you will find out. You have half an hour.'

'Half an hour! I'll need longer than that to do one of these dresses justice,' she exclaimed with real panic.

'You do them justice already.'

'Too smooth,' Lexi complained and shooed his grinning face out of the door.

When he closed it behind him she returned her attention to the dresses, not knowing which one to choose.

'Athens! You're taking me to Athens!' Lexi had felt sick the whole time they had been travelling in the helicopter that felt no safer than a tin box being tossed around by one of her toddlers. She had only just now prised her hands from her eyes at Leo's insistence.

Athens spread out below her like a bejewelled cloak, the Parthenon sitting atop it like a porcelain crown.

The helicopter circled lower and Lexi once again covered her face, ignoring Leo's husky chuckle but glad of his strong arm holding her close.

She felt a jolt and then Leo said, 'We're here, angel.'

He unclipped her safety belt as the whine of the rotors ebbed, then jumped down onto the ground and placed his hands around her waist as he lifted her out. 'Lucky you're so small,' he said huskily against her ear. 'Not to mention exquisite in that dress.'

'It's black,' Lexi said almost apologetically, 'but I loved the design.'

'It's beautiful.' Leo looked over her shimmering strapless dress, which fell in elegant waves to her feet with frankly male appreciation. 'I can't wait to tear it off you later on.'

'You will not.'

He laughed at her tone and she knew that if he wanted to tear it off her she could do nothing about it. Then she looked around and realised that they had landed on the top of a building with a clear view of the Parthenon. 'Oh, my…'

'You wanted to see the Acropolis at night. And here it is.'

Lexi swung her gaze back to his and tried not to let every one of her overawed emotions show on her face.

'Thank you. This is the nicest thing anyone has ever done for me.'

He seemed to be caught up by her gratitude and blinked before holding his hand out to her. 'Come. We have a booking in Athens' most revered restaurant and then you can take a tour.'

'Really? We can walk around it?'

'Of course. I didn't bring you all this way just to look at it from afar, angel *moy*.'

Lexi laughed and tried not to be dazzled by his arrogant confidence.

'My mother would love it here,' Lexi mused, gazing around the posh old-world restaurant, with tables set at discreet distances from each other and draped in heavy white linen. 'She's half Greek herself.'

Leo leaned back in his chair. 'That explains the dark hair and golden eyes.'

Lexi laughed. 'My eyes aren't golden; they're a hybrid.'

'Yes. Golden when you're angry and green when you're aroused. They're very alluring.'

The muscles deep within Lexi's pelvis clenched at his intimate tone and she knew from the way his eyes smouldered that he knew it. The man oozed sexuality when he wasn't even trying so when he was… Lexi felt heat sweep into her face and tried to think of something to say.

'I've always hated them. As a child I longed for blue eyes and blonde hair.'

'I love them.'

Okay, not helping.

'We need to change the subject.'

'We need to find a bed, you mean.'

Lexi felt a stupid grin split her face as he reached across the table and took her hand in his, drawing lazy circles around her palm.

'That's not helping either.'

'Have I told you how beautiful you look tonight?'

'Yes. Several times. As are you.'

'Beautiful? Sexy, maybe.'

'And modest.'

'You don't get anywhere being modest, angel.'

Lexi sipped her wine, feeling mellow and content. 'Speaking of getting anywhere, do you think you'll stay in the apartment, or do you think you might get a house with a garden now that Ty is staying with you?'

She'd said the wrong thing. She knew it even before he removed his hand from hers and picked up his water glass.

'Ty lives with Amanda.'

'But Amanda's email…'

'Is rubbish. Once my security team find her I'll sort out the problem and everything will be back to normal.'

Sort out the problem? Lexi felt slightly queasy. He had been *so* different this week. She had been *so* sure…and of course she knew why he thought he couldn't have Ty, but didn't he see he was different from his father? Or was there more to it? Was it that he just didn't want Ty, regardless? A thought Lexi had trouble formulating, let alone verbalising. And why was that? Why did she care so much…?

'You can stop looking at me with those shocked, wide eyes, angel. I know what you're thinking but life isn't a fairy tale.'

'I know that,' she snapped, but she knew part of her wished that it was.

'Then you know that I have to find Amanda.'

Lexi tried not to grimace. 'And if you don't?'

'I will.'

His certainty sent a frisson of dread darting down her spine and she was starting to feel sorry for Amanda. 'Don't be too hard on her, Leo. I think it's possible she suffered from post-natal depression after Ty was born.'

'You feel sorry for her?' His tone was incredulous and she cringed.

'I'm not taking her side, if that's what you mean. I know she tried to trap you into marriage, but I don't see the point in dwelling on that. Life is too short to waste on anger or guilt.'

He stared at her for a heartbeat, his body tense. 'It's also too short to talk about Amanda Weston. Come.' He stood up. 'The Parthenon awaits.'

Lexi was only half paying attention to their personal guide as she wandered through the ancient ruins, her mind on the conversation in the restaurant.

This week she had assumed Leo had changed his mind about Ty but she'd been wrong and it made her feel edgy. She wanted to ask him if he was ever planning to tell Ty that he was his father but the magical night already felt tainted by their earlier discussion and she didn't want to ruin it by getting into another argument. Which was probably very cowardly of her, but she needed more time to digest her feelings before she broached it again.

Thankfully, the flight back to the yacht was a little better than the flight over but that was because she was basically half asleep with her head on Leo's shoulder. Still, if she'd had the energy she would have kissed the deck when the helicopter landed safely on the yacht.

Leo scooped her up into his arms and carried her into his suite. Lexi stood before him, much as she had that first night but instead of ripping her dress in half he gently turned her and lowered the zip at the back. Then he peeled the fabric from her body and proceeded to kiss his way down her spine.

His lovemaking was surprisingly gentle and afterwards

Lexi lay in the crook of his shoulder and traced lazy patterns over the hair on his chest. Gradually his breathing eased as he slipped into sleep and, for all her earlier tiredness, she felt suddenly wide-awake.

He had told her a few nights ago that he had never slept as well as he had this week and she was glad. But she was also a fool. What she felt for Leo was ten times—no, a thousand times—deeper than what she had ever felt for Brandon. Because she hadn't really loved Brandon—at least not the way she loved Leo.

She let the words that had been edging into the front of her brain for days now take root and she knew without a shadow of a doubt that they were true.

She stared into the darkened room at nothing in particular and didn't know how she felt about that. Because she didn't know how *he* felt about *her*.

Yes, he'd done nice things for her and, yes, he had spent time with her, laughed with her, helped her whenever she needed it, but was she really any different from any other woman he had spent a week with?

Being on his mega-yacht and sailing around the Cyclades islands was like being in a fairy-tale bubble. In two days she would return to London. Return to work. Return to reality. And she had no idea if he would want to continue seeing her there.

She tried to imagine what it would be like if he did. Movie nights with Todd and Aimee? Dinner in her tiny flat? Or would she always have to go to his penthouse and enter his world? And would she want that?

Oh, it was too hard.

Leo shifted and mumbled in his sleep, his arms tightening and releasing around her. He tried to turn, his brow pleated, and Lexi realised he was starting to have a nightmare again. She instinctively smoothed her fingers over his forehead, trying to soothe him.

'Sasha?'

The whispered word was barely audible but Lexi heard it. And froze. 'No, it's me, Leo. Lexi.'

He seemed to relax at the sound of her voice and his lips whispered across her temple as he pulled her back down to him, immediately falling into a deep sleep. Unfortunately, it took Lexi a lot longer to do the same.

CHAPTER FIFTEEN

LEXI woke alone the next morning for the first time since they had started sleeping together and knew it didn't bode well.

Then she realised that she wasn't quite alone when she heard Leo talking into his telephone over by the window. He was as naked as the day he was born and the morning sun streaming in highlighted his toned butt and the defined dent where his back muscles met his spine.

She had seen him on the phone many times this week but she had never heard him speaking in such a low personal tone and her stomach clenched, a sixth sense telling her that he was talking to a woman.

Then she remembered how he had called out Sasha's name last night in his sleep. How he had thought *she* was Sasha? Lexi's heart hammered at the thought that he had remembered the dream and called Sasha while she lay sleeping.

Stop, take a breath, she ordered herself. He was not her father and she was not her mother. Hadn't she told him that his parents' story didn't have to be his own? So, ergo, nor did hers!

He switched off the phone and Lexi saw such a distressed look etched into his profile that her breath stalled in her lungs. She didn't want to intrude on what was clearly a private moment for him but nor could she keep quiet.

'Bad news?'

His head swivelled around at the sound of her voice. 'You're awake.'

Her eyebrows rose. 'Yep.'

She was desperate to ask who had been on the phone but he tossed it onto a nearby sofa and turned back to face the window, effectively shutting her out.

Lexi felt her face grow hot and her hands start to tremble at the silent rebuff. For the past few days, whenever the conversation had veered onto the personal he had clammed up and she had let him, not wanting to push him as her mother had pushed her father. But now it was different.

Now her heart was involved and she felt even more vulnerable than before. She remembered her father had had topics that were off-limits and it had meant that at times they had all felt as if they were walking on eggshells around him. Just as she felt she was doing now with Leo.

'Where are you going?' he demanded gruffly.

Lexi stopped at the sound of his voice. She had been so deep in thought she had put on Leo's linen robe and was halfway across the room and hadn't even realised she'd moved.

She hesitated, wishing he would put some clothes on. 'You didn't seem to be in the mood to talk.'

'I'm rarely in the mood for the type of conversation you want to have, angel.'

'A personal one?'

'An interrogation.'

Lexi thought of her parents. Of Brandon. And then an image of the family on Santorini swam into her consciousness. She wasn't silly enough to idealise that they were the perfect couple—everyone had some sort of issue to contend with—but the fact was they *were* a couple. They had *committed* to be together for the long haul. Lexi's father had never married her mother and if she continued sleeping with Leo she would be doing so knowing that the end of their relationship was also marked in the sand.

She thought of the needy, clinging woman her mother had become and Lexi didn't want that for herself. She didn't want to become a victim and right now she felt like both! She liked being in control of her life and falling in love with a man who had no intention of loving her back was certain to erode even the most confident woman's self-esteem.

And maybe it hadn't been the elusive Sasha on the phone. Maybe it had been Amanda. And maybe she could just quit with all the guesswork and ask him.

'I was curious as to who was on the phone,' she defended herself. 'I think that's fairly normal.'

He stared at her for so long Lexi's eyes started to drift down the impressive lines of his taut body, only to snap back up when he said, 'It was my mother.'

'Your mother?'

'She calls this time every year.'

He looked as if he regretted adding that but Lexi was not in the mood to let him off the hook. 'Why?'

His hesitation was fleeting, but Lexi caught it. 'It's my birthday, angel.' His smile didn't meet his eyes and Lexi stared dazedly as he moved towards the bathroom.

His birthday! 'Were you going to tell me?'

And his mother was still alive?

Lexi's mind reeled. His online biography had informed her that his mother had passed away and she'd forgotten it was false. Only half aware of what she was doing, she followed him into the bathroom and saw him shrug as he stopped in front of the mirror. 'I hadn't thought of it.'

'Birthdays are special, Leo.'

'Maybe in your world. In mine they are just another day.'

'I didn't realise your mother was still alive.'

He gazed into her eyes briefly in the mirror before they slid lower down her body, one hand rubbing his jaw. 'I noticed this morning that the inside of your thighs are a little red so I thought I might shave this off.'

Lexi's heart thundered at the image his words brought to mind but she ignored it. 'Do you still see her?'

His eyes narrowed on hers. 'What did I tell you? An interrogation.'

Lexi blew out a breath. He was right. She did want to interrogate him. But that was only because he wouldn't *talk* to her. And if he wasn't going to talk to her, why was she still standing there?

Shaking her head at herself, she walked out of the room, surprised when she heard his voice behind her.

'It's not like you to walk out on an argument, angel.'

She turned, glad that he had slung a towel around his hips. Not that it hid much… She forced her eyes to his and noticed he was looking at the necklace she was fondling. 'I just need some space.'

The scowl on his face deepened. 'Why?'

She threw her hands up in front of her. For an astute man, he could be terribly obtuse at times. 'Because you have things you don't want to discuss and I'm not good with that.'

He paced away from her. 'This is why I don't do relationships.'

'Is that what this is?'

'Obviously not.'

'Leo, people in relationships talk to each other and not just about safe topics. They talk about real issues. Like this. Only you won't discuss anything personal. You didn't even tell me it was your birthday!'

'What the hell is the problem with that? It was the day I was born. Get over it. I have.'

Lexi barely registered the harshness of his tone, still stung by how little she knew about him. And on the one hand that was completely normal. They had known each other for little more than a week. The problem was that if he asked her she would tell him anything and it scared her when he wouldn't do the same for her. 'I guess it just showed me how little of yourself you really share with me,' she said testily.

He shook his head. 'You don't understand.'

'No, you're right, I don't,' she fumed. 'I don't understand why you haven't told Ty you're his father and I don't understand why you won't tell me who Sasha is. You called out her name again last night, just so you know.'

He looked momentarily stunned and she figured that he hadn't remembered the dream after all. 'I've told you Sasha is not important.'

And neither, it seemed, was she.

'If that was really the case then you wouldn't mind talking about her.'

'*Chort vozmi*, Lexi. Sasha is not a woman. Sasha was my brother.'

His brother?

'You have a brother?'

'*Was*. I *had* a brother. He died when he was three.'

Ty's age.

'How old were you?'

He looked distinctly uncomfortable. 'Ten.'

The time he had said his father went to prison. Lexi swallowed, not sure she wanted to find out the two were somehow connected, but unable to stop herself from asking, 'How did he die?'

Leo blew out a frustrated breath and closed his eyes briefly before staring back at her. 'He got in between my parents arguing one day and my father backhanded him into the wall.'

'Oh, my God.' Lexi's hand flew to her mouth.

'I told you there are some secrets you're better off not knowing, angel,' he sneered, walking through the doorway to the sitting room.

His voice was so cold, so clinical, and Lexi knew his brother's death still cut deep. As it would.

She followed and sat on the sofa, her hands cupped between her knees as he made coffee. 'That was why your father went to prison. Why you got into fights,' she said softly. 'I'm so sorry, Leo. You must have been devastated.'

The muscles in his back tensed but he didn't say anything.

'And your poor mother,' Lexi continued, unable to comprehend how bad she would feel in the same situation. 'She must have been so overcome with guilt and grief… Was it any wonder she couldn't look after you properly after an event like that? It would have been so difficult.'

He flicked a switch on the coffee machine and the sound of hot water hissed into the room. Then he turned and pinned her with a hard stare. 'She didn't want to take care of me. But I was glad. I couldn't wait to get away from her either.'

Lexi was shocked by the harsh vehemence of his words. 'Why?'

His eyelids lowered to half-mast. 'You planning to finish this interrogation any time soon, angel? I need a shower. With you in it.'

Lexi stared at him. Was this the best it would be between them? Was this all he had to offer? More secrets?

She thought about her life back in London. Her friendship with Aimee. Her job. Her mother fostering children as a way of giving and receiving love. She felt a million miles from everything right now but *that* was her reality, not *this*. This was a potential fantasy and what had happened to her resolve to never enter into those again…?

Her sigh broke the silence and she stared at a point in the middle distance, despair weighing her down. She heard Leo move and glanced back at him. He was a man in pain and her heart gripped. She couldn't give up on him just yet.

'I realise that this is an intensely painful subject for you, but I think it's eating you alive, Leo. And I think you're still suffering from your mother's abandonment of you at a time when you needed her most.'

'She didn't have a choice.'

'So you keep saying, but…'

'I was responsible for Sasha's death.' The harsh words seemed wrenched from some deeply hidden place inside him.

'What do you mean?'

'I was supposed to be looking after him that night.'

His voice held a wealth of self-recrimination and Lexi's brows pulled together. 'Where were your parents?'

He made a harsh sound. 'Fighting. It was always my job to look after Sasha when they fought. Only that particular night I couldn't be bothered. I was more interested in my computer game than my baby brother.'

He stormed back into the bedroom and Lexi heard the sound of him dressing. His revelation had been shocking and her heart went out to him.

She got up slowly and went to the doorway. He ignored her and continued to button his shirt. 'Leo, you weren't responsible for your brother.'

He continued to ignore her.

'Your parents were wrong to burden you with his safety. You're not to blame for his death. You know that, right?'

When he looked at her his eyes were bleak. 'None of that changes the fact that he's gone. That I let him down. That he would *be* here now if not for me!'

Lexi felt a lump form in her throat at his hoarse tone.

'You didn't—'

'Enough! I've dealt with all this; it's in the past.' He tucked his shirt into his trousers and stalked away from her.

She hesitated briefly before persisting. 'I don't think you have dealt with it.' She eyed him carefully. 'Not if you think Sasha's death was somehow your fault.'

He stopped dressing. 'I was old enough to know better.'

'You were ten!'

He ignored her and Lexi shook her head. Did he seriously believe he should have known better? 'You were only a child yourself. But even if you refuse to see the truth in that, what does it mean? That you have to pay for Sasha's death for the rest of your life?'

He stopped and stared at her and Lexi felt a spurt of hope that he was hearing her. 'You have to forgive yourself, Leo. You have to stop playing God. But you also have to forgive your father. If you don't, you just might become him. A lonely, empty man who was obviously filled with anger and hate.'

His blue eyes were icy as he looked at her. 'Are you done?'

'Leo, Ty needs you. I n—' Lexi stopped on a sudden inhalation. What had she been about to say? That she needed him? No. She didn't *need* him. She *loved* him. There was a difference. One created a dependency, the other a partnership. But he didn't want that and she did. More than ever with him. 'I know you can be a great father to Ty and, no matter what you think, you deserve to be happy.'

'I asked if you were done.'

Lexi wrapped her arms around herself in an attempt to stop herself from going to him. She loved him and he was in pain and she felt it all the way to her bones.

'Leo, I feel sick to think of what you must have gone through as a child, but you don't have to live alone like your uncle, and you would *never* hurt Ty.'

He made a brittle sound in his throat. 'You say that with such confidence, angel.'

Lexi felt him slipping away from her. 'Because you're *different* from your father, Leo. You've already made different choices in your life but for some reason you refuse to see that.' She felt a spurt of anger at his cold detachment, desperate to reach him any way she could. 'You know I'm starting to think you like hanging onto the pain of your childhood. I think it gives you an excuse for never taking a chance on love.'

Lexi wished the words back as soon as they left her mouth because even though she thought they might be true, he most likely didn't need to hear them right now.

Leo turned on her. 'Is that what you imagine is going on

here, Lexi?' he snarled. 'Did you imagine I was falling in love with you? That you had beaten every other woman to the post and would get my ring on your finger?' He laughed harshly as if the idea was ludicrous. 'Because I'll tell you now, I'm not the type to hand out trinkets you can wear around your neck in the hope that one day I'll come back.'

Lexi felt as if she'd been punched. Not only because of what he had said, but also because she could see that she had just done what her mother had done—harangued a man into ending a relationship with her.

But she couldn't be sorry. Not like her mother had been. Because Lexi knew she deserved more from a man. Where her mother would have settled if her father had stayed, Lexi realised that she never would. So, as sick as she felt at losing the man that she loved, she couldn't be sorry that she had forced the confrontation. 'I wasn't talking about you taking a chance on me, Leo,' she said with quiet dignity. 'I was talking about Ty.'

'Leo? Hellooooo?'

Leo blinked at the sound of the cutesy female voice in front of him and landed back at the Duke of Greythorn's swanky London party with a thud.

He glanced down as the blonde curled her fingers around his forearm as she smiled up at him. 'For a minute there I didn't think you'd heard a word I said.'

Leo stared at her. For a minute? Try the last half an hour.

He rubbed the back of his neck and glanced around the opulent hotel room and thought that his investment team had done a good job in procuring it for his portfolio. But that was it. He couldn't care less about the party, or the people in it.

'Look, Sarah—'

'Samantha.'

'Samantha.' He smiled, but it felt like more of a wince. 'To be honest, I didn't. My son is at home with a cold and I'm a little distracted right now.'

'You have a son? Does he look like you?'

Yes. Yes, he did. And Leo felt his heart swell with pride at the fact. He shook his head slowly. 'You know, you're the first person who isn't in his inner circle who knows about him.'

The blonde tilted her head coquettishly. 'I feel privileged.'

Leo frowned. He hadn't told her because he wanted her to feel privileged, he'd told her because for the first time he actually felt like it. For the first time he actually *felt* like Ty's father and it pained him to think that Ty still didn't know who he really was.

'Do you have a wife as well?' Samantha purred.

'No.' He shook his head. 'I'm not that lucky.' Lucky? Where had that come from? 'If you'll excuse me, I have to go.'

'Of course. I hope your child feels better soon.'

Leo brooded about the evening he'd had all the way home. It wasn't the party that was the problem, or even most of the people in it. It was him. He'd changed. He wanted more from life than polite chitchat and a fleeting moment of losing himself inside a beautiul woman's body.

He'd only been back from Greece for a week but other than work and Ty, he had to admit that he was bored, and for once he didn't want to just carry on as if everything was okay. Because it wasn't. It was empty.

As if on cue, an image of Lexi's smiling face came to mind and he realised he'd never once been bored in her company. Phenomenally turned on—and exceptionally frustrated—but never bored.

He recalled the moment she had left the yacht exactly seven days ago. He hadn't gone after her straight after she'd walked out of his room, his emotions stripped bare when her pained expression had reminded him of how his mother had often looked at him when he'd disappointed her as a child.

He and his mother had an estranged relationship at best.

He sent her money she didn't use and she called him on his birthday, which made him feel guilty and hurt. The fact was, something had broken between them after she had asked the nursing staff to turn off Sasha's life support system and he didn't know how to get it back.

And Lexi had only exacerbated those feelings with her unrelenting questions that morning. So, instead of going to her straight away to apologise for his callous words, he had done what he always did when emotion threatened to swamp him—he'd switched off. Gone for a swim.

He would have gone to her after he had cooled down but he'd been too late. She had already boarded one of his choppers for Athens—supposedly under his instructions! He'd nearly called it back but he knew how much she hated them and it had been a mark of her desperation to get away from him so he'd decided to let her go. Ty had cried and then become remote. Just like he did when he was trying to stop himself from feeling anything.

'Good evening, Mr Aleksandrov.'

'Good evening, Mrs Parsons.' Leo pasted on a smile and walked through to his sitting room, shrugging out of his dinner jacket. 'How's Ty?'

'Sleeping like a little lamb. I told you the worst of his illness was over.'

'So you did.' He tossed his jacket onto the back of the sofa. 'Do you have that passport yet?'

'Not yet sir, but I'll be sure to tell you when it comes through.'

Leo nodded and walked her to the door once she had collected her bag. 'Goodnight, Mrs Parsons. I'll see you tomorrow afternoon.'

'Actually, I'm back in tomorrow morning, sir. Carolina has an appointment to attend to in the morning.'

'Fine. See you in the morning.'

He saw her out of the door and tugged at his bow tie.

He stopped outside Ty's room and opened the door a whisker to look inside. The room looked vastly different from the way it had before he'd gone to Greece. Gone was the double bed and modern furnishings and in its place was a racing car bed and half a toy store. Leo smiled at the thought of how much he would have loved this room as a child.

All he could see from the dim light given off from Ty's nightlight was a small lump under the covers and a shock of pale hair. He stood beside the bed and watched the steady rhythm of Ty's breathing for some time, automatically smoothing his hair back from his forehead when he stirred.

As if sensing his presence, Ty muttered in his sleep and rolled over. 'Grandma?'

Leo felt gutted as Ty called out for Amanda's deceased mother. How was it that he had got the care of his young son so wrong? How was it that he had been so blind to so many things? Lexi was right, he hadn't faced anything. He'd just buried it in a six-foot pit and piled a heap of manure on top.

He lay down on top of the covers and curled himself around Ty's sleeping body as he had seen Lexi do weeks earlier. A lump formed in his throat and his nose tingled as he fought to hold back tears. This was his son. His own flesh and blood and he'd used every excuse he could come up with to stop himself from feeling anything for him. To stop himself from loving him. And all because he was afraid.

Leo thought about himself as a boy, hiding under his blankets late at night as he listened to his parents fighting and then, full of worry for his mother, creeping into the hallway to make sure she was okay.

He remembered how lonely he had felt, sitting with his back to the wall in a tight huddle. How…stoic. How strong he had decided he needed to be to survive. He hadn't shown emotion even then.

No wonder his mother had said he was like his father! And yet she had still called him every year to maintain a connection with him. Maybe she *had* loved him. Maybe Lexi was right in saying that she had just been so overcome with grief that she had only *seemed* to close off from him. And, drowning in his own grief, he had pushed her away so that he didn't have to face his own guilt. His own fear of hearing how like his father he was.

Leo grimaced. He had unknowingly made himself over in his father's image anyway and he was still doing it.

Bohze; he didn't want that any more. He recalled the blissful nights on the yacht, with Lexi sleeping beside him all soft and warm. He'd convinced himself that it was just sex that had given him the sense of well-being he always experienced in her arms, but it wasn't.

It was her.

He thought again of that last morning they had been together and the moment he'd felt sure she had been about to tell him that she needed him. At the time it had sent him into a flat spin but now…now he was ready to admit that he needed her too. Needed her more than his next breath.

Bohze!

She'd made him care and he'd been so afraid of admitting it, he had driven her away. Had laughed in her face at the notion that he was falling in love with her. Which he was. Had.

He loved her.

The thought hit him with the force of a bullet.

What an ass he was. He loved her and he had pushed her away.

He had to tell her. He had to *have* her. And he was sure she felt the same way. He was sure she wouldn't have given herself to him, lain with him every night in his bed, if she hadn't had strong feelings for him. So okay, maybe not love—*yet*—but he'd move heaven and earth to change that.

'Grandma?'

Ty stirred again and Leo stroked his brow. 'It's not Grandma, Ty. It's Papa.'

He felt a sense of warmth he'd only ever experienced in one other person's arms steal over him and it was as if a lifetime of pain and suffering just melted away. He could feel Sasha in Ty's small body, but it was different.

When he'd held Sasha he'd done so with the arms of a child. Now he could feel Ty with the arms of a man. He could sense his own strength compared to Ty's vulnerability and realised that he didn't feel any of the vindictiveness his father had expressed through violence. He just felt love.

Lexi read and reread the email and knew she should feel happier.

'So Darth Vader has approved the loan?' Aimee said with a gleeful smile as she read over Lexi's shoulder. 'You are such a legend. Three weeks ago, I thought there was no chance we'd get the money but now…' She did a little jig. 'Now we move on to phase two.'

Lexi nodded. 'It's thanks to Leo Aleksandrov that we have the loan approved.'

She flicked through a couple more emails knowing that Aimee was watching her sympathetically. When she had returned from Greece a week ago she had been red-eyed and hadn't been able to hide her misery. Of course she'd told her friend everything. Including the full extent of the hurt Brandon had once caused her, which had been easy because it no longer had any effect on her at all. What hadn't been easy was waking up each morning with the memory of how it had felt to have Leo spooning her, of draping herself over his hard male body, and knowing she'd never experience that again.

'Don't look now,' Aimee whispered, 'but the man in question has just walked in.'

'Mr Hammond?' Lexi looked around despite her friend's warning.

'Not Darth Vader. Leo Aleksandrov.'

'Wha—' Lexi closed her mouth, her eyes fixed on Leo's

blond head as he walked through the main childcare room holding Ty's hand.

'I wondered whether Ty would be back,' Aimee mused. 'Do you want to go out and greet them?'

Did she…?

'No!' Not on your life. 'In fact—' Lexi stood up and looked around for a place to hide '—you go, and lock my door after you. If he asks, and I doubt he will, tell him I'm sick.'

Which she was.

Heartsick.

'Too la— Good morning,' Aimee trilled.

Lexi felt Leo's presence and deliberately kept her eyes on the cooling cup of tea on her desk.

'You must be Aimee.' His deep voice resonated inside every one of Lexi's cells. 'It's nice to meet you properly. I am Leo Aleksandrov.'

'I know.' Aimee sounded breathless and when Lexi looked up it wasn't hard to discern why. Leo filled the doorway of her office, wearing black low-riding jeans and a peacock blue T-shirt that matched his eyes and hugged every one of the hard muscles lining his chest. Wasn't today a work day?

She drew in a slow, discreet breath and tried to put on a brave face. If she had thought about Ty returning to the centre at all she hadn't considered that Leo would be the one to bring him. Amanda maybe, but not Leo.

She looked at him, her brain empty of everything but getting through the next few minutes.

She cleared her throat discreetly before speaking. 'If you want the sign-in sheet, then—'

'I don't want the sign-in sheet.' His dazzling eyes, which seemed impossibly blue, held hers. 'I want you.'

Lexi felt light-headed. *Oh, boy, how easy would it be to misconstrue that statement?*

Aimee made a squeaking noise. 'I think I have some wool

to wind.' She made a dash for the door and Leo stepped into the room to let her past.

Lexi's knees went weak and she dropped back down in her chair, not caring that it made him that much taller.

'So how can I help you?' she asked carefully, pleased with her moderated tone.

'You're wearing more make-up than usual,' he rasped. 'Why?'

Lexi felt herself redden. She was wearing more make-up because she was trying to hide the bags under her eyes from lack of sleep and too many hours pining over him.

'This is what I normally wear,' she lied.

'You don't need it.'

Lexi cleared her throat again. This was excruciating. 'I can't believe you stopped in here to discuss my make-up requirements,' she said, wishing he'd just say what he had to say and leave.

'No.' He rubbed the back of his neck and she noticed for the first time that his own eyes didn't look that rested either. Was Ty keeping him up? He wouldn't have been happy to see her leave the yacht, but he had seemed fine with Carolina...

'I came to tell you that I'm buying a new house.'

'A new house?'

'With a garden.'

'Oh.'

'And a pool.'

She nodded, not trusting herself to speak.

He pulled out the visitors' chair and sat down opposite her, looking far too big for the tiny structure. 'Don't you want to know why?' he asked carefully.

Lexi took a deep breath. 'If you want to tell me.'

'I'm keeping Ty.' His words were quiet and sure, his eyes shining. Then he shook his head. 'That makes him sound like a pet. What I meant to say was that I have agreed to take full custody of Ty and Amanda has agreed to see him during the holiday periods.'

Lexi swallowed and contained the surge in her heart with some difficulty. 'So…' she cleared her throat '…I need to amend his forms.'

'Damn it, Lexi, I don't give a stuff about Ty's forms.' He rose and stood in front of her as if he wasn't sure what to do next and then he paced to the back of the room. '*Bohze*, I'm making a hash of this.'

'Making a hash of what?'

He frowned. 'Of telling you how I feel. It's because I've never done it before.'

Lexi was pleased he wanted to tell her how he felt about Ty, but really she would have felt less pain stretched out on a rack of ten-inch nails with rats gnawing on her stomach.

'Leo, I couldn't be happier for you and Ty but—'

'I'm not here because of Ty. I'm here because of us.'

Lexi watched him warily. 'You made it pretty clear last week that there was no *us*.'

'I said a lot of stupid things that morning. Most of them, as you rightly pointed out, because I couldn't let go of the past. I'm sorry I hurt you. In my defence, I was feeling a little unhinged that morning.'

'Because your mother called?'

'Because my mother called. Because our lovemaking the night before had been so damned beautiful.' He paused, watching her as if trying to gauge her reaction to his words. 'For years I buried myself in work and refused to face Sasha's death because I was afraid to let emotion in. Only you made it impossible for me not to feel. Not to *care*. But the truth is angel…' his voice cracked '…the truth is that I love you.'

'You love me!'

'Not just love you. I adore you. I fell in love with you the minute I saw you and—' he grimaced '—I've been running—' He stopped. Stared at her. 'You took off your necklace.'

Lexi reflexively touched the place her necklace had hung for too many years, her mind still spinning from Leo's passionate declaration. 'It was time.'

'No; I ruined that for you.' His voice was soft, remorseful. 'I'm sorry.'

Lexi shook her head. 'Please don't apologise. I had some growing up to do where my father was concerned. For years I refused to face that he wasn't coming back, idealising him as much as my mother had, but I was living in the past. When I was younger I wore the necklace to keep a connection with him, but over the years it had become a habit. And I guess, as you said, I never wanted to admit that he chose his other family over us.'

Leo obviously heard the catch in her voice because he rounded her desk and pulled her out of her chair and into the warmth of his embrace. Lexi sank against him like a stone, her nostrils flaring as she drank in his familiar male scent. God, she had missed this. Missed him.

His hands ran over her back soothingly.

'Angel, he was a weak man. Like my father. They could never accept responsibility for their actions. I was like that for a time but you pointed out to me that life is a choice. We may have been given a bad start, but if we really want something different we can have it. At least I hope we can.'

She raised her head and dared to hope that maybe his declaration of love before wasn't just a fantasy she had conjured from thin air. 'What do you mean?'

He shook his head and moved back to perch on her desk, taking a deep breath. 'I need to touch you but…' he folded his arms tightly across his chest '…first I need you to know that, even though you refuse to see what I have inside of me, I nearly killed a man once.'

Lexi stilled. 'Tell me.'

'It was a month after my uncle's death. He was in a bar, spouting off about his promotion because of his cost-saving strategy. A cost-saving strategy that meant he'd bought substandard equipment that had ended my uncle's life.' He swallowed and she knew how hard it was for him to talk about this. 'I saw red. Hit him. And I didn't stop. Four men had to pull me off him. If they hadn't…' He shuddered.

'Leo, you were young, hurt. What you did was wrong, but I know that deep down you're not a violent person.'

'I nearly hit Tom Shepherd.'

'But you didn't.'

'Because of you.'

'No. You chose not to. Leo, you might have used your fists when you were younger, but—' she took a chance and stepped forward, cupping his face in her hands '—I know that's not who you are now.'

'Lexi, I love you. Marry me.'

'What? You don't do commitment.'

'That's because I've never been in love before. But I'm not letting you go, *moya milaya*.' His hands dug into her waist and his lips claimed hers in an elemental kiss that went on as long as time. Finally, when breathing once again became a necessity, he released her mouth and leant his forehead against hers. 'I used to think that love was to be avoided at all costs. That it meant nothing but pain. Now I know that one day with you in it is worth a thousand without you. I've missed you, angel. Say you'll marry me. Say you'll make me the happiest man alive and Ty the happiest child by giving him ten siblings.'

Lexi felt so choked she almost couldn't speak. 'Ten!'

'Okay, maybe I'm thinking of the practice more than the reality of ten kids, but at least two. Whatever you want. I will be yours to command for the rest of your life if you'll have me.'

She smiled. 'Really?'

'Yes.' The glint in his eye was devilish. 'Of course you will have to wear a very short skirt when you do it.'

Lexi's insides melted as she recalled their incredible love-making that night on his pool deck.

'I think I can manage that,' she murmured huskily.

'For ever?'

'It will take me that long to believe this is all true.'

'Oh, its true, angel, and I've a mind to show you just how true right here on this desk.'

'Only we're in the childcare centre and that's a really clean window,' she pointed out.

'I told you your standards were too exacting.'

'No, they're not. They've just been holding out for you.'

Leo groaned. 'I adore you Lexi Somers.'

He kissed her fiercely. 'And you haven't said it yet.' His voice had a rough quality that held a note of uncertainty.

Lexi stroked her hands over his chest and reached up to loop them around his neck. 'I love you.'

'And?'

'And yes, of course I'll marry you.'

A slow grin spread across his face. 'That's all I wanted to hear.'

'You're very easy to please.' Lexi laughed, feeling wildly ecstatic at the realisation that the man of her dreams loved her as much as she loved him.

'Actually, I'm not. No woman has ever come close to pleasing me the way you do. You're the most beautiful woman I know—inside and out—and I still don't think I deserve you.'

'You do, Leo. You definitely do.'

'Shall we go and tell Ty the good news?'

Lexi felt her heart swell. It felt as if she had loved Ty since the moment she'd first met him but... 'What if he doesn't accept me in such a permanent role in his life?'

'Lexi, he adores you. As do I. Come. You have nothing to worry about.' He looked at her fiercely. 'Ever again.'

Lexi knew her eyes were glowing with happiness. 'Have I told you that I love you?'

Leo smiled down at her and gathered her in tight. 'Not enough, angel.' He brought his mouth to hers. 'Not nearly enough.'

* * * * *

HOLIDAY WITH
THE MILLIONAIRE

SCARLET WILSON

This book is dedicated to my auntie, Margaret Wilson, and my honorary auntie, Mary Hamilton. Doris and Daisy with their holiday antics are based on you two!

CHAPTER ONE

Lara tried to hide her sniffles as the door opened and Addison's chin nearly hit the perfect hardwood flooring.

'Lara? What on earth...?'

She didn't wait for her to finish. Rain was dripping off the end of her nose and running down her back as she tried to bump her impossibly heavy case over the entranceway of the house. The case gave a squeak and one of the wheels catapulted merrily into the air, spinning off down the front steps and along the exclusive London street.

She swallowed the impossible lump in her throat. It pretty much summed up her life right now.

Addison pulled her by the elbow and slammed the door behind her. 'What's wrong? What's happened?'

Lara's stomach coiled up. She hated this. She hated turning up like this. Even though she tried to hide it, she knew Addison was stressed enough without adding anything else into the mix. Her pretty face had been marred by a permanent frown for the last few months Lara had been acting as a nanny for her and her husband, Caleb.

She took a deep breath. She was still in shock and the words just seemed to come out of nowhere. 'I had a *Sliding Doors* moment,' she breathed, before dissolving into tears.

'A what?' The frown was back. Addison had no idea what she was talking about.

Lara shook her head, her blonde hair sending raindrops splattering all around them. 'I went home earlier than he expected. I caught the earlier tube.' Her voice wobbled.

Addison took a deep breath and stood up a little taller. 'And?' She could be scary when she wanted to be.

'And Josh was in bed with the next-door neighbour.'

She wobbled and Addison caught hold of her elbow and steered her through to the kitchen. 'I'm sorry, Addison. I know you're just about to go on holiday but I had nowhere else to go. I just stuffed everything into my case and left.'

Addison flicked the switch on the coffee machine. 'That ratbag. How dare he? You've paid the rent on that flat for—how long? And he does this to you?'

She opened the cupboard and pulled out two cups then sat down on the stool opposite Lara. 'What are you going to do?'

Lara hesitated. The timing was, oh, so wrong. 'I'm sorry, Addison. I know you're leaving in the next few hours. This is the last thing you need.' It was the absolute last thing. Although to outsiders Addison and Caleb Connor had the perfect life, Lara could tell that things were strained. Their son, Tristan, was a dream to nanny, a happy, well-mannered little boy with the biggest smile in the world. But things in the household were far from happy. Addison had been strangely silent these last few weeks, and Caleb's presence had been virtually non-existent. Lara had the distinct impression this month-long holiday was make or break for the couple.

She bit her lip. 'I wondered…can I stay for the next couple of weeks? Just until I try and sort things out? I'll need to find somewhere else to stay.'

Addison didn't hesitate. 'Of course you can. No problem at all. Caleb and I will be gone in the next few hours. You can have the place to yourself and take some time to get sorted.'

She pressed some buttons on the state-of-the-art coffee machine. She frowned at Lara, 'Double shot?'

Lara nodded. Addison pressed a few more buttons for

the extra shot for Lara and decaf for herself and the steaming hot lattes appeared in seconds. She held up two syrup bottles. 'Gingerbread or caramel?'

'Vodka,' Lara groaned. It might only be three o'clock in the afternoon but after the day she'd had she wanted to cut straight to the chase. She pointed over at the one in Addison's left hand. 'Caramel.'

Addison poured a healthy amount of pure sugar syrup into the latte before adding the tiniest dash into her own.

She looked Lara straight in the eye. 'What are you going to do about your holiday?'

The holiday. Of course. Lara pressed her head down on the counter worktop. 'Oh, no.'

Addison reached over and squeezed her hand. 'You've been looking forward to this all year. Don't let him spoil this for you. You deserve a holiday. You need a holiday. Spend the next two weeks sorting yourself out, then go and lie in the sun. Relax. Chill out.'

'By myself?' The holiday she'd been looking forward to for months had instantly lost its shine. There was something really wrong about going on a cruise on your own. Talk about awkward.

Addison's glare had a steely edge. 'Yes, by yourself. Why not? You don't need a man to determine who you are in this life. You've saved hard for that holiday. Go and enjoy it.' She picked up her latte. 'Now, I need to finish packing. Will you be okay?'

Lara shifted on the stool. She really needed to get out of these rain-soaked clothes. Her stomach was churning. She could sense the tension in the air around Addison. It wasn't like her to say something so direct. She usually kept all her cards played safely close to her chest. Still, it wasn't her place to say anything. The line between employer and employee still existed and she shouldn't cross it. Her only concern should be Tristan, and from all her observations he was a happy, healthy little boy. Whatever was going on between the adults was up to them to solve.

She nodded her head in grateful relief. 'I'm not right now, but I will be. Thanks, Addison. I promise I'll take good care of the place.'

'I know you will,' Addison replied, with the quiet reassurance she always possessed. She paused for a second, 'I won't be able to call or email you. The place we're going—it doesn't have a phone line or internet.' She paused and gave a sad kind of smile. 'You'll be fine, Lara. You don't need him. He didn't deserve you—not at all. It's amazing how strong you can be on your own when you need to be.' She held Lara's gaze. 'The world needs good people like you. Look after yourself.' She gave a nod of her head and disappeared out into the hall.

Lara sucked in a deep breath, looked around the immaculate show kitchen and put her head back on the counter.

Two weeks to sort herself out. Perfect.

It was almost midnight. Reuben fumbled with the key in the lock yet again and swore under his breath.

Maybe he shouldn't have had that extra drink but his flight had been delayed six hours, jet-lag was kicking in and he'd decided to stop to try and something to eat before he got back to the house.

Only something to eat had turned into something to drink. The takeaway hadn't looked too appetising and the pub across the road had stopped serving food at seven p.m. So he'd just had a drink. That had turned into another. And then another. Watching a football match in a pub had that effect. After five minutes everyone was your best friend.

The key finally clicked into place and he shouldered the door open, falling over the front step and landing in a heap on the hardwood floor. The entrance hall was so big the noise echoed around him.

He picked himself up and tried to feel his way along the wall, seeking a light switch. When was the last time he'd been in Caleb's house? Must have been over a year ago—Addison wasn't exactly welcoming. She didn't seem to like her husband's bad-boy friend.

The light switch wasn't beckoning. All he felt was the flat walls. His eyes tried to adjust to the dark. If he remembered correctly the kitchen was to the right and the living room to the left, looking out over the exclusive London street.

He sighed and headed towards the living room. He'd collapse on the sofa and watch TV for a bit.

He froze in mid-step. What was that? Was that a noise?

He held his breath for a second. Caleb, Addison and their son should be on holiday. Caleb had said he could stay here for the next few weeks while his house was getting roof repairs. He tipped his head to the side and listened again.

No. Nothing.

He dumped his bag at his feet and walked over to the outline of the door to the living room and pushed it open. All he really wanted to do right now was sprawl out on the sofa.

But everything was wrong. And the jet-lag meant that all the senses in his brain were firing in slow-mo.

If he'd been firing on all cylinders he would have noticed immediately the glowing television on the wall, the sweet wrappers and wine bottle on the living-room table and the duvet on the sofa. *His sofa.*

Instead, all he noticed was the flash in the corner of his eye and the thudding pain at the back of his head. As he made contact with the floor and looked upwards all he could see was something pink and fuzzy.

Then everything went black.

* * *

She couldn't breathe. There was a tight strap across her chest and her heart was thudding wildly in her ears.

One minute she'd been lying half-dozing on the sofa, watching Saturday night TV, the next she'd heard footsteps walking across the entranceway. She'd gone into autopilot—years of watching too many TV shows—and picked up the nearest thing to hand. It was one of Caleb's awards and it was currently lying broken on the floor next to the burglar in black.

She picked up the phone and dialled the police. 'Emergency services. Which service do you require?'

'Police.'

'Police, how can we help you?'

'There's a burglar. In my house. I've hit him.'

'What's your name?'

'Lara. Lara Callaway.'

'Can you give me your address, Lara?'

'Seventeen Crawford Square, Belgravia.'

'Where is the suspect now, Lara?'

She gulped. 'At my feet.' Police, she'd asked for the police. Maybe she should have asked for an ambulance?

'Lara, what do you mean, the suspect is at your feet? Are you in any danger?'

Her mouth was suddenly dry. Maybe she shouldn't have drunk all that wine? 'No. I don't think so. He's unconscious. I hit him.'

The operator spoke slowly. 'Without putting yourself in any danger, can I ask you to check that he's breathing? I'm adding an ambulance to the dispatch call.'

Lara bent her knees and squinted at the guy on the floor. He was lit only by the TV glowing on the far wall. His chest was rising and falling slowly.

She took a deep breath. For a man who was breaking into people's homes he was actually very handsome. He didn't have that furtive, shady look about him. There was a hint of suntan under the shadow along his jawline. He gave a little groan and she jumped back.

'Yes, yes, he's breathing. But I think he's going to wake up.'

'Lara, take yourself to a safe place. The police are on their way and will be at your address in under two minutes. Keep this phone with you. You can keep talking to me if you're scared.'

She backed off out of the room and headed to the front door. Her head was starting to throb. This was turning into a nightmare.

Maybe this was her fault. This was a prestigious London address—of course they would be at risk of housebreaking. The house had a state-of-the-art alarm system—which she hadn't put on yet. She would have done on her way to bed. She just hadn't got that far yet.

Something struck her as strange. How had the burglar got in? The front door was still closed. None of the windows seemed open. What if he'd damaged the house somewhere? Through the window the glow of blue lights in the distance made her breathe a sigh of relief.

How was she going to explain this to Addison?

This was the worst jet-lag *ever*.

'Sir, can you open your eyes for me, please?'

And why was this bed so hard?

'Sir?'

'Yeow!' Someone had nipped the soft flesh on his hand. He sat bolt upright, ignoring the pounding headache.

Wow. He swayed. Dizzy. That was a new experience for him. He hadn't been dizzy since that time he'd been knocked out while playing football ten years ago.

Knocked out. He narrowed his gaze as the pieces started to fall into place. Two policemen. Two green-suited paramedics—one male, one female. And another female dressed in a pink fuzzy pyjama suit with her blonde hair in some kind of weird bundle on top of her head. She looked like some kind of giant kid's toy.

He lifted his hand to the back of his head and winced. 'Someone want to tell me what on earth is going on here?' He frowned and turned to face the pink teddy bear. 'And who the hell are you?'

The teddy-bear face looked indignant. He could tell she was trying to place his Irish accent, which got thicker the angrier he was. 'Who am I? Who are you? You broke into my house!'

One of the policemen stepped forward but Reuben held up his hand. 'Wait a minute—you're not Addison. This isn't *your* house.'

He stood up and dusted himself off. 'And I didn't break in anywhere. I have a key…' he pulled it from his back pocket '…because I am supposed to be staying here. So who are you exactly?'

The policeman looked from one to the other. 'It would probably help if you could both identify who you are.'

The paramedic stepped forward. 'I'm not finished yet.' She held up a penlight and shone it into Reuben's eyes. He flinched but didn't object. He knew better. After a second she gave a nod. 'Both pupils equal and reactive.' She stepped back to write some notes.

Reuben pulled his wallet out from his back pocket and handed it to one of the policemen. 'Reuben Tyler. I just landed from LA a few hours ago.' He folded his arms across his chest. 'My own apartment is under repair. It took damage during the recent storm and when they went to do repairs they discovered asbestos in the roof.' He turned to glare at the teddy bear again. She really was quite cute. If he hadn't been having such a bad day he might have been quite taken by her strange get-up, perfect skin and mussed-up hair. 'My friend Caleb Connor, who owns this place, said I could stay here while he and his family were on holiday.'

The policeman turned towards the teddy bear, who was shifting uncomfortably on her feet at the mention of Caleb's name. 'And you are?'

'I'm Lara Callaway. I work for the Connors. I'm their nanny.'

Ah, their nanny. Things were starting to fall into place in his brain. Caleb had said the last nanny had left and they'd hired someone new.

'And I can verify this with the Connors?'

He watched as she gulped and glanced at the clock. This was a girl who obviously wasn't used to being around the police.

'Well…not right now. They'll be midway across the Atlantic—and they're going to a place with no phone or internet.' She turned around to look at Reuben. 'You're not going to take him at his word, are you? I've never seen him before—and I've never heard Mr Connor mention his name. He could be anyone.'

Reuben rolled his eyes and sighed. The teddy bear was starting to get annoying. He glanced about the living room, his eyes fixing on a distant photo frame. He stalked across the room and picked it up, thrusting it towards the policeman while glaring at Lara. 'Here, photographic evidence. That's me and Caleb at an awards ceremony around five years ago. And…' he pulled his phone from his pocket '…here's a text from Caleb, telling me how to switch off his alarm.'

He ran his eyes up and down Lara's fuzzy-covered frame. She might be wearing the most unsexy nightwear in the world but it still gave a hint of her curves. She wiggled her pink painted toes as if she could sense his gaze on her. 'And as for the nanny…' he gestured with his head towards her '…I've never heard of her. According to Caleb, I would be the only one staying here.' He gave a little laugh. 'As for no phone and no internet? I'll bet Caleb didn't know that before he left. He might be on the other side of the Atlantic but I'm pretty sure we'll hear him blow up from here.'

All he really wanted to do was get his head down—and maybe find something to eat. His head ached and he couldn't believe the commotion. So much for some quiet downtime.

Lara looked flustered by his words. 'I've worked for the family for the last six months. The nanny before me left. Addison—Mrs Connor—said I could stay here for the next couple of weeks. I've had a bit of a…misunderstanding and she agreed at short notice.'

Reuben's ears pricked up at her words and he couldn't stop a smile appearing on his face. She was obviously easily flustered, not used to being around the police and feeling distinctly uneasy. Then again, she was in her nightwear—even if it did cover every part of her body—and it was obvious she'd decided to have feast in front of the TV. Probably not the scene you wanted all these people to see.

'What was the misunderstanding?' he pressed. He was amused now. 'The one that made you hit me over the head with something.'

He looked around the floor to see what she'd hit him with and saw the remains of something on the floor. He bent down and picked up the broken marble and gold trophy. His mouth fell open. 'You hit me with the Businessman of the Year award? Oh, wow, Caleb will be *mad*.' He pointed over to the photo of Caleb and himself, showing Caleb clearly holding up the award with pride.

If she'd been flustered before she looked positively pained now. 'But I didn't know who you were. And I thought you were a burglar. I thought you were going to attack me.' Her voice started to wobble and her eyes started to fill. 'I didn't know what to do.'

The policeman put a hand on her arm. 'We understand, but Mr Tyler does have a right to press charges.'

'Charges?' She could barely get the word out and he could see her start to shake.

'For assault.'

She wobbled. She looked as if her legs were going to give out completely.

Enough. He needed this to be over with.

'There won't be any charges. Not from me anyway. I'm sure Ms Callaway will be able to speak to Caleb about replacing his award.' He looked towards the other policeman, who'd been talking quietly into his radio. 'Have you verified us yet? Can we finish this?'

The paramedic raised her eyebrows at him. 'Actually, no, we can't. You were knocked out, Mr Tyler. We should really take you to hospital to be checked over.'

'No. No. I definitely don't want to do that.'

But as he shook his head he realised how dizzy he was. It was all he could do not to sway. He eyed the sofa for a second, wondering if he should sit down.

'We're obliged to take you, Mr Tyler. There can be serious repercussions from a head injury. It will only take a few hours.'

'In London on a Saturday night? You've got to be joking. Every A and E around here will have queues out the door.' He waved his hand. 'I'm fine.'

The paramedic frowned and her lips thinned. This woman was formidable. It was time to take a different tack.

'Look, I've just got off a long flight from the US and I'm tired. I just want to find something to eat and get to sleep. I haven't slept in the last thirty-six hours. You said my pupils were equal, surely that means I'm okay?'

She hesitated and glanced at her partner. 'After a head injury some symptoms take a while to appear. You might feel okay now, but in a few hours it could be different.'

The policemen were exchanging glances. The only person in the room who couldn't look at him was Lara—the giant teddy bear.

'I really don't want to go to hospital,' he said steadily.

The paramedic glanced from him to Lara. 'Well, I'll have to get you to sign something. Then I'll give you a final check and leave some head-injury instructions. You can't be left alone. There needs to be someone around you in case you feel unwell later and need to go to hospital.'

A smile broke across his face. 'Oh, I'm sure Ms Callaway will oblige.'

Her head shot up. 'What? Me? No!' She turned towards the policeman. 'You're not actually going to let him stay here, are you? I don't know him. I don't want to be left in a house with a stranger.' Her indignation made him smile even more.

The policeman looked at her. 'Then perhaps you'd like to stay somewhere else? You did say you made this arrangement at short notice. Maybe there's somewhere else you can stay?'

She cringed. 'What? No.' She was starting to look a bit panicked. But there was no way at this late stage that Reuben was going to ring around friends to find a bed for the night. He'd made this arrangement with Caleb and he was sticking to it—whether Ms Teddy Bear liked it or not.

The paramedic stood in front of Reuben. 'Can you sit down for a second while I do some final checks?'

She couldn't possibly know how grateful he was to sink down onto the comfortable overstuffed sofa. His stomach gave a little growl as he noticed all the sweet papers on the coffee table. The smell of chocolate and cheese and onion crisps was drifting in his direction. He didn't care who it belonged to. As soon as he got rid of these folks he was eating the entire lot.

A paramedic made a few final notes and handed him a clipboard and pen. 'Sign here.'

He scribbled his name and took the leaflet she proffered. She gave him a suspicious glance as she stood up. 'If you have any of the symptoms on the card you must attend the nearest A and E.' She gestured with her head. 'It's St David's, about a mile in that direction.'

He gave her a nod. 'Thanks.'

The policemen headed towards the door. 'We'll file a report but I take it things are settled now?'

Lara stood with her mouth gaping. She looked shell-shocked. 'But—'

'I'm sure everything will be fine,' the other policeman cut in. 'Goodnight, Ms Callaway, Mr Tyler,' he said, as all four people filed out the front door.

Reuben stood again, waiting for them all to leave before finally closing the front door behind them. His legs felt heavy, but nowhere near as heavy as the thudding in his head.

He stalked back through to the sitting room, collapsed on the couch and tore open one of the chocolate bars, grabbing the TV remote.

Lara hadn't moved. She was still rooted to the spot.

He grinned at her wickedly. 'Well, then, I guess it's just you and me.'

CHAPTER TWO

THIS COULDN'T BE HAPPENING.

An hour ago she'd been watching one of her favourite eighties movies as she'd sipped wine and eaten her body weight in chocolates.

Now it felt as if the Terminator had just invaded her comfortable living space. Except this terminator had an Irish accent that was almost musical to her ears.

Not that Reuben Tyler looked like Arnie. And with his black jeans and leather jacket he was maybe a little too stylish for a burglar. She was trying not to stare. She was trying not to look at him at all. What on earth was she going to do?

'So, do you always dress like a giant teddy bear?' he said as he flicked through the channels.

'What?' She stared down at her favourite nightwear. Oh, no. In all the chaos she'd forgotten how she was dressed. Hardly a good look for a first meeting.

She scowled at him and stuck her hands on her hips. 'Well, it wasn't like I was expecting guests, was I?'

The corner of his mouth turned upwards. 'Evidently.'

Okay, this guy could make her blood boil but was he a tiny bit hunky? She stole another glance. When he wasn't angry, he might be described as quite handsome in a rugged sort of way. His dark hair was thick and a little dishevelled. His white T-shirt showed off his tan—doubtless from his stay in the US since it had rained solidly for the last month in London. No wonder she was keeping her pale flesh covered. But it was those eyes that could probably melt the hearts of the female population of the city. Dark brown, like coffee or chocolate—both were her vices.

She gave a little shudder. What on earth was she thinking? She didn't know a single thing about this man.

'You can't possibly stay here. Addison told me I'd have the place to myself for the next few days.' She folded her arms across her chest. She was grasping at straws but Addison really hadn't mentioned a word about having to share the place with one of Caleb's friends. Which most likely meant that Addison hadn't known that Reuben would be here...

Darn it. There went the little shudder again. All of a sudden he wasn't so much a dangerous intruder as a slightly intriguing handsome stranger. But sharing the house with someone she didn't know still made her feel uncomfortable.

Reuben seemed completely uninterested in her comments. He grabbed a bar of chocolate from the table and started eating it. 'I think you should be more worried about smashing up Caleb's trophy. He was very proud of that.'

The trophy. Her eyes went to the floor. It was broken into three solid parts. No super-strength glue in the world could put it back together. She sagged down into one of the armchairs. 'I've no idea what to do about that,' she murmured.

Reuben sat up a little straighter. He gave his head a little shake and winced. 'Do you have any painkillers?'

She nodded. 'Come through to the kitchen. There are some in the cupboard.'

She flashed her hand over the light for the hall and it came on, flooding the entranceway with light. Reuben frowned and bent down. 'What on earth is that? I couldn't find the light switch when I came in.'

She walked past. 'It's one of Caleb's new inventions.

Light switches you don't touch. Just the motion of your hand switches it on. Do you know that light switches and doorhandles are the biggest places that harbour germs?'

She couldn't believe she was having a normal conversation with a guy she'd thought was breaking into the house. It was all so surreal. Maybe this was a dream? Maybe she'd drunk a little too much wine and fallen asleep in front of the TV? Because, truth be told, Reuben Tyler did look a little like a dream.

She stubbed her toe on the way into the kitchen. 'Youch!' She definitely wasn't dreaming. That had hurt too much.

She waved her hand over the switch to turn the light on and walked to the cupboard on the far wall to retrieve the tablets. Reuben sat on one of the stools at the kitchen island and gave a little sigh.

She grabbed a glass and filled it with water. 'Here you go.' She hesitated then added, 'I'm sorry about your head.'

He looked up at her through lazy, tired eyes. 'Yeah, yeah. I'm sure I'll get over it.'

He was looking at her with those chocolate eyes. The stare was so intense it almost felt as if it was burrowing through her thick pink onesie. It was *definitely* heading for the bin after this. His gaze made her feel uneasy and she started to ramble. 'There are a few free bedrooms upstairs. I'm on the second floor so I'd appreciate it if you could sleep on one of the other floors. Maybe the third? Since Addison, Caleb and Tristan all sleep on the first floor.'

'You're pushing me into the servants' quarters?' His voice was a lazy drawl.

'What? I am not.'

'Yes, you are. Don't you remember that in all these Georgian houses the servants stayed in the attics?'

'Did they?' She wrinkled her nose. 'I wasn't much of

a history buff, more a geography girl myself.' She waved her hand. 'Anyway the rooms upstairs are lovely. The biggest one has an en-suite bathroom, I'm sure you'll be comfortable there.'

He was still watching her, almost as if he was trying to size her up. But what alarmed her most was the fact there was a twinkle in his eye. He swallowed the painkillers and took a gulp of the water. 'Maybe I'll just crash on the sofa—next to your midnight feast. Were you actually going to eat all that?'

Colour heated her cheeks. She was about to be offended, but from the twinkle in his eye it was almost as if he was trying to bait her. She'd recovered enough from the shock of earlier to play him at his own game.

'I was going to eat all that. And you owe me. Don't think I didn't notice that you swiped one of my favourite chocolate bars.' She wagged her finger at him. 'Touch anything else and I'll give you more than a sore head.'

He surprised her. He threw back his head and laughed, just as his stomach growled loudly. He shrugged his shoulders. 'What can I say? I'm starving.' He stood up and started prowling around the kitchen, staring at the uniform white cupboards as if he didn't know which to open first. 'Is there anything to eat around here?'

Lara watched him for a few seconds. That was definitely a pair of well-fitting jeans. They hugged every inch of his thighs and backside, even though she could see the waist was a little loose. His white T-shirt was rumpled and there was tiny hint of curling dark hairs and flat abs. It was all she could do to tear her eyes away.

She sighed. 'As I was a late arrival too and Addison had run down most of the fresh food, there's only what I bought tonight.' She opened the fridge. 'I have bread, bacon and baked beans.'

He was smiling again and counted off on his fingers,

'And wine, and chocolate, and crisps, and some kind of cake I didn't even recognise.'

She smiled and shook her head. 'Don't even think about it—all of those are out of bounds.'

He leaned against one of the cupboards. 'Well, I've thought about it. I know how you can make it up to me.'

'Make what up to you?'

'The fact you assaulted me with one of Caleb's trophies.' He put his hand on his chin. 'I'm thinking a bacon-and-baked-bean sandwich might just cut it.'

'You don't put bacon and baked beans in a sandwich.' She shook her head in disgust. 'Especially not at one in the morning.'

The glint remained in his eyes as they swept up and down her body and he lifted his hand to his head. 'Ouch.' He gave the back of his head an exaggerated rub. 'I think one o'clock in the morning sounds a perfect time for a bacon-and-baked-bean sandwich. Hours past dinner and hours until breakfast.'

She pursed her lips. He was getting to her. He was definitely getting to her. She wasn't quite sure if it was the guilt trip working or the rising tension she could feel in the air between them.

'Fine.' She turned around and flicked a few switches on the coffee machine. 'What do you want to drink?'

He stared at the machine as his brow creased. She hid her smile. The first time she'd seen the coffee machine she had been bamboozled by it. It had taken a few attempts to finally get it right.

'What does that do—make coffee or beam you up?'

'Oh, if it could beam you up I'd press that button right away,' she said smartly, as she walked back over to the fridge, pulled out the bacon and fired up the grill.

He folded his arms across his chest. He looked amused,

maybe even intrigued by her sparky response. 'So, now we're getting to see the true you.'

'As opposed to what?'

He laughed. 'As opposed to the crazy ammunition-wielding giant pink teddy bear I met when I arrived.'

She glared at him as she put the bacon under the grill. 'Let's see.' She counted off on her fingers. 'You've ruined my night. It seems like you're going to interrupt the two weeks of sanctuary I was expecting to have here. You've insulted my favourite nightwear. Scared me half to death. Stolen my chocolate and blackmailed me into making you something to eat.' She folded her arms back at him. 'Why, Reuben, you're my favourite person in the world right now.'

He shook his head at her tone. 'I hope you're not serious.'

She opened the cupboard and pulled out a tin of baked beans. 'About which part?'

His cheeky smile reached from ear to ear. 'About the favourite nightwear part. I'm hoping you've got something much more appropriate than that.'

Had he really just said that? He must have because tiny electric sparks were currently shooting down her spine and making her toes curl.

She opened the tin of beans, poured them into a bowl and started to nuke them in the microwave. 'Why do I think you're going to be a pain in the neck to have around?'

He raised his eyebrows. 'You seem to have been hit with a sass attack. Exactly how much wine did you drink?'

'Obviously not enough.'

'Wow.' Reuben mocked being hit in the chest and fell against the wall. 'What's happened to you?'

She shrugged. 'I had an adrenaline surge when I thought someone was breaking in. You know, the old fight-or-flight thing. Then when the police arrived I started to panic.' She turned the bacon over in the grill pan. 'Both those things have left me now. It's late. I planned on being asleep around an hour ago. Instead, I'm playing hostess in a kitchen that isn't mine and plotting an elaborate lie to tell Caleb about his award.'

She stuck some bread in the toaster and walked back over to the coffee machine. 'Now, pick your poison or learn how to work this yourself.'

He laughed and walked over next to her. 'You know, the giant pink teddy bear is losing her appeal.'

'That's fine. I never wanted to be a cuddly toy.' She pressed some buttons and coffee and milk steamed out of the coffee maker.

'I'll have what you're having,' he said quickly. He obviously didn't want to miss out on the chance of coffee and would drink anything.

She made another latte, put the bacon on a plate on the middle of the kitchen island and lifted the steaming-hot bowl of baked beans from the microwave. The toast popped and she took the butter from the fridge and put everything down in front of him, handing him a plate and some cutlery and sitting at the other side of the island.

She could feel the intense brown eyes on her again. Part of her wondered what he was thinking. Part of her was too scared to even think that far.

He started buttering his toast. 'I thought I asked for a sandwich.' He kept buttering.

She could feel her anger starting to smart. This guy was a royal pain in the neck. The tranquil time she'd expected to get here had been ruined. Two weeks to get her head together and make some plans for when she came back from her holidays—hopefully enough time to secure another tenancy somewhere.

'I made an executive decision. Bread would be too squishy.'

The edges of his mouth turned upwards. He was trying to keep a straight face. He lifted the bacon onto his toast and grabbed a spoon for the beans. 'Squishy.'

'Squishy,' she said again as she put her bacon in the middle of her toast and spooned some beans onto the side of her plate.

She lifted the toast towards her mouth. 'Now I'm going to watch you eating that without getting beans all down the front of your white T-shirt.'

'That sounds like a challenge.'

'You bet it is.'

Things were beyond odd. He was beginning to like the pink teddy bear more and more—particularly now she was showing some added spark.

He could tell his mere presence annoyed her. Under normal circumstances he'd probably feel the same way. When Caleb had offered him somewhere to stay while his building work was done he'd been relieved. It wasn't as if he didn't have enough money to check into a hotel—he could have done that easily. But then he would have been constantly around people when what he really wanted was some peace and quiet in order to negotiate a deal with a troublesome sports star.

Even though Addison didn't really approve of him, his days of being a bad boy were more or less over. He just didn't have enough hours in the day any more.

He watched as Lara poked at her plate with a fork, trying to spear the baked beans individually.

'Slippery little suckers,' he said as he tried to hold his sandwich together. She glared at him as he took a bite. After a few seconds he spoke again. 'Okay, you got me. I'll admit it. It tastes great.'

She gave a hint of a smile. 'It is pretty good.'

'Better than chocolate and wine?'

'Never.'

This girl was fun. Or she could be fun if she'd just let her guard down a little.

'So, how did come to be working for Caleb and Addison?'

She sat back on her stool at little and sipped her coffee. 'I met Addison through a mutual friend. She was looking for a nanny at short notice and I had just got back from Australia.'

'What were you doing out there?'

She gave a little shrug. 'I went to see the world but ended up only seeing Perth. I met someone when I got there and ended up working as a nanny for a family there for nearly ten months.'

'Why did you come back?'

She rolled her eyes. 'My visa was going to expire and I hadn't met an Australian I could con into marrying me.'

The more she shot at him the more he liked her. 'I don't believe that for a second.'

She shook her head. 'The guy I met, Josh, was English. Let's just say I don't have a good record with guys. If he's a loser, I'm attracted to him. If he's a cheat, I can't spot it. If he's bad for me in any way, shape or form I seem to fall for him hook, line and sinker.'

Now he was definitely curious. 'You staying here—is this about a guy?'

She let out a sigh. 'Let's just say after today's *Sliding Doors* moment it looks like I'm going my dream holiday on my own.'

'*Sliding Doors?*'

'Yes, as in the movie.'

'Never seen it. What do you mean?'

'You've never seen it?' She shook her head. 'Where have you been? The girl gets out of work early and runs to catch the tube. In one version she makes the train, in the other she doesn't. In the version when she gets home early, she catches her boyfriend in bed with someone else.'

He sat back, bacon and beans forgotten. 'And that happened to you?' Maybe he should actually start watching these chick-flick movies.

She sighed again and nodded.

'Ouch. Blooming fool. Who is he? Do you want me to go and sort him out?'

Her head shot up. She looked surprised. 'Of course I don't.'

He shook his head. 'Oh, please. Don't tell me you still love the guy?'

She leaned her head on her hands. 'I'm not sure I ever really did. I just feel as if I've got "Mug" stamped across my forehead in big letters. I just shoved everything I could into a case and left.'

'How long did you stay together?'

'In London? Just the last six months. I met him when I went travelling to Australia and we rented the flat together when we came back.' She toyed with her coffee cup. 'Not that he actually paid any rent. He was…' she lifted her fingers in the air '"…writing" apparently. I guess that wasn't all he was doing.'

Reuben frowned. 'And who was the other woman?'

She groaned. 'The next-door neighbour. I couldn't even punch her. She's built like an Amazon and could probably squash me beneath one of her size-eight feet.'

He couldn't help it. He let out a laugh.

She picked up the dishtowel and flicked it at him. 'It's not funny!' His coffee cup tipped and few dark brown splashes splattered his white shirt.

He looked down. He'd been travelling for hours and was feeling grubby anyway. Perfect time to change.

He shook his head and started laughing as he undid the buttons. 'Tell me there's a washing machine around here somewhere?' Every white kitchen door looked identical. He had no idea what lay behind any one of them.

Lara had started to laugh but it seemed to die somewhere in her throat. He looked up to see what was wrong. Her eyes were fixed firmly on his chest. It was an automatic reaction. He sucked in his abs—even though he had no need to. He hadn't even thought twice about taking off his shirt. Maybe she was shyer than he'd thought?

'Give me a second till I grab a T-shirt,' he said quickly, walking back out and getting his bag from the hall. He rummaged around and grabbed a black T-shirt, pulling it over his head as he walked back in. 'Now...' he smiled '...where were we?'

Lara hadn't moved. It was as if the words were stuck somewhere at the back of her throat. She gave a little shudder and fixed him with her eyes.

Her very blue eyes.

He hadn't been paying enough attention.

He'd already noticed the hint of curves beneath her nightwear. While her blonde hair was currently piled on top of her head he could imagine it sitting in long waves past her shoulders.

He could also imagine her in a really sexy dress and heels.

He said the first thing that came into his head. 'You didn't have anyone else you could stay with?'

It was an innocent enough question. Trouble was, it made her insides curl up a little and made her feel a bit pathetic.

But he wasn't finished. 'Isn't it a bit strange to come and stay with your boss?'

She should have stopped to think for a second. But thinking wasn't really Lara's style—particularly not when she'd just had a glimpse of mind-numbing abs. 'I haven't been in London that long. I originally came from Sheffield so all my friends are up there. And because of the job—looking after Tristan—I haven't really had time to make any good friends since I got here.' She bit the inside of her cheek. 'To be honest, I'm not quite sure what I would have done if Addison had said I couldn't stay.'

She could feel the rush of heat into her cheeks. She felt a bit embarrassed and was definitely squirming. This was rubbish. She wasn't the person who had done anything wrong here. Not like Josh-gets-into-bed-with-the-wrong-woman or Reuben-breaks-into-houses-Tyler. It was time to turn the tables.

'Reuben?'

'Yeah?' He was trying to appear casual as he finished his coffee.

'How, exactly, do you know Caleb?'

She'd stood up to clear the plates away and started loading the dishwasher.

'Why do you want to know?'

'I guess I'm still trying to decide if I'm going to let you stay, or if I'm going to phone the police again.'

He rolled his eyes and gave a casual wave of his hand. 'I knew him years ago.'

She banged the dishwasher closed and pressed a few buttons before sliding back onto the stool across from him. '*Where* did you know him?'

He sighed. 'What's with the interrogation? Isn't it about time to go to bed?' He didn't mean it to come out that way but his voice just naturally inclined upwards as he spoke. It gave the sentence a hint of cheekiness.

Lara's cheeks flushed with colour as she pointedly ignored his comment. 'You asked me how I got the job. It's only fair I ask you how you know Caleb—particularly when I've never seen you around here before.'

Reuben held onto the worktop and leaned back on

the stool. His back was beginning to seize up. He really needed to lie down.

'Caleb and I went to school together.'

'Really? What school?'

He cringed. He knew exactly what came next. 'Eton.'

Her mouth fell open. 'Eton?' He should feel insulted. The surprise wasn't because Caleb had gone to Eton, the surprise was definitely directed at him.

He shrugged his shoulders. 'What can I say? I was a posh boy.'

The colour was starting to die down in her cheeks. It was obvious she was curious. 'It's a long way from Ireland,' she said. It was a natural thing to say but he barely blinked.

'Yes, it is.' It was almost as if he were drawing a line in the sand.

She put her elbows on the worktop and leaned towards him. 'You said you just got back from the US on business. What is it that you do?'

'A bit of this, a bit of that.'

She waggled her finger at him. 'Oh, no. Don't give me that. What is your job title exactly?'

'I'm a businessman.'

She waved her hands. 'And so says the entire population of London.'

'I'm a sports agent.' He said quickly, in the hope it would stop her asking questions.

Her eyes widened. 'You mean you're Jerry Maguire?'

He shook his head. 'If I had a pound for every time I've heard that...'

She perched back up on the stool. 'I like movies but I'm not what you'd call a sports fan. Well, truth be told, I hate sport, but will I know anyone you manage?'

He shrugged. 'If you hate sport, probably not. A few footballers, a few cricketers. One tennis player. Also some basketball and baseball players. A few big-name American footballers.'

She gave him a curious stare. 'So that's why you jet around?'

He paused for a second. 'Most of the time. I have clients in the US, Italy, Spain and England right now. And I'm always looking for the next big signing. Things get a bit crazy at times. It's a mad world out there and sometimes the whole business of a team is based on who they sign—and more importantly how that person behaves. One stupid interview comment can make a team's shares plummet. I sometimes have to do some troubleshooting or some collateral damage limitation. That can take me pretty much anywhere. The US this week, Spain last week. For the next two weeks I'm in London.'

'Lucky me,' she said quickly. He sucked in a breath. For a second he wasn't sure if it had been sarcasm or wit, but then the edges of her mouth turned upwards.

She leaned her head on one of her hands. 'So, if you and Caleb are such lifelong friends, how come you haven't been to see him once in all the time I've worked here?'

He paused to swallow the last of his coffee. 'While it's true that Caleb and I go way back, it's not the same with Addison. Though she's far too polite to come out and say it, I have a strong suspicion that she might not like me very much.'

Lara frowned. Sure, Reuben was annoying, verging on arrogant, but what possible reason did Addison have to actively dislike the man enough to discourage his presence in her home? Should she be worried?

'Why do you think it is exactly that Addison doesn't like you?' She strove to keep her tone neutral and the wobble out of her voice.

He took a few seconds before he answered. 'Let's just say I knew Caleb when we were relatively young guys—

long before Addison came on the scene—and we might have been involved in a few...' he paused to think of the right word '...boisterous activities.'

'Boisterous activities? That's it? That's all you're giving me?'

He nodded. 'I think that would be best.'

She folded her arms across her chest and looked through the kitchen window into the darkness. 'Looks like a long, rainy night out there to me...' She let her voice drift off.

'You've got to be joking? You'd actually ask me to leave?'

She started walking around the kitchen. 'Absolutely. And just think, there's a lovely king-sized bed up there, with fresh, clean sheets just waiting for you to jump in and ease your tired bones.' She folded her arms around herself and rubbed her hands up and down them. She knew exactly how to play him.

He sat down his coffee cup. 'You're a manipulator.'

'And you could be a murderer, a drug dealer or...' she scrunched up her nose '...even worse, a wannabe.'

'A what?' He couldn't hide the surprise in his voice. 'What are you talking about?'

She waved her hand. 'You tell me you're a sports agent, then you tell me you have to sort out badly behaved sports stars. You might just want to hang around them. You might even bring random dubious sport stars back to this place. They could wreck it.'

He shook his head. 'You honestly think I want to hang around these guys? Some of them are worse behaved than two-year-olds.'

She folded her arms across her chest again. 'Then give me a straight answer. Explain your "boisterous activities".'

Boy. She was good. He'd practically walked right into that one.

He stood up, put both hands at his waist and arched

his aching back. 'Fine. We did some cliff-jumping, some free running. There might have been a little police involvement back in the day. Then there was the usual girl stuff. That's probably why Addison doesn't like me. She probably thinks of me as a bad influence or something.'

Lara leaned against one of the white cupboards. 'Why? Because you encouraged her husband to take part in extreme sports, or because of the girl stuff?'

He ran his fingers through his hair. Jet-lag was definitely hitting right now. 'Truth? Probably a bit of both. But, remember, this was all before her time.' It wasn't exactly the truth. But that was as much as he was willing to say.

Lara gave a nod. She'd finished cleaning the kitchen and it was back to its original sparkling white show-home-kitchen appearance. The kind of kitchen that looked as if people didn't actually live in the house. 'Well, that's okay, then.'

She was still watching him with those wary blue eyes. He was trying not to think about the idiot who'd cheated on her and was obviously short of a few brain cells.

'I've got an idea,' he said, as he walked back through to the sitting room and picked up her half-empty bottle of wine and glass. 'Let's have a toast.'

'A toast to what?' She looked completely bewildered.

'A toast to the fact we'll need to share this house for the next two weeks.'

He poured some wine into her glass and handed it to her before she could object, then lifted the bottle up towards her. 'To an interesting two weeks.' He clinked the bottle to her glass before lifting it to his lips.

Her eyes never left his. 'To an interesting two weeks,' she repeated.

CHAPTER THREE

IT WAS THE weirdest feeling. Somewhere in the space up above her there was another body breathing in and out.

She'd bet Reuben wasn't having trouble sleeping. At first she'd thought she was too hot and had discarded the thick onesie. After tonight she'd probably never wear it again. Then she'd realised she didn't have PJs—and sleeping in the nude with a stranger in the house just wasn't an option. So she'd done something she'd never even thought about before and crept along the corridor to Addison and Caleb's room and rummaged through a few drawers until she'd found something suitable.

But it wasn't entirely suitable. Addison's sleeping apparel seemed to be short satin nighties—a whole variety of them. Even lying in bed she kept trying to tug it over her backside as it left her feeling strangely exposed. Or maybe that was just because Reuben was overhead.

She couldn't help it. She'd done an online search on him. Who wouldn't?

He seemed to be the darling of the acidic football critics. He'd brought two young, unknown Argentinian footballers to a Premiership team and had virtually saved it from bankruptcy. He'd negotiated a change of coach three times for his tennis player, which had helped him shoot up the rankings. He'd had seven baseball teams fighting over one of his players. And the dollar signs for his latest basketball signing made her eyes water.

Then there were the photos. Plenty with the latest sports

star but she was more interested in the ones with a beauty by his side. Granted, the beauty was never the same twice. But all were considerably more glamorous than she was—even when she was wearing one of Addison's satin night-dresses.

Eventually she heard noise downstairs. Had she slept at all? It didn't feel like it. It felt as if she'd tossed and turned all night, her head full of dark-clothed strangers breaking into the house.

By the sound of it Reuben was banging through all the cupboards in the kitchen. Lara sighed and threw back the bedclothes. She sat up, the cooler morning hair hitting her barely covered skin. She glanced around. She wasn't going to go downstairs dressed like this. She hesitated in the doorway, peering along the corridor before stealing down the corridor to Addison and Caleb's bedroom again in search of a dressing gown.

She should have guessed. There was a perfect matching bright pink satin dressing gown to the nightdress she was wearing. Bright pink trimmed with purple lace. She didn't even want to think what it had actually cost. She wrapped the dressing gown around her. That was much better. It covered all the parts of her it should, skimming just above her knees.

With a bit more confidence she opened the door to head towards the kitchen and almost barrelled straight into tea-bearing Reuben.

'Oops, sorry.'

She jumped back as the tea sloshed onto the carpet.

Caleb's eyes swept up and down her more exposed body. 'Nice change,' he said quickly. 'So you don't always dress as a teddy bear.' He squinted behind her. 'Is that Caleb's room?'

Heat flushed into her cheeks. How did this guy do that

to her? She bit her lip. 'Caught. Just don't tell. Let's just say I didn't bring a lot of nightwear with me.'

He looked as if he were going to say something but stopped and gave his head a shake. He held the tea out towards her. 'I made you tea.'

She stared at the cup. 'What are you up to?'

He gave her a smile. 'What makes you think I'm up to something?'

'It's written all over your face.'

He sighed. 'What are your plans for today?'

Her eyes dipped downwards to her pink-painted toes. She hadn't realised it but they actually matched her nightdress and gown. Her toes curled. 'I'm not actually sure.'

'You would have been on holiday, right? What were you going to do?'

She bit the inside of her cheek and said nothing.

This time it was Reuben's turn to blush as he realised her obvious change of plans. 'Oh, right. You were planning on spending time with that numbnut that you called a boyfriend. That means you're free for the next two weeks.'

Her head shot up. 'What did you call him?'

Reuben shrugged. 'A numbnut—which he obviously is. Does the guy think he's some kind of superhero? How dare he cheat on you?' His eyes narrowed. 'Want to get thinking creatively? We could plot some hideous revenge.'

Her hands closed around the cup of tea. 'Revenge means thinking about him—I'd rather not.'

Reuben nodded. 'I have some work to do. Do you fancy coming with me?' What was wrong with him? He had a mountain of work to get through. He knew there were six hundred emails in his inbox. But he had some other things to do. And he was feeling sorry for her. This time his eyes lingered on her curves and long bare legs.

'I suppose I'd better register somewhere to try and find a new rental in London.'

'Do you have the name of a reputable agency?'

She nodded. 'The one I used the last time was great. I guess I'll just register with them again.' She sighed. 'Once I've done that, I think I need to do a little shopping.'

'Food or clothes?' He'd already checked out the kitchen. After last night's feast there was hardly anything left.

She sighed again. 'Both, I suppose.'

'Well, come and hang out with me for a while, then we can do some shopping.'

She looked at him suspiciously.

He lifted his hands. 'What? It's only fair I foot the bill for shopping. I ate all your food last night.'

She nodded. 'Okay, then. Let me drink this tea and find some clothes.'

He gave a cheery nod and wandered back down the corridor. She watched his retreating back, but her eyes were drawn downwards. He was still wearing well-fitting jeans and a snug grey T-shirt.

Her two weeks of misery seemed to be looking up.

CHAPTER FOUR

HE MUST BE CRAZY. Why on earth had he invited Lara out for the day?

Sure, she was cute. Sure, they had to share a house for the next two weeks. But that didn't mean he had to try and be her new best friend.

But there had been something about her. When she'd been telling him about her ex and the pain had been etched in her eyes. The guy was clearly a fool.

He'd cringed last night when she'd asked him why Addison didn't like him. He tried his best not to think about that night at all. But Lara had seemed placated when he'd padded out his story with a little detail.

Too bad he'd left the biggest detail out.

Caleb had shrugged off what had happened between them. He knew how damaged Reuben had been by his parents' relationship. But Addison had no idea. He still wasn't Mr Popular with her.

She probably didn't even know that Caleb had invited him to stay here.

He finished sending a few emails as Lara walked into the kitchen. She was wearing a pink sequined T-shirt, a pair of hip-hugging blue jeans, black heeled boots and a fitted bright pink raincoat.

Her hair was soft and shiny and hanging in waves around her shoulders. She walked across the kitchen, smiling, pulled a pink lipstick from her pocket and painted it on her lips. 'Reuben, what exactly did you plan today? I should remind you, I'm not exactly a sports fan.'

He laughed. 'It will be fine, I promise. I need to visit one of the nearby football stadiums but I'll be less than half an hour. Then we can sort out some food and anything else you need to buy.'

She gave a thoughtful nod. 'I might have left some of my things behind.'

'Things like what?'

She sighed. 'My whole summer wardrobe. Just about everything I need to put in my case for my holiday is still at the flat. It's ready to be picked up. It's all sitting in another case.'

He blinked. 'No problem. We'll swing by later and you can collect it.'

Panic streaked across her face. 'But...I don't think... I'm not sure...'

'Calm down.' He reached over and took her hand, trying to ignore the little pulses he could feel in his palm, '*I'll* go and get your things.'

Her eyes widened, flooding with relief. 'You will?'

How on earth could he say no? 'Of course I will. No problem.'

He picked up his car keys. 'Now, can we go?'

For some strange reason the car seemed to be parting the traffic in London. Lara had never managed to get through the London streets so quickly—but, then again, she'd never been in a car like this one before either. The dark red colour alone seemed to command attention but it was so low, so sleek against the road that she wondered if she'd ever be able to get out again.

Reuben handled the car with ease. In the streets of London she would be terrified to drive a hundred yards but he took every corner without a second thought, pulling up outside the vast stadium only thirty minutes later.

He signalled to her to get out and she climbed out, looking up at the glass-fronted stadium. 'Come on, I won't be long,' he said, as he walked into the reception area, waving at the reception staff. 'Lydia, Carrie, where's the chairman?'

'Downstairs in the changing rooms. He's talking to the manager.'

Reuben gave a casual wave and opened a door to a flight of stairs. Lara struggled to keep up with his long strides, almost running to keep up as he turned corner after corner through a warren of tunnels underneath the club.

He paused outside one of the doors. 'Wait here,' he said, smiling. 'Don't want you to see anything you shouldn't.' He disappeared through the door.

She sighed and leaned against the concrete wall. This wasn't exactly her idea of fun. How long would this take?

A few seconds later there were shouts and one of the footballers came stomping along the corridor. His eyes only briefly brushed over her before he pulled his top over his head and banged through the changing-room door.

She sucked in a deep breath. Footballers were known for being temperamental, weren't they?

A few seconds later the door opened and another footballer came out. This time he had a hint of smile about his face. Which was just as well, since he wasn't wearing much. Lara sucked in an even deeper breath than before and fixed her eyes on her hands. This guy slammed through another door with 'Physio' emblazoned across it.

Then came another, then another, each man wearing a little less than the one before.

Did the players always walk around here practically naked? She had about a hundred friends who would think this a fabulous dream. Pity she wasn't one of them.

Lara focused on her fingernails. They weren't great. When was the last time she'd taken time out for a manicure? It had been on her to-do list. It would need to move further up. There was another bang. She couldn't possibly ignore it.

Her chin bounced off the floor. It was the team's star mega-million-pound footballer, with painted-on sculpted abs, a pair of teeny-weeny white tight briefs and the best spray tan she'd ever seen. His eyes looked her up and down lasciviously, making her stomach roll over—and not in a good way. His ego was so big there was barely room for the rest of him.

'Hey, baby,' he said, as he slid along the corridor towards her.

She gulped. Oh, no. Her worst nightmare. She was *so* out of her depth right now.

The door opened behind her and an arm slid around her shoulder. 'Chris, are you being a prat again?' He turned towards her. 'Sorry, Lara, I should have warned you about these guys. If there are any females around they like to do walk-bys with each one wearing less than the previous one. Ignore them.' Reuben had a wet towel in his hand and he flicked it at Chris, who leapt into the air like a big girl.

'Ouch!' He rubbed his thigh and stormed back into the changing room, muttering expletives under his breath.

Lara shook her head. 'You're joking—that's what they do?'

Reuben nodded. 'Every time. They can't help it. The average mental age around here is about twelve.'

He hadn't moved his arm from her shoulders and she wasn't quite sure how she felt about it. Exactly how many women did he bring here with him—and why did that matter to her? 'Can we get out of here now?'

He smiled. A white straight-toothed smile that reached all the way to those big brown eyes she was currently staring up into. It was odd. But it was one of the most genuine smiles she'd seen. Before, he'd been amused by her or he'd been sarcastic. This time it felt real and it sent a little wave of pulses skittering over her skin. Just what she needed while her brain was mush.

She gave a little shudder and put her head down as they walked down the corridor. But Reuben stopped. 'Hey, what is it?'

Her footsteps had stopped but she hadn't lifted her head. He stepped in front of her, his fingers reaching down and tilting her chin up towards him.

It seemed such a personal touch—an almost intimate touch. Or as intimate as you could be in a place filled with staff while you were fully clothed. 'What's wrong, Lara?'

It was the way he said her name. That Irish lilt that was guaranteed to turn any woman's legs to jelly. This guy could be Colin Farrell's brother.

Her body wanted to tremble. But she wouldn't let it. No way. No, sir.

She lifted her eyes to meet his. 'Let's just say I have an image from yesterday imprinted permanently on my brain. It keeps flashing back in there when it's least wanted.'

He gave a visible shudder. She didn't need to give an explicit description. He knew exactly what she was getting at.

He swung his arm back around her shoulders. 'It's time to move things on. Let's go and collect the stuff you need for your summer holidays and that way you're done—finished. For ever. You can forget about the loser and look forward to your holiday.'

He guided her back along the corridor. 'I meant to ask—where are you going on holiday anyway?'

He pushed the door open and held it for her. 'I'm booked to go on a cruise,' she sighed. 'I always wanted to cruise around the Med so I saved all my spare pennies for it.' She waved her hand. 'And if you're going to cruise, you need the clothes for it.'

He smiled as if an idea had just blossomed in his brain. 'You certainly do. Where does the ship sail to?'

She was starting to feel a little more comfortable around Reuben. Talking about travelling meant that they were on neutral ground. Small talk was about all she could handle right now. She smiled. 'Everywhere I've always wanted to visit—Barcelona, Monte Carlo, Pisa, Marseille, Sicily.' A little edge came to her voice. 'I'm not going to let him spoil it for me.'

Reuben nodded. 'And we won't. Let's get this over and done with.'

If someone had sat him down before he'd boarded the flight to London and told him what his next twenty-four hours would be like he wouldn't have believed them. Not for a second.

He rapped the door of the Camden flat once again, glancing down to the street to where his car was idling. Even from here he could see Lara's hands turning over and over in her lap.

There was a noise—a grunt—and the door finally opened.

Reuben blinked. Really? Lara was definitely hovering around a ten. This guy? He was lucky if he was a four. What's more, he could almost smell the arrogance coming from him. His fingers automatically balled into fists.

'Who are you?' said Mr Barely Dressed. That paunch really wasn't attractive. There was a tittering noise behind him. Great. The neighbour was still hanging around.

'I'm a friend of Lara's. I'm here to pick up the rest of her stuff.'

The guy's brow furrowed. 'A friend of Lara's? I've never met you before.'

'And you'll never meet me again. Now, she wants her case with her summer clothes in it. Give it to me and we'll be on our way.'

Now the guy looked really pleased with himself. 'Well, it's too late. I flung the rest of her stuff out of the flat yesterday after she stormed out. The bin men have already been.' He folded his arms across his chest.

'You what?' He couldn't stop himself. He had Mr Smarmy pinned against the wall in an instant. 'You did what?'

The guy panicked. 'Well, she was gone. And it's not like she'll be coming back. Why would I want to keep her stuff?'

Reuben shook his head. 'It's not bad enough you got caught in bed with another woman, you didn't even give Lara the chance to collect all her things. How dare you?'

The guy was still against the wall but he lifted his hands, doing his best impression of a shrug. 'Well, she was screaming and shouting yesterday. Calling me all kinds of names. There was no way she'd be back.'

A woman appeared at his elbow, holding a phone in her hand. 'If you don't get out of here now I'm calling the police.' She turned her nose up in a sneer. 'Tell Lara she's not welcome here.'

There was so much he could say. His temper was bubbling just beneath the surface. What a pair of low-lives. The woman was running her eyes up and down his body. It made him feel positively unclean. Both of them did.

He could feel adrenaline surging within him, closely followed by a red mist descending. Just like he had the night he'd punched out Caleb. Was it any wonder Addison didn't like him? He flinched. He didn't want to be that guy any more. He was *trying* not to be that guy any more.

He released his grip on the guy and looked at him in

disgust. 'You two deserve each other. Lara's worth ten of you.'

He turned on his heel, ignoring the shouts that followed him. The guy made him mad. The girl made him mad. Their utter disrespect of Lara made him mad. How had she ended mixed up with these two?

He strode back to the car, jumped inside and slammed the door, not thinking for a second about what he was going to say to her.

Her eyes widened at the expression on his face and she stared at his empty hands. 'Didn't you get my stuff?'

It was the wide-eyed innocence that made his stomach curl in knots. On a few fleeting moments Lara had appeared quite street savvy, but right now? He felt as if he were just about to grab her heart between both hands and squeeze hard.

She'd already told him she'd saved hard for her dream holiday—and from what he'd seen he could take a guess that the guy upstairs hadn't contributed at all. Just how much would it cost her to replace her entire summer holiday wardrobe?

'I'm picking your stuff up later,' he said quickly.

He turned the car onto the main road. 'Now, let's go and food shop.'

She wasn't quite sure when the house burglar turned into her kind of guardian angel. All she knew was thirty minutes after telling her they'd pick up her clothes later he pulled his sleek car up outside one of the most famous department stores in London with its gold and green sign.

Reuben walked around and opened the door for her. Her head flicked from side to side. 'You can't leave your car here…'

Her voice trailed off as a uniformed man slid into the driver's seat and the car mysteriously disappeared.

He smiled at the expression on her face and gestured towards the door. 'Let's hit the food court. We need to buy supplies.'

She watched the dark red car disappear around the corner, shaking her head as he slung his arm back around her shoulders and steered her towards the entrance. 'I didn't even know they did that,' she murmured.

'What can I say? I've friends in high places.'

What on earth did that mean? She looked down at her clothes. Jeans and a pink t-shirt. And come to think of it her boots could do with a polish. If she'd known they were shopping in style she might have dressed up a little.

They walked down the stairs to the food court. Even two steps down the aroma of everything expensive came up to meet them.

Reuben was smiling already, crossing over to the glass display cabinet of fine meats and truffles and *foie gras*.

'What do you like?' he asked.

She wrinkled her nose. 'Chicken.'

He raised his eyebrows. 'Chicken?' You'd think she'd sworn out loud.

She nodded. 'Chicken. I like chicken.'

She looked around at the massive department.

'And raspberry jam. And freshly baked bread—maybe a croissant or two. And some more bacon and eggs.'

Her legs had started walking, following her nose as she glanced from side to side.

'I love the chocolate digestives from here, and the rose and violet shortbread— Oh…' She spun round and put her hand on his chest. 'And those tiny dark chocolates filled with orange. Now, where on earth will they be?'

He put one hand on his hip as people filed past. 'We're in one of the finest food stores and you want bacon. And eggs. And raspberry jam.' His chest was right in front of her nose and now every time she breathed in she didn't get the wonderful food aromas around her, she just got Reuben Tyler. Every masculine, woody scent of him. If she could sell that aftershave she'd never have to work again.

She breathed in, trying not to look like a teenager. Her hand was still resting on his chest. Through his thin T-shirt she could feel the warmth of his skin and the roughened hairs underneath the palm of her hand. Her brain tried to make sense of things.

This time yesterday she hadn't known this man. She hadn't even known he existed.

'Chicken.' The word came out of nowhere. 'You forgot the chicken.'

She tilted her head and smiled up at him. Her nose was directly across from his chest. Too close for comfort really. Especially now she could see the tiny shadow along his jaw line. Why did her hand want to reach up and touch it?

His arm folded around her waist and he pulled her closer and spun her around as a large group of tourists swept past. He was looking down at her with those deep brown eyes. It was almost as if he knew she was a little mesmerised. Truth was, he must be used to it.

'Didn't want you to get trampled.' He laughed as his accent played havoc with her senses. 'And chicken.' He shook his head again. 'Let's not forget the chicken.'

He reached behind her, his chin brushing against her hair, and plucked a thin cylindrical box from a stand. 'Your orange creams, I suppose?'

She closed her hands around the tube. 'Perfect.'

He paused. It was almost as if something else flitted past his brain. He was leaning over her, seeing every part of her up close and personal. If he tilted his chin down just a touch…

She wished she'd put on more make-up—heavier foundation instead of her usual tinted moisturiser. Longer-lasting lipstick rather than her light lip tint.

She could almost feel herself disintegrate under his gaze. What did he see? And how did she compare to what he was used to?

She tried to squeeze that thought from her mind. Why should she care? She barely knew him. So what if he'd just gone out of his way to help her? The truth was he was still invading the space she'd thought she would have for the next two weeks. Her skin was prickling under his intense gaze. There was a whole wave of sensations sweeping across her. And she couldn't fathom any one of them.

Reuben gave a little shake and stepped back. It was almost as if nothing had happened. He pulled up a trolley next to them and started loading up his selection from the counter. He pointed to item after item and she blinked at the price tags. Chicken stuffed with haggis and wrapped in bacon. Chicken with chorizo and a tomato sauce. Chicken with peppered sauce and mushrooms all packaged up before her eyes. If she hadn't been hungry before she was definitely hungry now.

And it seemed once Reuben started to shop he could do it like a pro. Sirloin steaks—enough to last the fortnight. More pepper sauce. Salad. Fresh bread, pastries and croissants. Her raspberry jam. Bacon, eggs and sausages. A whole heap of vegetables. Biscuits, chocolates and a really, really good-looking fresh cream gateau.

Lara looked at the groaning trolley and nudged him.

'What?' he asked.

'I don't think people really do their weekly shop in here,' she whispered, her eyes taking in the other customers, who had maybe one or two items in their hands. 'At this rate we'll need to remortgage Caleb's house for the food bill.'

He looked surprised. 'I'm covering the food bill. Don't worry. You didn't expect me there and I should contribute something.'

He made it all sound so reasonable, while her purse was currently screaming out in relief. There was no way she could pay half of a bill like this. 'Fancy a bottle of wine?' he asked, as they walked further along.

She glanced at the nearest shelf. Two hundred pounds a bottle. 'Er…no, thanks.'

He moved the trolley forward then stopped again. 'It was rosé you were drinking last night, wasn't it?'

He put three bottles in the trolley before she had a chance to answer, then he picked a bottle of red and one of white too. She could feel herself breaking out in a cold sweat at these prices. It didn't matter that she wasn't footing the bill.

She leaned forward and hissed in his ear, 'Put those back. You can buy wine for less than ten pounds a bottle in the supermarket down the road.'

The corners of his lips turned up in amusement. He walked over to the nearest cash register and handed over his credit card without anything being run up. The cashier nodded, swiped it and handed it back, taking a note of the ticket for his car.

He slipped an arm around her back and led her to the stairs. Lara's head was turned backwards, staring at the cashier. 'Really? You don't even put in your PIN?'

He shook his head. 'I trust these people. By the time we want to leave the car will be loaded up and ready to go.'

She shook her head as she climbed the stairs. The jewellery section was right in front of them. 'Let's go upstairs for a coffee. Food shopping makes me hungry.' Now, *that* she could agree with.

She wandered through the jewellery department—most of the jewellery didn't have price tags, which told her everything she needed to know. While she didn't know how much things actually cost, she could just do her little-girl-in-a-shop state of mind and pretend that they could all be hers.

She stopped suddenly and Reuben walked right into her. She hadn't realised he was so close. 'Sorry,' she murmured.

He followed her eyeline to the side and pointed. 'You're looking at that?' His face was screwed up in that a-guy-will-never-understand kind of way.

She nodded. 'It's gorgeous. It's like something Cleopatra would wear.' She moved a little closer but resisted the temptation to touch the glass. Interlocked flat panels of white, yellow and rose gold. One of the fashion magazines would probably describe it as a showstopper. And it was.

She moved further along and stopped and pointed at a large square-cut pink diamond surrounded by white diamonds. She was too scared to even breathe next to it. 'Bet we'd really need to remortgage Caleb's house for that.'

Reuben shook his head and steered her towards the lift. The smell of coffee hit them as soon as the lift doors opened, in perfect timing with a loud growl from Reuben's stomach.

She laughed. 'Trying to tell me something?'

He nodded. 'My body is telling you that it's crying out for another bacon sandwich.' He pointed to the glass-fronted cabinet filled with tiny cakes. 'But that's not what you get here.'

She turned to face him. 'Did you want to go somewhere else?' She got the distinct impression he'd brought her here because he'd thought she'd prefer it. On most days she would be happy with a cup of tea in a local café. Why did she get the impression he was trying to keep on her good side?

He shook his head. 'The coffee is great in here. Makes up for the lack of bacon. What are you having?'

She stared at the board as the barista approached them. 'I'll have a skinny, sugar-free caramel latte,' she said.

'What?' He wrinkled his nose as the barista waved her hand.

'I've got it,' she said, as she turned to the large metal machine. 'Triple shot for you, Reuben?'

He nodded then turned back to Lara. 'Didn't take you for one of those mumbo-jumbo crazy coffee girls. Not after the amount of chocolate you consumed last night.'

She slapped his arm. 'Hey. Anyway, there's method in my madness. The skinny sugar-free counteracts the fact I'm going to have four of those little cakes.' She was feeling quite pleased with herself. The only problem would be choosing. She walked up and down the counter, trying to decide.

'Only four?' came the deep voice, right next to her ear.

She jumped. 'Stop it.' And turned back to the counter. The barista had finished preparing the coffees and placed them on a tray. She must be able to read minds because she was standing with an empty plate and a pair of tongs in her hand.

'A rhubarb and custard tart, a death by chocolate, a strawberry and vanilla pastry and a pecan pie.' The words were out before she could stop them and Reuben let out a muffled laugh behind her.

He pointed in the other direction. 'I'll have a piece of apple pie,' he said, before leaning over towards her ear again. 'Man-sized.'

Her head shot around and she felt heat sear into her cheeks. It was ridiculous. He was only winding her up. There was even a dangerous twinkle in his eyes.

She went into her bag to find her purse but he waved her away. 'You just bought the shopping. You've got to let me pay for something.'

'We'll talk about it later.' She sighed and made her

way over to a table, pulling out one of comfortable velvet chairs and sitting down.

Reuben sat down opposite her and put the tray of coffee and plates on the tables.

She pointed at his apple pie, which was obliterated from view with cream. 'Would you like some apple pie to go with your cream?'

He picked up his fork and speared the pie. 'You can talk. At least I've only got one instead of four.'

She picked up her tiny pecan pie. 'It's ridiculous calling this thing a pie. Look, it's barely bigger than my thumbnail. One bite and it'll be gone. Two if I nibble.' She eyed his plate again and couldn't hide her smile. 'You, on the other hand, could sink to the bottom of the Thames eating that lot.'

He shook his head and kept eating. There was something nice about this. Something easy. After yesterday morning she'd thought the next month would be an absolute disaster. She could write a book on the last twenty-four hours alone.

But being around Reuben Tyler wasn't as hard or as uncomfortable as she'd first thought. It didn't hurt that he was particularly easy on the eye. And that accent…

She watched him carefully from across the table. She could see a few women giving him a second glance then giving *her* a second glance too.

He may not be a footballer but he looked like the kind of guy who'd have a WAG hanging around him and there was no way she fitted the bill.

'So what did you plan to do for the next two weeks?' He'd finished demolishing his pie.

She shrugged her shoulders. 'I was just going to hang out with Josh, preparing for our holiday.' She wrinkled her face. 'I guess that won't be happening.'

Reuben's dark eyes were fixed on her. 'Do you want that to happen?'

'What? No, of course not. Not after what I saw yesterday.' She shuddered. 'It's going to take a long time to get that sight out of my mind.'

He was still watching. 'You sounded as if you were a bit sorry.'

She took a sip of her latte. 'About Josh?' It was hard to find the words. 'Part of me is, and part of me isn't.' She picked up her spoon and started stirring her latte. It was an unconscious act, keeping her eyes away from his penetrating gaze. 'I guess I've been looking forward to the holiday for so long that I just pushed the other stuff away.'

'What other stuff?'

Her insides started to squirm. It was bad enough having to think these thoughts to herself. They'd definitely come to fruition last night. But saying them out loud? That was something else entirely.

She kept stirring as the swirling coffee was easy to focus on. 'Probably the fact that Josh hadn't paid for any of the holiday. Hadn't paid rent since we moved in together after we got back from Oz, and didn't seem particularly bothered about finding a job. He was just happy that I was working and paying the bills.'

Her fingers clenched around the long spoon. 'Now I just think what an idiot I was. Out working while he was at home, doing goodness knows what.'

His hand reached across the table and covered hers. 'Don't put yourself down, Lara. You're a gorgeous girl who just got stuck with a loser. Lesson learned. Move on.'

She gulped. All of a sudden her mouth was dry and the rhubarb and custard tart had just stuck midway down her throat. It was his hand. The way it just enveloped hers. The warmth. That little touch of compassion.

After the rubbish day she'd had yesterday, she hadn't

really expected anyone to reach out to her. To make her feel valued again.

It gave her a warm feeling. The kind that had always spread over her when she used to be around her gran. Her parents had been great, but she'd always had a special connection with her gran. She'd encouraged her studies in English and had been so proud of her when she'd been accepted at university. But when her gran had died one month later it had all been too much for her. Her mum and dad loved her lots—but had never had the same ambitions for her that her gran had. She'd needed some time away—some space. She'd deferred her university placement and drifted from one bad job and bad relationship to the next, finally ending up in Australia then back here.

Tears were brimming in her eyes. Thank goodness Reuben hadn't noticed. Was he getting a tiny pulse shooting up his arm too?

He gave her hand another squeeze and went back to his coffee. Obviously not.

She was an idiot.

It was almost as if he could read part of her mind. See that she was trying to hide the parts of her that were hurt. His tongue ran along his lips, catching some of the sugar from the apple tart, and she swallowed, trying not to stare.

'Caleb's been good for me.' It was as if he chose the words carefully.

She was curious. 'How?'

He pressed his lips together. 'He keeps me focused. Keeps me grounded. Addison might not like me much, but when I go to their house and see Caleb with his son…' His voice tailed off and he gave a little shrug, 'It makes me see what a family should be like. I don't doubt for a second Caleb would give his life for his wife or his son in a heartbeat. They're his whole world.'

There was something about the way he said the words

that sent a little prickle down her spine. She didn't doubt for a second her mum and dad would do the same thing for her. Reuben hadn't mentioned his family at all. 'Aren't all families like that?' she asked carefully.

His gaze caught hers for a second and he shook his head. 'That's one of the things I like about you, Lara—your idealism.' He took another swig of his coffee. 'So what are your plans now for the rest of this week?'

It was clear that part of the conversation was over. She couldn't pry—she barely knew him—so she swallowed the remainder of her tart and said the first thing that came into her head. 'I've decided to do some touristy stuff. I never really got the chance when I first moved to London, so it might be quite nice.'

He looked amused. He tilted his head to the side. 'What kind of thing?'

'I'm going to do the Buckingham Palace tour.' Where had that come from? It was the first thing that had popped into her head and right now she didn't want to look like an idiot in front of Reuben. She certainly didn't want to act like a woman who'd been cheated on and mope about the place. This was the new improved version of herself.

A woman swept by their table in red-soled black patent stiletto heels and a long sweeping cream wool coat. Her long blonde hair was like a sheen from a TV advert and Lara sensed the cool blonde's eyes sweeping over her and then Reuben.

'Reuben Tyler?'

Perfect pouting pink lips appeared at the table, along with a waft of expensive perfume and a remortgage-your-house handbag. Lara shrank back in her chair.

Reuben froze for a few milliseconds then seemed to move into his default charm position. 'Millicent. How nice to see you.' He stood up for a second and let her do the kiss-on-both-cheeks move.

'When did you get back?' Millicent's voice was a little sharp.

'Last night.'

'Really? I didn't notice your car.' Lara could feel the edges of her mouth start to turn upwards. Watching the body language here was a real treat. For a few seconds she'd felt intimidated by the gorgeous statuesque blonde. But while Reuben had his charm face in place it was clear the woman was about as welcome as a box of frogs.

She lifted her latte for a sip and prepared to attack her death by chocolate. Better settle in. This could be fun.

Reuben shook his head. 'There's work being done of the roof. Asbestos. So I can't stay there right now.'

Millicent tilted her head to the side, the tone of her voice changing automatically. 'Why didn't you say? You're more than welcome to come and bunk in with me.' She let out a shrill little laugh.

'I hardly think that would be appropriate,' said Reuben. 'Millicent, meet Lara, my girlfriend.'

The perfectly formed death by chocolate cake somersaulted out of her hand and landed upside down on the white and black tiled floor. She stared in disbelief at her little piece of heaven before shooting Reuben a laser glare.

Millicent was practically sneering as her eyes swept over Lara's less-than-perfect hairstyle, minimal make-up and non-designer clothes.

Her recovery was swift. 'Oh, how nice. Reuben...' she glared at him '...was obviously keeping you a secret.'

She extended her expertly manicured hand towards Lara. Lara stared at her chocolate-smudged fingers and wiped them on a napkin, reaching over and shaking Millicent's hand. 'You too.'

'Where do you live?' asked Millicent quickly.

A thousand tempting answers flooded through her brain. Part of her wanted to give the world's most exclusive address—to say *Buckingham Palace*—and the other part of her wanted to pretend to live in the most notorious part of London, just to see how Millicent would react.

She put on her best face as she nudged Reuben under the table with her boot. To his credit he didn't even flinch.

'Belgravia,' she said. It wasn't exactly a lie. She *was* living there—for the next two weeks at least.

'Oh…' Millicent gave an almost disbelieving nod of her head. 'How lovely.'

'Well, it was lovely to see you again, Millicent,' Reuben said quickly. He might as well have put a sign above their heads saying, *Go away. Now.*

Instead, he did something much more unexpected. He leaned across the table and grabbed hold of the lapel of Lara's jacket. It pulled her forward just a few inches and that was enough for Reuben to lock his lips onto hers.

For a second she couldn't breathe. He'd stood up and leaned all the way across the table. She could taste coffee. She could taste apple. But what she didn't get—not for a second—was how good his lips felt against hers.

This was no tender kiss. No tiny peck. His other hand reached across and fastened at the back of her head, almost holding her in position. She could have objected. She should have objected. But something else was happening. Her lips were starting to move against his. For some unknown reason her body was starting to waken and fire on all cylinders. He didn't need his hand at the back of her head. She couldn't have pulled away even if she'd wanted to.

The kiss deepened, his lips opened against hers, his tongue nudging along the edges of her lips. It was only natural to let her own lips open to his. Her brain was in a swirl. What on earth was she doing?

Then, almost as soon as it had begun, it was over. Reuben pulled away, sitting back with a cheeky gleam in his eyes and leaving her stunned.

After a few seconds she almost remembered to breathe.

Millicent gave an almost discernible sniff then swept away in her stilettos as if she had been born to wear them—and she probably had been. Lara watched in slight awe. If that had been her she would be sprawled on her back by now.

She turned her steely gaze to Reuben and arched her brows. She couldn't have formed words if she'd tried.

He actually shifted a little in his seat. Apart from when she'd bashed him over the head this was the first time he'd actually looked a little uncomfortable. Good.

He gave a little gulp. 'I think I might have just crossed the line there.'

'You're so far over the line, you can't even see it any more. It's just a speck on the landscape. Is that how you roll? You just grab unsuspecting women for a kiss?'

He had the decency to look a little sheepish. He pointed towards the food. 'I try to soften the blow first with coffee and cake.'

She stared hard at him. Her mind was still tumbling over and over *that kiss.* The kiss that had made her heart race erratically, her mind go numb and woken up parts of her she'd thought were dead. Kisses weren't meant to do that. Or certainly not a kiss with no preamble, no flirting, and in a public place.

'I know. I'm sorry.' He leaned across the table towards her. 'Desperate times call for desperate measures. Want to know what my friends and I actually call Millicent?'

Her curiosity spiked immediately. She just hoped it wasn't some crude boy thing. She was trying not to focus on the logical part of her brain that had recognised he'd just said he'd had to be desperate to kiss her. 'Okay,' she said cautiously.

He glanced around, almost as if he expected Millicent to spring out again from behind the nearest pillar. 'The barracuda.'

Lara choked. 'What?'

He nodded. 'Honestly. She's a nightmare. So I'm sorry about the girlfriend thing and the kiss thing, but it was the quickest way to get rid of her without being rude.'

'So ignoring her and kissing me wasn't rude, then?'

Reuben's eyes twinkled as he leaned back in his chair. 'You can't say it was all bad, was it?'

She ignored the cheeky comment. The guy was a player. And she was feeling a little wicked. It seemed like kissing a bad boy brought out the worst in her.

Lara fiddled with her last tiny cake—the strawberry and vanilla pastry. 'I have a price, you know,' she said carefully.

Reuben sat back. He looked a tiny bit worried. 'What do you mean?'

She pointed behind him to the glass cabinet. 'It will take at least another four deaths by chocolate since you killed my last one.'

He breathed a sigh of relief and grinned. 'Absolutely.' He stood up and walked back over to the counter, coming back moments later with a pile of tiny chocolate cakes all topped with cream. He pushed them across the table towards her. 'Go on. Do your worst.'

She pulled the plate towards her and picked up a fork. 'If you keep feeding me like this I won't be able to fit into my bikinis and summer dresses.'

Something flickered across his face. She'd no idea what. He looked as if he'd just swallowed something unpleasant but he recovered quickly.

She wasn't entirely sure what she thought of Reuben Tyler, but it might be fun finding out.

* * *

His insides coiled up. He was going to have to tell her soon. Lara wasn't a designer shopper, but any woman's high street summer wardrobe would still cost a lot to replace. He got the distinct impression that while she managed, Lara wasn't exactly flush with money and given that she'd now have to scrape together the deposit to rent a new flat, the last thing he wanted to do was let her know she needed to buy a whole new summer wardrobe.

'I've been thinking about the cruise,' she said, gazing across the café. 'I think I'll need to get a few more things. A new pair of sandals and maybe another skirt. But I won't know for sure until I can go through the rest of my summer clothes.'

Reuben shifted uncomfortably in his chair. It was now or never. He really needed to be honest with her. He licked his dry lips. 'About your summer clothes…' he started.

'What?' All of a sudden her voice and eyes were razor sharp. He could almost feel her gaze penetrate his skin. What was it with women and their senses? They could practically smell when something was wrong.

For the first time in his life words stuck in his throat. What was wrong with him? He'd never been a stranger to the truth—in fact, he'd often been criticised for his direct approach.

'Maybe you should get some new things,' he said slowly, trying to pick his words carefully. 'Cruises are quite glamorous, aren't they?'

'You don't think I'm glamorous enough?' The words shot out and he cringed.

'No. No, that's not what I meant at all.'

'Then what did you mean?' Women didn't usually make him squirm. This was a first for Reuben Tyler.

Her gaze was fixed on him. Like some kind of female superhero with laser vision. Who could have guessed the girl that had been the giant pink teddy bear could do a complete turnaround?

She was doing her best to appear direct. To have a little edge. Trouble was, he already knew her a little better than that. He'd seen the vulnerability in her eyes. He'd seen the hurt. And he didn't want to be the person responsible for that.

He leaned his elbow on the table and rested his head on his hand. 'There might have been a bit of an issue with Josh.'

Her eyes narrowed. 'What kind of issue?'

'He might have disposed of the rest of your clothes.'

'He *what*?'

Heads all over shot round. A few of the counter staff stood up on their toes, trying to see who'd yelled, but since Lara was on her feet it was pretty obvious.

Reuben could feel all the gazes turn to him. Yeah, right. This was all his fault.

He gave the slightest shrug. 'Sorry. The guy's obviously an idiot. He said he'd dumped all your stuff when I asked.'

She leaned across the table towards him. 'And you knew this? You knew this a few hours ago and you didn't tell me?'

There was a loud tut behind them. Reuben shook his head and turned, giving a smile to the elderly woman behind him who was looking at him as if he'd just run over her cat.

He lifted his hand towards Lara. 'I thought you might be upset.'

The colour in her cheeks was building. If he'd thought her eyes had been lasers before, now they were definitely shooting sparks.

He was surprised by how cute she was when she was angry.

'I guess I was right,' he said, as he picked up his coffee and drained his cup.

Lara's fists were clenched on the tabletop. It took a few seconds for the blanched knuckles to be gently released and Lara sagged down into her chair.

'All my things…gone?' she asked.

He nodded his head. This was what he'd wanted to avoid. Her shoulders slumped and the high colour in her cheeks started to disperse, replaced with a white pallor.

She blinked. Oh, no. Her eyes were getting that sheeny way—the way they did before a woman burst into tears.

She started murmuring. 'But what am I going to do? That was my entire summer wardrobe.' She shook her head. 'I have nothing—not a single thing to take with me on the cruise.' One fat, hot tear spilled down her cheek. 'And I certainly didn't budget for this.'

She took a deep, ragged kind of breath. She was twisting a napkin between her fingers. 'It's not just the clothes. I had other things in that case. Things that meant a lot to me. Things I can't replace.' Her voice was getting shakier as she spoke.

'What kind of things?' He could feel the march of a thousand cold feet down his spine. What else had Josh flung out to the trash?

'There…there was something special.' A tear rolled down her cheek.

'What was it?'

She shook her head and brushed away the tear. 'It was nothing. It wasn't valuable. Just a keepsake. Something I've had since childhood.'

He was curious now. It must have been something special for her to be reacting this way. He reached over and touched her hand.

She gulped. 'It's silly, really. It was a book. A copy of *Alice in Wonderland*. My gran bought it for me when I was little. We used to read it all the time. And it doesn't matter that I could walk into any bookshop and buy another copy. It wouldn't be this one. The one we read for hours.'

Reuben spoke quietly. 'And it was in the case with the summer clothes?'

He shouldn't just have held Josh against the wall. He should have done much, much worse.

She gave a little nod. 'I just can't bear the thought I won't see it again.' She pressed her hand against her heart. 'It was full of memories for me. Every time I opened the pages again I thought about my gran. She died just after I'd been accepted for university.'

Something clicked in his brain. 'And you didn't go?'

Lara bit her lip. It was obvious she was thinking about how to reply. He didn't do this. He didn't form emotional attachments with women. He didn't like tears and sniffles. It was his first cue to walk away.

Or his first cue to do his natural alternative—throw money at a situation.

He reached across the table and grabbed Lara's hand. 'Come on.' He pulled her to her feet and started walking.

He could sense she could barely keep with his long strides but he didn't want to think about that too much.

'Reuben, where are we going?' she sniffed.

For some reason he couldn't even bear to look at her. Here was a woman he barely knew—but he couldn't stand to see her upset. It did strange things to his brain. Strange things to his equilibrium. And he couldn't quite fathom why.

This wasn't his fault. None of it was his fault, but that wasn't helping.

There was one thing he could do here—one thing that he had. The thing that seemed the quickest fix for most people in the world. Money.

CHAPTER FIVE

LARA COULD FEEL panic begin to set in. Where on earth could she get some money? She had a tiny bit of spending money for the cruise, put away every month and hidden in an account that Josh had known nothing about. She'd hoped it would cover the gratuity charge for the trip and whatever drinks package she wanted to buy. She'd pre-paid a few excursions when she'd booked the trip and had thought she wouldn't need much more money.

If only she'd known.

She cringed, putting her head between her hands. Five weeks ago she'd bought a pink dress with tiny glittery beads. More money than she'd ever spent on one item. But it had practically called out to her from the shop window. And it was perfect for a cruise. And she'd had the rest of her wardrobe—or so she'd thought.

She started to think frantically. Borrow. She could borrow clothes. But who from? One of her best friends was in Australia and the other in the US. She had a couple of acquaintances in London but none of them were the same size as her.

She started fingering the edge of her jacket. There was a whole wardrobe full of clothes upstairs in the house. She'd already borrowed a nightdress from Addison—but that had been an emergency situation. There was no way she could let herself borrow any of Addison's clothes. They were way out of her league. And what if she damaged something? How on earth would she replace it?

She swallowed. Her mouth was dry. She could do with some water. She could feel herself starting to panic. Control. It was slipping away from her just when she'd thought she could capture it back. Josh had been quite controlling. Comments about her hair, her make-up and her clothes. She'd tried to ignore them, but after more than a year together he'd chipped away at her self-confidence. Now, just when she thought she could shake him off, he'd done something else to control her. This wasn't just about the clothes. It was about taking back charge of her life.

Reuben had ushered her into a lift. She hadn't been paying attention but the doors swished open right in the heart of the designer womenswear section. Right now she couldn't even afford to buy a pair of sunglasses—not when her finances were in such dire straits.

Reuben was still muttering into his phone. It was obvious from the expression on his face and his tone that he wasn't the slightest bit happy.

His eyes flickered towards her and he gave a start as he realised the lift doors had opened. 'I'm busy,' he hissed into the phone, jamming it back in his pocket.

Lara couldn't even think straight. Her head was still full of every item of clothing that she'd need to replace with unknown funds so by the time he'd steered her in and out of the lift she didn't have a clue where she was.

An elegant young woman in a dark suit with a jaunty scarf at her neck greeted them. 'Mr Tyler?' she asked. 'I'm Bree, your personal shopper.'

Reuben nodded, his hand firmly in the small of Lara's back. 'This is my friend, Lara Callaway,' he said swiftly. 'She's had a mishap with her summer wardrobe and needs some replacements.' He glanced around the dazzling array of clothes. 'Things that will be suitable for a summer cruise she'll be enjoying in a couple of weeks.'

This time Lara did blink. She was trying to suck in a breath between her tightly clenched lips.

The dark-haired, red-lipped woman nodded attentively. She was so neat. So tidy. So professional that Lara felt entirely dowdy. But Bree nodded as if she were the most important person on the planet and steered her towards a room. 'What kind of things would you like? Dresses? Skirts? Or trousers? Is there a particular colour you prefer? And would you like daywear as well as nightwear?'

Lara felt herself nod along and murmur, 'Pink, or blue, or green. Any summer colours really.' How come she already knew that Bree had that ruthless efficiency edge to her personality type?

Her hands pressed self-consciously against her stomach. 'Do you need to know my size?'

Bree shook her head, her eyes running up and down her body. 'No problem. I've got your size,' she said confidently. She ushered Lara behind a set of velvet curtains. 'Get undressed and I'll be back in a few minutes.'

Reuben hadn't even lifted his head from his phone. He was answering some text or email as he sat down in the velvet-covered chair in the corner of the room.

Another assistant appeared with some glasses and a bottle of champagne. She poured them without a word and set one glass down on the table next to Reuben and the other in the dressing room next to Lara. 'Would you like some chocolates?'

Lara shook her head wordlessly. If she couldn't afford a cup of tea in here, she certainly couldn't afford any clothes.

She stood behind the curtains and stared out at Reuben for a few seconds. He looked furious. She was almost scared to speak.

She grabbed hold of the edge of one of the purple velvet curtains. 'Reuben,' she hissed.

He didn't even acknowledge that she'd spoken.

She tried again. 'Reuben!' This time she was louder. He looked up.

'What?'

She blinked back the tears that were threatening to fill her eyes again. 'Why did you bring me here? I can't afford any of this stuff.' Her stomach clenched. 'You should have told me. You should have told me about my clothes this morning. Then I might have had a chance to get something sorted instead of wasting time over coffee and cakes!'

He frowned. 'What are you worrying about? I'll cover the cost of your clothes.' He waved his hand and went back to his email.

Her mouth fell open. 'What? No.' She couldn't believe it. Why would someone she barely knew offer to restock her wardrobe for her?

He gave a little shrug as he kept bashing away at his phone.

She opened her mouth to speak but Bree swept back into the private changing room with half the contents of the store held effortlessly over her arm.

She stood behind the curtains with Lara and systematically hung things up. 'You're not ready yet?' she asked as everything was slotted into place. 'Summer dresses, skirts and matching tops, Capri pants and a variety of matching items. You get started and I'll find some eveningwear for you and some shoes.' She regarded the rainbow of clothes hanging in front of her nose. 'I've brought the colours I thought would suit you best, but we can change that if there's anything you don't particularly like.'

She swept back out without another word and Lara gulped. She wasn't sure she'd have the heart to tell Bree she didn't like anything she'd chosen.

She stared down at her skinny jeans, brown boots and simple top. Talk about being out of place.

She picked up the glass of champagne and stared at it for a second before taking a nervous gulp. Bree wasn't making her uncomfortable. She'd been nothing but efficient. Lara was making herself uncomfortable.

She fingered one of the pale pink summer dresses hanging in front of her. It was gorgeous and would suit her pale complexion and blonde hair perfectly. But there was no way she was even looking at the price tag.

Where was the harm in trying on a few nice things? There was no way she'd let Reuben buy them for her, but on an ordinary day she would never dare to come in here and try on all these clothes. It was a bit like being a child in a sweetie shop, surrounded by a million fabulous sweeties crammed in jars all around her.

She kicked off her boots and jeans, leaving them in a rumpled heap on the floor, tossing her T-shirt on top. It took only a few seconds to slip the dress over her shoulders and slide the zip into place. She stood back a little to get a look in the mirror.

That was what a dress that probably cost more than her monthly salary looked like.

Nice. More than nice. She ran the palms over the fabric. Gorgeous.

The curtain moved behind her and Bree appeared at her elbow. 'Oh…very nice,' she said, as she deposited some glittering eveningwear on the hooks on the wall. 'Step outside and get a proper look. The light is better there.'

Bree swept back the curtain before Lara had a chance to object. The noise attracted Reuben's attention and he looked up. There was a slight rise of his eyebrows. 'Very Monte Carlo,' he quipped.

She wasn't used to having a guy around while she tried on clothes. Parts of her favourite movie were springing to mind. On one hand it brought a smile to her face, and on the other she was feeling slightly uncomfortable.

She stepped in front of one of the other mirrors. It was a gorgeous dress. Perfect for sitting in the café opposite the Casino in Monte Carlo. Oh, she already had her whole visit planned out.

Bree held up another summer dress. This one was pale yellow dotted with tiny flowers—not dissimilar to a top she owned. 'Try this one too,' she urged. 'I think it will look just as nice and be a good contrast for you.' She gave a wave of her hand. 'I'll get you some sandals.' She wrinkled her nose. 'Will you be doing any walking?'

Lara nodded. 'I expect to be doing lots of walking.'

Bree nodded. 'I'll get you some wedges, then.' She disappeared again and Lara stared over at Reuben. She might as well not exist right now. He was talking on the phone again. Someone was getting the benefit of his full attention—but she wasn't entirely sure she wanted that to change.

She took a few steps back and her hands settled at the edge of the velvet curtains—it was almost as if she was peeking around at him.

From here she was beginning to get the whole 'bad boy' experience. Trouble was, it was making her blood rush quicker around her body. The skin at the back of her neck prickled as he started full-on ranting at the person at the end of the phone. He'd taken off his jacket and laid it across another chair, giving her a bird's-eye view of the muscles rippling underneath the thin fabric of his T-shirt.

There was a hint of stubble along his jaw line and even from here—at the other side of the room—she could see his dark brown eyes blazing. She ducked back behind the curtain and wriggled her way out of the pink dress, taking the yellow one off the hanger. It really was cute, she liked it, she could imagine herself standing in front of the Leaning Tower in this dress and taking a photo. Right now she would be standing in front of the Leaning Tower in her underwear. She shook her head and took another little gulp of her drink. Too quick, and this time the bubbles shot up her nose, making her cough and splutter.

A head appeared around the curtain followed by a warm hand that thudded her back.

'Reuben!' she gasped as she held the dress up in front of herself.

It was no use. He had a rear view anyway and from his amused expression he was taking full advantage.

'What?' Even though the word was innocent, with his Irish accent it sounded like pure cheek.

'Get out!' she hissed.

He disappeared back behind the curtain and she pulled on the dress as quickly as she could, yanking back the curtains, ready to tell him exactly what she thought.

Bree breezed back into the room with two pairs of wedges in each hand. Her footsteps faltered and she looked from one to the other.

Lara was mad but Reuben was sitting with his arms folded, one leg slung over the other with a look of pure amusement on his face.

'Should I come back?' Bree asked hesitantly.

'Don't mind me.' He shrugged.

'I thought you were on the phone,' Lara snapped.

He shrugged again. 'I was. That was round one.' He glanced at his watch. 'I'd say round two will start in about five minutes. Let's see how much you can try on in that space of time.'

He stood up and walked over to her, flooding her with a waft of his aftershave. 'The dress is perfect for you.' He looked towards Bree and pointed at the wedges. 'And I like the natural-coloured ones. Not so plastic looking. Get them.'

His phone buzzed in his pocket and he ignored it. He

looked at the huge amount of clothing hanging from the hooks. 'What else do you like?'

She was stunned. She wasn't quite sure what to make of this. There was no way on this planet that Reuben Tyler was the least bit interested in women's clothes. Not unless he was removing them. What was he playing at?

Bree was smiling anxiously behind him. It would be rude not to respond. She ran her hand down some of the items hanging in front of her. 'I like this one, and this one. Not so much that one or that one.' She pulled out a pair of white Capri pants. 'I still need to try these on.'

Reuben's eyes fixed on something else, and his hand brushed across hers as he reached between the clothes and pulled out something shimmering underneath. It was a gold evening dress. Almost invisible net fabric covered in tiny gold sequins and jewels adorned with fringes— almost like a really chic flapper-style dress.

He held it up against her. 'I think this will really suit you.'

She gulped. It was gorgeous but she could tell from just looking it was way out of price range. On a normal day she'd be too scared to even touch a dress like this.

She shook her head. 'It's probably too fancy for a cruise ship.' Her voice came out almost as a squeak.

Reuben's phone sounded in his pocket again. He completely ignored it, his eyes fixed firmly on hers. He leaned forward, the stubble at the side of his jaw scraping her cheek as he whispered in her ear, 'Go on, try it on. For me.' He stood back.

Bree was wide-eyed behind him. 'I have the perfect sandals for that dress,' she said quietly, before turning on her heel and disappearing.

It was weird, the effect he was having on her skin. Was it the voice? The smell? Or just the masculinity that seemed to exude from his pores? A million little butterflies were currently beating their wings against her skin, making her unable to focus on anything else.

It didn't help that she couldn't seem to draw her eyes away from his hypnotic gaze. Those deep brown eyes just kept pulling her in and she felt her body drift towards his almost subconsciously. And his was moving too, as if pulled by an invisible magnet. His hand caught at the back of her head, tangling in her hair.

She had a wave of déjà vu. Back to earlier in the café downstairs. Back to the feel of his lips against hers. Back to feeling stunned when they'd finally pulled away.

'These ones! I told you they were per...' Bree's voice tailed off as both parties jumped back.

Reuben muttered a curse under his breath and stalked back over to the chair. Lara tried to suck in the air around her but that was a bad idea. Because all she inhaled in was the remnants of his aftershave and that did funny things to her ability to concentrate. She made a grab for the shoes. 'Thanks.' And whipped the curtain closed in front of the stunned Bree's face before sagging against the mirror.

She squeezed her eyes closed. It could have been so much worse. They could have actually been kissing. Come to think of it, she was quite sure people had been caught in much more compromising positions than they had in these fitting rooms.

Something coiled inside her. Something odd. She might be feeling a little off balance but part of her felt cheated. Cheated out of what might actually have come next.

Her hand went automatically to the glass but it was already empty. Her throat had never felt so dry but the last thing she should do right now was ask for more. It had obviously gone to her head already.

She peered round the curtain to locate Bree. 'Could I trouble you for a glass of still water, please?'

Bree nodded and disappeared, leaving Lara with a few seconds to try and think straight.

She took a deep breath and looked at the dress again. It was gorgeous. Better than she could ever have imagined. Reuben had asked to see her in it, and how wrong was it to play princess for five minutes?

The dress slipped over her shoulders as if it had been made just for her. It covered everything but gave the illusion of not quite covering everything at all. The gold jewelled sandals did match perfectly, with just enough of a heel to give her some elegance without having the fear of falling on her face.

Her hand toyed with the curtain. She loved it. But what would Reuben think—and why on earth was that important?

She pulled the curtain back and stepped out into the room. The brighter lights in the larger room caught the beadwork, sequins and fringes on her dress, sending little shards of colour scattering all around the room.

The rainbow effect made Reuben look up from his phone. His eyes widened and his tongue ran slowly along his lower lip. 'Oh, wow...' His voice was low and throaty.

Bree reappeared with the glass of water in her hand. 'Gorgeous,' she breathed.

He waved his hand towards Bree without taking his eyes off Lara. 'This one's definitely a keeper.'

She was caught. She loved this dress. She loved everything about it. But it was just a dream. Like the rest of the clothes behind the curtain. A dream that could never be hers.

'We'll take it.' He'd lost his huskiness. Now his voice was determined.

'What? No. No, we can't. I don't even know how much it costs.' *And probably don't want to know, because that would definitely spoil the dream.*

'It doesn't matter. I'd said I'd cover it. That…' he glanced down at her bare legs '…and the shoes. And the rest of the clothes she tried on and liked.' He walked back over to the range of clothes and picked up a slinky electric-blue dress. 'I like this one too, it matches your eyes. Try it on and if you like it we'll have it too.' He nodded towards a bright pink dress with sparkling circular beads. 'And that one.'

He punched a number into his phone and put it to his ear.

Bree started flapping around her, a wide smile reaching from ear to ear. She lifted out the clothes that Lara had preferred. 'Okay, I'll put these ones over here.' She pointed to the capri pants and blue dress. 'Take your time and try those on too. I've got a gorgeous pink printed blouse that will match those pants.' She disappeared before Lara had a chance to speak again.

Lara looked down. It would be so easy right now to say yes. But she couldn't. She just couldn't. She didn't want to feel as if she owed anything to Reuben. And it didn't matter that he didn't give her that vibe—money was no object to a man like him. She just didn't want to feel like that.

Reuben's voice started to rise. 'That's enough. You have a responsibility to the club. If you renege on the deal now it could affect the club's shares.'

Lara was hesitating behind the curtain. It didn't look like now was a good time to talk to Reuben. She shifted from foot to foot then grabbed the white capri pants and tried them on. Bree was back a few seconds later with the printed pink shirt.

Bree's taste was impeccable. She hadn't picked a single thing that hadn't complemented Lara's skin tone and shape. The pink shirt was printed with little birds and tied at the front. It was perfect.

Bree gave a little sigh. 'That's fantastic. Is there any-thing else I can get you?'

'No.' Lara said the words quickly before she could change her mind. This was getting out of hand.

She slid the shirt and pants back off and handed them to Bree, who disappeared while she pulled her skinny jeans and T-shirt on again. She pulled back the curtain as she tugged on her boots and shouted over to Reuben. 'Reuben, we really need to talk.'

He glanced up from his phone and waved his hand at her. This was getting old.

She marched over in front of him. It was clear he was mad. His voice had risen even more and now he was just plain shouting. 'I'm tired of this. Fed up having to try and placate an adult who is acting like a two-year-old. Enough! I'm done dealing with you.' He hung up and jammed his phone in his pocket as his other hand kneaded the side of his temple.

If Reuben had been in the same room as that player he would probably have killed him with his bare hands. Trou-bleshooting was becoming exasperating. This one foot-baller had signed for a lesser-known club, taken part in the announcements and then decided to back out of the deal—after the club's shares had already soared and they'd spent a huge amount of funds on printing his name across their shirts. Kids were already fighting to get one.

The player's temper tantrum and bad behaviour could bankrupt a club that had already been on the brink.

He blinked and looked up. Lara was standing in front of him with her hands on her hips. His stomach did that crazy thing it had in the last few hours and flipped over. She'd been the one bright thing in the past twenty-four hours.

'What?'

She shook her head. 'You can't buy those clothes for me.' She held out her hands. 'Reuben, I shouldn't even be in a place like this. I probably can't afford a bra from this place, let alone anything else.'

'You need a bra?' That was creating pictures in his mind it shouldn't. Every time they'd appeared in his brain these last few hours he'd tried to force his memories back to the pink onesie. That usually killed any hormones plain dead.

Lara's brow creased into a frown. 'No. I don't need a bra. I need to be able to pay for my own clothes.'

He stared at her. 'Why?'

Lara threw up her hands and stared at him in disbelief. 'Why? *Why?* Because I hardly know you. Because these clothes are for me, not you. Because I like to walk around in things that I've bought with money that I've *earned*. Because it's important to me to be independent.'

He didn't get it. Not really. Every other woman he'd ever dealt with loved it when he threw money at them.

He gave a little smile. 'But you looked beautiful in the clothes. They'd be perfect for the cruise.'

Her shoulders sagged. 'I know that. But I can't afford them. And it's important for me to be able to look after myself.'

Okay. Maybe she was making sense. He'd thought this was an easy get-out clause after not telling her about her disposed-of summer wardrobe.

His phone rang again and he flinched. A wave of concern washed over her face and she reached over and took his hand, her argument about money momentarily forgotten. 'You know what? Maybe you need to think about something else. You've spent an hour constantly fighting with that guy on the phone. When was the last time *you* had a holiday?'

That was easy. 'Spring. Four years ago. My dad was in hospital.'

'You haven't had a holiday in four years? That's ridiculous. It's about time you had a break.'

He shook his head. Ugh. Bad idea. 'Breaks don't make you money. I don't do holidays. They're a waste of time.'

She let out a laugh. 'I guess you and I have different priorities. My holiday is the one thing I look forward to every year.' Her voice tailed off and she looked outside the dressing room.

There it was again. That expression on her face. The one that made him feel like the worst person in the world. He hated it when she looked like that. It didn't matter that none of this was really his fault. His only crime had been his act of omission. But he still didn't like the fact that right now he'd do anything to take that look off her face.

A tiny seed was starting to sprout in his brain. Lara was looking up at him with those clear blue eyes. What on earth had that clown Josh been thinking? The guy must have had rocks in his head.

She was shaking her head again, glancing over her shoulder to make sure Bree wasn't around. 'This was a nice idea, Reuben. It really was.' She ran her hand over her own skinny jeans. 'But it can't happen. This…today… It was a bit like being a fairy princess for an hour or so. But time's up. It's back to real life and the fact I'll probably need to raid some of the second-hand shops to see if I can restock my summer wardrobe.'

He tried to interrupt but she held up her hand. 'Don't. I don't want charity—and I know you don't mean it like that. I know you're just trying to do something nice.' She gave him a rueful smile and pressed her hand against her heart. 'But your something nice makes me feel bad in here. It makes me feel as if I can't look after myself. It makes me feel as if I need someone to bail me out.' She shook her head. 'I don't want to feel like that. I *can't* feel like that right now. Finding Josh in bed with someone else is doing enough damage to my self-esteem right now. You need to let me find my own way with this too.' She stood up. This time her flat abdomen was right in front of his face.

It was probably an unwitting action. She reached out with her hand and ran her fingers through his hair. 'Come on, Reuben, let's get out of here before your favourite foot-baller calls back and you spontaneously combust.'

As if by magic his phone buzzed in his pocket again and he could feel his rage rising. He'd spent the last few years working non-stop. For the most part he'd liked it. It wasn't as if he had a wife and child to come home to and the lifestyle suited him. He loved the energy of his job, even thrived on the stress a little, but the last day had made him stop to breathe for a moment.

When was the last time he'd taken a holiday? When was the last time he'd even *thought* about taking a holiday?

He'd always had a take-no-prisoners attitude and it had served him well in his line of work, which was full of in-flated egos. He called things as he saw them and worked hard for any team he dealt with. But now? If he had five minutes alone in a room with the current diva he was dealing with it was likely he'd do something he shouldn't.

The truth was he needed some time out. He needed some time away.

He stood up quickly, his hand catching Lara's waist.

She didn't flinch, just wrapped her hand over his and moved a little closer, putting her other hand on his shoulder. 'You okay?'

He could hear the genuine concern in her voice. Her light floral perfume with tinges of orange was floating up around him. She brushed her hand against his cheek.

The unanswered phone buzzed again and Lara let out a sigh of exasperation. She dipped into the pocket of his jeans, retrieved the phone and pressed the button. 'Reuben Tyler is unavailable to take your call,' she said sharply.

After a few seconds her eyebrows rose. The footballer was obviously on a tirade. She shot Reuben a cheeky smile as she shook her head. 'Finished?' she enquired into the phone. 'In that case, the answers to your questions were no, no and no. And don't call us, we'll call you.' She hung up and put his phone in her bag.

He'd never actually had anyone take charge of him before. It was a whole new experience. Lara just shrugged. 'I didn't like him much.' She started heading towards the door. 'You should make yourself unavailable for a while until he sorts himself out.'

She was so matter-of-fact about it. Her head wasn't thumping with stocks, shares and the livelihoods of everyone attached to the club. It was almost like a light-bulb moment for him.

He followed her out to the main department, wincing at the bright lights. Bree was standing behind the nearest counter with a whole range of beautifully folded clothes, awaiting payment.

Lara's footsteps faltered. 'Oh, no,' she whispered.

He walked right into the back of her and slid his hand around her waist. 'Don't panic. I have the perfect solution.'

She spun around to face him, her lips just inches from his. It struck him that to anyone looking they must appear a couple. 'Does she work on commission?' Lara whispered. 'Have I just ruined her entire day?'

He reached for his wallet. 'I'm going to pay.'

She grabbed hold of his hand. 'No, Reuben. We've spoken about this.'

He gave her a smile. 'Not entirely. I'm paying you back.'

She frowned. 'Paying me back for what?'

He waved his hand and stopped Bree from wrapping

the pink dress. 'Here,' he said with a flourish. 'Go and put that back on.'

'Why on earth would I do that?'

'I'll let you know what I'm paying you back for once we get out of here. Let's test-drive your fancy new clothes.'

She was bewildered. But Reuben had already swiped his credit card. Bree reached behind her and pulled the silver sandals back out of the bag. 'Here, take these too. You can change back in the dressing room.'

Lara held the glittering pink dress in her hand. Was she finally losing her mind? Maybe this was all just some crazy dream and any second now she'd wake up and find out the last few days hadn't happened at all.

The bright lights of the shop made the dress glitter even more. It was gorgeous. It was a beautiful dress. She'd actually looked at herself in the mirror and held her breath.

She shrugged. Where was the harm in this? It was only temporary. Most of the clothes she could still return. The pink dress?

Well, that might just be destiny.

The bar was beautiful. In one of the most well-known five-star hotels in London, it was sleek, chic and discreet. It was definitely the place to bring a date you wanted to impress. The opulent art deco setting couldn't be any sexier—smouldering black lacquer, burnished gold alcoves, velvet upholstery and the kind of low lighting that showed off everyone to their best advantage.

Normally Lara would have shied away from a place like this, but with her shimmering pink designer dress and silver sandals, for once she didn't feel out of place.

Reuben obviously knew the cocktail bar well. He nodded to the barman and handed her a cocktail menu. 'What would you like?'

She was too busy staring at the chandelier directly above her head. She gave a shrug. 'Something fruity.'

He shook his head and leaned across the bar to place an order. 'What do you think of the place?'

She glanced around at all the elegant couples in the room. They looked like they did this every day. 'It's beautiful,' she said quietly. 'Very elegant.'

Reuben pointed over to the corner. 'Over there? That's the former cabaret stage where George Gershwin and Frank Sinatra performed.'

She sucked in her breath as the barman slid some orange-coloured drinks towards them. The drinks were just as glamorous as the place. Served in stunning, long-stemmed crystal glassware, she was almost too afraid to even take a sip.

The peach-flavoured icy drink was delicious. A few more of these and she would drift off into a world all of her own. And from where she was currently sitting, she would take the sexy Irish man right with her.

No. She shook her head. Silly thoughts. Ridiculous thoughts. It was just…she couldn't stop focusing on those lips. Those lips that had kissed her earlier like she'd never been kissed before. Was that what kisses were meant to be like? How come it had taken this long for her to find out?

She took another sip of the peach cocktail. It was gorgeous, just the right amount of sweetness with a little bit of tartness. It was so easy to get carried away in a place like this, with its decadence and splendour. Particularly when she was dressed like this and had the handsomest man in the room on her arm. It was almost like being in a movie. Time for a reality check.

She owed Reuben a huge amount of money. And in spite of the glamour and ambience of a place like this, that made her feel distinctly uncomfortable. He didn't give her controlling vibes at all. But she wanted to be in charge of

84 HOLIDAY WITH THE MILLIONAIRE

her own life. She wanted every decision she made to be based only on what she wanted—no more outside influences. She really needed to clear the air about this before she could move forward. And there was no time like the present.

She looked over at him and took a deep breath. 'So, tell me, Reuben. How am I going to pay you back?'

Reuben was relaxed. He was feeling chilled. And it was the first time he'd felt like this in weeks—perhaps months.

Lara looked absolutely stunning. She'd pulled her blonde hair up in some kind of silver clasp, leaving little tendrils around her ears. She'd found some pink lipstick somewhere and it matched her dress to perfection. She looked as if she'd spent all day getting ready when the reality was he knew it had only taken ten minutes.

Another thing he liked about her. Along with a whole host of others.

He couldn't understand why she wasn't more confident about herself. It was one of the reasons he'd suggested she test-drive her new clothes. He'd known just how stunning she looked in them. And so did every other guy in the room. All eyes had been on Lara from the second they'd walked in here. Only she didn't seem to notice.

It had come to him in a blinding flash exactly how he should play this. There was chemistry between them. No one could deny it. And after one taste of her lips he was sure he wanted to taste a whole lot more.

He got it that she was proud. He got it that she didn't want a handout. And while he admired that—and he certainly wasn't used to it—it put him in a bit of a difficult position.

Then she'd made the suggestion herself. Reuben should have a holiday.

The idea had never appealed before.

But the idea had never had a blonde-haired, pink-dressed beautiful woman dangling before his eyes. Maybe a quick fling would get Lara Callaway out of his system?

Sure, Caleb might kill him. But from where he was standing it would be worth it.

More than worth it.

And maybe some time together would instil a little more confidence into this gorgeous woman? Maybe, if she had the holiday she'd always dreamed of, and didn't have to worry about money, she'd be able to see herself the way he saw her. A sexy, gorgeous woman with the world at her feet.

She was still waiting for him to answer as she sipped at her straw through those delectable lips.

'That's easy.' He gave her one of his dazzling smiles. 'You'll pay me back by letting me go on the cruise with you.'

She blinked, then her brow furrowed. 'Wait a minute. I'm lost. Want to run this by me again?'

Maybe he should buy her another cocktail. 'It's simple. You told me I need to take a holiday, and you don't want me to pay to replace your clothes. This is the easy solution. I come on the cruise with you—and instead of refunding your cash for my share, I buy you a new wardrobe.' He let his eyes roam up and down her body in the glittering pink dress. Boy, did she wear it well. 'That way you don't feel indebted to me because you're officially buying your own clothes.'

She made a noise. Maybe it was a whimper. 'But... but...' The words just wouldn't form. 'But you don't do holidays,' she finally squeaked.

He lifted one eyebrow. 'It seems like I do now.'

She lifted up her hands. 'But you hardly know me.'

She looked panicked and it made the edges of his

mouth curl up in amusement. 'Then clearly that's about to change.'

She wasn't talking. Her mouth was hanging open. It was the first time he'd really seen Lara lost for words. It made him want to laugh.

He walked smoothly behind her, pressing his chest against her shoulders and looking into the glass in the gantry ahead of them. He bent down and whispered in her ear.

'Stop panicking, Lara. Let the rational side of your brain kick in for a few seconds.'

She was staring straight ahead, watching their reflections in the glass gantry. It was the first time he'd really seen them together—seen what the rest of the world must see when they looked at them.

He smiled. He was absolutely doing the right thing. Two weeks on a cruise with this woman? He'd have to be crazy to let her go alone.

She was staring right back. Watching him, with his head at her shoulder and his arm slipping around her waist. She still looked pretty stunned.

'You know it makes sense,' he said smoothly. 'Technically, you're paying for your own clothes. I'm just refunding you for the half of the cruise that I'll be taking in Josh's place.'

It seemed almost reasonable. If she jumbled it around in her head for long enough she could find arguments and counter-arguments everywhere.

The cruise was days away.

She really, really wanted to go.

And she really needed something to wear.

Did she want to spend two weeks on a cruise ship alone?

None of this was normal. None of this was rational. That kiss must have driven her crazy because she couldn't think a single sensible thought.

She took a huge sip of her cocktail. 'Okay,' she said quickly, as she felt his fingers at her waist. She lifted her cocktail glass towards him. 'Two weeks on the cruise of a lifetime.'

Reuben walked around to her side and picked up his glass. His fingers hadn't left her waist. He clinked his glass against hers. The look on his face was almost predatory.

He gave her a wicked smile. 'My first holiday in four years. This could be fun.'

CHAPTER SIX

LARA HADN'T STOPPED chattering for the last thirty minutes. All the way on the transfer from the airport to the cruise-ship terminal.

Reuben pushed his credit card towards the red-lipped hostess who'd just given them the hard sell. 'Yes to the drinks package and yes to the excursion package.'

The woman beamed at them both and swiped his card in the blink of an eye.

'Reuben,' hissed Lara. 'That's probably way more expensive that it ought to be. I'd already prepaid a few excursions.'

He shook his head and put his arm behind her back, pressing gently to urge her to move forward. He wasn't going to argue about this. 'Why come on a cruise and only go on a few excursions? Let's just enjoy them all.' The ship was gleaming next to them.

'Didn't you say you wanted to do the excursions to Monaco, Rome and Pisa?'

She nodded.

'And don't you think it's likely we'll drink a couple of glasses of wine with dinner each day?'

She pressed her lips together and nodded again.

He gave her back a little push again towards the embarkation point. Her footsteps faltered as she tried to push her passport back in her bag. Her hands were trembling.

He blinked. Over in the corner of the room a child was jumping up and down with excitement. Another couple—

clearly on their honeymoon—kept stopping on the gang-way to take pictures. The whole check-in hall was buzzing.

He hadn't been on a holiday in so long that he'd forgotten about the build-up and the expectations. Last time he'd gone on holiday a few years ago he'd booked a flight and hotel and had left later that day. Nothing had been planned.

But according to Lara she'd planned this for years. She'd wanted to go on a cruise ship since she was a child and after finally saving up the money had spent weeks choosing between different cruise liners and itineraries. No wonder she was nervous. It was kind of cute.

He stopped her in front of the ship. 'Wait a minute. Let's take your picture before you board.'

She gave him a smile as she glanced up at the gleaming hull. For the next two weeks four thousand passengers would live in a different world, leaving one port at night and waking up in another. Would not have to worry about making breakfast, lunch or dinner and be able to choose between relaxing on board or visiting a different city every day.

On paper it actually sounded quite good. The reality of being trapped on a ship with four thousand people he might not actually like for a fortnight gave him a whole host of other thoughts.

Lara pulled her sunglasses down from her head. She was wearing the sunny yellow dress and wedges. It suited her—complimenting her long legs—even though he'd noticed her pulling it down a few times. He lifted up his phone. 'Smile. We finally got here. You're about to have the holiday of a lifetime.'

Her smile wavered for a second and he could see her take a deep breath. She'd spent the last two days in a complete flurry. To be frank, he was surprised they'd even got here. He'd never known anyone double-check on twenty occasions that they had their passports, tickets, itineraries and boarding passes. He snapped the picture quickly. 'Come on,' he said. 'Let's get on board before they leave without us.'

His hand was at the small of her back again. Although her summer dress covered every part of her, the fabric was thin and she could feel the warmth from his palm. It didn't matter that the summer sun was scorching down on her shoulders and face, all she could concentrate on was the heat at the base of her spine.

All the crew were impeccably dressed in white and nodded and greeted each of the guests in turn.

The main reception area of the cruise ship had a central open space, right up the middle of the ship, with a grand piano at the bottom with a curved bar. Lara let out a squeal when she saw the stairs. 'Look, Reuben, they've got crystals in them. Aren't they gorgeous?'

He was obviously amused at her delight. 'Want your picture taken on the stairs?'

She glanced down at her dress. 'Should I wait until I'm wearing one of the evening dresses?'

'Why don't we take a picture in every outfit?' The easy smile he gave her sent little ripples up her spine. She could see a few other guests smile at his accent. Sex appeal just dripped from this man.

'Sure, why not?'

It was odd. At Addison's house in London she'd been comfortable around Reuben. When the two of them were in the house together there was definite underlying current. But it was pleasant. It made the air around them buzz.

But here—somewhere new—the buzz felt a little different. Sparkier. More sexual. Maybe it was because she could see other people reacting to the man she was with. Maybe it was because she was officially on holiday and was just excited by the cruise. But she had a sneaking suspicion it was more to do with the man, rather than the place.

There was something more restrictive about being under the roof of her employer and Reuben's friend. Here, there was no one to answer to. No one to catch them doing something they shouldn't.

Where had that come from?

Reuben had pressed the button for the glass elevator and gestured her over. 'Let's check out the cabin then we can go up on deck and grab a drink for the cast off.'

The elevator slid up smoothly to their floor and they walked along to their cabin. Part of the expense of the trip had been her superior cabin selection, larger than average with a balcony she intended to sit on every night.

But the number of this cabin corresponded with a higher floor. She was curious.

He slid the card they'd received at check-in into the door as her stomach flip-flopped over. And it nearly flip-flopped over onto her new wedges.

This wasn't a cabin—it was a suite.

The place was stunning. A deep red carpet covered the floor of what looked like a sitting room. There was a huge comfortable sofa and a large-screen TV fixed on the wall. One side of the room didn't have a wall—it was pure full-length glass windows with a balcony running along the length of the cabin giving spectacular views.

She almost couldn't speak. 'Great,' said Reuben, walking easily across the room to the small bar in the corner. Her feet carried her forward. The first door on her right led to the bathroom. Second on the right was the bedroom. Now she nearly did fall over.

One enormous king-sized bed took up most of the room.

'I phoned them,' she said quickly. 'I phoned them to ask for it to be changed to two beds.' She spun around and held out her hands. 'And this can't possibly be ours. I didn't pay for a suite—just a superior cabin. There must have been some mistake.'

Reuben didn't blink, just strode over and jumped on the bed, lying back amongst the array of pillows with his arms behind his head. 'No mistake. I paid to upgrade us. Figured we might as well do this in style.' He gave her a wink. 'As for the bed, I don't mind if you don't.'

Her feet were frozen to the floor as her stomach tumbled over. This wasn't supposed to happen. Of course she'd booked a king-size bed when she'd thought she'd been coming on the cruise with rat boyfriend. But as soon as Reuben had suggested he come along instead, she'd amended her booking.

'Let…let me go and speak to the concierge,' she stumbled. 'Maybe they could put two beds in here instead?'

Reuben rolled on his side, head on his hand, facing towards her. 'Why bother? Look at the view you've got from that balcony. What if the only other cabin is down in the bowels of the ship? No view. No balcony. I imagine a cruise like this is pretty much booked out.'

She swallowed. He was probably right. But surely it couldn't hurt to check?

He propped himself up a little further. 'Look at the view we have of Venice right now. Imagine coming into port at Barcelona and getting to see the whole city. And what about Monte Carlo? There'd be a view of the race track, the casino and all the mountains.'

He was right. She knew he was right. But the thought of sharing a bed with Reuben Tyler was doing strange things to her senses. It was almost as if his woody aftershave, laced with pheromones, was snaking its way across the room to her like a big lasso. If this was how it was just being in the same room, what would it be like sharing a bed?

She knew it. She should have brought the onesie.

And he was relishing every second of her uncomfortable squirming. She could see the gleam in his eye from here.

'Come on, Lara. I don't bite. You've lived under the same roof as me for the last two weeks. You know that.'

'But we haven't been in the same bed.' The words were out before she could stop them as the heat flushed into her cheeks.

He starfished across the bed. 'But look how big it is.'

His T-shirt had crept up a little, revealing the dark hairs leading down to...

He turned on his side again as she gulped. 'Look, this bed is enormous. If you find me that irresistible you can put some pillows down the middle to stop you from sneaking over to my side.' He demonstrated by moving some of the pillows from behind his head into the middle of the bed. The ratfink. He was enjoying every second of this.

'What do you wear in bed?' she blurted out.

'Nothing.' It was a rapid-fire answer complete with wicked gleam.

The heat from her cheeks was starting to spread down the rest of her body. Soon she'd light up the room like a glow-worm. 'You can't wear nothing!'

He grinned and put his arms behind his head again. 'What do you want me to wear?'

'Something. Anything.'

He moved off the bed and walked over to her, grabbing her arm, pulling her away from the doorway and letting the door slam behind her. The room instantly shrank in size. The suite didn't feel so extra-large any more.

Now her nostrils were full of his scents—aftershave, soap and the biggest whiff of pheromones possible. Her vision was completely taken up by his chest and shoulders. And he hadn't let go of her hand. 'I'm sure when it comes to bedtime,' he said huskily, 'I'll find something entirely appropriate to wear.'

She could almost feel his voice skitter over her skin. That Irish accent was so sexy, so enchanting that one tiny Amazonian part of her wanted to drag him back to the bed right now, throw him down and just leap on board.

She wasn't normally as uptight around other people as she was around Reuben.

She sucked in a breath and looked up at him. Those dark brown eyes were fixed on her face. The intensity was shocking. Thank goodness for the little twinkle that was still there.

'You'd better,' she said firmly, 'or this is going to be a long two weeks for you on a hard floor.'

The edges of his lips turned upwards. His breath touched her skin. 'Whatever you say, Lara.'

She nudged her shoulder into his chest and pushed past him. 'Let's get changed,' she said quickly. 'There's a whole world out there and I don't want to miss a second of it.'

And just like that she'd agreed to share her bed with a man she'd only known for two weeks.

CHAPTER SEVEN

THE SHIP GLIDED along the Grand Canal. It was one of the final cruise ships allowed along the Grand Canal before plans changed and they all had to moor outside the canal.

Reuben hadn't expected any of this. Everything about this had been last minute for him and, to be honest, he'd been treating it all like a bit of a joke.

Yes. He needed a holiday. After four years with none at all he deserved one.

More importantly he needed some time away from his current business dealings before his partial eruptions turned into a full-blown Vesuvius version.

Lara's face in the cabin had been a picture. He hadn't even given any thought at all to the sleeping arrangements but it seemed she had and her plans had gone awry.

It was clear she didn't realise just how cute and sexy she looked with that wrinkled nose and wide eyes.

So the wonder of Lara, coupled with the wonder of Venice, was doing strange things to him.

The thought of a short fling with Lara was growing more appealing by the second.

They stood on one side of the ship as they passed the Piazza San Marco, the Doge's Palace and the campanile of San Giorgio Maggiore. The multicoloured buildings, some old and tired with peeling plasterwork, others still proud and pristine with arched windows, balconies and overflowing window boxes, kept them enthralled. There was something about Venice that couldn't actually be captured in a photo or in a travel book. You had to actually *be* there to experience the colours, the sights, the noise.

It seemed that every holidaymaker on the cruise ship was standing on deck to watch their passage out to sea. The sun was beating down on them and after a few minutes Lara gave a little sigh and leaned against him, taking a sip of her cocktail. 'This is just how I imagined it would be.' Her voice sounded sad and without even thinking about it his hand slid around her waist and anchored her to him.

'It's gorgeous,' he said quietly. 'I never even gave this much thought. I knew that Venice was a group of islands but I didn't realise quite how many. Or how different they all are.'

The ship had moved on, passing the island where Murano glass was made and moving past one with that was used mainly as a cemetery. He turned his head a little to face Lara. There was a tear gently rolling down her cheek.

'Hey.' Reuben caught her shoulders and turned her to face him. 'What's wrong? Isn't this the trip of a lifetime? The one you always dreamed of?'

Was this because of him? His teasing earlier about the sleeping arrangements? Lara had always seemed able to play him at his own game, but maybe he'd just stepped too far.

She gave a little nod of her head. 'It is. I know it is. It's just…different from what I expected.'

'How?' Now he could feel his insides curling up.

She gave the tiniest shake of her head and sighed, wiping away another tear. 'I expected to be really excited to be here. To love every minute. But the last few weeks and all the trouble with Josh have just…taken the gloss off things for me. I spent so much time thinking about where we would be going, what we would see.'

She gave the wryest smile he'd seen. 'Now I'm standing here, watching Venice glide past, I'm just realising I've been dumped in the most horrible way. He wasn't even sorry. He didn't really care that I'd caught them. Then to throw away all my things, knowing how that would upset me, and that I wouldn't be able to replace them.' She gave her head a little shake.

'I know it's silly to get upset over an old book.' She pressed her hand against her heart. 'But it meant something to me. I guess things have just hit me all at once. I've been treated like I'm not good enough by a man who is lower than the belly of snake. It doesn't really say that much for me, does it?'

There was an instant burn inside him. He recognised it well. Rage. Fury. The kind of feelings usually channelled into his business dealings. It helped when dealing with some of the volatile sports stars. Not the kind of rage he used in everyday life.

Not since that night with Caleb.

'Garbage.' He grabbed her hand and pulled her towards a set of steps, ushering her up towards one of the exclusive bars.

'Where are we going?'

He pointed to one of the bar stools that gave a view out of the full-length glass windows and gestured to the barman, pointing to a bottle of pink champagne.

The barman didn't hesitate. He produced two champagne glasses, an ice bucket and popped the cork quickly.

Reuben took the champagne and poured it into glasses, the froth and bubbles almost spilling over the edges of the glasses. 'Here.' He handed her one.

'What are we doing?' Her brow was furrowed.

'We're toasting the end of a bad relationship. We're celebrating the fact that Josh didn't manage to ruin your dream. We're saying goodbye to feeling like rubbish and raising our glasses to a new future and a new adventure. No negative thoughts allowed. From here on, it's fun, fun, fun.'

He clinked his glass against hers. He wasn't usually so gung-ho. So nice really. But there it was again. That weird thing about being around Lara and her sad face doing strange things to his insides. He seemed to have a low threshold for her being down.

When he'd first met her two weeks ago she'd been fiery—and still quite angry. And even though she still joked with him it was almost as if uncertainty was taking her over. She'd obviously had too much time to think about all this—too much time to let her confidence falter.

He looked around. In his opinion Lara Callaway was the best-looking woman around here. And apart from being funny, she was quirky and she had a good heart. She had passion. She said she loved looking after Tristan and after a few false starts in life obviously thrived in the job she was currently doing. Maybe if she'd been working the last two weeks she might have been too distracted to get down. Now he was feeling guilty for not being around much, contract negotiations and temperamental clients having filled up most of his days and evenings in London.

But the next two weeks would be entirely different. The next two weeks he'd be around her morning, noon and night. And where might that lead?

Maybe Lara would consider a fling? Some fun on the cruise? Because that's all it could be. He wouldn't be able to offer the Caleb and Addison lifestyle. The happy-ever-after and for ever. He wasn't that kind of guy. He didn't come from that kind of family. But two weeks to try and build a beautiful girl's self-confidence? He could do that.

He shifted on his bar stool. That single thought had sent an imaginary cool breeze over his skin and blood rushing to places it shouldn't. Strange how these things sneaked up on you.

Lara gave him a smile that almost made him sigh with relief. She clinked her glass against his. 'You're right. I know you're right. This year is the end of all ratbag boyfriends. And the start of something new entirely.' She tipped back her head to swallow some of the champagne.

He gulped. Her scent was drifting around him—the same scent she'd worn that day he'd kissed her in the café. And right now he had a prime view of that soft skin at the bottom of her neck...

What was wrong with him?

Reuben Tyler didn't take time to fantasise about women. Normally, he didn't *have* the time. Plus the fact he usually just acted on instinct. He could spot a flirtatious glance from a million miles away. All he usually had to do was decide whether to go with the flow or not. But Lara was entirely different.

Sure, there was buzz between them. Sure, her lips tasted like no others.

But most of all he'd actually got to know her a little. He knew what kind of coffee she liked. What kind of cake. He knew the type of wine she liked to drink and what kind of takeout food she enjoyed best. All of these superfluous things usually just passed him by. But living under the same roof as Lara for the last two weeks had kind of imprinted them on his brain in a way he couldn't really understand.

She reached over and touched his hand. 'This is great, thanks. Do you want to go and sit back outside? We could look at the information they gave us and decide what trips we want to do at the different ports.'

There was that innocence to her voice. A purity that he'd really never encountered before. Most of the women he met were players. They knew exactly what they wanted and when they wanted it. Lara didn't even have a sniff of that around her. It was refreshing. It was different. And it was clear that he'd been moving in the wrong circles for far too long.

He resisted the urge to say the words hovering on the edge of his tongue. *We'll go wherever you want.*

Maybe it was the nature of holidays that played havoc with the senses. Maybe it was the freedom that he was going to be able to ignore his emails and phone for two weeks.

Or maybe it was the Lara effect.

It made him wary. Was a two-week fling really what Lara would want?

Would that really help rebuild her confidence?

He gave his head a shake. Whatever it was, he had two weeks to figure it out. He refilled the glasses. 'Sure, why not? Let's watch the rest of the Venice lagoon go by.'

His hand went naturally to the small of her back as they headed to the door and he resisted the temptation to let it slide further down.

This could be a long two weeks.

CHAPTER EIGHT

'Do you want to hit the casino?'

'What?' She was sitting on the balcony, reading a book and letting the sun warm her shoulders.

Reuben didn't do relaxation well. He'd been pacing around the cabin for the last hour. He'd already gone for a couple of walks around the ship and flicked through the various channels on the ship's TV.

'Do you want to go to the casino? Put on one of those fancy dresses we bought and let's live a little.'

She lifted her feet down from the table they were resting on and leaned forward, watching Reuben as he paced the room, trying to use up some of his nervous energy. What on earth was wrong with him?

'I've never been to a casino before. What do you actually do in them?'

He looked stunned. 'You've never been to a casino before?'

She shook her head and shrugged her shoulders. 'The only casinos I've seen are the ones James Bond is usually in.'

Reuben walked out and grabbed her hand. 'Well, the casino on board might be quite small, but it's a perfect start. Come and get changed.'

She let him pull her to her feet.

'It'll be the perfect start for the mother of all casinos, the one in Monte Carlo.'

Her eyes widened. 'We can't possibly go there.'

'Why not? We're mooring at Monte Carlo overnight. There's no curfew on the ship. We can be out as long as we like.'

She wasn't sure if he was conscious of his movements but as he said the words he stepped closer to her. Other people might be intimidated by a guy moving into their personal space but things were getting odd with Reuben.

They weren't in a relationship. They weren't actually anything to each other. But from that first stormy meeting every day just seemed to step up a little notch. There was almost expectation now. That waiting...for something. She wasn't quite sure what.

But every time Reuben took a step into her personal space those expectations rose. The electric buzz had been rising slowly, first to a simmer then to some definite bubbles. Everything was just beneath the surface. All it would take was one move, one look, one connection to make everything erupt.

She just wasn't sure she was ready for it.

She'd just broken up with Josh. She should be distraught. She should be giving herself some time to heal and collect her thoughts.

But everything about her was jittery. Her stomach was permanently clenched. Reuben hadn't offered anything. Hadn't mentioned anything. He was here with her now after inviting himself on her holiday.

He was sharing her cabin—sharing her bed with no discussion of what on earth was going on between them. And she couldn't ask. Because then she would be admitting there *was* something.

It was official. Reuben Tyler was the most exasperating man she'd ever met.

She looked up at the brown eyes that were fixed on hers. What would he do right now if she stood up on tiptoe, wrapped her arms around his neck and kissed him—just like he'd kissed her in the store in London?

Maybe it was time she kept him on his toes too?

But right now she couldn't. She gave a tiny shake of her head and a little smile. 'Monte Carlo it is. I can hardly wait.'

Holidays seemed to do strange things to Reuben. He was talking to complete and utter strangers at dinner every night and actually finding their company enjoyable. He was having conversations about things other than sport and stocks and shares.

Every time someone assumed that Lara was his partner he couldn't find the words to correct them. And that was definitely a first for him. He actually liked it that people assumed they were together. He'd nearly blown a quiet gasket when he'd seen some guy leer at her at the bar. But Lara was no shrinking violet. She'd accidentally-on-purpose dropped her iced drink in his lap and promptly left.

Now he was drumming his fingers on the sumptuous piano bar, waiting for Lara to appear before their visit to Monte Carlo's casino tonight. They'd only arrived in port an hour ago and he'd quickly dressed and left her to get ready. He'd been able to tell she was nervous.

Funny thing was he was a little nervous too.

The man next to him made a little strangled noise, choking on his rich Merlot. Reuben spun around to follow his gaze and almost choked himself. Lara was wearing the gold dress, the one that looked completely sheer and was covered with jewels and gold sequins. It gave the illusion of nakedness where there was really none. Just as well he actually knew that—the rest of the men in the bar would continue to keep their eyes entirely on her.

But Reuben couldn't have dragged his eyes away if he'd tried.

Lara's skin had only the tiniest hint of colour, her long blonde hair resting in gently cascading curls down her shoulders. Her only jewellery was a thin gold locket around her neck and her long bare legs finished with her jewelled wedges drew almost as much attention as the dress itself.

She was every inch the belle of the Monte Carlo ball.

His feet moved automatically to meet her. It was almost self-preservation. If he wasn't by her side in an instant some other guy would be. Without even thinking, he slipped an arm around her waist and gave her a kiss on the cheek. 'You look amazing, Lara.'

There was still a glimmer of uncertainty in her face, the tiniest part of her still lacking in self-confidence. He couldn't for a second understand why—and he'd bet every person in the room wouldn't understand either.

But this was Lara. They didn't know her like he did.

She gave a little nod of her head and sucked in a breath. 'Thank you,' she said, running her eyes up and down his formal suit.

This time it was his turn to suck in his breath, even though he didn't understand why. He pointed towards the bar. 'Do you want to have a drink before we go?'

She shook her head. 'No.' Her gaze meshed with his. 'I'd rather just get this night started.'

The words sent a buzz through his entire body. If any other woman had said those words he would immediately have assumed something. Something intimate. But with Lara? He just wasn't sure.

He held out his elbow towards her. 'Then Monte Carlo here we come.'

She slid her arm into his. 'I can't wait.'

* * *

The journey from the ship to the edge of Monte Carlo took only a few minutes. The ship was moored directly underneath the race track and casino.

There were guards standing at the entrance to the world-famous casino and her stomach gave a little flip-flop as they started up the steps. Trouble was she didn't know if the flip-flop was for the venue or the handsome man on her arm.

She hadn't bothered with a jacket but the night air was warm and the lamplight in the street made the jewels and sequins on her dress send scattered lights all around them. She was like her own little kaleidoscope. The kind she'd pressed to her eye as a child. It made her heart flutter in strange little ways. It was like being the star in your own fairy tale.

Reuben's hand was securely placed at the bottom of her spine and from the second they'd stepped off the ship things had seemed different. As if something had just stepped up a notch.

They entered the Salon Renaissance and had their IDs checked quickly. 'I can't believe people from Monaco can't gamble here,' she whispered.

'Neither can I,' he replied in a low voice. 'But the law was made over a hundred years ago. They didn't want to corrupt their own citizens but they're happy to take money from any visitors.' He glanced around as a famous racing driver entered the casino. 'And remember the foreign nationals who reside in Monaco can come here.'

'So I see,' she replied, as she watched the racing driver and his model girlfriend, dressed in a slinky red dress, nod to the doorman and walk in like old friends.

The Salon Renaissance was sumptuous. Everything about the place spoke of opulence and money. There was

a variety of gaming rooms all around them. Lara had no
clue what was going on in any one of them.

Reuben gave a smile of amusement at the look on her
face. 'How about we go and get a cocktail first? Then I'll
get us some chips and we can look through the gaming
rooms and decide what you want to play.'

'I'm not sure about this,' she murmured, starting to
feel a little panicked. Someone like her could easily lose
their entire year's income on the turn of a hand of cards.
She was completely out of her depth here.

They walked through to the bar. Like everything else
it was elegant and immaculate. Lara poised herself on
one of the bar stools. The biggest surprise was how busy
the casino was. It was still early evening, but everywhere
she looked she could see well-dressed people laughing
and chatting as if visiting the casino was an everyday
occurrence.

She shifted on her stool. The little jewels and sequins
on her dress caught the lights from the chandelier above
the bar. Thank goodness for the gold dress. Even if she
had retrieved her original wardrobe she would never have
had anything suitable to wear in here.

Reuben handed her the cocktail list. It didn't even have
prices listed and for once she decided not to ask. She
scanned the list quickly. 'I'll have a mango daiquiri,' she
said with a smile. 'I'd usually have strawberry, but it might
be time to try something new.'

She lifted her gaze to meet his just as the breath was
sucked out of her body as she realised how that might
sound.

Nothing was lost on Reuben—he just had a way of acting *way* much cooler than she did. There was the tiniest
flicker in his eyes. Then a little quirk as the corner of his
lips turned upwards. His beer was much more straightfor-

ward, but once they had their drinks he raised his glass to hers. 'To trying something new.'

Her hand trembled. The flirtation was definitely increasing, along the heat between them. Right now they could probably heat up the whole building on their own. She took a sip of the frozen daiquiri and tried not to groan with pleasure at the sharp and sweet cold sensation.

He held his hand towards her. 'Want to have a look around?'

She nodded. There were doors to different rooms all around them. 'Do you know where to go?'

He smiled and pointed with one hand. 'The Hall of the Americas has blackjack, craps, American roulette and baccarat. The White Hall has slot machines. The Salon Europe has English and European roulette, stud poker and thirty forty.'

He might as well have been talking a foreign language. A vaguely familiar-looking woman walked past, glittering with diamonds, her face completely wrinkle-free. Hadn't she won an acting award a few years ago? It was like being the new girl in school all over again. She didn't have a clue where to go or who to talk to. Reuben was the only familiar factor in this whole scenario. She turned to face him. 'Does anywhere play snap or gin rummy?'

He turned to face her, his hand automatically going to her hip. It made her feel a tiny bit more secure. Maybe he would find her lack of knowledge exasperating. Maybe he would get fed up with her and want to go and spend some time at the tables on his own. Her stomach was currently clenching as she watched him.

His fingers moved at her hip, pulling her just a few inches closer. She could almost see something flash in his eyes but it wasn't the usual amusement or tease. This was something different. Almost a form of endearment. 'You don't know how to play any of these games?'

She shook her head and blonde curls cascaded forward over her shoulders. 'No. But I'm sure I could kiss your dice for luck.'

Her whole body was tingling right now. Maybe she was reading this all wrong. Let's face it—she'd hardly been astute when it came to Josh.

But this situation and this *man* felt like a million miles away from her last. Reuben reached up and brushed his finger next to her cheek. Any second now she might actually see stars.

This time she moved. She stepped forward, letting the aroma of him drift through her senses. He leaned forward.

She could smell his shaving gel, the one he'd used as he'd got ready. For some reason she was holding her breath, caught in the gaze of his dark brown eyes. His sexy smile seemed entirely for her only. 'I think you're right.' His voice was low and husky. 'I think you might be my good-luck charm.'

The effect was instant. Butterfly wings against her skin, beating in tiny frantic movements. All parts of her skin. Even parts that were apparently covered.

This couldn't be happening. This just wasn't right.

The hand holding her cocktail glass trembled, even though she tried to steady it.

He was still only inches from her. She could see tiny lines around the corners of his eyes, the hint of shadow around his jaw line and a pair of lips just asking to be kissed.

Her fingers tightened around the stem of her glass. Everything about this was, oh, so wrong. She shouldn't even be thinking like this. Shouldn't even let these thoughts enter her head.

But from the second they'd arrived it was almost as if a fanfare was erupting all around them. Back home in England there had been several moments, several flashes that might have made her think about Reuben Tyler a little differently.

But once he'd kissed her, once he'd made her lips sting and toes curl it had been like a tiny seed in her brain that just unfurled into a giant chestnut tree. With acres of room to swing on. *Stop it!*

She swallowed nervously. It didn't matter she'd already drunk half her cocktail. Her lips were bone dry. Especially when he was staring at them.

Her automatic response was to lick them. But Reuben's gaze didn't move. Normally she would have felt uncomfortable, felt as though she were under the microscope. But everything about this—the grandeur of the surroundings, the volume of people around them, the feel of the expensive dress against her skin, and the way his cologne was weaving its way around her—made her feel a little bold. It was like starring in her own private movie.

She licked her lips again and watched as he straightened his shoulders a little. She matched his move, pressing lightly towards him and letting her breasts almost touch the lapel of his jacket. She bit her lip and kept watch on his dark eyes.

It was the first time she'd ever overtly flirted with a man. Lara was used to speaking her mind, but she wasn't a girl of action, and she'd never been a tease.

Maybe she was having an allergic reaction to the mangoes in the daiquiri? They weren't exactly her normal fruit of choice. It could be that they'd had some strange effect on her body and lowered her inhibitions. Or maybe it was just the giant rush of pheromones emanating from them both and exploding somewhere in the middle.

Whatever it was, the sparkle coming off her dress didn't even begin to capture what was happening between them.

Reuben shifted on his feet, a little uncomfortable. Was

he adjusting himself? She couldn't help the smile that reached from ear to ear.

'Come on,' he said briskly, covering her free hand with his own. 'Let's teach you how to play European roulette.'

He crossed the Salon Renaissance in such long strides she almost had to run to catch up. Now she had pulses shooting up her arm too.

He stopped abruptly and turned to face her, not dropping her hand. 'Did you want to eat first? There are restaurants here.'

She shook her head. Eating was absolutely the last thing she wanted to do right now. Her stomach wouldn't be able to keep a single thing down.

Reuben walked smartly to a booth and changed some money for chips. He turned and handed them to her. She frowned and stared at the multicoloured pile in her hands. 'How much are these worth?'

He paused, as if he was hesitating to tell her. 'They're in euros. The value is on them. It ranges from twenty-five euros to one hundred, five hundred and a thousand.'

'A thousand euros? Are you mad?' She could see heads turn at her rising voice. But she didn't care. She started riffling through the chips. 'Which ones are those? I don't want those. I don't really want the five hundreds either. Even the hundreds make me feel a bit faint.'

'Relax.' He closed both hands over hers, his voice as smooth as silk. 'What can go wrong? You're my lucky charm.'

He slid an arm around her waist and directed her to one of the rooms where they were playing roulette. She watched for a few minutes, her eyes wide. She didn't have a clue what was going on and everyone else looked like they'd been doing this for years.

'I thought we were doing the one where all I had to do was kiss the dice?' she murmured.

He raised his eyebrows. 'Craps? It's complicated. That's in the other hall. I thought I'd introduce you to something a little easier.'

He gave a nod to the croupier and gestured for Lara to sit on a stool.

Lara was so out of her comfort zone that she had no idea she was by far the most stunning woman in the room. She'd started to line up the chips into little coloured piles. It seemed to keep her focused.

Reuben had his arm around her, the length of his body up against her back. Her orange-flowered scent was snaking its way up his nostrils. On anyone else he would hardly notice. On Lara it was tantalising, evocative.

He could see the glances from the other people around the table. They were curious about the new players.

Lara leaned back against his chest and turned her head to whisper to him, 'What on earth do we do now?'

He reached up his hand and pulled her silky soft curls back from her ear to reply. He couldn't help it, his reaction was automatic, but his finger trailed down the soft skin behind her ear and down to the nape of her neck. She twitched against him and he resisted the temptation to do it again. He'd already had one waking up of his anatomy tonight and it seemed like any second there would be another.

He took a deep breath and spoke in her ear in a low voice, his lips brushing against her earlobe.

'You can do lots of different things. The most straightforward way is to bet on red or black. Or you can choose between odd or even numbers. The stakes are lower then. If you want to be a bit more risky you can bet on a column of twelve numbers or a row of three.' His left hand moved to her hip. 'You can put your chip on a line and bet on two numbers—that's a split bet, or you can put a chip on a corner—between four lines.'

She nodded slowly as she studied the table, as if she were trying to take it all in.

He took a final step forward, moving his right hand from the edge of the table and directly onto her thigh. He heard her suck in a breath, but the action just pushed her body further back against his. 'Or you can play things dangerously and only bet on one number. That's the most risky play.'

He let the words hang in the air between them.

They were good at this. Talking innocently about one thing when they were actually implying another. Or maybe it was just he who thought that way? Maybe this was all going completely over Lara's head?

But then she rested back fully against his chest, shifting her hips backwards on the chair and coming into contact with another part of him. She didn't flinch. She didn't move. Instead, she picked up one of the chips, turned it on its edge and rolled it over the back of his hand, which was still firmly on her thigh.

'I'm not quite sure how I want to play,' she said cheekily.

A waiter came past and nodded at their near-empty drinks. 'Same again?' he asked.

Lara shook her head. 'I'll have a lavender fizz.'

Reuben smiled and turned towards her, his lips almost coming into contact with her cheek.

'What on earth's that?'

She smiled. 'Champagne, lavender syrup and raspberry purée.'

He raised his eyebrows. 'You memorised the whole cocktail menu?'

She shook her head. 'No,' she answered innocently. 'Just the ones I liked the look of.'

Reuben nodded to the waiter. 'I'll have the same again and the lady will have a lavender fizz.'

His fingers slid a little further up her thigh. *Her bare thigh*.

He'd seen plenty of glimpses of her thighs in the last few days but he hadn't actually felt how silky smooth they were until right now. If he wasn't careful the roulette table was going to start blurring in front of him.

Lara stood up quickly, leaning across the table and putting her chip down on the number seventeen. He could see the gentlemen on either side of him glimpse the rapidly rising short dress and he moved to block their view.

She gave him a playful smile. 'I think I've decided to take the biggest risk.'

That was it. The blood was roaring in his ears. The palms of his hands were tingling. This was ridiculous. He was in the finest casino in the world and was supposed to be showing Lara around. Instead, he felt like a teenage boy with hormones erupting all over the place.

This was *so* not him. What was different here?

The croupier gave a nod. 'All bets placed?' he said, as he looked around the table.

Ten seconds later his white-gloved hand spun the roulette wheel and sent the ball spinning in the other direction.

Lara was still standing but she backed up against him. 'My first-ever bet,' she whispered.

He was surprised. 'What? You don't even bet on the Grand National?'

She shrugged. 'I don't know a thing about horse racing and wouldn't have a clue how to put on a bet. I've never been in a betting shop in my life. My parents didn't bother with things like that. I used to just pick my favourite jockey outfit from the newspaper and shout for that horse.'

He liked her. He liked her more and more. And it was beginning to creep around him like a big coiling snake. He'd never really felt that connected to any woman before. And he'd never believed in love at first sight. In his world, that was for fools.

It was ironic really but from that first impact—that first blow on the head and that murky blackness as he'd come round and got his first look at Lara, the giant pink teddy bear, something weird had happened to him. He couldn't put his finger on it. He couldn't describe it. Because he didn't really know what it was.

He just knew that he didn't like to see her sad. He'd probably do or tell her anything to help her blink back her tears. And he would have been more than happy to knock her ex into next week. It had taken all his self-control not to.

And here in the casino, he could see her attracting attention. But what struck him most was that Lara hadn't noticed. Her attention was focused entirely on him. And that gave him the biggest buzz in the world.

This place was probably full of billionaires—but that hadn't even crossed Lara's mind. She wasn't calculating. She wasn't a player. He'd spent the last few years mixing in the wrong circles. Lara was like a breath of fresh air.

She sounded as if she might have been a little flighty in the past but it was clear she loved her job and wanted to do the best she could for Tristan. It was refreshing to find a woman who wanted to pay her own way and take care of herself. And it was more than a little infuriating to know she'd been subsidising and taken advantage of by another man.

The wheel was spinning round and round and his hand slipped around her waist and rested on her stomach. He smiled. She was holding her breath, waiting for the ball

to rest in one of the numbers on the roulette wheel. Her
fingers were clenched into tight fists.

Watching the ball spin round the roulette wheel was
almost mesmerising. He could see how people could become addicted to the game but the only thing he was addicted to right now was the look on Lara's face.

The wheel started to slow, the ball moving more slowly
almost tripping past the numbers. 'Come on!' she urged.

Her stomach muscles were clenched under his palm.
The ball tripped alongside the last few numbers, moving
steadily past twenty-five, then seventeen, then thirty-four,
before finally coming to rest on number six.

'Oh, no.' Lara sagged back against him and without
even thinking he tightened his grip a little. She spun
around in his arms, their noses practically touching. It
seemed almost natural that her arms lifted and rested on
his shoulders. 'Rats,' she said. 'My first bet was a complete
doozy. Maybe I should just give up on all this?'

The waiter appeared back with their drinks and set
them down on the table next to them. Reuben was conscious of the eyes of people around them watching. They
must look like a couple. It was an intimate pose. It spoke
of complete and utter knowledge of the other person. And
right now he wished that was true.

'Let's finish these drinks.' He smiled. 'We can place
a few more bets and then just people-watch if you want.'

She glanced to the side as a well-known movie actor
walked past with his entourage. She tilted her head to the
side. 'Well, I guess if we want to people-watch, this is the
place to do it.'

She picked up her lavender fizz and took a sip. She gave
a little hiccup as the bubbles caught in her throat. 'Wow.'
She laughed. 'It's delicious.'

He moved forward, this time with him sitting on the
stool at the roulette table and positioning her perched

against his thigh. It was the oddest feeling but he wanted everyone around—with their admiring glances—to realise that Lara Callaway was with him. *Just him.*

Lara seemed to rest comfortably there, sipping her cocktail as she watched him place a few bets. The casino was getting busier, the tables more crowded, and the Mediterranean heat was rising.

He brushed his hand against her leg again. 'Let's say you try again? One more time—for luck. Betting in the casino at Monte Carlo is something you can tell your kids about.'

Her gaze faltered and dropped down to his hands then slowly up to his face. He wondered what she was about to say and it made his gut twist a little. But after a few seconds Lara smiled and laughed. 'Or when I'm old and grey and in my rocking chair on the porch I can tell my grandkids about this man who hijacked my cruise and introduced me to the high life.'

Something inside him plummeted. Was that really how he wanted to be remembered? As the man who'd hijacked her cruise? It wasn't exactly complimentary. It certainly didn't have any emotion attached to it. He could be anyone—anyone at all. And that's what bothered him most.

It was almost like putting up an automatic shield around himself. 'Introduced you to the high life, eh? Was that what you wanted?' The words didn't seem to come out quite right.

She shook her head. Her hands were still on both of his shoulders and his hands lifted and settled on her hips. She shifted her head from side to side before locking her blue eyes on his. Her voice was low.

'I think this is definitely how the other half lives. Even in another lifetime I couldn't fit in here if I tried.' Her voice sounded a little melancholy and a rueful smile spread across her face. 'But I don't know that I'd want to.'

She pointed to her drink. 'It's nice for one evening—to feel like another person, with the world at their feet. But I kind of like being grounded in reality, and there's nothing like cleaning the muddy football boots of a five-year-old and sticking plasters on bloody knees for that.'

He couldn't help but smile. Just when he'd thought she might disappoint him—even a little—she brought him back to earth with a bang.

Several other women flitted through his mind—women who would have put the entire stash of chips on one bet without a moment's thought. Lara had only used one. She didn't seem that interested in using any more. She knew the value of money better than he did. It was humbling.

He spun her around. 'Let's try once more before we leave the table.'

She gave a nod and picked up one more chip.

'Wouldn't you like to raise the stakes a little higher?'

She met his gaze again. 'I think the stakes are high enough already, don't you?'

He swallowed. For a woman with a certain vulnerability about her she was much better at this than she should be.

She reached across the table and set her chip on the line between fourteen and seventeen. 'There you go. This time I'll try a split bet. Let's see if I can get lucky tonight.' Her cheeks flushed a little.

He laughed. The innuendo level was going off the scale. He pulled her back against him, letting her make no mistake about what her words were doing to him.

The croupier spun the wheel and set the ball in motion. Lara leaned forward again to watch the spinning wheel. Her dress hitched up a little at the back and he tried his best to avert his eyes but the hormones flooding through his system really didn't want to.

The wheel started to slow and Lara shifted from foot to foot.

Her hands clasped together in front of her chest as the wheel and ball simultaneously slowed. She leaned even further forward, her attention rapt. The ball seemed to tease tantalisingly as it jumped from number to number, easily slipping past seventeen.

As it moved excruciatingly slower Lara couldn't hide her excitement. She started to clap her hands together and shift more rapidly from foot to foot. 'Oh…look, look, it's getting closer.' The ball tripped over one, then twenty, then seemed to dangle between twenty and fourteen before finally falling over into the red fourteen.

'I've won!' Lara's shout echoed around the casino, much to the amusement of some of the turned heads. She flung her arms in the air and spun in Reuben's grasp, wrapping her arms around his neck and planting her lips firmly on his.

For a second he was stunned. He knew it was excitement. He knew it was the thrill. But there wasn't a single cell in his body that didn't ache in response.

She tasted of raspberry—and of champagne. His hands slid from her hips to her bottom as he edged her lips apart.

This was totally different from their first kiss. The first kiss had been instinctual. An act of self-preservation—all on his part, with no real thought or consideration about Lara. Until he'd got one hint of her hidden passion and only scratched what lay beneath the surface.

This time it was pure, unadulterated pleasure.

Right now he was wearing his bad-boy label with pride. A more sedate man might have decided those few drinks were enough to impair Lara's decision-making processes.

But Reuben didn't doubt her decision-making at all. Not right now anyway. She was finally letting the walls and barriers she'd built up around herself tumble down.

Tonight she had an edge of confidence he hadn't seen before.

Deliberately or not, she'd just aligned her hips with his, pressing the length of her body with its warm curves against him. It was hitting all the right spots.

His fingers trailed down the side of her cheek to the base of her neck where her pulse was beating a rapid tune against his fingers.

She tilted her head to the side. He could sense one leg lifting from the floor as she tilted her pelvis towards his. Her lips parted, her tongue brushed along his bottom lip. Tantalising.

A wave of anticipation swept his body, making his stomach clench. All of a sudden the walls of the sumptuous casino were pressing in around them. The tiny hairs at the back of his neck stood on end. It felt as if every eye in the house was on them.

He drew back. Lara's heavy eyelids fluttered open, her eyes dark with desire. Her lips were swollen, still open, and her breathing choppy.

She looked almost stung that he'd pulled his lips from hers.

It seemed he wasn't the only one caught in the wave of anticipation.

He sucked in a steady breath, ignoring the amused eyes around them, and picked up their chips from table. He nodded his head at their fellow players. 'Ladies, gentlemen, if you'll excuse us?'

He didn't wait for their acknowledgement, didn't need to see their knowing glances.

He just grasped Lara's hand firmly in his and crossed the casino floor in swift steps.

She hadn't said a single word and he could hear her footsteps pitter-patter behind him as they crossed the impeccably tiled floor. They burst through the casino doors and back out into the cool evening air.

This time he did stop. The fresh air was just what he needed. His arm slid around her waist.

He expected her just to stand there for a few seconds, to let the air cool her heated skin and dampen the electricity between them.

But it seemed he didn't know Lara as well as he thought.

She stepped directly into his line of vision. Her bright blue eyes were flooded with passion and a steely determination. She placed one hand on his chest, under his jacket, the palm of her hand pressing against his thudding heart. Her other hand rested on his jawline.

It was an intimate gesture. A gesture almost of promise.

'What was that?' There was no vulnerability to her voice. No uncertainty. Lara Callaway wanted an answer to her question.

'I don't know,' he said quickly. Because he didn't. He wasn't used to a woman putting him on the spot and calling him on his actions. Mainly because his actions were always invited and definitely reciprocated. He was always straight with women. Things were never going anywhere—his job and lifestyle dictated that, so he made no pretences.

But everything with Lara had started differently. He hadn't met her in a club or restaurant. They hadn't gone for a few drinks together, knowing exactly where things would end.

It didn't matter that they had a room together. In fact, it was probably the biggest problem of all. The biggest elephant in the room.

For Reuben, going to a hotel room with a woman meant just that. One night, sex, with a quick retreat in the morning.

Here, there was no retreat. Nowhere to hide.

Lara's eyes flashed at him again. She leaned forward. For a second he thought she was going to kiss him. Thought he might have a chance to taste those lips again.

There was a roaring in his ears. A flashback to the other day and the hurt and pain he'd witnessed in her eyes. Lara Callaway wasn't someone to be played with. She wasn't someone to have a casual fling with and dump when they got back to London.

He knew her.

And if this went any further he would be the person causing the hurt in her eyes.

He took a step back, removing himself from the warmth of her skin and smell of her perfume. He gave a shake of his head. 'This isn't right, Lara. Not for you. Not for me. I'm not your kind of guy. I can't give you any kind of promise.'

His body was screaming at him, *Fool! Fool!*

The irony of how he normally acted was killing him. But he just couldn't do this.

He couldn't do this to her.

Something flashed in her eyes and she leaned forward. Her soft skin came into contact with his cheek, her voice low. 'Don't give me that. You and I both know we move in different circles. I'm not your barracuda girl. And I don't need any guy treating me as if I'm not good enough. I'm past that.'

She spun on her impossibly high heels. The gold jewels and fringes on her dress spun out as she turned, catching the lamplight from the casino, refracting and lighting up the street around them like disco balls as she ran down the steps and jumped into the nearest cab.

Reuben's breath had caught somewhere in his throat. He could hear the theme tune of a movie play in his ears.

Every part of him was cringing. He'd handled this so

badly. She didn't realise he was walking away because he actually *felt* something for her.

If anything, he wasn't good enough for her, not the other way around.

He turned his head towards the ship moored beneath them as he kicked his heels.

Maybe the walk back would cool him off?

One thing was for sure. He certainly needed it.

CHAPTER NINE

LARA WAS MORE than mad. Reuben Tyler had ruined her night's sleep in the world's most comfortable bed, with a stunning view of Monte Carlo. Selfish git.

He hadn't kissed her since that day in the café, so when she'd kissed him last night in the casino she hadn't expected to have to draw him a diagram of what came next.

The guy was supposed to be a bad boy.

So bad, that he'd pulled away from their kiss and practically frog-marched her out of the casino. What on earth had she done that had been so wrong?

Was it against the law in Monte Carlo to kiss in the casino?

She wasn't even sure where he'd gone last night and that made her even madder. She'd been too tense to sleep. Had Reuben gone back to the casino to find a more 'suitable' woman? She had visions right now of finding a huge pair of scissors and shredding all his clothes and tossing them over the balcony.

Now she was lying in bed wondering what on earth to say when he finally showed up.

She hated feeling like this, hated feeling as if she wasn't good enough. She'd already had one dose of that from Josh and she certainly didn't need it from Reuben.

What made her cringe was the fact that she must have read much more into their kiss than he had. He couldn't possibly know the way it had sent electric pulses racing through her senses. The way it had scrambled every sensible thought in her brain. And the way it had sent her imagination into overdrive.

She hadn't wanted him to stop. She'd had very vivid ideas of what she'd wanted to happen next—but he obviously hadn't.

It was embarrassing. It was humiliating. Maybe this was normal behaviour for Reuben because, let's face it, she didn't really know him that well. Two weeks trapped under the same roof as someone didn't mean that you got to know them. It was clear she'd barely scratched the surface.

He'd mentioned no relationships. He hadn't even talked about his family. Just a few hints about bad blood between him and his parents. There were enough pictures of him online with pretty girls to fill a hundred albums. So this was it for him. Find a girl. Kiss her.

Something twisted inside her gut. There was no way bad-boy Reuben didn't follow through to the next event. So what exactly was wrong with *her*?

She flung the covers back, grabbed some clothes and stomped into the shower. Today's stop was Château d'If. She didn't care one bit what Reuben's plans were. She'd dreamt about this place since she'd first read *The Count of Monte Cristo*. There was no way she was missing this place for any man.

Reuben's face creased into a rueful smile as he opened the door of the suite and heard the bang of the bathroom door.

She was up. The fireworks would start any time.

He'd spent the night in one of Monte Carlo's sumptuous five-star hotels. Surprisingly, the bed had felt strangely empty and cold. It might have been just what he'd needed last night, but this morning he could do with a little heat again. And that little flash of satin nightdress and glimpse of leg might be all it would take.

What was wrong with him? He was a fully functioning man. It was inevitable that women would have instinctual reactions to parts of his anatomy. Normally, when he knew the attraction was mutual he wouldn't hesitate to pursue it.

But with Lara? Things felt entirely different.

He was getting to know her in ways he didn't normally get to know other women.

He'd seen the primal fight for survival when he'd first met her, closely followed by the hurt in her eyes and a glimpse of vulnerability. That's what had done it for him.

That's what had made him want to pound Josh into the nearest wall. That's what had made him want to make sure that he didn't hurt her in a similar way.

He loved her one-liners and quick comebacks. He knew that part of it was self-preservation—that wall that she kept around herself. He just wasn't entirely sure what was stopping him from bursting through it to get exactly what he wanted.

Lara had wanted him last night.

Just like he'd wanted her.

The mood, the atmosphere, the surroundings, the way she'd looked, everything had been perfect. If you could plan the perfect evening, that would have been it.

So why had it ended with him sleeping in an empty hotel room?

Because after he'd kissed her, after his hormones had threatened to sweep him away, she'd called him on it. She'd asked him what this was. And he'd been unable to answer. All he'd been able to do was step back. Step away.

Because Reuben Tyler didn't have a clue.

Everything about this was alien to him. A crazy little

thought was starting to spin around in his head. Was this what things were like when you started to fall for a person?

How could people live like this? How could they function?

One hand didn't know what the other was doing. Should he kiss her? Shouldn't he? How could he walk away from Lara the next morning and carry on as normal? Because that's what he'd normally do. But every instinct in his body, every cell was crying out and telling him that this time he couldn't do that.

Caleb. That's the only person he would talk to about any of this kind of stuff. And Caleb would probably laugh him out of the room, because Reuben would *never* bring up this kind of thing. He just wasn't built this way. Or so he'd thought.

He could remember a few years ago Caleb bursting into his flat to tell him he'd met her. He'd met the one. Addison. The woman who'd seemed to hate every single thing about him. The woman that Lara seemed to hold in high regard.

He hadn't got it. He just hadn't. It wasn't that Addison wasn't beautiful and charming, because she was—or at least she could be if she wanted to. And what had been crystal-clear was the love and devotion in her eyes for Caleb. He had never doubted for a second how Addison felt about his friend.

There was a quiet confidence about Addison that made her different. She'd never scream. She'd never shout. Reuben had experienced a few of Caleb's previous girlfriends. At one point he'd asked him if he shopped in Tantrums-R-Us.

And it didn't matter that Addison didn't really like him. What mattered was what he saw when Caleb and Addison were in a room together. The way their eyes could find each other across a crowded room. The way Caleb would stop in mid-sentence just to catch his wife's eye and send her a smile.

A special kind of smile that made you wonder what it meant.

All of this had been in some silly cosmic cloud above Reuben's head. He'd never got it. But more importantly he'd never *wondered*. And now he did.

He'd certainly never witnessed it at home. His parents could barely stand to be in the same room together. They had been hateful to each other—more obsessed with money and prestige. It hadn't been an environment to bring a child up in. He could testify to that.

But Reuben always knew how to play a deal. Years of being a sports agent had made him able to read people and know how to deal with them.

Now, for the first time, he'd no idea what to do next.

And it unnerved him. Lara Callaway unnerved him.

He'd thought that nigh on impossible.

She was ready. She was ready to face the world and come out fighting. Bree had a good eye. The white Capri pants and pink printed shirt covered in flying birds was knotted at her waist. She pulled her blonde hair into a ponytail and finished with a slick of pink lipstick. All she needed now was her wedges.

She flung open the bathroom door and stepped straight into Reuben's broad chest. This suite wasn't really as big as it needed to be.

'Owf!'

He held up his hand. Her wedges were dangling from his finger. 'Thought you might need these.'

She stared up at his face. He was smiling. There was no trace of last night. He'd changed into a short-sleeved shirt and trousers. It was clear he was ready to go to Château d'If. Where on earth had he been?

She sniffed unconsciously—trying to find the smell of another woman on him. But there was nothing. All she got was a huge whiff of Reuben Tyler's pheromones. The thing that drove her nigh on crazy.

'Have a good night?' she snapped.

It was stupid. Even though she was still mad with him, he was here. Here, with her.

He gave a nonchalant nod. Or he tried to. She could see the glimmer of worry behind his eyes. 'I checked into a hotel in Monte Carlo. Didn't want to upset you any more.'

Her stomach flipped over and unwanted tears brimmed behind her eyes. That made him sound considerate. As if he'd actually thought about what had happened between them last night. As if she wasn't quite as unworthy as last night had made her feel.

It still didn't help the fact that he looked relaxed and refreshed after sleeping in a comfortable hotel last night while she'd tossed and turned all night.

'The tour doesn't leave for another hour. We've plenty time for breakfast. Let's go to the restaurant this morning. The buffet is always a bit frantic.'

He was talking as if nothing had happened. But, then, to Reuben, obviously nothing had happened. She didn't know whether to react or not.

He leaned against the wardrobe and folded his arms across his chest. 'You know, some people might ask questions about why you want a visit a prison on an island so much?'

How should she play this? She could hit with all her emotions from last night. But in the cool light of day they seemed a bit out of place. A bit over-dramatic. Maybe she should do what he was doing? Act as if nothing had happened.

She picked up her bag. 'Some people might find that's none of their business,' she answered smartly, as she grabbed her wedges and pushed her feet into them.

She headed for the door, pretending not to notice that Reuben was following her. It was obvious he fully intended to accompany her as usual this morning. Confusion was fluttering through her mind. Didn't he even want to talk about last night? Want to talk about that kiss?

They rode up in the central glass elevator and stepped out at the restaurant. Reuben had been right. It was much calmer here. Sometimes the breakfast buffet felt like survival of the fittest. Why hadn't she thought to come to the restaurant before?

A waiter showed them to their table and took their order. 'Toast and poached eggs and lemon tea, please.'

'Toast, bacon, a fried egg and some coffee, please.' Reuben nodded.

The waiter disappeared quickly.

Lara licked her lips. She was determined not to speak first, determined that he not know how much his rejection last night had hurt.

The ship was due to dock at Marseille later this morning. There was a variety of excursions available but Lara had already pre-booked the one to Château d'If. It had been one of the reasons she'd picked this particular cruise.

'What's the attraction with Château d'If?' he asked again.

She picked at the white linen tablecloth. 'I read a lot as a kid. I know that Alexander Dumas used it for inspiration for *The Count of Monte Cristo*. I've always wanted to visit it.'

'You wouldn't rather browse the shops in Marseille?'

She shook her head. 'And look at more things I can't afford? No, thanks. I'd much rather see the island that inspired my favourite book.'

The waiter appeared again with the coffee and lemon tea. Lara poured her tea and took a sip just as Reuben's phone buzzed.

She frowned as he pulled it from his pocket. 'Who needs hand-holding today?'

He glanced at the screen and pushed the phone back into his pocket. 'Nobody.'

She kept her gaze steady. 'Is that the footballer again? Are you still ignoring his calls?'

He sighed. 'And his voice mails and his texts and his emails.'

She smiled. 'He's persistent, then?'

Reuben nodded.

The waiter appeared and placed their breakfasts down before them. Lara started buttering her toast. 'Is that a good or a bad thing?'

This time it was Reuben who frowned. 'I'm not sure. If you'd asked me last week I would have told you that an agent should always be available for his clients.'

She paused her knife. 'And now?'

He met her gaze. 'I don't know. I've answered any queries from all my other clients. But none of them are as demanding as he is. They can all have their moments— but none of those are quite like his.'

'Does he even know he's being unreasonable?'

Reuben shrugged. 'That's the biggest issue. I don't think so. By the time he finally gets me he'll be furious and probably give me an earful.'

She picked up the salt and pepper. 'So why haven't you dumped him?'

He took a sip of his coffee. 'That's exactly what Caleb asked me. He doesn't like him either.'

Lara shook her head. 'Then I don't get it. The guy gives you constant headaches. He's disrespectful to those around him. He treats the people at the club poorly. In fact, he treats most people in life poorly. Why continue to represent someone like that? Surely his behaviour reflects badly on you too?' She paused for a second as she cut her eggs. 'Or is the pay cheque just too much?'

His fork stopped midway to his mouth. 'Why would it be about the money?' he snapped.

She raised her eyebrows. 'Because there doesn't seem to be another single good reason to keep him on your books.'

Reuben shifted in his chair. It was one of the few times she'd actually seen him looking uncomfortable.

He sighed again. 'It's not quite as easy as that.'

She sat down her knife and fork. 'Well, explain it to me.'

Reuben ran his fingers through his hair. 'Not everyone has a fairy-tale life, Lara. I brought him here from Brazil. He might not have come from the slums but he wasn't far off it. He started with one of the lower-league clubs, but as soon as his talent was noticed, the offers came in thick and fast. He wasn't used to having money. He's not used to fame or the way celebrity is here. I feel as if I've left him exposed to something he wasn't ready for.'

She could see the worry etched on his face. 'How long has he been here now?'

'Four years.'

She tried to be reasonable. 'In that case, he's had four years to learn how to deal with things. He's had four years with English clubs. He's had plenty of time to learn some manners and how to conduct himself. If he hasn't learned by now, it's unlikely he will.'

She took a deep breath. He'd made that little comment about fairy-tale lives. It seemed to have opened a door for her.

'Tell me about Ireland,' she said.

'What do you want me to tell you?' His reply was kind of sharp.

'You haven't mentioned much about your family. Do you have brothers, sisters? Do you see a lot of your mum and dad?'

He twitched. Or was it a visible shudder? 'I'm an only child.'

'And do you go back home much?' she pressed.

He almost rolled his eyes. 'Not if I can help it.'

She put down her knife and fork. 'What does that mean? Surely you never got into that much trouble at home?'

He shook his head. 'Even if I had, no one would have noticed. Not everyone has the idyllic parents that you do, Lara.'

She felt offended. 'What's that supposed to mean?'

He shrugged as he kept eating. 'You've said that your mum and dad are great. They'd be happy to have you back home and you'd be happy to go back if you could.' He shook his head. 'Let's just say I'm at the other end of the spectrum.'

She frowned. 'What does that mean?'

'It means my parents couldn't wait to send me to boarding school and I couldn't wait to go.'

Her stomach twisted. This was all so wrong. No kid should feel like that. 'You don't see your parents?'

'Not if I can help it. I went to see Dad four years ago in hospital and that was it. In all my life I can't remember my mother and father being in the same room and not fighting. Most of the time they didn't even realise I was there.'

Lara sucked in a sharp breath. 'That's awful. Why haven't they just divorced?'

He shook his head. 'Strict Catholics. They prefer to make each other—and everyone around them—miserable.' He paused for a second. 'Don't get me wrong—I've always had a roof over my head, clothes on my back, food on the table. Did I ever have anyone ask me how my day was? Give me a hug or a kiss? Not a chance.'

Lara couldn't eat any more. 'That's terrible. I'm sorry, Reuben, no kid should experience life like that.'

He sat down his knife and fork. 'I guess I should appreciate the fact they sent me to school and I met Caleb. His family are great. They were my first real example of what a family should be. Up until that point I thought most people lived like I did. Once I realised the love and attention Caleb had from his mum and dad it made me resentful and angry.' He took a sip of his coffee. 'Now, a few years on, I'm adult enough to realise I don't need toxic people in my life and step away.'

Lara could feel tears in her eyes. She reached across the table and squeezed his hand. 'You told me before that you knew Caleb would give up his life for his wife and his child. And I know you're right. He's a great dad and a great husband.' She smiled. 'He might have a bit of the workaholic in him, like you, but I've never doubted his devotion to his family. I'm glad you had a chance to see that not all parents are like yours.'

There was silence for a few minutes. She didn't feel the need to fill it with endless chatter. She was trying to get her head around what he'd just told her. It was making her see Reuben in a whole new light. Maybe the way he'd been brought up was affecting his ability to make connections in life? Maybe that was why he had trouble letting people in?

Reuben shook his head a little. 'I was jealous, you know.'

Lara looked up. 'What do you mean?'

He sighed. 'Caleb and I always spent a lot of time together. Once he met Addison...' His voice tailed off.

She tilted her head to the side. 'You got dumped?'

She probably didn't mean it quite like that but the notion was close enough.

He gave a hollow laugh. 'It introduced me to the concept of happily-ever-after. I'd never believed in it. I still don't know if I do and Caleb called me on it. That—and a few other things.'

'You fell out?'

She got the distinct impression there was much more to this.

'Not quite.' He shook his head and stood up, holding out his hand towards her.

She hesitated. After last night did she really want to hold hands with him? But something had changed. His bad-boy edges had chipped off a little. He wasn't as full of bravado as he'd originally seemed.

She pushed her chair back, slipped her hand into his and headed towards the shore and the coaches that were lined up ready to take them on their tour.

It was only a short journey along the coast to where the small boats waited to take them across to Château d'If.

As she stepped down from the coach Lara gave a little gasp. 'It's even more perfect than I imagined.'

Reuben looked at her in surprise. 'A prison? Perfect? That's an unusual description.'

He held out his hand again for hers as she took the last few steps down and walked to board the boat. The white limestone island seemed to rise out of the perfect blue sea with the fortress taking up most of the area. 'I know it's supposed to be one mile away but it looks almost close enough to touch,' she said in wonder.

The boat ride only took ten minutes and the water was much choppier than it had originally looked.

They stepped onto the island to be met by a tour guide who showed them around.

'The history of this place is amazing,' Reuben agreed. 'I can't believe that one of the prisoners was here for nearly twenty years.'

'I like how the cells are all so quirky and different,' Lara said, as she walked up the flight of stairs and peered inside one of them, fingering the sign outside where previous prisoners' names were inscribed.

'You do know that the *Man in the Iron Mask* wasn't actually imprisoned here?'

She smiled and moved to stand behind some bars. 'I know that. But I like the legend. It makes the whole place a little more magical.'

They moved outside and stood at edge of the fortress looking back over the Bay of Marseille. Lara leaned against the fortress wall. 'Look how close Marseille looks. I wonder how many people died trying to reach it and getting caught in the currents.'

He was smiling at her again. 'You like to capture the whole moment, don't you?'

She turned back to face him, her hair getting blown around like crazy in the wind. His hand reached up brushed the side of her face. 'Why else come?' she said quietly. 'There isn't much point if you can't try and get into the spirit of things.'

His gaze locked with hers. It hadn't come out quite as she'd meant. She hadn't been talking about last night. She really hadn't. But now she couldn't drag her gaze away from his. The brisk breeze had made all the little hairs on her arms stand on end. He took a step closer to her. 'So, tell me what you really think.'

Her mouth was instantly dry. His body had blocked out some of the wind sweeping around her, stilled her hair and kind of caught the air between them. For a few seconds she couldn't hear the squawking birds around them. The voices of the other tourists were lost. It was just him and her.

She licked her lips. She was determined not to let those brown eyes pull her in. She'd let that happen in the casino the night before—and where had that got her? The wind was rippling his shirt against the muscles of his chest. It was hard not to look. Hard not to let her hand automatically reach up and rest itself there.

She lifted her chin towards him. 'That's one thing you can count on, Reuben. I'll always tell you what I really think.'

He sucked in a breath. She could feel it beneath her palm and his fingers curled at the side of her cheek. He didn't miss a beat. 'And that's why I'm here, Lara.' There was something in the way his Irish accent folded around her name. Held it there for a few seconds. Cherished it even.

The edges of his mouth turned upwards and a glint of gold lightened those dark eyes. It lightened the moment, letting the breath she hadn't realised she was holding escape from her lips.

His hand dropped and rested behind her waist, exerting the tiniest bit of pressure to turn them both towards the view. She relaxed a little, taking in the sweeping sights of Marseille and the multitude of white yachts in the harbour. It really was another life—another world. A whole other bank balance.

She rested her head against his shoulder. 'This place seems as if it should be something else entirely.'

His fingers drummed against her waistband. 'What do you mean?'

'I kind of wonder why some billionaire hasn't swept in here with some ridiculous offer and tried to buy this island. Couldn't you imagine this place with the fortress transformed into some sumptuous private dwelling with a whole host of glass glinting in the sun? It could be like something from a James Bond movie, you know, with lots of glamorous women in floor-length sweeping gowns drinking cocktails with men in tuxedos.' She glanced around. 'I bet this place could even have its own helipad.'

She waved her hand in front of her. 'And all the beautiful people of Marseille would stare over at the island and wonder exactly what was going on here.'

She turned to face Reuben. He gave an almost imperceptible shake of his head and a grin was plastered to his face.

'What?' she asked.

'You,' he said. 'I had no idea you had such a wild imagination.' He reached over and tapped his finger on her forehead. 'What on earth else goes on in there?'

'Wouldn't you like to know?' she quipped, as she started to walk away.

It was impossible to ignore the curvy bottom in the white capri pants sashaying in front of him. Bree, the personal shopper, had been right. The pants and shirt knotted right at her navel made the most of all Lara's assets, hugging her curves in all the right places. As she walked ahead she reached up and caught her blonde hair, tying it back up in a ponytail.

He preferred it down, but she looked good no matter how she wore it.

He could sense the admiring glances around them. Everyone here must think that he and Lara were a couple. And that wouldn't be a surprise—because they seemed to act like it. He wasn't afraid to touch her—just like she wasn't afraid to touch him. She regularly took his hand, put her hands on his arm or chest, or reached out and touched his face.

The strange thing was he was beginning to ache for her touch. It all seemed so natural. It all just seemed to fit. And he was beginning to wonder what things would be like when they got back to reality.

Back in London, he wouldn't spend much time at Caleb's house. The work on his own property should be complete, and Addison didn't exactly roll out the welcome wagon for him. And she certainly wouldn't appreciate him trying to hang around her nanny.

The thought of not being able to see Lara every day didn't sit comfortably with him. But what on earth could he do about it?

He knew that she hadn't been happy last night—she probably thought he'd screwed things up between them. He'd have liked nothing more to have taken her back to the cabin and undressed her—but where would that have left them?

He didn't want to have a fling with Lara. He didn't want to wake up the next day and make some excuse to leave. But talking about relationships and feelings just wasn't his thing. Guys just didn't have those conversations. Or maybe he was just hanging around with the wrong people?

His parents had certainly never encouraged it. They couldn't face up to their own relationship failings so they couldn't possibly offer any advice that he would take notice of. They'd never been that interested in him. And as he'd grown older he'd been wise enough to distance himself from them completely.

Lara had stopped to chat to a couple of elderly ladies who were also on the cruise. One of them threw back her head, laughing, as Lara's cheeks flushed pink.

He walked over and slid his arm around her waist. 'What have I missed?'

The pinkness in her cheeks deepened and she waved her hand as the ladies dissolved into another fit of laughter. 'Oh, nothing, we were just chatting.'

One of them tapped Reuben on the arm. 'And I wonder who we could have been talking about?' she said coyly. She reached over and grabbed Reuben's phone from his hand. 'Here, let me take a picture of you two lovebirds. You make such a gorgeous couple.'

They barely had time to pose before she handed the phone back and the two ladies walked away, still laughing.

Reuben turned to face her, his fingertips coming into contact with the sliver of bare skin at her waistline. 'James Bond again?'

She shook her head. 'Unfortunately not.'

'Then what?'

She shook her head again. 'Nothing.'

'Come on, tell, it's half the fun.'

She put her hand over his and started to walk back towards the boat. 'Believe me, my imagination has *nothing* on theirs.'

'Now, that sounds *really* interesting.'

She tapped her finger on his chest and gave him a wink. 'Just as well I don't kiss and tell.'

She walked across the gangplank back on board as he stared down at his phone. Two photos had been taken in rapid succession. One showed them posing and smiling a little awkwardly, and another showed him with his arm around her waist and her hand touching his chest. They were looking at each other with the beautiful backdrop of Marseille behind them. This one had no pose about it. It was entirely natural. Their smiles were genuine and the chemistry reached out to grab him.

He gulped and pushed the phone deep down into his pocket.

There were a million pictures of him with glamorous women on the internet. But one thing was for sure—none of them looked like that.

* * *

Two hours later they were back on the cruise ship, lying next to the pool. Lara had changed into her pink bikini and sarong and was trying her best to read the latest bestseller.

Sunglasses were a godsend. She could hold the book in her lap while she secretly spent the whole time sneaking glances at the guy next to her on the sun lounger.

She'd had a few views of Reuben's bare chest before. His muscles were well defined, there was a definite hint of a tan and a fair sprinkling of dark hairs. But couple that with the dark hairs on his defined calves and she was seeing a whole lot more than she normally did.

She gave a little smile as an Italian guy at the other side of pool dived in wearing barely-there white Speedos.

Reuben groaned and rolled over onto his belly. 'Don't tell me you're watching the guy on parade.'

She leaned forward. 'What if I am?'

'Should I have pulled my Speedos out of my bag? Is that what it takes to get some attention around here?'

She laughed and put her book down. 'All it takes to get some attention around here is the promise of a cocktail over at the bar.'

Reuben stretched his arms above his head. It was so easy when her eyes were hidden to have a quick glance at the dark curling hairs on his abdomen leading in one direction.

He sat back up and reached out his hand. 'Done. A cocktail it is.' He nodded his head towards the pool. 'I can't take the competition here anyway.'

They walked over to the nearby bar and sat down. Lara picked up the menu and started to peruse it as the bartender approached. 'What will it be?' He smiled.

Reuben gave her shoulder a nudge. 'What takes your fancy?'

She shook her head at the obvious innuendo. 'Speedos,' she whispered under her breath.

He groaned and turned to the bartender. 'I'll have a beer.'

The bartender nodded. 'And for the lady?'

She sighed and put the menu down again. 'I'm not sure. What do you recommend? I prefer cocktails with rum.'

He pointed to one on the menu. 'How about this one? The sunset cruiser? It has rum, peach, melon, a dash of lime and some Angostura Bitters.'

She grinned. 'Sounds tempting. Count me in.'

Reuben leaned his arm against the bar and raised his eyebrows at her. 'Are you going to taunt me all day?'

She gave a little nod. 'I think you deserve it.'

The sun was shining brightly above them, warming their backs and making her feel more relaxed. 'You should try and catch me,' she teased. 'I'm probably on the re-bound.'

The bartender placed their drinks down and Reuben picked them up and carried them over to a table shaded by a parasol, his lips set in a firm line.

She sat down in the shade and took a sip of her cock-tail. Gorgeous. It hit the right spot.

Reuben was chewing his lip but his dark eyes were fixed firmly on her.

'What if I don't want you on the rebound?'

'You don't seem to want me at all.'

She could almost feel the temperature around them plummet and it was nothing to do with the shade.

'I guess I'm not good enough.' Her stomach curled as she said the words. 'But I don't really want to be a vacant blonde, hanging on to your arm in a designer dress, like all the others.'

His back straightened and she could see him bristle.

He was mad, but trying to control it. He took a swig of his beer. His jaw tightened. 'I like you,' was all that came out.

'Just not that much,' she said swiftly, as she took another sip.

This wasn't nearly as uncomfortable as it should be. The ship had just set sail again. There really was no escape for either of them. She was confused about last night. Surely she hadn't read things wrong? Their chemistry had practically lit up the whole of Monte Carlo.

And it was kind of amusing to see Reuben Tyler struggle to find words.

A cool breeze swept over her skin. Maybe he was just trying to be kind, when what he really wanted to say was that he just wasn't attracted to her at all. Now, that really *did* make her stomach lurch in all the wrong ways.

She was already feeling exposed—and sitting in her bikini and sarong didn't exactly help. She took another sip of the cocktail, hoping the rum would calm her nerves.

She could see a little tic in Reuben's jaw.

He took another swig of his beer. Did he need Dutch courage too? He sighed and set the bottle down with a clunk. 'I like the fact you're not a vacant blonde.'

She licked her lips. 'Really?'

He shifted in his seat. 'I like being around you.'

It was like getting blood out of a stone. It seemed that when it came to the emotional stuff Reuben was hard work.

'I like being around you too,' she replied.

He wasn't looking at her any more. He'd fixed his eyes on the horizon. 'But it's awkward.'

'Awkward how?' This didn't seem to be going so well.

He ran his fingers through his dark hair. 'I'm not good at relationships.'

'Is that what this is? A relationship? I wasn't sure we'd got that far.' She started playing with the straw in her drink. Nothing like talking about feelings to make you feel like an awkward teenager again.

He lifted his hands up and let out a huge sigh. 'I don't really know how to do this.'

She almost laughed out loud. 'What do you normally do, Reuben? See a girl, ask her out? Date once, and that's it?'

'Usually.'

'Haven't you ever had a proper girlfriend? Lived with someone before? Had someone you would introduce to the family?'

This time he spoke a little more quietly. 'If I introduced anyone to my family they'd have to be wearing a suit of armour.'

She reached over and squeezed his hand. She had such a great relationship with her mum and dad that she couldn't really imagine how it was for him. They'd been having such a wonderful time she didn't want to darken his mood, so she pulled her hand back and lifted her eyebrows. 'My mum's getting desperate for grandkids. I think the next guy I bring back home she'll lasso for me and drag him down to the church!'

Reuben threw back his head and laughed. 'I'd better watch out, then.'

She nodded. 'You'd better. What's your maximum number of dates, then?'

'Honestly? I think it was six.' He shrugged his shoulders. 'And I spent two weeks with you in London, then our time on board, of course.' There was a little sparkle in his dark eyes again. 'You've already beaten the record.' The more he spoke the thicker his accent got. It was doing crazy things to her pulse.

'Even though we've barely kissed?'

He gave a tiny nod of his head. 'You think I didn't want to?'

Her gaze meshed with his. 'Oh, I could *feel* you wanted to.'

He leaned back in his chair and threw up his hands again. 'That's just it. You know I want to. But I like you. I don't want to hurt you. I have no idea where this could go.'

She stirred her drink again. 'And you don't want to find out?'

He folded his arms across his chest. 'You know I do. But you see the kind of job I have, Lara. I'm hardly in the country for any time at all. I spend most of my life in mid-air. How can something work when one of us is never here?' He picked up his beer again and leaned his elbows on the table. 'Anyway, you might have forgotten but you've got a bit of a reputation.'

She jerked back. 'I have?'

He was teasing again. She could tell. Every time he did it, a little glint appeared in his eyes again.

He looked up through heavy lids. This man could be *so* sexy. 'You have. You've got a bit of a reputation for picking losers. I'm worried I'll get labelled.'

She picked up her drink mat and flung it at him. 'I can think of a whole host of other words.'

He laughed. 'Seriously, though, what are you going to do when we get back home?'

She shrugged. 'What else would I do? I'm going to look after Tristan. Caleb and Addison will be back by then and I love my job, he's a great kid.'

A few lines appeared on his forehead. 'Did you always want to be a nanny?'

She shook her head. 'No, I told you. I kind of fell into it.' She counted off on her fingers. 'So far, I've been a nanny, a strawberry picker, worked in a bar, waitressed, spent three dismal months in a call centre, lost someone's messages as a PA and...' she paused and raised her eyebrows '... I even spent two months volunteering at a zoo.'

'What?'

She giggled. 'Believe me, the penguins *stink*!'

He looked serious again. 'So, what was your dream job when you were a kid?'

She sat back for a moment. 'Wow. I think the last person to ask me that my gran.'

'And what did you say?'

A wave of disappointment swept over her. It was odd. It had been a long time since she'd felt like this—as if she hadn't really fulfilled her potential. But the worst part about it was the way she couldn't stop hostile thoughts towards Reuben because he'd asked the question.

She took a few seconds before she finally answered. 'I used to have lots of romantic ideas about working at NASA—even though I couldn't pass physics. Or owning a florist shop or being a TV presenter.'

He gave a little nod. 'Interesting choices.'

'It gets better. I even wanted to be the female version of Indiana Jones and study archaeology.'

He held out his hands. 'Every day's just a surprise with you, isn't it?'

She gave a rueful smile. 'What I really wanted to do was study English at university. I wanted to study English then maybe go on to be a journalist. I got the grades, got the place and then…Gran died. It was as if all my energy and focus disappeared. I couldn't get my head in the right place to study. I decided to take some time off and the rest—as they say—is history.'

'And you'd never consider going back?'

She shook her head. 'I'm twenty-six, Reuben. I'd be the oldest student in the class. They'd call me Grandma.'

He finished his beer and stood up, holding out his hand towards her. 'Then they'd have me to deal with. Come on, let's go and get changed for dinner. We need to plan for Pisa tomorrow.'

She took the last sip of her cocktail and slipped her hand into his. It felt as if it belonged there.

She'd dreamed about coming on this cruise for so long—but her dream had never quite looked like this. Reuben was having a whole host of effects on her she hadn't banked on. And it was clear that the chemistry was still simmering beneath the surface.

Now he had her brain spinning in a whole host of other ways. She wasn't just distracted by the handsome man in front of her—she was also distracted about the things she'd pushed to the back of her brain. Was applying to university again really an option for her? She hadn't even considered it until now. And was this really a time to start thinking about another relationship? She'd just got out of one and was getting her life back on track, having the space and control to make decisions for herself. Did she want anything more? The sun warmed her shoulders as they crossed the deck towards the bar again.

Reuben Tyler was full of surprises. What would come next?

CHAPTER TEN

THE PHONE BUZZED in his pocket again. His footballer client was getting beyond obnoxious. Lara had no idea that he'd actually had three different conversations with the guy since he'd got here—every time telling him to smarten up his act. None of those words seemed to be having an effect.

It was just as well he was in the middle of the Med right now because if he was in the same room as his client he might actually bounce Mr Arrogant into next week.

Any day now the club would cancel his contract because of his antics and Reuben was secretly counting down the days.

Lara was chatting to the two elderly, mischievous women—Doris and Daisy—again. They seemed to be spending most of their time teasing her. All three were currently trying on a whole array of wide-brimmed hats from a street vendor. The Italian sun was positively scorching today.

He walked over swiftly and thrust some bills at the street vendor, paying for all three hats. 'It's on me, ladies,' he said swiftly. 'I don't think I've ever seen anything so ridiculous in my life.'

All three faces turned towards him, laughing. The hats *were* ridiculous. Lara's was pink with a huge yellow flower, Doris and Daisy's bright green and bright blue respectively, both adorned with bright orange flowers.

Doris wagged her finger at him. 'Thank you kindly.

But don't come moaning to me when you've got sunstroke or blisters on the back of your neck.'

They wandered off as Lara put her bag over her shoulder. She was wearing the pale pink dress they'd bought in London and looked as pretty as a picture. The bright pink hat actually suited her. It was quirky. Just like Lara.

His heart stopped. That was it. That tiny little thought had just caused a ricochet around his body.

This was it. This must be exactly how Caleb felt about Addison.

And it had taken until today, watching her laughing in the sunlight, for him to realise exactly how he felt.

He didn't want to wake up next week without Lara in his life. He didn't want to have to skulk around to Caleb's house in order to see her again.

Was this what it was like to be in love?

He couldn't help himself. He wrinkled up his nose and shifted on his feet. It wasn't as if he had an example to follow. His mother and father had spent most of their married life fighting. He'd never seen a single moment between them to make him think they'd ever been in love. And although he'd missed Ireland when he'd been sent to Eton as a teenager, it had actually been a relief to get away from the atmosphere in the house. And once he'd left he'd had no intention of returning on a permanent basis.

So love was a bit of stranger to Reuben. Sure, he'd watched as many corny movies as the next guy—but even they made him feel uncomfortable. He'd loved his grandmother and his grandfather but that kind of deep love and affection was different from the way his heart was beating a rapid tune against his chest now.

That kind of love didn't cause pins and needles down his arms and legs and make him bite his lips to stop them tingling. He took the tiniest step backwards.

He wasn't entirely sure he liked this. He didn't doubt

for a second the kind of person Lara was. She was good. She brought out a whole side of him he hadn't even known was there.

But certain things twisted away at his gut. Things he wouldn't say out loud for fear of offending her. Lara already had some ridiculous idea in her head that she wasn't good enough. The last thing he wanted to do was perpetuate that myth.

But deep down it bothered him that the woman he loved worked for his best friend. It shouldn't matter. He shouldn't care. She'd already told him she was doing a job that she loved.

Was it wrong that he thought she had so much more potential? Was it wrong that he really wanted her to fulfil her dreams?

She was proud. She was independent. He already knew these things. She wanted to pay her own way in life and save hard for the things that she wanted.

He squirmed as he thought about how he hadn't had to consider money in a long time. He was no billionaire. But he was definitely in the category directly below that—in his line of work most agents were. And living in London certainly didn't come cheaply. He hadn't even admitted to her that he actually had more than one property.

The places in the US had become essential since he spent so much time over there—one on the west coast and an apartment on the east coast. Having his own space was so much better than constantly living in hotels. In the next few weeks he would close on a property in Ireland too. He hadn't even viewed it personally—just online. But he knew the area well and it felt good to buy something in Ireland that wouldn't have any ties to his parents and their complicated relationship.

'Reuben, what are you doing?' Lara shouted from the end of the row of street vendors lining the outside of the

Piazza del Miracoli, which held the Baptistery, the Leaning Tower and the cathedral. 'Come on!'

He smiled and hurried after her, reaching the entranceway to the square. The brilliant sunshine was glinting off the white marble of the three buildings. It was dazzling. A real suck-in-your-breath moment. Lara had stopped dead in front of him and he stepped closer putting a hand on each of her hips.

'That was a bit unexpected,' he murmured in her ear. He was talking about the view. Of course he was talking about the view.

He could see the smile painted across her face. It reached from ear to ear. She'd lifted her hands and placed them on her chest. 'Wow,' she breathed. 'Just, wow.'

She leaned back a little against him. It was odd how he was beginning to appreciate the little things. Before he hadn't really gone for any touchy-feely stuff with women. He'd never really had that kind of connection before. But with Lara things felt entirely natural and had done from the beginning. He was relishing it. Liking how much he actually enjoyed it.

'What do you want to do first?'

She eyed the line of cafés across from the three monuments. 'Did the tour guide give you tickets for the tower?'

He nodded and pulled them from his pocket. They had a time stamped on them. Her stomach gave a little growl. 'How about we stop for something to drink first and then work our way around the monuments?' She slid her hand into his as he nodded and headed towards the first café with empty tables out front.

Lara ducked her head in the shop door. 'Nope, not this one.'

He frowned and followed her to the next one. 'What was wrong with that one?'

She stuck her head inside the next one, eyed the glass

cabinet full of cakes and shook her head again. 'Not this one either.'

He looked at the huge array of cakes and pastries and held out his other hand. 'What? Not enough cakes for you?'

She led him to the next doorway, peeked inside and turned around with a wide smile on her face. 'Now, this one will be perfect.'

He glanced inside. It seemed exactly the same as the others. 'What is it?' he whispered. 'What did I miss?'

She pointed with her finger. 'That.'

He followed her finger to the hugely stacked sponge cake layered with strawberries and cream. 'What is it?'

'Strawberry cassata cake—ricotta, whipped cream, Chambord, sponge and strawberries. That's what I've been searching for. What more could a girl possibly need?'

He laughed. 'I could be quite insulted by that.' He glanced back at the cake. 'Instead, I think I'll just order two.'

They sat at a table just across from the monuments and ordered the cake and two cappuccinos. One taste was enough. She was right. It was delicious.

'How on earth did you find out about this?' He was trying hard not to stare as she licked her fork.

'They had it at a café in London. Addison told me when I got to Italy I had to try the real thing.' She leaned back in her chair and looked first at the view and then at Reuben. She sighed. 'I think I'm in heaven.'

There was something about the way she said it that made his heart swell. It was absurd. It didn't matter that she'd been looking at him while she'd said it. He knew that she was talking about the whole experience. Was it wrong that he hoped she considered him part of it?

Four hours later, Lara was slumped against him as they walked slowly back to the bus. Today was officially the hottest day Italy had experienced in years. And every part of their bodies felt it. 'I can't believe my phone is full,' she grumped, her hat crushed beneath her fingers. She'd given up wearing it on her head, claiming it made her sweaty, and had started using it as an impromptu fan instead. Both of them agreed it was entirely useless.

Reuben pulled his T-shirt away from his back for about the tenth time that afternoon. They'd walked around the cathedral, the Baptistery and climbed the two hundred and ninety-seven steps to the top floor of the Leaning Tower. Lara had almost wept when they'd reached the top as, although the cathedral and Baptistery had been cooler, outside on the tower the heat was scorching. Their tour guide's joke about frying an egg on the pavement had been met with hard, exhausted stares.

'When we get back I'm going for a sleep,' Lara said, her head still resting on his shoulder.

'Me too,' he agreed. He could hardly believe he was used to working sixteen-hour days and yet a tour of Pisa had just about finished him. It didn't matter that there was something oddly comforting about having Lara slumped against him. She just seemed to fit so well.

He closed his eyes and it seemed like only a few seconds later that the tour guide was brushing against his arm. 'Wakey-wakey, everyone, we're back at the ship.'

Reuben stretched his back and stood up, holding out his hand towards Lara. Maybe it was time to have a conversation about what happened when they got back? They'd danced around the subject a few times. But after today's recognition about how he felt, maybe it was time to find out if his feelings were reciprocated. His stomach did a few flip-flops. The scary thing for him? Right now, he felt about as far away from his bad-boy reputation as humanly possible. There was a gorgeous woman only a few inches away who could potentially mash up his heart like modelling clay. Was he really brave enough to find out if she would?

He touched her shoulder and gave her a shake. 'Come on, Sleeping Beauty. We need to decide if we want to go to the theatre after dinner or just go for a few drinks.'

Her eyelids flickered open, revealing her blue eyes— a perfect match to the Mediterranean. He leaned forward a little. 'Maybe you should wear that blue dress tonight? It looked gorgeous and you haven't had a chance to show it off.'

Something caught his attention from the corner of his eye. The two elderly ladies from the cruise ship—Doris and Daisy. Doris's voice was getting louder and her actions more frantic as she tried to wake her counterpart. 'Daisy? Daisy? What's wrong? It's time to wake up. We're back at the ship now. Come on.'

Reuben didn't hesitate. He took a few steps closer. He was no doctor—he'd had no medical training at all—but that didn't mean he couldn't help. Daisy's colour was terrible, she was ashen and slumped to one side.

He touched Doris's arm. 'Why don't you go forward and speak to the coach driver?' He could see the pink of Lara's dress at his side. 'Lara will go with you and get some help. Let me sit next to Daisy for a few minutes.'

He glanced towards Lara, giving her all the information she could possibly need. Her lips pressed together as he almost lifted Doris from the seat and steered her forward. Lara took his place easily as he slipped into the seat next to Daisy.

He took a deep breath. He'd watched enough movies to know what he should do. They were right next to the cruise ship. Someone from the medical team would be here in moments. He put his fingers gently at Doris's wrist to feel for a pulse and watched her chest for any rise and fall. He felt a minor second of panic until he adjusted the position of his fingers and felt a rapid fluttering pulse. There was no way he could count that.

Doris's chest was rising and falling very slowly. Her pulse was fast and her breaths slow—what on earth did that mean? Reuben didn't have a clue. Her lips were tinged blue so he repositioned her slumped head, hoping her airway would be a little clearer and started to talk to her softly. 'Hi, Doris. It's Reuben here. I don't think you're feeling too good but don't worry. Daisy has gone to get some help.' He slid his hand into hers. 'It's been a really warm day. Maybe the heat just got a little too much for you? Whatever it is, don't panic. Help will be here soon. If you can hear me at all, give my hand a little squeeze.'

The rest of the passengers were filing off the bus, casting a few anxious glances in his direction. He sent up a silent prayer that one of them would be a doctor or nurse and offer to help. But it seemed like everyone was in the same boat as him. No medical expertise at all.

He could see some commotion on the dockside. Lara was talking anxiously to someone who was nodding and talking into a radio.

He kept his voice low and steady, sliding his other hand over to reassure himself she did actually still have the rapid pulse. Poor Daisy. The two old ladies had kept them entertained for days—even though he and Lara had been the butt of most of their jokes. The last thing he wanted was for something bad to happen.

A few minutes later the white-uniformed ship's doctor appeared with a whole host of equipment. Reuben was relieved to slide out of the way—and, when asked to assist carry Daisy in a stretcher a few minutes later—he was only too happy to help.

She was sped back to the ship on one of the golf-type buggies they used on the dockside.

Lara was standing outside the bus, waiting for him,

wringing her hands in front of her, lines of worry etching her face.

He slung his arm around her shoulder. 'Let's forget about the sleep. I need a drink and so do you. Something long and cold.'

She nodded and slipped her arm around his waist. 'Absolutely,' she agreed, as she watched the golf buggy pull up next to the ship.

Three hours later they'd found out that Daisy had suffered a mild case of sunstroke. She'd be monitored in the cruise medical centre overnight and even though they'd invited Doris to join them for dinner she'd insisted on staying with her friend.

Reuben was waiting in the sports bar for Lara. She'd asked him to give her a little time and space to get ready and he'd been happy to agree. He'd wanted to make a few calls to some of his clients and watch a Spanish football game to monitor another client.

It was odd how her stomach kept fluttering round and round. They'd already spent ten nights on this cruise ship. Ten nights sleeping in the same cabin.

But tonight felt different. Their relationship was changing. It was beginning to actually look like a relationship as opposed to two strangers just sharing a room. And she wasn't quite sure what that meant.

She put the finishing touches to her lipstick and hung some dangly earrings from her ears. Done. She opened the wardrobe door for a quick check in the full-length mirror, putting her hands on her hips and swinging from side to side.

The electric-blue dress was gorgeous. The slinky material hugged her skin without clinging, the fuller skirt swinging out as she moved from side to side. The wraparound style suited her. The tiny beads around the

V-shaped neckline caught the light as she moved in her silver sandals.

She picked up her silver bag and headed to the door. The ship was busy tonight, with more passengers having boarded in Livorno. She threaded her way through the crowd to the sports bar. It was packed. It seemed that every male on the ship had headed here to watch the game between two of the main Spanish football clubs. She spotted Reuben easily. He was sitting—no, almost standing—on a bar stool next to the main bar, his eyes fixed on a big screen. A deafening roar erupted around her as one of the teams scored and Reuben punched the air.

She couldn't hide her smile as she started to weave her way through the crowd.

It was hard to ignore the appreciative stares around her. It gave her confidence, confidence that had disappeared in the weeks since Josh had cheated on her.

She loved this holiday. She loved this ship. And she loved being in Reuben's company. He'd helped her realise that none of this was down to her. When she allowed herself to think back she knew things would never have worked with Josh. With hindsight, it was obvious he'd been using her. And even though she hated acknowledging it, she had to in order to move forward.

And that was exactly how she felt now—as if she was moving forward.

Reuben was wearing a pale blue shirt and dark trousers. She could see the outline of his muscles and defined waist beneath the fine fabric of his shirt. He'd caught her gaze and was watching her weave her way through the crowd. And this time there was something different in his look. It had always been there—simmering just beneath the surface—but now his gaze was full of pure unadulterated lust.

Her stomach muscles clenched and she could feel her

heartbeat starting to quicken. His eyes seemed to caress her as she moved towards him, skimming the way the dress clung to her curves. She lifted her chin, enjoying his gaze.

His brown eyes met hers. Unspoken words passed between them. None of this had been a figment of her imagination. Reuben Tyler, sports agents and a man with an income she couldn't even comprehend, was interested in her, Lara Callaway, nanny.

In any other lifetime she wouldn't have believed it.

But she wasn't interested in Reuben Tyler, sports agent.

She was interested in Reuben Tyler, the guy with a sexy accent that made her knees tremble and who was happy to eat cake and drink coffee with her. The guy had even taken her shopping—she hadn't met a guy like that before.

And she didn't have a fancy job title. She didn't even have anywhere to stay right now. And he certainly wasn't after her for her money. Here's hoping he just liked her for herself.

Her footsteps faltered, even though the floor was smooth and even. Recognition dawned in her. She'd been annoyed by Reuben's questions before. But he'd asked her the things she should have asked herself. She loved working for Addison and Caleb. She loved looking after Tristan. But was it really the job of her dreams, or had she just temporarily landed on her feet?

A tiny little part of her had always wanted to go back to university. She had the qualifications—all she had to do was reapply and save some money. She could do that. She could. Her footsteps started again with renewed confidence. Part of her felt guilty. She'd have to tell Addison her plans, and Addison had been good to her. But in a few years Tristan would be grown and wouldn't need her any more. He was due to start school after the summer. Her role would be reduced. It made sense to plan ahead now.

Reuben's brow had creased as her steps had slowed but now she gave him another smile. A smile of assurance. A smile of determination.

The momentum of her footsteps carried her onward, even though her stomach was still clenching a little. Confidence was a wonderful thing. But it could also be a curse.

She knew the attraction between her and Reuben was off the charts. But what next? She didn't want to be the next girl he was photographed with in the press. She wasn't interested in a fling or short-term thing. She wanted to be good enough for Reuben on a permanent basis. Not just a temporary one.

And tonight that's what she intended to find out.

CHAPTER ELEVEN

REUBEN HAD LOST all interest in the football game the second he'd spotted Lara across the room. It was impossible—he knew it but it was almost as if he could spot her sparkling blue eyes from the doorway and kept fixed on them as she moved towards him.

He didn't want to miss a single moment. The dress was perfect, hugging her curves and giving more than a hint of what lay beneath.

He sucked in a breath as for a few seconds her footsteps faltered. But it was only temporary. She met his gaze again and took the final steps towards him, coming closer than he would ever have expected, placing her hands firmly on his chest.

'So, what about this dinner, then?'

It was so direct. Straight to the point. And every cell in his body loved that.

But there was still that tiny part of him that was holding back. He liked this woman so much that he didn't want to do anything to hurt her. The surge of hormones was overwhelming. And they all gave one clear, direct message. Those blue, unblinking eyes were staring straight into his soul. Asking the question *What is this?* all over again.

Was he really brave enough to answer?

Her eyes were bewitching. Pulling him in. Making him feel as if things were really out of his control. Their flirtation had been going on from that first direct hit over his head. From the second he'd had his first view of the giant pink teddy bear. But that teddy bear had morphed into a real-life siren.

A siren that he couldn't even have imagined. Couldn't even have dreamed of.

He licked his lips and she unconsciously mimicked his act. He bent a little lower—more for him than for her. Now he could suck in her scent—the smell of shampoo, floral perfume and soap. Delicious. Now he could brush his lips against her ear and push back her silky soft hair. 'We've got seven to choose from. Which would you like to try?'

She turned her head slightly and fixed him with her gaze. 'Surprise me.'

There was a rush of blood around his body and a roaring in his ears. There was no way he could last the night. It was inevitable. Things had been building to this point from the very first moment. Tonight they were heading straight into the eye of the storm—straight into the climax.

He crooked his elbow towards her. 'Well, Ms Callaway, let's see where the night takes us.'

She raised her eyebrows as she tucked her arm into his elbow. 'Let's see indeed.'

They finally decided on the French restaurant. It had a quiet ambience with candlelit tables and a view of the ocean, a pianist on a grand piano in the corner and waiters who seemed to move without making a sound.

The plates of succulent food appeared and disappeared like moves in a carefully choreographed dance. She hardly tasted a thing. All she could think about was the main event.

Reuben appeared much calmer than she was. He spent the evening specialising in small talk, asking about her job, her plans and if she'd heard anything from the agent in London trying to find her a flat.

She'd almost forgotten about that.

She stared down at the trio of desserts in front of her. Every one of them she loved. But her stomach was too busy doing flip-flops to eat. 'I'll need to email her back. I'll do it tomorrow. I'm sure she's found me somewhere.'

'Hasn't she already sent you an email with some rentals?'

Lara sighed. 'Yeah, but one was too far away, another way too expensive and the other one was a shared flat with three other people. I'm not sure about that one.'

He gave a wicked smile. 'Are you worried they'll complain about your snoring?'

'What?' She flung her napkin towards him. 'I do not snore.' Then she stopped to think for a second and leaned forward. How would she know? 'At least, I don't think I do. Do I?'

The thought of Reuben listening to her snoring for the last ten nights filled her with complete dread.

He laughed and tossed her napkin back. 'Of course you don't.' He winked. 'I would have woken you up if you did.'

She tilted her head to the side. 'You talk in your sleep, you know.'

His eyes widened. He actually looked shocked. 'What?'

She smiled. 'Yeah, you do. Quite a lot, actually. Sometimes you have full conversations as if you're really talking to someone.'

He shifted in his seat and she couldn't help but feel amused at Reuben looking a little sheepish. 'What do I say?'

She gave a wicked smile and lifted her wine glass. 'Lots of things you probably shouldn't.'

He shifted again. 'I'm not sure I like the sound of that.' There was a rasp in his voice. It sent tiny tremors down her spine. Her imagination was working overtime.

She looked at him carefully. She didn't want to do anything to spoil the chemistry between them—but it was time to get it out there.

'You mutter mainly. Sometimes about your mum and dad, sometimes about Caleb.'

It was as if he froze. His hand was midway to his glass and it just stopped.

'Oh.'

'Oh? Is that all I'm going to get?'

His eyes were fixed on the table. For the first time all night he wasn't looking at her. It didn't feel right. It didn't feel natural. Eventually he ran his hand through his hair with a sigh.

He lifted his brown eyes to meet hers. 'I might not have been entirely truthful about why Addison doesn't like me much.'

It was like a little cool breeze over her skin. She set down her wine glass. 'Tell me.'

He stared out of the window at the gorgeous view. 'Addison came in at the wrong moment. Caleb had just called me on my behaviour.'

'What kind of behaviour?'

'He knew my parents. He knew what they were like. I was being childish. He'd told me he loved Addison and was going to marry her and I told him that love didn't exist and he was wasting his time on some fantasy.'

She wasn't sure where this was going. 'And?'

He sighed again. 'And, then he told me to grow up. He told me every kind of relationship wasn't like my mum and dad's. The world was full of people who loved each other just as much as he loved Addison and not to judge their relationship by the warped one my parents had.'

She pressed her lips together. 'Tough words.'

He gave the slightest shake of his head. 'Not really. They were all true. But I lashed out—I punched him— just as Addison walked through the door.'

Her hand went up automatically her mouth. 'Oh, no.'

He gave a sorry kind of smile. 'Oh, yes. Bad boy through

and through. No wonder she doesn't like me. I think she can't believe Caleb and I are still friends ten years later.'

Lara shook her head. There was something about the way he'd said the words. 'You're not all bad,' she said quietly, as she reached across the table and squeezed his hand.

His brown eyes fixed on hers. She lifted up her other hand. 'Look what you've done. Look what you've done for me.' She gave him a little smile. 'You've broken my run of loser boyfriends.' She laughed. 'And that's been going for my entire life. That's quite a feat, you know.'

He turned her hand over and started to trace little circles in her palm. 'I'm sorry, Lara. You've no idea how much I like you. I've never told anyone about my parents before—I've never told anyone about my fight with Caleb before. But with you? It's just easy. It's just as if it's meant to happen.'

Their gazes connected again. It was like a little zing in the air.

It's meant to happen.

She took a deep breath. 'You've given me confidence again, Reuben. Confidence I haven't had since I was a fifteen-year-old girl. You've made me question myself. You've made me question my potential and whether I'm doing what I really want to. I needed that. I needed that *so* badly. So thank you.'

His fingers stopped tracing the circles. 'What happens now?'

She licked her lips. 'Now we do what we're supposed to.'

He signalled to the waiter that they were finished and stood up. It was kind of hard not to stare at the part of his body that was right in front of her. But he seemed to be reading her mind, because he caught her hand and pulled her close to him.

Close enough to get the full effect.

She gulped. There was no chance of misunderstanding.

One hand splayed across her back, the other stroked a finger down her cheek. 'Want to go see the show?'

She shook her head. 'I think we should make our own show,' she whispered.

Her heart was clamouring inside her chest. She was conscious of the fact that every time she inhaled her breasts brushed against him. Conscious of the fact his eyes were fixed entirely on hers.

A tiny little part of her brain was screaming, *If you wanted to capture the bad boy, you've got him.*

She ignored every red flag that tried to raise itself above the parapet. For the first time in the last few weeks she felt entirely in control.

She felt confident in herself and her actions.

She didn't expect this to go anywhere. She had no expectations except for the here and now. She'd never thought like that before. But if she put up walls around herself then when Reuben walked away she'd be protected.

She slid her hand around his waist and grabbed his bum. This power thing was intoxicating. 'Shall we?'

The walk to the cabin had never felt so short. When she fumbled with the card Reuben's hand closed over hers, his breath at the back of her neck.

His voice was low, throaty. 'Lara, are you sure about this?'

The door clicked open and she spun to face him.

He'd never looked more handsome. Those dark brown eyes were pulling her into a warm chocolate oblivion. She reached up and ran her fingers through his hair, tugging him towards her.

'I've never been surer.'

CHAPTER TWELVE

REUBEN WAS DRUNK. Drunk entirely on Lara Callaway. She was like an infectious disease. A drug. And at some point he would tell her how he actually felt.

Just not right now.

Right now he'd just watch her sleep and wonder how on earth to play things when she woke up.

Because he should say something—shouldn't he?

He should talk to her about her job. About finding somewhere to stay. He could offer that she come and stay with him—it's not like he didn't have the room.

But it was almost as if something was stopping his tongue from functioning. It was the weirdest thing in the world. Every time he tried to imagine himself in a different place from where he was now he just couldn't see it. Couldn't see himself as part of the partnership. Couldn't see himself in a loving, reciprocal relationship.

It was ridiculous. He was adult enough to know that he was capable of whatever he wanted to be. But there were still those ingrained memories from childhood—and even now his reluctance to visit his family home. His associations of family were different from other people's. He hadn't realised how much it had scarred him.

He winced at the thought. He wasn't the type of guy to admit that anything scarred him. In lots of ways he'd been lucky. He'd had a roof over his head, clothes on his back and parents who did seem to care—in some part—about him. They just didn't care about each other.

Lara sighed in her sleep and turned towards him, one hand tucked under the pillow, the other reaching out towards him.

Lara had always had this crazy idea that she wasn't good enough. But it wasn't her that wasn't good enough—it was him.

A horrible cold sensation swept his body. What if he turned out like his dad? What if after a few years all they did was fight? And what if they brought kids into the equation and exposed them to same relationship he'd witnessed between his mum and dad?

That really made him feel sick.

Just as all these thoughts jumbled around his head Lara's eyes flickered open, those perfect blue eyes the same shade as the Mediterranean Sea outside.

She gave a lazy smile. 'Hey,' she whispered.

'Hey,' he replied. But it didn't come out quite right. Hers was sexy and content. His was terse.

A frown creased her brow and she leaned her head on her hand. 'What's wrong with you?'

'There's nothing wrong with me. I'm just not so sure this was the best idea.' *Where had that come from?* Sometimes his brain and mouth were completely detached from one another.

Something flickered across her face as she sat up in the bed and pulled the sheet up over her naked body. It was too late. He'd hurt her already. 'Well, it's a bit too late for that.' Her voice was matter-of-fact then she gave her head a little shake as if she couldn't believe what she was hearing. 'What is this—the morning after the night before?'

He winced. That made him feel terrible. He got out of bed—trying to get a little distance—and pulled on his jeans. 'Don't you have regrets?' The words were out before he really thought about them.

She hesitated for the tiniest second. 'No, not really. I

didn't think you'd propose marriage the next day, but at the least I hoped we'd still be friends.'

She'd hesitated. It didn't matter that he was the person who'd started this. It didn't matter that all of these insecurities were his, not hers. Now the only thing he could focus on was the fact she'd hesitated for the tiniest second when he'd asked her if she had regrets.

Lara shook her head, her hair fanning out around her shoulders. 'What's the problem? We're both adults. Look at us. It was inevitable that this was going to happen. We've been dancing around each other for the last few weeks.'

'And now we're not.' His response was automatic.

She halted.

He hated himself. He could almost see the shutters close across her eyes. He'd been too abrupt. He wasn't good at this kind of thing. Which was probably why he never got himself into these situations. His whole objective this morning had been to make sure he didn't hurt Lara and he'd completely blown that out of the water. He couldn't have made more of a mess of this if he'd tried.

It was just the words. They were jumbling around in his head. He couldn't think straight. He couldn't say what he really wanted to say.

He couldn't tell her that he thought he'd fallen in love with her and wanted her to be around permanently.

She stood up, wrapping herself in the sheet, and crossed to stand directly under his nose. 'What is this, Reuben?'

He pulled a T-shirt over his head. 'What's what?' he snapped. He couldn't help it. She'd already called him on this before. He'd hoped if it ever happened again he would be better prepared. Have an answer at his disposal.

If she'd asked him last night during dinner he would have told her it could be exactly what they wanted it to be.

So why couldn't he do that now?

Why were all his defences in place and every cell in his body telling him to get out of there?

Lara's face was an open book. He could see her confusion. He could see her hurt. He could see the pain in her eyes that he had caused.

His hand reached up automatically to touch her face but her body jerked away from him.

This was why he shouldn't do this. This was why relationships didn't work for him.

'You haven't answered me.' Her voice was shaking.

He hated the way his insides were twisting. Part of him wanted to congratulate her on her persistent questioning and the determined angle of her jaw.

He looked into her eyes. *This* was where he should tell her that he loved her. *This* was where he should tell her he wanted to spend the rest of his life with her.

This was where he should tell her that he was just being stupid. He was letting childhood experiences colour his adult life. But the words just wouldn't come.

He hated himself. And from the look on Lara's face she hated him too.

She pressed her finger to his chest. 'Why can't you let anyone in? Are you so damaged from your childhood that you can't let yourself love anyone just a little—or even try?' She was shouting now, furious with him. 'I thought you were an adult. I thought you said you'd put all that behind you—cut the toxic people out of your life. You know what people who love each other look like—you've seen Addison and Caleb. You know what things can be like if you'll only give them a chance.'

He couldn't speak. He was frozen. He could see the fury on her face and hear all the hurt in her voice, but he just couldn't reach out. He just couldn't take that step.

'Get out of my cabin, Reuben,' she said quietly.

And in the worst example of bad boy ever, he picked up his jacket and left.

Lara couldn't breathe. It was as if her lungs couldn't pull in any air. It didn't matter that she was only dressed in a sheet. Her head felt fuzzy and her legs weak as she yanked open the door to the balcony.

The warm outside air hit her immediately. She wasn't sure if it was better or worse. She leaned over the balcony, trying to suck in deep breaths.

After a few minutes her heart stopped clamouring against her chest and her head started to clear.

Still wrapped in the sheet, she took a few steps back. A few people down on the dockside were already staring up at her. She leaned against one of the glass doors.

Nightmare. Absolute nightmare.

She'd gone from the perfect night to the worst morning possible.

But the thing that hurt most hadn't been the look of confusion in his eyes, or the fact he'd more or less rejected her this morning. It was how she felt inside.

That little glimmer of confidence that had been seeded inside her since she'd first met Reuben had bloomed and grown. It had made her look at herself, realise she was worthy and make her look at the decisions she made in this life.

She wouldn't let him take that away from her. Not now. Not when she'd just got it back.

She stepped back inside the suite and stared around. She knew exactly what she needed to do.

Money didn't matter any more. She could easily put a flight on her credit card.

For her, this dream cruise was over.

It was time to get back to reality and make the changes she wanted and deserved.

She *was* worthy. And now she believed it.

But first she would see the Colosseum.

CHAPTER THIRTEEN

REUBEN HAD NO idea what he was doing. He had no idea where he was going. He just kept walking. It was amazing how far you could actually walk on a cruise ship.

He needed to clear his head. Everything he needed to say to Lara was actually in there. But from the way his heart was currently squeezing in his chest he would be lucky if he could ever form words again.

He stopped and leaned over the deck railing, trying to breathe in some fresh air. The ship had docked in Civitavecchia for Rome. His heart sunk.

This should be a great day. Lara had raved about visiting Rome. She'd been so looking forward to touring the city and visiting the Colosseum—they'd already signed up for the trips. Another black mark against his name.

He had to sort this out. He had to. In his working life he never had problems speaking his mind and putting things straight.

It was only his personal life that was such a screw-up. Trouble was, he'd never met anyone like Lara before. He'd never considered a long-term relationship. He'd never had one.

He stepped back from the railing and started walking again. His brain was spinning the whole time, trying to formulate an answer to the question, *What is this?* At this point an answer would not be enough. What he really needed was an answer followed by a heartfelt apology and whatever it would take to persuade her to give him a chance.

He kept walking. And walking. And walking.

The corridors of the ships were like a maze. All similar, with no real sense of direction. Eventually he came upon a sign: 'Medical Centre'.

Doris. Of course. He took five minutes to check and see how she was doing.

'Where's Lara?' she enquired.

He waved his hand and tried to brush off the remark. 'She's fine. She's getting changed. I'm sure she'll come and see you later.'

Doris gave him a careful look. It was almost as if she were looking directly into his brain and not liking what she was seeing. 'Okay, then,' she said stiffly.

He left. He had to. He had too much else to think about.

If he didn't get a grip he would lose Lara completely. Someone else would get her—with her pink teddy-bear suit, quirky sense of humour and giant blue eyes. Someone else would get to wake up next to her every morning. Someone else would get to hear about how her day had gone and get to feel the touch of those lips against theirs.

What could he offer?

Lara wasn't interested in the money or the celebrity. Lara was interested in *him*.

Probably more than he was interested in himself.

What did he really have to offer her?

Could he say those all-important words and tell her that he loved her? Because he couldn't last night. And he couldn't this morning.

They'd stuck in his throat.

And Lara had challenged him. She'd asked him again what this was.

She wasn't stupid. She was trying to sort out things

for herself, as much as for him. She'd been hurt already. Didn't need to be hurt again.

He had to leave.

The thought came like a blinding flash. If he couldn't find the words then he wasn't worthy of the relationship.

He wasn't worthy of Lara.

Caleb had told him grow up. It was finally time.

This wasn't the fairy-tale dream cruise he'd thought it would be. It had exposed him to feelings and emotions he hadn't expected.

He'd never connected to another person the way he'd connected to Lara.

And the truth was—he just didn't know what came next.

And now he'd hurt her.

The same look that he'd seen in her eyes when she'd spoken about Josh was now there when she looked at him.

The irony of her thinking she'd got away from loser boyfriends made him cringe.

Turned out Reuben Tyler was the biggest loser of them all.

All relationships weren't like the one his parents had. He was old enough, and had seen enough of life, to know it. So why did he let it still hold him back? He pushed the thought from his mind.

His feet started walking. He could leave. He could leave right now and let her enjoy the last few days of the cruise without him.

That was for the best.

That was exactly what he should do.

His legs powered him towards the suite. His brain was spinning. How would be explain he was leaving?

The door of the suite was ajar. He pushed it wide open.

The whole room was in disarray. The drawers were open and coat hangers were on the floor and on the bed.

He looked in the corner for her case. Gone.

He opened the door to the bathroom. All her items that had littered the little shelf below the mirror and driven him crazy had vanished.

There wasn't a single trace of her left.

Lara Callaway had bested him once again.

CHAPTER FOURTEEN

'I'VE HAD IT with you. I've had it with you and your bad attitude. You've let your team down, let the fans down and you've let your family down. Finally, you need to worry about the fact you've let me down. I'm done with you. I won't represent someone who thinks it's okay to treat other people with such disrespect. The club has sacked you and I won't be finding you another. This is finished. Find another agent.'

Reuben put down the phone. The rage was bubbling just beneath the surface but he'd managed to contain it. Coming home to the story that his client had punched a toilet attendant, groped some woman in the street and reneged on a visit to a children's hospital because he 'couldn't be bothered' had been enough for him.

And it was like a huge weight off his shoulders.

His secretary motioned to him through the glass. He walked outside and she handed him a brown paper package. 'Special delivery arrived for you. Want me to open it?'

Something squeezed around his heart.

He knew exactly what this would be.

'No. It's fine. Thank you.'

He walked back through to his office in The Shard and stared down at the city below.

He couldn't explain how it had been since he'd got back. He'd just felt…empty.

And he knew exactly why.

A figure on the street caught his eye. A woman with

blonde hair, jeans and brown leather boots. It couldn't be, could it? She was striding down the street with confidence, nodding to people as they passed.

She looked up as she reached the end of the street and broke into a run. A kind of strangled sound came out of his throat as she leapt up into the arms of a tall guy, putting her legs around him and clinging around his neck.

It wasn't Lara. Of course it wasn't Lara.

But it could be.

The wave of emotions that swept over him took what little breath he had left.

Caleb had been so right. It was time to put the past behind him. It was time to start living again.

He'd been a fool. He should have just grabbed hold of her with both hands and told her he wanted to give this a shot. He should have told her that from that first look she'd wound her way into his heart and his brain.

He should have told her he could spend the rest of his life watching her sleep, with her blonde hair splayed around her and the sun kissing her skin.

He should have told her that he loved her.

He watched the couple beneath him start to kiss passionately and his heart twisted in his chest.

That's what he was missing out on.

That's what he could have.

He picked up the parcel from his desk. The time to tell her that he loved her was now.

He could only hope and pray that she'd listen.

Lara looked out of the window onto the London street. It had been raining solidly since she'd got back. Her phone had been permanently switched off and all the messages on the house phone had naturally been for Addison and Caleb.

Her mood felt as wet as the weather.

Addison had left her a message, saying they'd be back a few days later. There had been no explanation and Lara was a little curious. It wasn't like she'd anything else to do to fill her time.

She opened another window on the internet. Last night she'd listed all her fancy clothes to resell. When on earth would she get the chance to wear them again? But her finger had hovered over the 'sell' button for too long. She'd just been unable to press it. She'd never owned clothes like that before and likely wouldn't again. She might keep them for an extra few weeks.

All the other windows opened were wishful thinking. On a whim last night she'd pulled up the prospectus for the university she'd wanted to attend. The entrance requirements hadn't changed. She could still make the cut.

Then she pulled up another—and another. Degrees had changed in the last few years. She could study English and French, English and German, English and History, English and Philosophy, even English and Creative Writing or English and Media. The list was endless. She'd spent a long time considering the English and Egyptology degree. How interesting would that be?

All she had to do was fill out the form. It was silly. As a mature student her application would be looked at differently. She didn't need to start at the beginning of the academic year. She would be able to start midterm if she wanted.

Her fingers hovered above the keyboard again. The key question was—did she?

She had confidence now. Confidence that Reuben had helped instil in her. She bit her lip and selected the university she'd always dreamed of and the degree that looked best. After half an hour she pressed 'send'. Done.

A noise at the door startled her. She stood up swiftly and strode over to the door. A delivery guy handed her a thick envelope and asked her to sign for it. She did it without even thinking—she signed for parcels for Addison and Caleb all the time.

But this one was different. This one was addressed to her.

She tore open the envelope, tipped it up and a data stick fell into her hand.

What?

She peered inside the envelope again There was a small sticky note. She pulled it out. *Watch me.* That was all it said.

She frowned and walked back to her laptop. Her hand hesitated next to the port. What if this was one of those things with a funny virus—one that would read her bank accounts and empty them?

She gave a rueful smile. Good luck with that, then. She might have got there first.

She stuck the stick in and waited until a message appeared on the screen, asking her what to do next. It only took a few seconds to get it to play.

A video screen appeared in front of her.

She blinked. Reuben Tyler. No way. What in the world…?

He held up a few pieces of white card with black writing, one after the other.

Her hand covered her mouth. She knew exactly what he was doing. He was imitating one of the films they'd watched together.

The words appeared quickly.

You might have guessed…
I'm not too good at this stuff…
You might even say…

I'm the worst in the world.
Words don't come easy to me...
And I'm afraid the ones that I do say...
Will be the wrong ones...
So I decided...
To get by...
With a little help from my friends.

She smiled at the song reference as he threw the last card away.

A few seconds later someone else sat down in front of the camera. It was a face she recognised instantly. Red Lennox, the baseball player Reuben represented.

He held one card in front of him.

What are we?

His trademark smile reached from side of his face to the other. It was clear he was highly amused by this. Her ears were flooded with his thick Texas accent.

'What are we? It's a good question—particularly for a man who is used to having all the answers. But it seems that he struggled with this one. So he asked for some help.'

Red held up a little piece of paper and held it front of him. He leaned towards the screen.

'Lara Callaway, I can't wait to meet you. It seems you're the one that got away. The one that he made a big mistake with.' His hands drew a wide circle in the air. 'Massive.' He winked at the camera. 'But it seems you are always on my mind.'

Red frowned at the card and glanced back at the camera.

'Should I be singing here?' He shook his head. 'I'm not sure. Anyway, it seems that Reuben wants to apologise, he wants to tell you that he knows exactly what you are.'

He leaned into the camera one more time and gave her a cheeky wink.

The camera picture faded out and in again. It was a different room. A different person sat down in the front of the camera.

Lara sucked in a breath. The tennis player Craig Robertson. He'd won Wimbledon twice. He was holding the white card too.

What are we?

Craig shook his head and shrugged his shoulders. 'I can't believe the guy who helped me propose to my girlfriend has made such a mess of things for himself. But here I am anyway. Anything to help a friend.'

He gave a smile.

'Love is a strange thing. I know. You don't realise it until it hits you over the head—or, in my case, throws you into a strange pool in France.'

He held up his hands.

'And then, when you do realise it's love, you're scared. Scared the other person won't feel the same way, scared you'll be out there on a limb. It can be hard to put it out there.' He winked at the camera too. 'But apparently some of us have a better gift of the blarney than others.'

Lara had stopped breathing. *Love.* These people were talking about love.

The tennis player tossed the card over his shoulder. 'Anyway, the point is, Reuben Tyler knows exactly what you are.'

The screen faded again. Another one?

Oh, yes. The billionaire footballer with the looks that had sold everyone in the world a bottle of aftershave. Dylan Bates. He had a card too.

What are we?

She let out her breath in one huge gasp. How on earth had Reuben managed this?

Dylan smiled. He was known across the planet as one of the nicest guys ever.

'It seems Reuben Tyler has just let the love of his life slip through his fingers because he couldn't find the right words. It's not that he didn't know them—he did. He just couldn't bring himself to say them. And now he feels like a total idiot.'

There was a huge twinkle in Dylan Bates's eyes. He leaned forward.

'I've waited a long time to see Reuben slayed by the love god, and it seems that it's finally happened. Lara Callaway, come and stay with me and my family in Los Angeles.' He tapped the side of his nose. 'I can give you lots of stories from years ago that you'll be able to use as blackmail material for years.'

He sat back.

'In the meantime, give him a chance. Everyone deserves a chance. Particularly this guy.' He held up his hands. 'What are we? You can bet Reuben Tyler knows.'

The screen faded to black.

Lara looked over her shoulder. It was almost as if she expected him to be standing there. That was it. Nothing else.

She looked back at the screen. Surely he would appear next and say something—anything?

But, no, the screen remained blank. She didn't know whether to laugh or cry.

For some reason her feet carried her to the door. She had no idea what she expected. Maybe the delivery guy would still be there with some other kind of message?

She yanked the door open and went to step outside. But her foot stopped midway. The step was blocked.

By a familiar shape dressed in a leather jacket and jeans. Beside him was a huge cake box. His head turned at the noise of the door opening.

Every little hair on her body stood on end, prickling her skin. Her breath caught in her throat. She left the door open and thudded down on the step next to him.

This was the oddest apology she'd ever had.

'Hey,' she said.

'Hey,' he replied. He gestured towards the box. 'I brought you a present.'

She gave a little nod and lifted the lid on the box. It was biggest strawberry cassata cake she'd ever seen. She tried not to smile. There was a spoon right next to it. She picked it up and dug right into the middle of the cake, pretending not to notice his eyebrows rising, and lifted a huge spoonful into her mouth. It was the real thing. She could almost hear the noise of the Piazza del Miracoli around her. She swallowed and waited a few seconds. It would take more than a cake to win her round. 'That was some video. Were you trying to tell me something?'

He threw back his head and laughed. 'You're not going to make this easy, are you?'

She gave a little smile. 'I think I'm going to make it as hard as possible.'

He shook his head. 'Call it like you see it. That's why I love you, Lara Callaway.'

Now she really couldn't speak.

'You what?' It was more of a squeak than anything else.

He turned on the step towards her, sucked in a breath and blew it out slowly through his lips. When his brown eyes fixed on hers she thought she would melt. 'It's kind of hard when you don't know what it is. It means when it hits you in the face like a wrecking ball you don't actually know what's happened.' The lilt in his accent sent shivers down her spine. It must get stronger the more emotional he was feeling.

She could see from his face how much he was struggling with all this. The easiest thing in the world would be to reach out and touch him. Run her fingers through his dark hair, feel his stubble under the palm of her hand.

But he still hadn't answered the question. And she really needed to hear him say it out loud.

'So, what happened, Reuben? What are we? I seem to have half the planet telling me that you know.'

He gave a nod and looked a bit rueful. 'I might have been a bit bad-tempered for a few days and some of my clients got together to bang my head on a brick wall.' He held up his hands. 'When I told them how much of a mess I'd made of things they were only too happy to tell me what they thought. I wasn't sure if you'd speak to me so I decided to ask them to help me out.'

'I think I just got the equivalent of a million-pound video clip.'

He sighed. 'I think it might have been a bit more.' His hand reached over slowly towards hers. 'I'm sorry, Lara. I'm sorry I didn't tell you exactly how I feel. I'm sorry I didn't tell you outside the casino in Monte Carlo that I loved you and thought you were the most beautiful woman that I'd ever seen.'

Tears prickled in the backs of her eyes. Finally, they were getting somewhere.

She lifted her gaze to meet his. 'Love can be a beautiful thing, Reuben. If you'll let it in.'

She let her words hang in the air between them. There was no need to say more. He knew exactly what she meant. He fumbled behind his back and pulled out a brown paper package.

It wasn't the most prestigious gift she'd ever seen. But it

charmed with its simplicity. The wrapping was uneven—
it seemed that Reuben had done this himself.

His hand closed over hers. 'I listened to what you said
to me. I've had a few days to think about it.' He handed
her the package.

She turned it over in her hands and released one of the
edges, sliding her hand inside to pull out the gift.

It wasn't what she'd expected. And part of her heart
skipped a few beats as the smile spread slowly across her
face. It was the most perfect, personal gift in the world.

'*Alice in Wonderland*! You found it. How did you do
that? It's exactly the same as the one I had when I was
a kid.'

His brown eyes fixed on hers as he smiled. 'I worked
out what year you were born and what edition you were
likely to have had.' He leaned forward and whispered into
her ear. 'I'll let you into a secret. I have another three in
case that was the wrong one.'

She ran her hand over the pale blue cover of the book.
'No. This is definitely the right one. It's perfect. Thank
you.'

He hesitated then pointed at the book. 'Open it.'

She took a deep breath and opened the hardback cover.
A silver key on a red ribbon was sitting on the first page.

'You told me I had to let people in. And I think you
were right.' He held up the key, 'So, this is how I start.
I'd like to let you in. I'd like to give us a chance. And this
is my way. A key to my house and a key to my heart.' He
gave a wary little smile that warmed her heart.

He was nervous. He was *really* nervous about this.
And this was what she loved. It didn't matter about his
bad-boy reputation. She knew the real Reuben Tyler. Not
the guy who was the hotshot agent. Not the guy who had
lots of money.

She knew the guy who'd practically had to bring himself up. The guy who'd had no real example of what love was. She knew the truly laid-bare Reuben Tyler—that was the guy she loved.

The key was dangling in the air. She reached out with an open palm and held it underneath. She had to push him just a little bit further. 'So, what does this mean, Reuben? What are we?'

It was the million-dollar question. The thing she really needed him to embrace.

She heard him suck in a breath. 'We're whatever we want to be, Lara.'

She still hadn't taken the key. She really wanted to just swoop in and grab it. But a little part of her heart needed a little more. She knew this was an enormous step for Reuben, but she didn't just want a little part of him—she wanted the whole thing. The real deal.

She tried her best to stop her voice from wobbling. 'And what do you want us to be?'

He turned to face her, dropping the key in the palm of her hand and putting both his hands on her face. 'I want us to be together. I want you to be the person I see first thing every day. I want you to be the person to tell me when I'm being cranky. I want you to be the person I share amazing sunrises and sunsets with all around the world. I want to know when I get off a plane I have the girl who's captured my heart to talk to, no matter where I am. I want to look forward to coming home to you. I want to feel as if I'm coming home because I've got a reason to come home. I've found the person I want to love for the rest of my life.' He stopped for a second, and she could tell he was trying to keep himself in check. His voice was beginning to waver.

Tears brimmed in her eyes. She didn't doubt that this was the most emotionally open Reuben had ever been.

And it was with her. Because he loved her—just like she loved him.

She reached up and covered one of his hands with hers. 'I have too.' She gave him a heartfelt smile. 'But we might have a few issues.'

A frown creased his brow. 'Why?'

She ran her fingers down the outside of his palm. 'Because you think you're getting a girl with a job as a nanny.'

She saw the little light of recognition flicker in his eyes. A smile hinted at his lips. 'What am I actually getting?'

She couldn't help her smile. 'You're getting the world's lousiest student. I'm going to have to learn a whole heap of new skills. And for that I'm going to need a guy who is patient, understanding and who can put up with take-aways, books spread everywhere, and lots of moans and groans at exam times.'

He pulled her into his arms. 'You've applied?'

She nodded. 'I've applied.'

His lips hovered next to hers. 'Well, I guess we've got that in common. I'm applying too. For a job that I've no idea if I'll be any good at—but I want to spend the rest of my life finding out.' He ran a finger down her cheek and stared into her eyes. She'd never loved him more. 'But I haven't found out yet if my application has been accepted. Thing is, I think the panel pretty's tough.' His lips brushed against hers.

She tried to respond instantly but he held himself just a few millimetres away, teasing her. 'When do you think I'll find out?'

She ran her hand down his chest. 'Oh, I think you can find out almost immediately. There's just one tiny little thing.'

'What's that?'

'Do I have to share the cake?'

Reuben threw back his head and laughed then cap-

tured her mouth with his. And as her fist closed around
the shiny key in her palm she knew.

She knew this was the man she'd spend the rest of her
life loving and she couldn't wait to start.

* * * * *

MORE THAN
HE EXPECTED

ANDREA LAURENCE

To Mavens Linda Howard and Linda Winstead Jones—

You are more than mentors. More than friends.
You believe in me, push me and give invaluable advice
for both career and life. I only hope that one day I can
be as generous of knowledge and spirit as you are.

And to Maven Beverly Barton —
I miss your laugh. I wish I could've shared this
experience with you, but I like to think that wherever
you are…you're proud of what I've accomplished.

Prologue

Saturday, October 20
The Wedding Reception of Will and Adrienne Taylor

It was terribly cliché for the best man to seduce the maid of honor, but damn, that was one sexy woman.

Alex had no intention of using his best friend's wedding as an opportunity to pick up women. Usually, weddings were filled with misty-eyed romantics wanting more than Alex was willing to offer. He'd planned only to wear the tux and wave goodbye as another of his friends crossed over to the dark side.

But Gwen Wright had thrown a petite, slinky wrench into his plans the minute she had strolled into the welcome breakfast. She'd been wearing a tight brown skirt and beige blouse that made her dark brown eyes pop against peaches-and-cream skin. She'd cast a quick glance at him that morning, appraising him with a small smile curving her peach lips. When their eyes met, the light of mischievousness there had intrigued him.

Will had introduced them a few minutes later, and Alex was pleased to discover she was the maid of honor and his partner in crime for the big day. He'd politely taken her hand, marveling at how soft her skin felt against his. He'd wanted to spend more time talking to her, but he didn't get the chance. She was swept into the wedding chaos and the moment passed.

He hadn't had another chance to really talk to her, much less touch her, but the anticipation was building with each hour that ticked by. He tried to focus on Will and what his job as best man entailed, since that evening had been dedicated to bachelor activities with the guys.

But tonight was a different matter. When he'd stood at the rose-covered archway beside Will and watched Gwen come toward him in that clingy pink gown, he thought he might not be able to wait much longer. As he'd escorted her down the aisle at the end of the ceremony, he'd pulled her aside and whispered, "Later," into her ear. The blush of her cheeks let him know the brief message had come across loud and clear.

And later it would be. Later than he'd planned, actually. Gwen was running the show like a seasoned professional. The first opportunity he had to talk to her was during their obligatory dance, but despite holding her in his arms, he could tell she was a million miles away—making lists, planning the cake cutting… She was a woman on a mission, and he hadn't made an inch of real progress in his pursuit of her.

Now the bride and groom had departed and the crowd had started to thin. They were quickly closing in on a "now or never" moment. From the other side of the room, he watched her direct the few men charged with taking the wedding gifts back to the apartment. Every gesture, every smile intrigued him. Alex wished he could figure out what it was about Gwen that drew him to her. The impact of her presence had been direct and immediate. If she had some kind of sexual kryptonite that weakened him, he wanted to know it.

And there must be. She'd had his undivided attention for a good part of the last thirty-six hours, and she didn't even know it. There was no argument that she was beautiful. He loved the way her curly ash-blond hair framed her heart-shaped face and the dark eyes that watched him beneath full lashes. Her petite frame was highlighted by her bridesmaid gown, showing off those shapely calves.

But there was something else about her. Something that drew him in and wouldn't let him look away. And he was determined to find out what it was.

"It's later." Gwen had been sitting for less than forty-five seconds when she heard a man's voice over her shoulder. Forty-five seconds were not nearly enough to make up for the hours she'd spent on her feet.

She was the maid of honor. It was her job to scurry about and ensure everything was on track. But she was tired. Dog tired. Regardless of what the man wanted from her, he could forget it. Even dancing with Prince Harry had less appeal than kicking off her shoes and face-planting in her bed right now.

Then she looked up and found herself smack-dab in the laser sights of none other than the best man, Alex Stanton. He was looking extraordinarily handsome tonight in his Armani tuxedo, his golden hair tamed for the special occasion. The hazel-eyed bachelor had been charming and friendly toward her for the last few days, but like Gwen, he'd been busy with wedding responsibilities of his own.

She'd tried to ignore the tingle of electricity she'd felt dance across her skin when he'd taken her arm to walk down the aisle. But then, in a brief moment alone, he'd leaned close to her ear and whispered the word "later." The single utterance was laced with such heavy meaning that it was hard to breathe for a moment. How he'd managed to roll *"I want you," "I'm going to rock your world tonight,"* and *"I hope you're prepared"* into a single word, she'd never know. He'd followed the promise with a sly smile and wink before he'd pulled away and embraced the newlyweds.

"Miss Wright, may I have this dance?"

Gwen wasn't sure if she had the strength to make it through another dance with Alex. During their first turn on the dance floor, the electric feeling had intensified; this pull that urged her to press inappropriately close to him while they swayed. She'd spent the song thinking of cheesy knock-knock jokes to distract herself. She didn't want Alex to think she was throwing herself at him. Regardless of what she'd read into his words earlier, he was dancing with her because he had to. You dance with your cousin if that's who you're paired up with in the wedding party.

But several times over the last few hours, she had felt the prickle of awareness on the nape of her neck and caught Alex watching her from across the room. There was an unabashed appreciation in his eyes as he had looked her over, making a warm flush rise to her cheeks. But instead of approaching her, he would flash his trademark smile and disappear into the crowd like a circling shark.

The reception was virtually over now. She had pretty

much given up on anything but a quiet cab ride back to her apartment, since by her estimation, "later" had come and gone a long time ago.

And yet here he was asking her to dance. His heated glance sent a shiver down her spine, a tingle of excitement overriding the pain in her toes and sending her heart racing.

Most men did not jump-start a reaction in her like this, but Alex was not most men. To say the millionaire real estate developer was out of her league was an understatement. But he didn't seem to notice.

As he held his hand out to her, there was no denying what he was offering. He wanted to fulfill his earlier promise and then some. Alex was interested in more than a dance, and by taking his hand, she was agreeing to it all. The building ache of need low in her belly and the suddenly tight press of her breasts against the confines of her fitted gown told her she was anxious to accept his offer.

Gwen looked up at her suitor. He was handsome, charming, rich…. When would she ever have another opportunity like this? She'd had her share of lovers over the years, but few could hold a candle to Alex. His reputation set tongues wagging, and she'd be lying if she'd said she didn't want some firsthand experience. She deserved a night of fun with a man who knew how to have a good time. She'd been working so hard at the hospital and helping Adrienne. Next year would be just as hectic and, if all went as planned, quite lonely. A no-strings liaison with the playboy might be just what she needed.

One last drink before rehab, so to speak.

Her eyes locked on his, her answer clear as she reached out to offer him her hand. With a triumphant smile, he eased her from her seat and swung her gently around to face him on the seamless, white dance floor.

Without hesitation, Alex wrapped his arm around Gwen's waist and pressed her tight against him. His bare palm splayed across her lower back, the heat of his touch only intensifying the pulsating desire stirring just under the surface.

She was surprised by her sudden, physical reaction to his touch. It was like a floodgate had opened. She had to suck in a ragged breath to cover the shudder that accompanied the rush of adrenaline through her veins. The spicy scent of Alex's cologne swirled in her head, mixing with the soft fragrance of roses and candle wax and making her almost light-headed. Gwen could only cling to his shoulders as they rocked back and forth to the slow, seductive music.

They stilled on the floor as the music continued but didn't pull away from one another. Instead, Alex leaned down and kissed her. It started off soft but quickly intensified once he got a taste—his tongue invading her, his mouth and hands demanding more. And she gave it to him. Gwen arched her back to press her soft body against his hard contours. He growled low in his throat, the vibration rumbling through his chest and teasing the firm peaks of her aching nipples.

Finally, the last few notes of music silenced, breaking the seductive spell that cocooned them from the surrounding world. But Alex didn't let go, as she had expected. He looked down at her, the gold flecks in his eyes almost glittering with arousal. His jaw was tense, his shoulders rising and falling with his own rapid breathing.

It was time to leave. The *how*s and *where*s and *what*s were still up in the air, but they couldn't stay on the dance floor forever. "I need to get my things out of the bridal room," she said, her voice breathy.

Alex nodded, releasing her from his embrace, and Gwen headed toward the dark hallway at the back of the boathouse.

"Keep it together, girl," she whispered to herself as she turned the knob and entered the small space. Set up for brides, the room had a vanity and mirror, a chaise lounge, a wardrobe for hanging clothes and its own bathroom. They had cleared out all of Adrienne's things earlier, but Gwen still had a few items scattered around.

She quickly checked her hair and makeup in the mirror. Her hands trembled as she grabbed her compact and mascara, stuffing them into her purse. She wasn't sure if it was nerves or arousal rattling her composure.

Gwen was reaching for her hairbrush when she heard the soft click of the door closing, then locking, behind her. She didn't turn. She only needed to look up to see Alex's reflection in the vanity's mirror, his back pressed against the door as he watched her with passion blazing in his eyes.

The *where* had apparently been decided. And she was glad.

One

Eight Months Later

"I'm almost there," Alex said. "Fashionably late, as always."

The voice of his best friend, Will Taylor, sounded through the Bluetooth-enabled sound system of his Corvette. "I'm not really worried. Just wanted to make sure you remembered how to get here."

"I'm making the last turn now," Alex lied. He was at least another fifteen minutes from the house in Sag Harbor, but it would soothe his friend's concerns. This was supposed to be a vacation. The Fourth of July was one of those laid-back holidays with no obligations. There were no schedules, so he couldn't possibly be late. "Is everyone else already there?" he asked.

"Yes."

Alex hesitated before asking one last question. "Did

ANDREA LAURENCE 15

Gwen end up bringing someone with her?" It was a
dangerous question to ask, but he had to know. He'd re-
arranged his entire schedule to come out here because
she would be there.

"No, she came alone. She rode up with us this morning."

Excellent, Alex thought, although he didn't speak
the word aloud. As far as he could tell, no one, including Will and Adrienne, knew about what had happened
between him and Gwen last fall. So of course they
wouldn't understand his interest in seeing her again.
Or his burning desire to have her in his bed every night
for the next five days of this trip.

"So what does that make? Ten of us?" Alex tried
not to sound like he was fishing. "That's a nice, round
number. I'm glad she was able to take the time off. I
haven't seen her since the wedding, but I figured Adrienne would have her up for the holiday."

Will made a thoughtful sound but didn't elaborate.
"We'll see you shortly then."

"Bye," Alex said, pressing the button on his steering
wheel to terminate the call. Easing back into the soft
leather seat, he gripped the wheel tightly and pressed
his foot down on the pedal to accelerate.

Gwen would be with them in the Hamptons this
week. Alone.

He'd been hopeful, but he hadn't let himself ask until
now. The two weeks they'd spent together after Adrienne and Will's wedding had been incredible. She was
the smartest, funniest, sexiest woman he'd ever been
with. It had been quite the pleasant surprise to find such
an intriguing woman in such a small package. But to
underestimate the spark inside that petite frame was a
serious mistake. She was a firecracker in bed and out.

Their two weeks together had flown by, and before he knew it, he'd had to leave for New Orleans. Like all his relationships, it was short and without strings. Just a fun, sexy fling. But unlike most of the women he dated, Gwen hadn't wanted any more than that. She didn't eye his bank account or bare ring finger with burning ambition. She was just in it for a good time. He got the feeling she was busy, just as he was, and didn't want the complication of something serious. It was perfect.

So perfect he was hoping she'd be up for another round.

Apparently their short time together had not been enough for Alex to get his fill of Gwen. He typically grew bored with a woman after a few dates. If they pushed for more, he pushed the end button on his cell phone. He was always open about it, but most women seemed to think they might be the one to tame him. None had come close.

At best, Gwen had managed to stay on his mind amid the distractions. For the last seven months, Alex had been working on a new real estate development project in New Orleans that had sucked up a lot of his free time. Despite everything, thoughts of her would occasionally sneak into his brain while he was sitting in a boring meeting or lying in his bed at night. She'd even slipped into his thoughts as he'd trolled Bourbon Street. After their time together, it seemed that none of the women he met, especially in a setting like that, were up to par. Night after night he'd slink back to his hotel, alone.

Alex just couldn't shake the memory of Gwen. The soft caress of her hands across his stomach, the scent of her lavender shampoo, the sharp sass of her wit wrapped in the soft contrast of the Tennessee accent that came out when she was flustered...

Another week together ought to get her out of his system. Then he could get back on the prowl and reaffirm his reputation as a notorious bachelor.

Now that his project had gotten rolling, he could take a step back and let Tabitha and his management team run the show. When he and his friend Wade had started their first real estate development business, they'd been hands-on, start to finish. Now that he'd spun off and had the money to hire talented staff, he could do what he wanted and keep from getting bogged down in the details. He was looking forward to more time to play than he'd had in a long time. A few days in the Hamptons for the Fourth of July holiday was a great way to kick it off.

Alex turned onto the road that would lead to Will and Adrienne's waterfront vacation estate. Adrienne had concluded the family's ten-thousand-square-foot summerhouse was far too large for just the two of them and decided to make an event out of it. About eight other people would be joining them this week for some relaxation and fun.

At first, he hadn't planned to come, but when he realized Gwen would be there, too, he'd changed his mind. Although they'd agreed not to contact each other, there was a part of him that wished she had texted him every now and then. He missed the sound of her laughter and her bright smile. A few days with her could scratch that itch.

What he hadn't known until now was whether Gwen was bringing someone with her. He was hoping she would be up for Fling 2.0, but he couldn't be sure. If she'd shown up with another man, this would have been a long, boring week of clambakes, pool parties and cold beds.

A small, worn wooden sign marked the circular

driveway to the house. Alex slowed his Corvette and turned in, pulling behind a Range Rover and a silver Mercedes convertible.

He popped his fist against the horn to announce his arrival and climbed out of the car. His khakis and polo shirt had been a touch too warm in the city, but near the water there was a nice breeze making it cooler and much less humid. Perfect for being outside.

"Alex!" Adrienne called out from the front porch. "Will, Alex is here."

She started down the steps to greet him, and Alex noticed that his best friend's bride was looking as lovely as ever. She wore a pair of denim shorts with a light green sleeveless blouse tucked in, and her dark hair was pulled into a ponytail, her complexion a bit pink from the sun. To see her now, you'd never know she'd once survived a plane crash and undergone multiple reconstructive surgeries.

As Adrienne held out her arms to hug him, only the thin, white line of a scar up her left forearm remained. Alex pulled her into his embrace and gave her a tight squeeze. He'd been so busy lately he really hadn't seen much of them, either. In his business, it was feast or famine. Either he was working almost nonstop for months at a time, or he was home, freewheeling while his manager, Tabitha, handled the rest. The project in New Orleans was a big one and sucked up more of his time than he had expected.

"Do you need help with your bags?" she asked. "Will is out back fighting with the new grill."

The thought of Will grilling brought a smile to Alex's face. They'd likely starve or call in a caterer before the trip was over. "Nope," he said, pulling a duffel bag from the passenger's seat. "This is all I have."

"I'll show you to your room, then."

Alex followed Adrienne and her flip-flops into the house and up the grand, circular staircase that wrapped around the living room. They traveled down a long, white hallway with alternating doorways and artwork on each side.

"Here it is," she said, opening the door and waving him inside.

Alex went in and tossed his bag down on the queen-size sleigh bed that dominated the room. The bed was covered in an intricately designed quilt and large, fluffy pillows. The light oak wood of the bed matched the tall dresser and bedside stand. There was a flat-screen television, an overstuffed chair and ottoman, and a ceiling fan turning gently to keep air circulating. Honestly, it was far nicer than the hotel room he'd been living in the last few months in New Orleans, and he'd paid quite a bit for the privilege.

"You have your own bathroom," Adrienne said, gesturing toward a door on the far wall.

"Great. Where is everyone else staying?" Alex wanted to know exactly how far he might have to go in his underwear to get back from Gwen's room before everyone woke up. If he was lucky, it was her door he could see across the way.

"Emma, Peter and Helena are staying down the hall. Sabine, Jack and Wade are in those rooms across from you. Will and I have the suite downstairs, and Gwen's room is just off the kitchen."

Damn. She was about as far from his room as logistically possible. Just great. That would make sneaking around quite a bit more difficult. Alex tried not to frown. He didn't need Adrienne asking questions.

"Looks like I have everything I need, then."

"Great. I'll let you get settled, and we'll see you downstairs."

Adrienne slipped out of the room, leaving him alone. He heard the dull slap of her footsteps down the wooden staircase, then pulled back the curtains and watched for her to step out onto the patio. He could see Will out there, hovering over the stainless steel grill that was built into the L-shaped outdoor kitchen they'd added since his last visit. Adrienne kissed him on the cheek and assisted him in investigating the mysteries of the new cooktop.

With the coast clear, he unzipped his bag and pulled out a bottle of wine and a bundle of crimson roses he'd picked up for Gwen on his way out of town. His father had always taught him that a gift was never a bad way to start off on the right foot, especially with women. Alex would've gotten her some jewelry, but the last time he'd tried, she'd pretty much laughed in his face. To avoid a repeat, he'd opted for something a little more low-key. With Gwen, he'd learned he had to strike a balance between thoughtful, nice and too expensive.

Hiding them behind his back, he headed downstairs in search of Gwen's room. He'd stayed in that bedroom a few years back at another summertime Taylor gathering, so now he easily found it near the laundry room and kitchen, tucked away in a remote corner. At one time, it had been the maid's quarters.

The door was halfway open. From his vantage point, he could see an open suitcase lying on the bed. Alex approached the entry and poked his head around the corner. Gwen was putting clothes away in her dresser.

Her back was to him, so he took a moment to admire her. A strapless cotton sundress flowed in bright colors to her ankles and bare feet. Her curly, ash-blond hair was pulled up in a clip that left soft tendrils at her bare neck. He was suddenly filled with the undeniable urge to kiss her there.

Alex slipped silently into the room, creeping across the plush rug to come up behind her.

"Hello again, gorgeous," he said, wrapping his arms around her to display the wine and roses and planting a warm kiss at the apex of her neck and shoulder. "These are for you." He felt her tremble slightly at his touch, then stiffen beneath his hands.

She didn't turn to him or take the gifts. Instead, a soft, hesitant voice politely replied, "Hello, Alex."

A feeling of unease nagged at Alex's brain and threatened to override the longing building in his gut. This wasn't the welcome he'd expected from her at all. He'd anticipated a smile, a hug, maybe an enthusiastic "Hello, sugar"…or at the very least, a thank-you for the flowers. Perhaps he had miscalculated. Her less than enthusiastic greeting made him wonder if she was upset with him. Had she expected him to call even though they'd agreed not to? At the time, she'd seemed to understand what they had together, but she wouldn't be the first woman to be disappointed or upset when the relationship ended as planned.

She finally took the roses and the wine, setting them on top of the dresser without really looking at them, her back still facing him. Note to self—Gwen wasn't a fan of expensive jewelry, roses or red wine. What *did* she like?

"How have you been?" she asked. Her voice sounded more normal now, less timid. Perhaps he'd just startled her.

"Busy," he said, his free hands now planting at her waist. She didn't pull away, but she didn't lean back against him, either. The flowers hadn't done their magic, but he knew just how to thaw out a woman's cold reception. The feel of his arousal pressed against her back would certainly soothe her pride and let her know how badly she'd been missed. "You?" he asked, letting his palms glide around to her stomach to pull her reluctant body into him.

At least, that was the idea. As his hands ran over a soft, rounded belly instead of the flat, firm one he remembered, Alex paused.

The realization washed over him like a tidal wave. The breath was knocked from his lungs and his muscles seized, allowing him to neither pull away nor spin her around to see the truth with his own two eyes.

"Busy," she whispered, repeating his words. "And as you may have noticed, pregnant."

The hands on Gwen's rounded stomach had turned from a gentle caress to a grip of immovable stone in an instant. The pressing of his fingertips into her belly were almost painful in their intensity. She put her hands over his and pried them away so she could turn around and finally face him.

Gwen hadn't been sure how she would feel seeing Alex again. The boyishly handsome face was just as she remembered it, sending her heart racing unexpectedly in her chest. Her fingers itched to run through his messy, blond hair. Her lips ached to leave a trail of kisses along the faint stubble of his jaw. In an instant, it was as if the last few months apart had never happened.

But at the same time, Gwen wondered if coming here had been a mistake.

The golden-hazel eyes that had once sparkled with mischievous passion were now wide with unexpressed emotions and burrowing into her stomach. Granted, it was hard to ignore. To say she'd blossomed in the last month was an understatement. She'd gone from a small pooch of a belly to full-blown second trimester almost overnight.

But it wasn't the surprise on Alex's face that concerned her. She expected that. It was the red blotches spreading across his skin and the hard, angry line of his jaw. He was always so laid-back and carefree. She'd never seen him upset, but she supposed when you had enough money, you could fix any problem. Now his personality had taken a one-eighty swing, and Gwen wasn't even certain he'd taken a breath for the last two minutes.

"Breathe, honey, before you pass right out."

His gaze darted to meet hers, the intensity of it making her chest tight. She wanted to squirm and move away from him, but she stood her ground. She hadn't done anything wrong. Why should she run?

"Breathe?" he said at last. "You show up here pregnant without saying a word to me about it and tell me to breathe? Were you saving the news for my birthday or something?"

"It's none of your business what I do. We aren't an item. Why would I…?" Gwen started to argue, then stopped, realizing her mistake. She'd never thought for a minute that Alex would think this child was his. She was only five months along, but the furious set of his jaw indicated he wasn't familiar enough with a female gestational cycle to make that distinction.

They'd slept together and now she was pregnant. He'd obviously jumped to the wrong conclusion.

"This isn't your baby," Gwen quickly clarified.

Alex opened his mouth to start arguing with her, but her sudden and unexpected response stopped him short.

"Are you certain?" he asked, his face almost pained by the words.

"One hundred percent. I haven't seen you since November, and I'm only at twenty-two weeks. Unless some of your li'l swimmers decided to camp out in my apartment for the holidays and attack when I was least expecting it, you're in the clear."

His brow furrowed, and she could see the anger slowly fade away as the muscles in his neck relaxed. His whole body started to uncoil and he took a deep breath, the casual, easygoing posture she remembered finally gaining hold.

Alex ran a hand through the shaggy strands of his golden hair and shook his head. "You really scared the hell out of me, Gwen."

She was certain of that. Blended in with the anger glittering in his amber eyes had been a healthy dose of fear. When they were together, they'd been quite meticulous when it came to taking all the proper precautions. They both had their reasons. Alex said he didn't want the entanglement of a child, although she expected there was more to it than just that. And as for Gwen, well, she was sure he couldn't guess why it had been so important for her at the time, but an unexpected pregnancy would've derailed everything.

"I'm sorry," Gwen said, the words coming easier with the tension in the room fading. "If you were the father, I would've told you. I couldn't keep a secret like that for long, and Adrienne would've had my hide for even trying."

For her own self-preservation, Gwen had kept her fling with Alex a secret. Adrienne would make a bigger deal out of it than it was intended to be. And by the time her friend had returned from her honeymoon in

Bali, Alex was gone and there wasn't much point in mentioning it. It was just one fantastic last hoorah before her man-break. Nothing more.

Instead, she'd tried to pretend it never happened. The holidays and her pregnancy had done well to distract her. To a point. She blamed the hormones for her more emotional moments when thoughts of Alex slipped through her defenses.

Now Alex looked a touch uncomfortable, shifting his weight and burying his hands in the pockets of his khakis. It was about as close to repentant as she'd ever seen him. "I wish I'd known about all this," he said. "I mean, Will had no reason to think I would care, but I never would've touched you like that. Or brought you wine, obviously."

Gwen smiled. After eight months without a man, his brief touch had been the highlight of her week. Month, maybe. It was right up there with feeling the baby flutter inside her for the first time. "That's okay. Pregnancy isn't contagious."

Alex laughed, breaking the last of the nervous tension in her bedroom and reminding her of the lover she knew. During those two weeks, they'd spent as much time laughing and talking as they had making love. They'd walked around the city, dined in new restaurants and just enjoyed being in one another's company. It was easy to be with Alex.

Looking at him now with his bright, charming smile made her long to touch him again. For Alex to hold her and whisper into her ear the way he had before. But that was a pointless fantasy. Alex was just the latest in a long line of men destined not to stick around. As relationships went, Gwen had a miserable track record. She was always drawn to the men that would leave. A guy that was steady, loyal and committed to a woman didn't even show up on her radar. Probably because she didn't want one hanging around that long.

"That's not what I meant," he said. "I meant I shouldn't have presumed you were free for us to, uh… I mean, I hope if the father finds out about this that you let him know I didn't realize you were taken. Will said you came up alone."

Gwen frowned. "'Taken'?" Truth be told, she was anything but. Occupied, perhaps, but not taken.

Alex's glance darted to her left hand as it rested on the swell of her stomach. "I guess I assumed since you were having some guy's baby that he might mind me groping you. I know I'd probably be crazy with jealousy if someone put the moves on the mother of my child."

That was one thing Gwen certainly didn't have to worry about. "I assure you that Robert isn't really concerned with what I do or with whom."

In an instant, a touch of Alex's previous anger returned, and a dark pink colored the outer shell of his ears. His hazel gaze pinned her on the spot. "Robert who? Tell me the bastard's name."

Gwen's eyes widened in shock. She wasn't quite sure if it was because Alex looked as though he was ready to punch the baby's father in the face, or because he cared enough to go to the trouble. She thought she was just another notch in the proverbial bedpost. Certainly it wouldn't warrant such a protective response from him. "What does it matter? What are you going to do about it?"

"I'm going to sit him down and make sure he does right by you and his child."

"Good lord." Gwen laughed. "You sound like my Paw-Paw. Are you going to take your shotgun, too?"

"If I had one. I might go buy a gun just for the occasion."

Gwen's lower back was beginning to throb from standing in one place for too long. It was just one of the joys the second trimester had brought, along with insatiable hunger and an aching, expanding belly. A fair trade for the end of morning sickness, she supposed. She moved over to the bed to sit at the edge. "I appreciate the offer, but that won't be necessary. The situation is complicated and will take more than a few minutes to explain. But trust me when I tell you Robert is a perfectly wonderful husband and will be just as good a father."

"He's married? Jesus, Gwen. Maybe you need a talking-to as well."

Gwen sighed and patted the mattress beside her. "Sit down, Alex."

He hesitated for a moment, then settled down beside her. He maintained what he probably thought was the proper distance from a mother-to-be, but she could still feel the warmth of him, and the scent of his cologne hovered in the air she breathed. It took everything she had not to close her eyes and imagine being in his arms again. Not that she ever would be. Even if he had been interested initially, there was nothing quite like a surprise pregnancy to kill the mood.

"Listen, you've got the wrong idea about all of this. The father hasn't done anything wrong. In fact, his wife knows about everything and approves. Robert and Susan are good people who suffered a horrible tragedy that no one should ever have to face. I had the power to help them, so I did."

Alex watched her speak, visibly struggling to see where she was going with this. She understood the confusion. Her own mother hadn't approved, even when she had all the details. *Especially* when she had all the details. Only Adrienne, who knew Gwen was a marshmallow underneath her hard candy shell, could see why she had to do this for people who were practically strangers.

She took a deep breath. "I told you this wasn't your baby, but I didn't tell you the whole story. The truth is this isn't my baby, either."

Two

"I'm a surrogate."

Alex fully understood the meaning of the term, but somehow he couldn't connect it in his brain where Gwen was concerned. "This isn't your baby?"

"No. Someone else's bun is baking in my oven. I'm just a rental. This is Robert and Susan's baby biologically, and as soon as the adoption paperwork is filed, it will be theirs legally as well."

This was certainly unexpected. The pendulum of his emotions had swung wildly from one side to the other and back over the last few minutes. First, he was a father. Then he wasn't. Now she wasn't even a mother. He'd never anticipated that procreation could be this complicated. "Why would you agree to do something like that?"

Gwen shrugged. "Why wouldn't I? It wasn't like I was in a serious relationship or had other plans that would interfere. I spend a lot of my time at the hospital, and that's where I met them. Susan was a patient on my floor for several weeks after being in a severe car wreck in the Lincoln Tunnel. She was seven months pregnant at the time. Not only did she lose the baby, but she isn't able to carry another child. They were such a sweet couple, going through so much pain. How could I turn down the opportunity to help them?"

"You're being compensated, right?"

Gwen frowned, her nose wrinkling delicately. "Of course not. You sound like my mother. They're paying my medical expenses, but that's it. I didn't do this for the money, and frankly, they aren't in a position to pay even if it wasn't illegal. This isn't some fancy work-around for a rich, thin society woman who doesn't want to ruin her figure with pregnancy."

Alex wasn't quite sure what to say. She was a damn saint and probably the only woman on his roster who could come close to qualifying. He wasn't used to being around women like that. "Are you getting anything out of this other than a warm, fuzzy feeling?"

"Some distance," she said. "When I volunteered to do this, I decided I would use the time to take a break from relationships."

"So, what, you've sworn off men?"

Gwen smiled. "Yes, for now."

He wasn't quite sure what to say to that. He lived in a world where people of means indulged in whatever, whenever they wanted. Alex let his gaze drop to Gwen's hand as it rested on the soft swell of her stomach. Around her wrist was a silver charm bracelet with a heart-shaped lock charm. The one he'd bought her at Tiffany during their previous time together. "You're wearing your bracelet," he said.

Gwen smiled and held out her wrist to look at it. "I've worn it every day since you bought it for me."

Alex shook his head. He'd practically had to force the gift on Gwen. She'd finally chosen the bracelet under the threat of not leaving the store until she picked something. She'd refused diamond earrings. The roses and wine had been a complete failure. But at least she liked the bracelet.

"It's my chastity bracelet."

"What?" Alex nearly choked. "Like a chastity belt?"

"Slightly less medieval, but the same basic idea. I wear it as a reminder."

"You're using my gift as a reminder to avoid men? The irony is rich."

Gwen shrugged. "It was perfect timing. You insisted I buy something. I saw the lock charm in the case, and I knew it was the perfect symbol of the new journey I was starting on. A subtle reminder to stay on track, as if being pregnant wouldn't do that for me already. I mean, who'd want me like this? It was the perfect time to quit dating."

Alex was about to tell her that he, for one, would still want her, when Adrienne's voice in the kitchen caught their attention. "Gwen?" she called.

"You'd better go," Gwen said, standing quickly. She picked up the roses and wine from the dresser and thrust them back at him. "Take these with you. I don't want to explain where they came from."

Alex wasn't quite ready to leave, but he wasn't ready to explain to Adrienne why he was alone with Gwen, either. Jumping up, he stuck his head out the doorway toward the kitchen, then dashed off in the other direction. He rounded the corner into the living room unseen and opted to head back to his room to finish unpacking.

Or at least, to decompress. He'd had too big a shock in the last few minutes to go out onto the patio and be the life of the party just yet.

Talk about a game changer! For the most part, Alex thought he had women figured out. Between his mother and the list of ladies who had drifted in and out over his lifetime, he had a pretty solid understanding of the female of the species.

The exception was Gwen.

Somehow she took all his expectations and tossed them out the window. She was a genuinely good person. The first moment he'd laid eyes on her, she had been running herself ragged to make Will and Adrienne's wedding special. Later, he'd discovered she spent her working hours taking care of the sick, and from the looks of things now, she sacrificed her precious personal time for others, too. He couldn't imagine even one of the women he'd dated over the last ten years agreeing to anything like that. The majority of them were looking for some hedonistic pleasure or a sugar daddy. Either way, it was all about them. Selfish and spoiled, every last one of them. It was no wonder he never wanted to keep them around for long.

But Gwen…having a stranger's baby and asking for nothing in return? To subject her body to the ravages of childbearing without the benefit of having her own child when she was done? That wasn't exactly like loaning your neighbor a cup of sugar or donating an old coat to the homeless shelter. She was taking charity to a whole new level.

Alex slipped into his bedroom and shut the door behind him to block out the rest of the world. It wasn't until his weight sank down into the soft mattress that

the rush of adrenaline coursing through his veins finally seemed to subside.

Gwen was a remarkable woman. Smart, funny, caring, but saint or no, Alex had to admit he was still relieved to find that wasn't his child. There were worse
women in Manhattan to be bound to through the bonds
of shared custody, but that had been close. Too close.

Since he'd started his heated pursuit of women, Alex
had been nearly religious about using protection. It was
the only way to shield himself. Not only from disease
but from the women out there who would like nothing
better than to have his child and a permanent connection
to his bank accounts. The Stanton Steel company had
made a fortune during the race to build railroads across
the United States. The generations since then had done
well investing it. And Alex was the sole heir to it all.

By necessity, his record with women was flawless.
To the dismay of women everywhere, no one had conceived Alex Stanton's child. And for that, he was eter-
nally grateful. He wasn't interested in the emotional,
physical and financial entanglements. If his parents had
taught him nothing else, they had shown him that marriage for the sake of a child made everyone miserable
in the end. He had no intention of becoming a workaholic who bought his son's affections, like his father,
or an emotionally abusive recluse like his mother, who
blamed her son for her own wretched existence.

If he died single and childless, Alex would consider
that a victory. He'd rather donate his fortune to charity
just to hear the collective sound of the hearts of every
ambitious socialite in Manhattan breaking.

And yet…for half a heartbeat when he'd thought
Gwen was having his baby…there'd been this feeling
he hadn't anticipated. Sure, he was angry with her for

keeping it from him and sort of freaked out in general, but he'd also had a touch of excitement. He'd told himself after their weeks together that his thoughts of Gwen would fade. Continuing in any kind of real relationship with her would just lead to expectations he couldn't fulfill.

But in that moment, fate had very nearly made the decision for him. If that child was his, then perhaps Gwen could be, too. Not just a holiday fling, but something beyond that. Maybe they wouldn't have the kind of family pictured on Christmas cards, but there could be more than what they'd had. And he'd wanted it. The thought had flashed through his mind almost as quickly as his heart had raced in his chest.

And then it was gone.

Alex would never tell another living soul about his moment of weakness. Nor would he admit that, when she'd said the baby wasn't his, he'd felt a pang of regret and jealousy mingled in with the rush of relief.

What the hell was wrong with him?

Certainly he didn't require a baby as an excuse to have Gwen in his arms again. That was a life-changing complication he simply didn't need. But knowing that she was still single, albeit a bit preoccupied, meant his plans for this week hadn't completely fallen apart yet. If she was interested, they could still have a little fun and, hopefully, this time he'd be able to move on when it was over.

Alex heard a familiar melody of a woman's laughter from the patio. He strode to the window and pulled aside the curtain. Gwen had joined the others outside. She was standing near the sparkling turquoise pool, talking to Adrienne and another woman he didn't know.

He couldn't hear their conversation, but Adrienne spoke and Gwen laughed again.

He had missed that sound. When Gwen was really tickled, she laughed wholeheartedly. No polite, uptight chuckles from her. He loved how she could let herself go. Whether it was laughter or pleasure, she allowed herself to just feel it and react without worrying what other people thought. As he watched, her head tipped back and she giggled in unrestrained amusement. Her eyes closed, her white smile flashing up at him. Her movement allowed the golden sunlight to highlight the creamy expanse of her chest and shoulders exposed by her dress.

Alex had been too preoccupied earlier to notice how Gwen had changed since he had seen her in November. Last year, long hours at the hospital and attempts to diet before the wedding had trimmed her petite frame to the point of being almost too thin, in his opinion. Women always worried too much about those last few vanity pounds. In his experience, a woman with curves and a healthy appetite was more fun both in bed and out.

Now, as he watched her from the window, he could see Gwen was obviously pregnant, but everything about her seemed to be softer and more welcoming. Her skin radiated a rosy, maternal glow. Her breasts were fuller and her hips a touch rounder. Pregnancy really suited her.

And him.

The fire in his gut that had been building since he had gotten into the car this morning returned. The shock of their previous discussion had dulled it, but now it was back with renewed fervor. The woman he'd fantasized about for months was here, looking more beautiful than he remembered. Standing in the sunlight with her long, flowing dress, she looked more like some ancient Greek fertility goddess than a nurse.

The tightness in his groin forced him to shift his stance uncomfortably. Alex was surprised by his visceral reaction to her. There was something primal piqued by her new, soft curves. Typically the sight of a pregnant woman threw up red flags declaring her off-limits. It was something he'd never considered, given he never planned to settle down and start a family.

But Gwen wasn't off-limits. Her situation was unique and certainly complicated, but he didn't see any barriers between them. If she could be coaxed into continuing their affair, they could spend another fantastic week in bed together. Alex wanted that week to start as soon as possible.

"Sworn off men, have you, Gwen? We'll just see about that."

Letting the curtain drop, he headed downstairs to join the party and begin his heated pursuit of Gwen Wright.

"About damn time!" Will shouted toward the house.

Gwen turned that direction in time to see Alex strut onto the blue flagstone patio that arched out from the house. The tall, white pergola that lined the back of the house was covered in clematis vines this time of year, and it shaded almost everything below. Patches of dark and light danced across his face as he approached the outdoor kitchen, where everyone had congregated.

"The party can officially start," he announced, giving Gwen a brilliant smile before he bent down to pull a cold bottle of locally microbrewed beer out of the small refrigerator inset to the right of the grill.

The small gesture brought a wave of warmth to her

cheeks that had nothing to do with the sun. Perhaps she'd worried for nothing. When Adrienne had first invited her up here for the Independence Day holiday, she'd had doubts. Her friend had promised her a relaxing vacation by the ocean with nothing but fun and friends. It sounded like a dream.

The time away from work would be a godsend, as would going a couple days without having to climb the four flights of stairs to her apartment. Her daily routine got rougher as each week ticked by. She couldn't imagine what it would be like in the last few months. She needed this break more than she'd realized.

But she'd known seeing Alex again would be awkward. Her being pregnant made it doubly so. It wasn't because they had parted on bad terms. They had both known it was nothing more than a little short-term fun. He'd had a business trip to go on, and it had seemed like the right time to end whatever they had going. But once he was gone, she'd been left with this restless, icky feeling she'd never felt before.

Eventually the complications of her life had put those concerns out of her head, but it had just confirmed some of the thoughts she'd been having about her choices in men. As in—she always made bad ones. Alex was no different. And it just wasn't working for her anymore. The decision to take the next year off from dating was obviously a wise choice.

But Alex didn't know how she felt about things. Their relationship had ended on a positive note as far as he was concerned. And given the firm arousal that had pressed into her back less than an hour ago, he'd arrived alone and interested in having another go at it.

At least he *had*. Until twenty-two weeks of belly had come between them. Now he probably thought she was

as sexy as a beluga whale—or worse in Alex's mind—
a pregnant woman.

It was probably for the best. There was a reason
why she'd planned her man-break to coincide with the
pregnancy. It was built-in willpower. And lately, she'd
needed it. The months of celibacy and the second-tri-
mester hormones had done a number on her libido. If
Alex was still interested, she'd be tempted to use him
for a couple nights of hot sex, the way he used every
other woman in his life. Turnabout was fair play, right?

But, fortunately, she didn't have to worry. Alex would
stay at arm's length from her all week, and she wouldn't
need the strength necessary to turn him down. And
she *would* have to turn him down. She'd done so well.
She didn't want to fall off the wagon, even for a guy
like Alex.

"Alex, have you met everybody?" Adrienne set down
her glass of tea on the table and began fulfilling her role
as hostess by introducing her guests.

Gwen had heard it all before, but she listened a second time in the hope she would actually retain the information. First was Emma, Adrienne's half sister of
sorts. She was actually the child of George and Pauline Dempsey, who had lost their older daughter in the
same wreck that had nearly killed Adrienne. They'd
unofficially adopted Adrienne and let her take Emma
shopping or on trips from time to time. Emma had just
graduated from high school, and when she got home,
she had to pack up and get ready for her freshman year
at Yale.

Next was Sabine, a somewhat funky twentysome-
thing who managed Adrienne's boutique. She had a nose
piercing and a bright purple stripe in her black hair, so

Gwen wasn't quite sure what to make of her. Adrienne ran in diverse circles.

Peter and Helena were a middle-aged couple who lived in the brownstone next to Will and Adrienne's new place on the Upper West Side. Rounding off the crowd was Wade, one of Will and Alex's friends from Yale and Alex's former business partner, and Jack, an editor for one of the big New York publishing houses. Apparently he had worked with Will at the paper a few years back.

It was a blur of names and faces that Gwen would forget the minute the next name was called. She'd blame her short-term memory loss on the pregnancy—it was easy to label almost anything as a symptom of her condition—but the truth of the matter was that she was simply bad with names. At work, it was easy. All the staff had name tags, and all the patients had their names on a plaque outside their door or a clipboard hanging at the foot of their bed.

When the introductions were finished, she decided her time standing in the sun was over. It had felt good at first, but now she was a minute or two from starting to burn. Taking her glass of iced tea, Gwen returned to the shade of the pergola and sat down on one of the cushioned Adirondack chairs.

Leaning back into the cool comfort of her chair, she instantly felt better. Thank goodness she wasn't full-term in the heat of the summer. Gwen wasn't sure she could bear that. Her apartment didn't have central air, just a small unit in the bedroom window. Most of the time she was cold natured and it suited her fine, but she'd had fire running through her veins the last few months.

Taking a refreshing sip of the sweet tea she'd brewed earlier, she watched the men gather around the grill.

Apparently millionaires could run companies and build empires, but outdoor cooking was a challenge. She watched Alex open the cabinet beneath it and make some adjustments to the propane line. A few minutes later, a roar of success sounded from the group.

"We have fire!" the editor guy—Jack?—shouted triumphantly.

Adrienne patted them all on the back and headed toward the house. "I'm off to prepare the meat," she said with a smile as she slipped inside.

Sabine with the purple hair quickly grew bored with the sight of an operating gas grill and came to sit in the shade with Gwen. They hadn't spoken much since she'd arrived. She was sure the woman was perfectly nice—Adrienne was a good judge of people—but Gwen just didn't know what they had in common to discuss.

"When are you due?" Sabine asked before taking a sip from her beer.

"Mid-October," Gwen said, although watching the other woman made her think the day couldn't come soon enough. Of all the lifestyle changes she'd had to make, the hardest had been giving up her favorite beer. She didn't drink much, but there was just something soothing about popping the top on a cold one after a long shift, plopping onto the couch and watching a few hours of reality television on her DVR.

"My son will be two in October, so I understand where you're at. Do you know what you're having yet?"

Gwen tried not to look too surprised to learn Sabine was a mother. Imagining her own mother with purple hair was just impossible. "A little girl. I had the ultrasound last week."

Susan and Robert had been over the moon in the doctor's office. It was hard to see the fuzzy image on the screen from her vantage point, but she tried not to be too disappointed. This was their baby after all, not hers. They did give her a copy of the latest ultrasound picture to show off. Unfortunately, it was in her purse on her bed when she needed it.

"Do you have any names picked out yet?"

The more pregnant Gwen became, the more of these questions she had to field. It had been easy when no one could tell she was pregnant. Now, unless it was just a quick comment from a stranger on the subway, it was best to tell them about her situation before they pressed on.

"No, actually, I'm a surrogate, so the baby technically isn't mine to name. I think her parents are considering Caroline Joy and Abigail Rose. Every time I talk to them they've changed it again. For now I just call her Peanut, because that's what she looked like on the first sonogram."

Sabine's eyes had grown wider as Gwen talked. Apparently dropping a detail like that and carrying on without pause had thrown her off her guard. "A surrogate? Wow. I don't think I could ever do that," she finally said.

"Why is that?"

"Being pregnant is such a life-changing experience. Whether or not the child is yours, you're going to bond with it. To go through months with that baby inside you and then to give it away... I just couldn't do it."

Gwen tried not to frown at Sabine. She probably didn't realize how her words would affect her. But they struck a chord. Gwen had never been interested in having a family of her own. She'd spent too much of her childhood being pushed aside by her mother when a new man came into her life. She wasn't about to do that to a child of her own. Acting as a surrogate seemed like an intriguing opportunity. Since she'd never thought she'd have kids, she'd never thought she would experience pregnancy.

Never once did she consider that she'd form an emotional attachment to another person's child. But Sabine was right. She'd underestimated what it was like to have life growing inside her. The moment she'd felt the first flutter in her stomach, Peanut had become a real person to her. She'd gotten in the habit of talking to the baby when she was alone in her apartment. She was the one who helped Gwen pick out what she would have for lunch. The silent child had become her main companion when her crowd of bar-hopping friends didn't know how to act around her anymore.

Gwen hadn't really realized it until that moment, but she *had* bonded with the baby. With four more months to go, how much worse would it get? She didn't even want to think about it. She was too prone to getting emotional lately.

Confused, she turned away from Sabine and found Alex watching her from across the patio. He was leaning casually against one of the white wooden posts, while either Jack or Wade, she couldn't be sure, talked to him. But he wasn't looking at them or even pretending to. He was looking at her. There was an intensity in his hazel eyes, but there was something different there than the desire he'd directed at her in the past. It almost felt like admiration, although she had no idea why Alex would look at her that way. She was pregnant, broke and overworked. That was no condition to admire.

"He is one sexy piece of man," Sabine commented, still oblivious to the effect her words had on Gwen.

The comment startled Gwen into turning back to the

woman beside her. Sabine's gaze was focused exactly
in Alex's direction. Gwen had no claim to him, but the
thought of him and Sabine together brought on a surge
of jealousy that chased away the last of her confusing
emotions. She opted to play dumb. "Who? Wade?"

"No, the guy who came late. Alex."

"Ahh," Gwen said, not trusting herself to comment
further without sounding either bitter or jealous to the
other woman's ears.

"Pity for me, but I think he's into you."

That perked Gwen's attention. Her head snapped
toward him, but he had returned to his conversation.
"Why would you say that?"

"Because he keeps watching you."

"Maybe I'm just funny-looking." She sighed.

"Nope," Sabine said with certainty. "When you're
not watching, he's looking at you like you're the sweetest strawberry tart in the bakery window. He definitely
wants a taste."

Gwen subconsciously stroked her rounded stomach
and shook her head. "I appreciate you thinking so, but
somehow I doubt he wants to take a bite out of this."

At that, Sabine cracked a crooked, knowing grin.
"Oh, he does," she assured.

"Well, even if that were true, my life is a little complicated right now. I'm not interested."

Sabine laughed and shook her head. "I hardly think
that matters. I've had my share of experience with those
rich, cocky types. They get what they want, and they
don't care who they have to roll over in the process. If I
were you, I'd let him have his way with you. And let me
tell you something if you don't already know. Between
all the hormones and the increased blood flow, sex in
the second trimester can be absolutely mind-blowing.

I bet that in the experienced hands of a man like Alex, you can multiply that by ten at least."

Gwen's jaw dropped open, but she didn't have the words to respond. Instead, she shifted her gaze back to Alex. This time he was watching her, and his obvious, heated appraisal was enough to send a surprising surge of desire down her spine.

Well, hell. She hadn't counted on him still being attracted to her. That certainly complicated things.

Willpower, she reminded herself as she sucked in a deep breath and began fidgeting with her bracelet. She was on a man-break, and Alex was just the kind of man who had necessitated the break to begin with. Her attraction to him was nothing more than hormones and months of celibacy conspiring against her. But she could fight it. She had to. It didn't matter what Alex wanted. He couldn't just snap his fingers and get his way.

And yet, as she looked at him across the patio, Gwen was fairly certain her celibacy streak was on the verge of coming to a wild, passionate end.

Three

By the time Gwen had taken the last bite of her dinner, she thought she might literally burst. She'd recently regained her appetite, and everything tasted so good, she couldn't help herself. She'd had a grilled chicken breast and a cheeseburger in addition to the array of sides Adrienne had prepared. She was stuffed.

At least for an hour or so.

Given that Alex was watching her with his predatory gaze the whole time, she probably should've curbed her ravenous appetite and picked delicately at her food, but Peanut would have her way. After a rough first trimester living on saltines and lemon-lime soda, the hunger and the ability to keep it down were welcome. Even if the extra pounds were not. The doctor said she was right on track with her weight gain, but after a lifetime of trying to get smaller, not bigger, it was hard to change how she thought about things.

After they were done eating, several of the ladies started rounding up dishes, and the guys went inside for what promised to be a rowdy and high-stakes game of poker. Gwen scooped up her plate and a nearby bowl of potato salad and followed the other women into the kitchen.

"What are you doing?" Helena chided, snatching the items away from her the moment she crossed the threshold into the house. "You need to rest."

Gwen frowned. "I'm pregnant, not paralyzed. If washing dishes is hazardous to my condition, someone needs to tell me, because I've been doing it the whole time."

"Of course not. But take the opportunity to relax for once," Adrienne said, brushing past her with a platter and another bowl. "We can handle it."

The cherry-and-granite kitchen was quite large, but even Gwen realized that the four women already in there were bumping elbows and dancing around to clean up. A fifth one with a protruding belly probably wouldn't be much help.

With a sigh, she snatched one of her favorite peppermint candies from the bag she left on the counter, turned, and went back outside. The sun had set, but the sky was still bright with orange-and-red hues streaking across it. Beyond the pool and the expansive lawn that extended on both sides of the house, she spied the boathouse and pier that led out into the harbor.

A walk would probably help things settle, she decided. She slipped out of her sandals and kicked them to the side, then headed across the perfectly manicured lawn. The blades of grass were soft and cool, welcoming the bottoms of her feet to sink into them. It was a beautiful evening, one like she hadn't experienced in a long time. Along the tree line, she could see the blinking dance of fireflies as they appeared for the night. The breeze coming off the water was warm and salty, mingling with the scent of freshly mown grass.

It reminded her of her home in Tennessee. There, of course, the water was the creek that ran behind her grandparents' house, but the grass and the flashing lightning bugs were just the same. She had the urge to climb into the tire swing her Paw-Paw had hung for her and sway for hours, as she used to.

For a brief moment, Gwen was overcome with homesickness. She loved Manhattan—the energy, the excitement, the culture. But it had never felt like home to her. It made her wonder if she ever would've left Tennessee if it hadn't been the only way to get away from her mother. Following a guy she barely had lukewarm feelings for wasn't very smart, but it was a sure ticket out of her mother's clutches.

In the end, she and Ty went their separate ways, but she had gotten what she wanted from him—about six hundred miles of breathing room and her very own apartment, albeit tiny.

Gwen reached the pier and opted to walk out to the edge and watch the water. The occasional boat would sail by and send a ripple across the surface, but for the most part, the water was calm and still this time of day. At the end of the rough, wooden planks, she sucked in a lungful of ocean air and sighed.

She enjoyed getting away from the chaos more than she'd expected. There was a serenity out here that seemed to sink into her bones and force her muscles to unknot. Even Peanut had settled down and stopped squirming around. It was a shame she wasn't in the right tax bracket to live out here. She'd have to take a job as a live-in nurse for some old, rich Hamptons resident to do that. Unfortunately, caring for an entitled hypochondriac didn't really work for her.

Perhaps, after the baby was born, she should give some more thought about going back to Tennessee. That would probably make it easier on everyone with no awkward, obligatory visits. Robert and Susan could just take their baby and continue life as it was before their accident, and Gwen could return to the life she knew and start fresh.

The black, still waters around her beckoned. She couldn't remember the last time she'd been in a body of water that wasn't chlorinated, and she wanted to put her feet in it. Easing back, she sat on the boards and pulled her dress up to her knees. The water was cool and refreshing as she slipped her bare feet in to just above the ankles.

Looking out, she realized, as she had every time the idea of moving home hit, that going back to Tennessee really wasn't an option, as nice as all this seemed. For one thing, her romanticized memories of home would never hold up to reality. Paw-Paw and Gran were dead, and their old farmhouse and cornfields had been leveled to put up a housing subdivision. Returning would mean an apartment in Knoxville, which was a pretty sizable city, especially when the University of Tennessee, her alma mater, was in session.

And for another thing, she'd have to deal with her mother. She wasn't a powerless five-year-old girl anymore, but the less angst Gwen had to handle, the better.

Cheryl Wright was a desperate single mom on a never-ending quest for love.

When her relationships were going well, Gwen had been in the way and would get shipped off to her grandparents. When the relationship fell apart, Gwen would come home and take care of the house, as her mother was too distraught to get out of bed for days at a time. As Gwen got older, she was really more of a housekeeper than a daughter, although a housekeeper wouldn't have to hear about how she was the reason her mother couldn't keep a man.

Ever the expert, her mother had given Gwen an earful when she'd told her she was moving to New York City with Ty. He was a no-good loser just like her father, she'd warned. Of course, her mother was probably more concerned about who would make her dinner than Gwen's emotional health. Either way, it didn't matter. Gwen was gone and she couldn't go back.

With a sigh, she gazed across the harbor at a sailboat passing through. The mast was lined with white lights that twinkled across the surface as it moved. The boat called to her and made her want to swim out to it. Maybe she could convince the captain to take her on as first mate and she could just sail away from her problems. It seemed like a solid enough plan. That's what she'd done by coming to New York, minus the boat.

And that was why returning to Tennessee would feel like a defeat. Even though it would have nothing to do with Ty, her mother would get too much satisfaction from telling her she was right. Her life in Manhattan was hectic, but exciting. She worked at one of the top hospitals in the country and got to help so many people. She'd built a life for herself here over the past five years. She had friends. She was happy. At least until recently.

About a year ago, after another failed and mostly pointless relationship, she'd started having this nagging feeling that something was missing from her life. She didn't know what. Gwen had never wanted to chase the marriage and family that eluded her mother. But at the same time, whatever she was doing wasn't working, either. She was content, most days, but never really happy.

That's what her man-break was all about. A year off from the roller coaster of her dating life. Her hope was that, by the time it was over, she'd have a better idea of what she wanted. With four months left in her pregnancy, she was still pretty clueless on that front.

"You know, I hear sharks like to come up into these cooler waters and feed on the toes of pregnant women. It's a delicacy in their culture. Like sushi."

Gwen would've been startled, but she'd heard the faint tread of his footsteps on the planks of the pier. She didn't bother to turn around and look at him. "No. Everyone knows they all go to Florida for the holiday. It's like a buffet down there. Nothing hits the spot like a suntanned boogie boarder."

"Hmm. Quantity over quality, then." Alex sat down alongside her, crossing his legs to keep his khakis, loafers and argyle socks from getting wet. "What are you doing out here all by yourself?"

"I got banned from the kitchen by the other ladies, so I went for a walk and ended up out here. Why aren't you in there playing poker?"

Alex shrugged and looked across the harbor. "It's not really my game. I might as well just hand them each a couple thousand dollars and be done with it." With a smile he turned to her. "I'd kick their asses at racquetball, though."

Gwen smiled back. She'd always thought of Alex as more athletic and outgoing, so she wasn't surprised he could whip a bunch of corporate types at any kind of physical activity. His endurance was incredible. She blushed at the thought and hoped the rapidly darkening evening would disguise it. She didn't want to give him any more encouragement.

"So, how have you been lately? Aside from pregnant and all? We didn't really get to talk much earlier."

"I've been okay." She shrugged dismissively. "Work always takes up a lot of time. Preparing for the baby was a big deal, too. Lots of doctor visits and paperwork. It's a lot more complicated than just getting pregnant the old-fashioned way."

"And not nearly as fun, I'd wager," Alex said, leaning conspiratorially into her.

Gwen sighed. "No, not at all. Sadly, it's been so long, I can hardly draw much of a comparison."

Alex wrapped an arm around her shoulder and tugged her against his side. "Why has my lovely Gwen suffered such a long dry spell? I find it hard to believe."

"You flatter me," she said, shaking her head. "For one thing, they pumped me so full of hormones to get ready for the surrogacy that a man could've held a door for me and gotten me pregnant. Sex was out of the question. It was also the wrong time to start up anything serious. Do you wait until the third or fourth date to tell a man you can't go out next week because you'll be busy getting pregnant?"

"The fourth, definitely." Alex grinned. "But now that the deed is done, aren't you free to try dating again?"

Gwen couldn't suppress a chuckle. "In theory, but dating? Do you see this?" She looked down and pointed at her stomach. "This is man-repellant. And I'd be afraid of the men that *are* interested in me at this point. They might have some creepy pregnancy fetish, and that's the last thing I need."

Alex put a finger under her chin, tipped Gwen's face up to him and pinned her in place with his intense gaze.

"Let me assure you that nothing about you is repellant, and I'm most certainly a man."

The light mood instantly changed. A sizzle of electricity spanned the small gap between them, and Gwen could feel the beat of her heart thumping wildly in her chest.

Darkness had blanketed them, but she could still see the lights of the harbor reflecting in his eyes and the silver glow the moonlight cast across one side of his face. He was a beautiful man. Gwen would never say so—it wasn't the kind of thing he would want to hear—but it was true. Something about the lines and angles of his face drew her interest. His wide, disarming smile and mischievous eyes pulled her in. The shaggy, loose strands of his golden hair made her palms itch to run through them.

Alex was like some rogue angel in a painting that should be hanging in a museum somewhere. Perfect, alluring and untouchable.

He was so close. A part of Gwen wanted to lean in and kiss him. To take Sabine's advice and use Alex for all he was worth. The other part of her knew it would just mess with her mind.

Instead, Gwen rested her head on his shoulder, indulging in the comfortable cocoon of being in his arms again and making it impossible for her to kiss him. "And on top of everything," she said, pointedly ignoring his words, "I told you earlier I've sworn off men until after the baby is born. Being with you was my one last hoorah before all this," she said, rubbing her stomach. "I needed some time to myself."

Alex had watched the moonlight and shadows accentuate the battle going on inside Gwen's head until she finally hid from view. Unlike the Botoxed beauties he was usually bombarded with, she was the kind of woman whose every thought or feeling was plastered across her face. She didn't even try to disguise it, which made him wonder if she even knew. He wasn't going to let her hide from him. Not tonight.

"Stop," he whispered.

She sat up and frowned, a pout thrusting her full lower lip out to tease him. "What do you mean, 'stop'?"

"Stop using this pregnancy as an excuse to push people away. It won't work on me."

Gwen swallowed hard, her dark eyes widening slightly as she searched for meaning in his face. Apparently she was clueless about how transparent she was. Or how much attention he'd really paid to her when they were together before. "I don't know what you're—"

"You want me," he interrupted. "And I want you just as badly as I did all those months ago. There's nothing wrong with that. There's no reason to try to defuse the attraction between us just because of some artificial barrier you've put in place. If you want me, give in to your feelings."

She opened her mouth to argue, but his words seemed to have struck her temporarily mute. Alex thought this might be his opportunity to finally kiss her again the way he ached to, but she recovered more quickly than he'd hoped.

"What's your angle, Alex?"

He eased back a little, an eyebrow arching suspiciously at her. "Angle?"

"Yes. We both know I'm not the type of woman you usually go for. I'm not some tall, thin, surgically enhanced glamazon with aspirations of marrying well. Last time I was looking pretty good, but now I'm pregnant and celibate. Both are adjectives that fly in the face of everything you hold dear. I haven't been to a salon in months or splurged on a new outfit that wasn't from a maternity store. What are you getting out of this?"

Alex smiled his most mischievous grin and gazed into her eyes in the way that sent most women melting into his arms. "It hasn't been that long since we spent those fantastic few weeks together. Unless the hormones have scrambled your memory, I think we both know full well what benefit I'd be getting out of this."

Gwen's cheeks flushed red, her gaze breaking from his to look down at her hand as it rested on her stomach. "What we had last year was great, but I don't understand why you're putting the moves on me. Again. Especially considering everything else going on. Have you alienated every woman of consenting age in Manhattan? Are you that hard up?"

Alex snorted. "Hardly." There were plenty to choose from, in New York and New Orleans. He just hadn't found any that caught his attention as Gwen did.

"Then why me?" She looked up at him, a challenge in her dark brown eyes.

She honestly didn't think she was his type. Fortunately, Alex had a very broad and adventurous palate where women were concerned. But even then, Gwen was a beautiful, smart, funny, caring woman. What about that was unappealing to a secure and confident man? It sounded as though her experiences with less than worthy men had planted unwarranted doubts in her mind. She wouldn't need a break from men if she'd been involved with decent ones.

"Why not?" he retorted. "The two weeks we spent together were fun. Neither of us had any overly romantic ideas about what was going on. It was a perfect fling from start to finish. One of the many things I like about you, Gwen, is that you don't want more from me. So many women think they're going to change me, somehow. But I'm not about to tie myself down and be miserable for the rest of my life. With you, I feel like I can put my defensive walls down, relax and have a good time. To me, there's nothing sexier."

"Well, hell." Gwen looked as though she had a smart retort ready, but his explanation put all of it aside. "Alex, I—"

He charged in, capturing her mouth with his own and smothering any words. Gwen was stiff against him for just a moment of surprise, then her reservations were silenced and she gave in to the kiss. She softened, leaning forward to mold against him and bring her hand up to gently caress his face.

She tasted just like Christmas. She'd told him once that she kept handfuls of hard peppermint candies in the pockets of her scrubs at work. Gwen almost always had one in her mouth. He'd nearly forgotten until the spice assaulted his tongue and lured him to explore further.

Alex placed his hand on her hip and allowed it to slide up her side, pulling her as close to him as their position on the pier would allow. His fingertips stroked her heated skin through the thin, cotton fabric of her sundress. The touch coaxed a soft moan from her mouth.

Her encouragement made him bolder. His right hand glided up higher to cup the full swell of her breast. This time, his own groan of pleasure muffled hers. She was so much fuller and rounder than the last time he'd touched her. She was like a juicy, ripe peach in his hands, ready to be devoured. He couldn't wait to taste every inch of her and remind himself of anything he may have forgotten about Gwen in the last few months.

"Stop."

It was the word no man wanted to hear when he was caressing a woman's breast, but the soft whisper couldn't be ignored. Alex reluctantly pulled away, their warm breath still lingering in the space between them. He expected Gwen to distance herself, since she had called the cease-fire, but even she seemed hesitant to let the moment between them pass just yet.

"Why?" he asked, leaning his forehead against hers and closing his eyes.

"I just… I can't do this, Alex."

With a sigh, Alex moved away and unfolded his legs to stand on the pier. He reached down and took Gwen's hands in his own. The touch of her skin sent a tingle across his palms and up his arms, tightening every muscle in his body with anticipation. Gwen eased her feet out of the water and planted them firmly on the wooden planks as he pulled her up.

Instead of letting go, he tugged the full length of her body against him for one last touch, one last kiss, in the hope she might change her mind.

He'd forgotten she was pregnant until the only part of her body to make contact was the press of her breasts and the round curve of her belly. Their positioning was suddenly awkward, both of them pausing to see what had halted the progress of their physical connection.

The heated moment between them suddenly disintegrated as Gwen looked down and started giggling. "See, I told you. It is quite literally man-repellant." She brought a hand up to cover her mouth, but there was no stopping her contagious laughter once she got started.

What she didn't know was that her laughter was as

big a turn-on as anything else about her. Gripping her face with both hands, he leaned down and kissed her again.

The laughter silenced immediately as she stiffened in his arms. She didn't pull away, but she didn't give in to the kiss the way she had the first time, either. There was a hesitation in her touch, even as the smashed orbs of her breasts against the hard wall of his chest made him wild with arousal.

When she refused to give in, Alex pulled away and shook his head. He didn't understand how she could deny herself something they both wanted. This situation didn't need to be as complicated as she was making it. But he wasn't giving up on this seduction. Eventually he would convince her that he was right. This time Gwen took her own step back, looking up at him with confused black eyes that twinkled with the lights of the house. Her breath was ragged, every rise and fall of her chest tempting him with her out of his reach.

"I'm sorry. I just can't. Good night, Alex," she said. At that, she turned and walked back down the pier alone, disappearing into the night.

Four

Gwen awoke the next morning to the sounds of voices in the kitchen. Rolling onto her side, she picked up her watch from the nightstand and groaned. It was after nine. How had she slept so late?

She knew. Tossing and turning until well past three in the morning probably had something to do with it. But she just couldn't sleep. Her mind was still racing from her kiss with Alex. Every time she closed her eyes, she could see his smile. Every breath she sucked into her lungs was laced with his scent.

There was no getting away from Alex and how badly she wanted him. Break or no break, she couldn't help her reaction to him. Her body remembered his touch, and the taste she got last night wasn't nearly enough to soothe the need he easily built inside her.

But last night also brought the memories of their time together back in full Technicolor. As much fun as their fling had been, it had worked then because she was in a different place. An uncomplicated place.

Wanting Alex didn't change the fact that the kiss on the pier was a mistake. A fantastic, soul-stirring, spine-tingling mistake. She couldn't take it back, but she could keep things from going any further.

If she was that desperate for sex, she should try throwing herself at Wade or Jack. Or the first guy she could find once she returned to the city. Just not Alex. Giving in to him would be a bad idea. It might not seem like it at first, especially when the rush of his touch surged through her veins, but before the last of the holiday fireworks exploded, so would what they had together.

This time, she just knew it would end badly. The pregnancy had made her more emotional than normal. She didn't want to make the mistake of letting herself get too attached. Gwen could easily let herself get swept into some kind of fantasy. Out of all her past lovers, Alex was the least likely to stick around. Normally, that would be okay, but at this time in her life, there was no point in even starting something when finishing it would be so difficult.

Gwen ran her hand over her belly, pressing her palm in on one side to feel the baby stirring. "When you grow up, you be sure not to fall for a man like Alex, Peanut. You deserve the kind of man that will stick around and offer more than just sex and some flashy gifts. That's not enough."

She felt Peanut roll in response, then drive an elbow or a foot or something squarely into her bladder. Apparently she disagreed. The move sent Gwen leaping out of bed and scurrying into the bathroom. It was just as

well. The day needed to begin, and Peanut was ready
to go even if she wasn't.

Last night Will had mentioned something about VIP
tickets they'd gotten everyone for a charity polo tournament today. It was supposedly one of the highlights
of the trip, and she had no doubt they'd paid a small
fortune for it. Both he and Alex had played on the Yale
team in college, and everyone was gushing about how
great it would be. Adrienne and Helena were putting together a gourmet picnic for dinner at the field. Emma
had paraded around in a variety of hats, getting everyone's opinion on which one she should wear. It seemed
like a big deal to the others.

Gwen knew very little about sports outside of college football. She was Southern, after all, so a basic
knowledge of college football was provided by her father in her DNA. She occasionally followed the basketball team and even spent a semester as a little sister
to the swim team, but that was about it where athletics
were concerned.

Polo was up there with croquet and badminton in
the "obscure sports for rich people" category. In the
last two years of her friendship with Adrienne, they'd
both undergone a sort of baptism by fire into Manhattan society. Neither was used to being around these
kinds of social situations. Adrienne had adapted fairly
well. Gwen still struggled, but she quickly learned there
were few things rich people liked more than horses and
wine. This polo tournament was sponsored by a large,
prestigious winery, so it was the best of both for those
who cared. No matter what situation Adrienne dragged
her into, a basic knowledge of equestrian activities and
how the rainfall was in Napa this year could save her
from an awkward night out.

But the polo match should be fun anyway. She missed the energy and roar of excitement of UT football games, although she knew this would hardly come close.

By the time she emerged from her room, showered and dressed, the rest of the house was up and about as well. Several of the ladies were outside on the patio, but Gwen opted to crawl up onto one of the barstools in the kitchen and keep Adrienne company while she straightened up.

"Good morning, mama," Adrienne said with a smile. "Did you sleep well?"

"Yes," she lied. "Did I miss breakfast?"

"Not at all. The guys got up early to play a couple holes of golf, so they ate a long time ago. The rest of us just finished." Adrienne pulled out a plate and scooped some scrambled eggs, bacon, fruit salad and a biscuit onto it. "Here you go. I used your grandmother's biscuit recipe, and everyone was raving about them."

The scent was heavenly. Gwen started eating, washing the tasty bites down with the glass of milk Adrienne poured. Normally she hated milk, but it was just one more sacrifice she was making for Peanut's welfare.

"When do we leave for the polo match?" she asked.

"It doesn't start until four, but we have to drive to Bridgehampton for it, and I'm sure the men will want to arrive early. We've got plenty of time if there's something you wanted to do today."

Gwen shrugged. "Actually, I'm happy to do nothing. I just wasn't sure when I needed to be ready."

Adrienne smiled and leaned onto the counter. "I think you should make the most of doing nothing while you can. That's what this whole week is about. I know polo isn't your thing. You don't have to go to the match if you don't want to."

"Don't be silly," Gwen chided. "Of course I'll go. I don't even want to know how much those tickets cost you, so I'm not about to waste one. Anyway, anything we do here is better than working a twelve-hour shift and sitting alone in my apartment."

"You know, Will and I were talking…."

"Nope," Gwen interrupted, immediately recognizing her mistake. They'd had this conversation at least three times, and she wasn't interested in rehashing it.

"Come stay with us," Adrienne pressed. "You'd have your own room and bath. You wouldn't have to climb up all those stairs. Someone would be there at night if there was an emergency with the baby."

"I'm not living with you two."

"It's only temporary. Keep your apartment if you want, or let the lease expire and save up a couple months of rent to take a great trip or something when it's over. You let me stay with you when I had no place to go. Let me return the favor."

Gwen appreciated her friend's generosity, but there was no way she was going to accept the offer. "That was completely different. You were broke and homeless. I am absolutely, one hundred percent not hauling my pregnant hind end into your honeymoon bungalow."

"We've been married eight months. And a three-thousand-square-foot brownstone hardly qualifies as a bungalow."

"You're still newlyweds," Gwen said with a firm shake of her head. "Single women without elevators have babies all the time. I will be fine. Really, I'll be better off than most of them, since when it's over, I won't have a baby and all its crap to haul up and down the stairs."

"What about staying with Robert and Susan? It's their baby, after all."

"Robert and Susan live in a tiny place in Hoboken. They'd take me in, in a heartbeat, but it wouldn't be very comfortable for anyone. And I'd have a longer commute to work. No thanks."

Gwen could see the wheels turning in Adrienne's brain. Her silence made it appear as if she was backing down, but Gwen knew better.

Fortunately, the conversation was interrupted by the return of the golfing posse. The five guys strolled into the house, dumping their golf bags in the foyer and arguing loudly. Apparently there was some disagreement over Wade's handicap, the wind helping Jack cheat and whether or not it was illegal to move your ball if it fell in the cart path.

She had no real idea what they were talking about and continued to eat before her eggs got cold.

Will swept into the kitchen and wrapped his arms possessively around Adrienne, pulling her into a kiss that elicited a catcall from one of the other guys. That, precisely, was one reason Gwen wasn't going to stay with them. She wouldn't be a lumpy third wheel in their romance. And she was pretty sure she'd get depressed surrounded by all that mushy love stuff.

Alex followed Will into the kitchen and pulled a bottle of water out of the refrigerator. "Get a room," he challenged, looking at Gwen when he spoke, giving her a wide smile and winking when no one was looking.

The eggs in her mouth were suddenly dry as Styrofoam. Her cheeks were burning. Good lord. How could something as innocent as a flirtatious wink have that kind of effect on her? This man-break was going to backfire. It was supposed to help her get some perspective, but so far, all it had done was make her more vulnerable to the same type of charming man who made her want to take a break from dating in the first place.

Gwen took a big swig of her milk and stuffed a piece of cantaloupe in her mouth as a distraction. She didn't dare look up at him again.

But she did catch Adrienne watching her curiously. Her green eyes narrowed at Gwen for a moment before she turned and spoke to Alex.

"How long are you going to be back in New York this time, Alex?"

He shrugged, chugging half the bottle of water. "The project in New Orleans is under way, so I really don't need to go back down there for a while. My project manager, Tabitha, has it well under control. I was thinking of doing a little traveling this summer, though. Maybe scoping out a couple potential sites for my next project. Why do you ask?"

Yes, Gwen thought curiously. Why did Adrienne ask? And did she really want to know the answer? Probably not.

"Well," Adrienne began, "I'm worried about Gwen and that apartment of hers. It's just too many stairs, and she's all alone without air-conditioning."

"I have a window unit," Gwen grumbled.

"Like that is going to make an ounce of difference in the end of August when you're pushing eight months."

Gwen shrugged. She'd made it through the last five summers without AC. If she had to, she'd spend all her free time loitering at the ice cream place up the block from her building.

"I want her to come stay with us until the baby is born, but she's being stubborn about it."

"Are you trying to rally a gang to bully me into it?" Gwen asked, hearing the edge of her accent creeping into her voice. After five years in New York, it had mostly faded, but when she got agitated or tired, it came out in full force.

"No, actually, I had another idea. Alex's place is huge, and he's almost never there."

Gwen nearly choked on the piece of bacon she was attempting to swallow. Certainly Adrienne couldn't be suggesting that Gwen stay with Alex? As far as Adrienne knew, the two of them were casual acquaintances at best. If she knew the truth, she'd certainly keep her mouth shut on that topic.

"I know you pay some woman to water plants and collect your mail while you're away. Why couldn't Gwen stay there instead? You have that huge guest suite that no one ever uses."

Gwen's eyes widened in panic. She would not go stay with Alex whether he was there or not. It would just be weird. She turned to Alex, expecting to see him appearing equally horrified. Instead, he was just sipping his water and looking as though he were actually considering the idea. Surely a man who couldn't commit past two weeks wouldn't dream of letting a woman move in with him, even temporarily.

"I think it's a little presumptuous to invite someone to move into Alex's place without talking to him first," Will said.

Finally someone was speaking sensibly. "Especially since it's completely unnecessary." Too annoyed to continue eating, Gwen slid off her stool and planted her hands on her hips. "I am a grown woman. Y'all aren't going to railroad me into moving in with anybody. So stop wasting yer breath talkin' 'bout it."

She winced at the sound of her Tennessee roots slipping into her angry words. Before anyone could respond, she ended the conversation by spinning on her heel and dashing out of the kitchen and into her room.

Alex watched the players move back and forth across the field, but he wasn't really paying attention to the game. Normally, he liked polo. He had played for years in college, and the group they'd assembled for the charity match was like the dream team of players. But he just couldn't focus on the game. Not when thoughts of Gwen kept creeping into his mind.

He glanced to his left and saw where she was sitting with Adrienne in the VIP tent. Her bright teal dress and wide-brimmed white hat made her easy to spot in the crowd. He was glad to see she was staying out of the sun and resting for a while. The heat had been brutal today, and even though it was late afternoon, it was too hot for *him,* much less a woman in her condition.

And truth be told, he was going mad watching the beads of sweat roll into the forbidden depths of her cleavage. The plunging neckline of her dress had put her full breasts on display. She was wearing a gold-and-turquoise beaded necklace that accented the pale breadth of her skin, but it had a large teardrop medallion that rested just at the valley between the creamy orbs. He had a hard time tearing his eyes away, and eventually, someone was going to catch him.

Having her a hundred yards away and shaded from the sun removed the temptation. It also helped that Gwen had continued to keep her distance today.

After last night and the way she'd bolted after their kiss by the water, he shouldn't have been surprised. He was hoping a little time alone thinking about him would soften her resolve, but if it had, he couldn't tell. Perhaps he'd moved too fast. She hadn't minded the first time they were together, but she seemed as though she was in a different place now, mentally and emotionally. Maybe the baby had planted seeds in her mind about a family of her own. Or maybe she really was serious about this man-break thing. He could see the confusion in her eyes when he got too close. It was cloaked beneath a layer of desire, but she was obviously conflicted about getting involved with him again.

Maybe there was a reason he never returned to the same fishing hole, so to speak. Since he'd hit puberty, he hadn't spent more than a few weeks with any one woman, and not once had he seen the same woman a second time after they parted ways. Alex had convinced himself that since there were over three billion women in the world—four million of them in New York City—there was absolutely no reason for him to taste the same fruit twice.

But maybe the truth of the matter was that he knew the second bite might be sour. He knew how women thought. Even though they smiled and told you they were okay, they were lying. And when they said they weren't looking for anything serious, that just meant that you could wait a year or two before proposing. His mother had told his father something like that, then had immediately gotten pregnant so he would marry her. As far as Alex knew, they'd been miserable nearly every day since.

That would never be Alex. Unfortunately, women always wanted more than he could give, so he drew his line in the sand. One time around the block and on to the next woman before things got hairy. His methods had served him well over the years. Every romantic entanglement had an escape hatch large enough to drive his Corvette through it.

But Gwen was different.

Alex had had that thought a hundred times since he had first seen her at the welcome breakfast, and it was always about a different facet of her. She aroused him. Surprised him. Irritated him. Stirred a ridiculously protective instinct in him. And worst of all, Gwen had kept his interest. Months had gone by without him seeing her, yet she regularly plagued his dreams. The temptation of her had him breaking his own rule and rearranging his Fourth of July plans to see her again. That had never happened before.

And it was only so she could end up rejecting him. That was a new thing, too. He wasn't so pleased with how things had gone so far, but it wasn't over. He had no doubt he'd be victorious and get Gwen back into his bed.

The sound of a whistle caught his attention. The first half of the match was over. A man announced over the loudspeakers that it was time for the divot stomp and invited everyone out onto the field.

Alex watched as Gwen and Adrienne joined the others on the lawn. They laughed at each other, flipping over stray tufts of grass and looking fairly ridiculous. Gwen seemed to be having a lot of fun. He had the urge to go to her and wrap his arm around her waist to keep her steady as she hopped across the field. He wanted to hear her laughter up close. But she didn't want him there, so he held his spot, leaning against an ancient oak tree with his hands in white-knuckled fists at his sides.

Things between them had ended okay before, he thought. She hadn't asked him for more from their relationship. At the same time, she hadn't jumped at the opportunity to be with him again. Gwen was a contradiction. He didn't know where he stood with her. That alone was enough to make him want to push her and find out. That and his own burning need to possess her like the latest and greatest Apple gadget.

Alex still hadn't gotten to the bottom of what drew him to Gwen. Whatever it happened to be was as strong as ever. Strong enough to urge him to break down her walls, even though she claimed to be happy in her isolation. But what was the point, really? If he pushed her the way he wanted to, what could he give her in return? He'd tried to buy her jewelry all those months ago. He thought he'd been successful at the time, only to find out she'd relented because she'd found the perfect symbol of abstinence. That wasn't exactly what he'd had in mind.

Gwen had pushed away his physical advances. All Alex had in his arsenal was sex and money. If she wasn't interested in either, he was out of luck unless he could find another way to get her attention.

If she was after some kind of domestic existence like the one he'd very nearly dodged the day before, he couldn't help her there. But he wasn't sure she even knew what she was after. The way she'd blown hot and cold last night, he didn't know if the promise of something different between them would win her favor or send her running in the opposite direction. She'd said that she wasn't in the right place for something serious. Moments later, she wasn't receptive to something casual.

Certainly there had to be a middle ground where he could have Gwen back in his bed without grand, sweeping, romantic promises he couldn't keep. Being up-front and honest about that seemed kinder than promising what he couldn't deliver. If laughter and passion and excitement weren't enough for Gwen, then this whole week would be a waste of his time.

"Why aren't you out there stomping?" Will asked, coming up from behind him with a glass of chardonnay in each hand. He held one out and Alex gratefully accepted.

He swallowed a large gulp and let the dry bite of the wine chase away his unwelcome thoughts. "I just had these shoes polished," he said, knowing it was a lame excuse.

"Does Adrienne know you and Gwen slept together?"

Will's blunt question nearly sent a burning stream of wine up through Alex's nostrils. Instead, he fought to choke it down, swallowing and taking a painful, deep breath before he spoke. "No, she doesn't," he sputtered, and coughed into his fist. There was no sense in playing dumb. Will knew him too well and had watched him move through a line of women over the years. "Gwen doesn't want her to know."

Will nodded as he lifted his wineglass to drink. "She'd get overly romantic ideas about the two of you."

"Probably." Alex knew Will's bride was the best thing to ever happen to his friend, but she was softhearted and idealistic to a fault. "How did you know?"

Will glanced across the field, and Alex followed the direction of his gaze to the two women. The stomping was nearly over, and they were making their way off the field as best they could in a giggling fit. "The tension between you two is palpable. I've seen you watching her when you think no one is paying attention. When did it happen? It had to be right after the wedding."

"Yes. While you and Adrienne were on your honeymoon in Bali."

"It's been a long time since you've seen her, then."

"Yeah. You know I've been in New Orleans for months. Hell, I hadn't even spoken to her since November."

"That's certainly interesting."

Alex tried not to frown. He didn't like the implication of his friend's tone. "What do you mean by that?"

"You're still into her after all this time."

He certainly was. But he knew what Will was inferring—that perhaps he had real feelings for Gwen. He liked Gwen. He enjoyed her company. But feelings? Alex didn't have feelings about women. Not even for her.

"Why not?" he asked, dismissively. "I'd be stupid to pass up the opportunity to be with her again. She's a beautiful, uncomplicated woman who happens to be an exceptional lover. There's nothing else to it."

Will chuckled and slapped Alex on the back. "You just keep telling yourself that and maybe it will become the truth."

Alex's brow furrowed. "It *is* the truth. And besides that, she's turned me down, so there's even less than nothing to it."

Will tried to smother a smile, but failed. "Gwen turned you down? Is that an Alex Stanton first?"

He shrugged. "Maybe. But it's not over yet, so don't count me out. There's four days left to this trip. Eventually I'll convince her that I'm worth abandoning her vows of celibacy while she's here. Then she can go back to living like a nun, I'll be back on my game and Gwen will be in my past, just like all the others."

Adrienne waved at them and Will raised a hand to her. "Whatever you say, man. But if you want to keep whatever it is you two are or aren't having a secret, you'd better be more careful. I've never seen you look at a woman the way you look at Gwen. Adrienne will pick up on it in an instant." He started off across the lawn to join his wife.

"And how is that, exactly?" Alex called out to him.

Will stopped and turned, his face drawn and serious. "Almost like you wish that baby was yours."

Five

It was an exhausting day. Too much sun and noise and walking around. Too much energy spent dodging Alex's watchful gaze and Adrienne's continued arguments about her unfit living situation. By the time their parade of cars pulled into the circular driveway, Gwen was ready to sleep until her third trimester. Some of the group was talking about watching a movie, but she wasn't interested in anything but getting up close and personal with her pillow. She ignored both Adrienne and Alex's pointed looks as she excused herself and went to bed.

She resisted the urge to sleep in her clothes and managed to stay awake long enough to take off her jewelry and slip into her oversized University of Tennessee T-shirt. After that, she fell into a restless sleep pretty quickly.

Sometime after midnight, she woke up with a

miserably aching lower back. She propped a pillow between her knees and curled onto her side, but after another twenty minutes, her back still hurt and she was now wide awake.

Gwen flipped on the lamp and sat up in bed, defeated. At home, she would take a hot shower to ease her muscles, but the sight of her swimsuit on the dresser gave her a better idea. A swim in the pool would help take the pressure of the pregnancy off her body and allow her to stretch her sore muscles.

Gwen listened for noises outside her bedroom door, but it seemed that everyone had already gone to bed. Good. This would be her first time wearing her bikini since she'd gotten pregnant, and she wasn't quite ready to debut it to the world yet. She had a one-piece maternity suit that she would wear during the day with the others.

But tonight, she was free to swim as she pleased, and it would be easier to wrestle out of a wet two-piece. It was her favorite swimsuit, navy blue with tiny, white polka dots. As she slipped it on, she was pleased to find it still seemed to fit okay, although the bottoms rode lower on her hips to accommodate her belly. Gwen unlatched her bracelet, leaving it on the dresser, grabbed her towel and stepped quietly into the dark hallway. She took the direct route through the kitchen, creeping out the back door without so much as a creaking hinge.

Outside, the night was dark, but the lights of the pool were still on, giving it a shimmering turquoise glow. Wavy silver lines reflecting from the water danced along the back of the house and across the round, exposed orb of her stomach.

She tossed her towel across one of the lounge chairs and stepped to the stairs. Dipping her toe, she found the water to be cool, but not too cold. It was heated by solar panels to take the chill off. She stepped down slowly, submerging her body inch by inch until the water reached her waist. Letting go of the railing, she surged forward, cutting through the water. She resurfaced at the far end of the pool, taking a breath and pushing her wet hair back from her face.

It felt so good. Not only the water, but the weightlessness. The ache in her back immediately began to fade. She seriously needed to look into a membership somewhere with an indoor pool for the last few months of this pregnancy. Maybe a gym where she could work to get back in shape after Peanut was born. But either way, it would be worth the money, even if she just soaked in the water like a giant tea bag.

Gwen pushed off the wall and started back to the other side, stretching and pulling herself through the water. After several laps, she leaned back and let herself float at the surface. The water covered her ears and muffled the sounds around her, leaving nothing but the silent, starry night above her. She sighed, looking up at the twinkling scattershot of stars she couldn't see in the city. She hadn't realized how much she missed them until this moment.

As a teenager, she'd spent a hundred nights lying on the trampoline in the backyard doing this same thing. Watching the stars. Making wishes if one fell to Earth. Dreaming that one day she'd get out of Tennessee and do something grand and important with her life. Even at fifteen she knew she wanted to be a nurse. She wanted to help people and make a difference in someone's life.

Gwen supposed that was why she'd offered to help Robert and Susan. She'd worked for years as a nurse and had wanted to do more. Short of treating soldiers on the battlefield or children in third world countries, she wasn't sure what more she could do. But helping them have a baby was special. That would make a difference in their lives.

She let her hands drift up over her head, then brought them quickly to her sides, sending her gliding over the surface of the water. As Gwen drifted to a stop, she saw a meteor streak across the sky and dissolve into the atmosphere.

"We need to make a wish, Peanut," she said. "What shall we wish for?"

There were so many choices, Gwen had a hard time trying to decide. Of course she wanted a healthy, happy baby girl for Robert and Susan, but she didn't want to use her wish for that tonight. Every decision she made in her life was to make things better for others. Usually, knowing she'd helped someone when they'd needed it most was enough for her. But tonight, as selfish as it might seem, this wish, this star, was just for her.

But what did she want? She spent so much time worrying about other people that she didn't have a clue. Her career wasn't enough anymore. Even having a child for someone else wasn't as satisfying as she'd hoped it would be. It had been more confusing than anything. What did she want? Freedom? Family? Passion? Excitement?

"What do I want?" she said aloud to the night. Maybe the stars would point her in the right direction. As the question turned in her head, thoughts immediately drifted to Alex's bright, disarming smile. His messy hair. She could almost hear his muffled laughter through the water.

Gwen wanted to wish for Alex. She might as well wish for the moon. It would be a better use of a falling star to ask for immunity from his charms instead. Then she could get through the week without giving in to him. That seductive grin of his was nothing but trouble for a girl sworn to temporary celibacy.

"But I want him, Peanut. And I shouldn't. What should I do?"

"Personally, I'm not big on self-sacrifice, so I say if you want him, then have him."

The muffled voice made it through the water to her ears. Startled, Gwen shot upright, sinking under the surface and then bobbing back up to the top.

Wiping the water from her eyes, she saw Alex standing at the edge of the pool. He was wearing a pair of unbuttoned jeans and nothing else. The sight of his bare chest with its hard angles and defined musculature sucked the breath from her lungs. She remembered what it felt like to run her finger over the ridges and how the sprinkle of dark blond chest hair tickled her nose when she rested her head on him. Her eyes followed the trail of hair as it darkened and disappeared into his low-slung jeans. There didn't appear to be anything under them, as though he'd just tugged them on to run downstairs.

A sudden heat flushed through her body. She wanted Alex, but she certainly hadn't wanted to announce it to him. Not when she was fighting the feelings. It just gave him ammunition to use against her. How long had he been standing there? Listening to her? Watching her white belly float along the surface? Anger quickly dampened her desire. Gwen furiously splashed a handful of water at him, sending him flying back a few steps to avoid it.

"What's that for?" he asked.

"For sneaking up on me," she snapped, her legs furiously kicking to keep her petite body at the surface in the deep end of the pool. "What are you doing out here?"

"I couldn't sleep. I came down to get some water and see if there was any of Helena's pound cake left. I saw you through the kitchen window. What are you doing swimming alone in the middle of the night? Isn't that one of the basic no-no's for pool safety?"

Gwen ignored his question, swimming toward the shallow end so she could touch the bottom of the pool. Alex followed her, walking along the concrete edge in bare feet.

"My back was killing me," she said. "It woke me up, actually. I thought the pool might help. I certainly wasn't going to wake any of y'all up to babysit me while I swim."

Alex's eyes narrowed at her with concern. He seemed to be doing that a lot the last few days. She wished he'd just go back to glaring at her with poorly masked desire. That, she knew how to deal with. Sorta.

"Would you like me to rub your back for you? I give great massages."

Gwen's gaze darted to meet his. The concern was gone, the playful, seductive Alex returning. Yes, he gave good massages. She'd been treated to one in his apartment, complete with musky-scented massage oil and a happy ending for them both. His hands had been like slick magic on her skin. But that was then. Letting him try it after going months without a man's touch, even for something as innocent as a back rub, would ruin her plans. She'd fall off the wagon so fast, she'd be rolling in the dirt behind it.

Instead, she just shook her head. "That's a nice offer, but no thanks."

Alex crouched down at the edge of the pool. "You've been avoiding me since I kissed you."

Gwen opened her mouth to deny it, but there really wasn't much point. It was true. "Yes."

"Why?" His golden eyes were shrouded in the darkness, but she could still see the slightly pained expression on his face. Why her refusal would hurt him was a mystery when he could have any woman he wanted.

"Because I told you I am off men right now. You just don't listen. I'm trying to take some time for me, to organize my priorities, and I'm sorry, but you nibbling on my ear doesn't help. I don't need the distraction. It's just not a good idea."

"I don't agree. Seeing those curves of yours in that tiny bikini makes me think it's a marvelous idea. We could have a couple great days together, then you can go back to prioritizing all by your lonesome. What could it hurt?"

Gwen planted her feet on the floor of the pool and pushed herself to stand. "Me," she said, the water swirling around her stomach with the sudden motion. "It can hurt *me,* Alex. I really don't know what I'm doing anymore. This surrogacy was supposed to help me figure out what I want, but with only a few months left, I still don't know. But I'm trying to make some positive changes in my life. And, yes, I might want you. But, and I'm sorry if this offends you, I can't help thinking that getting involved with you again is a step back for me, not a step forward."

"I don't think I've ever had a woman tell me that before. Usually, I'm an upgrade." The playful glint faded from his eyes. "Gwen, you know that I—"

"—don't do relationships," she interrupted. "I know. And I was okay with that the first time. I certainly wasn't looking for anything serious." Gwen brought her hand to her stomach and stroked it beneath the water. "And I'm not looking for something serious now. I'm not looking for anything at all. But when I'm ready, I think I want something better for myself. And I don't think you're the man to give it to me."

"Gwen, I'm sorry I—" He reached out, but the wide moat of water kept her out of his grasp.

"Don't apologize, Alex. You are always up front about what you're selling. This time, I'm just not in the market to buy it."

Alex watched from the side of the pool as Gwen looked away, uncomfortably, to study one of the deck chairs. She'd spoken forcefully, putting up a brave front, probably hoping he'd just nod and go away so she didn't have to keep it up any longer. He could see she was struggling. Walking in on her private conversation had just proven to him that he was right. Gwen did want him. She was just being stubborn about it. He didn't get it. But there was only one way to get her to confess the truth. Alex would goad her into saying it.

"You're a chicken," he said.

Gwen's head snapped back toward him, her eyes wide with confusion and irritation. "What makes you think you know so much about me, Alex? I was nothing but Miss October to you."

"Maybe, but October is my favorite month, and I have an eye for details. My business wouldn't be doing as well as it is if I didn't understand people and what makes them tick. I know exactly what will capture their imagination and make them trip over themselves to buy one of my properties. And in my years with women, I've figured out quite a few additional things about them. And you."

"Like what?" she challenged.

Alex crouched down at the edge of the water to get closer to her. "Like how you never take any time for yourself. From the first moment I saw you, you've been killing yourself to make other people happy. For Adrienne's wedding. For the hospital and your patients. For your friends. Even for me during our brief time together. Now you've taken it to a whole new level, and you're having a baby for someone else."

"What's wrong with that?"

"Nothing," he argued, "unless you're suffering because of it. There's a fine line between a saint and a martyr. You don't have to be miserable to do what's important to you. It's about balance. When was the last time you did something just for you?"

Gwen frowned at him. He could see her struggling to come up with an answer, her cheeks flushing red with anger because it was taking longer than she wanted it to. "The last time I did something selfish was giving in to my fling with you."

He'd been expecting her to admit to something like splurging on a new dress or a pedicure. He never dreamed her answer would be something that had happened eight months ago. She was more caught up in this than he thought. "Why is doing something just for you selfish? The opposite of a giving person isn't a selfish one."

Gwen sighed and shook her head. "Okay, fine. You win. What do you want me to say, Alex?"

"I want you to admit that you want me."

Her jaw tightened, her dark eyes glittering with the night lights. "What does it—?"

She started to argue, but Alex cut her off. "Say it," he demanded.

"I want you," she said, but there was more irritation than passion behind her words. He wanted her to say it as though she meant it. And she would before the night was over.

Alex stood and suddenly walked off the edge of the pool, splashing into the water, jeans and all. Gwen leaped back in surprise, but she didn't have her protective moat any longer. Alex lunged at her, wrapping his arms around her waist and pulling her close.

"What are you doing?" she gasped.

"Say it like you mean it, Gwen."

Her eyes widened and she squirmed uncomfortably under his scrutinizing gaze. "It doesn't matter. I already told you I'm not interested in another fling," she argued.

"So you've said, but you're deluding yourself." He looked down and noticed the hands pressing against his chest. "You've taken your chastity bracelet off."

"The chlorine is bad for the silver," she sputtered. "It is not some subconscious invitation."

Alex smiled. She could say all she wanted, but he took it as a sign. "You and I both know there's no point in spending this whole trip denying the fantastic connection between us."

She immediately stilled, her breath catching in her throat.

"I know it would be easier if I just went back into the house and never touched you again. But I don't want to. It might be selfish, but I'm not ready to give up what we have yet. I can't stop thinking about how badly I want you, Gwen."

He didn't wait for Gwen's response. Instead, he brought a hand up to her face and cupped her cheek.

Her chocolate-brown eyes were still wide with surprise, but now a faint smile curved her full lips. That was all the invitation he needed. He leaned down to her, lifting her easily from the water that made her feel light as a feather.

When his lips touched hers, a surge of white-hot need knifed through his body, but he fought to control it. He wanted Gwen, but he didn't want to rush this. He needed to take it slowly and help her navigate her way back to trusting their sexual chemistry.

Gwen's mouth was soft and hesitant at first. She opened up to him slowly, her silky tongue gliding along his lip and teeth, teasing him. It took every ounce of restraint Alex had not to crush her against him and devour her with his mouth. Instead he let his tongue seek her out, tasting her, savoring the feel of her in his arms. She was like a rare wine. He wanted to take in her scent, let the flavor of her roll around in his mouth so he could truly appreciate it, and commit her to his memory.

His hands moved down the slick contours of her body. They glided over the cool silk of her skin, teasing him with her soft contrast to his hardness. Stepping back through the water, Alex moved them to the edge of the pool. Without his mouth leaving hers, he lifted her up to sit on the edge and erased the disadvantage of their height difference.

Gwen gasped as her backside met with the cold concrete, but she quickly recovered by opening her thighs and tugging him closer to her. The chilled pebbles of her breasts dug into his chest and echoed the heat of his arousal that pressed into her bare thigh.

Alex dipped his head to lick a drop of water that traveled down to the hollow of her throat. The sharp taste of it mingled with the salt of her skin, tempting him to run his tongue along the soft curve of her neck. She tipped her head back, her fingers lacing through his hair and urging him on.

He wanted her. Every touch, every taste, every soft cry that escaped her lips demanded that he have her. His fingers tugged at the bow of her bikini top. The blue scrap of fabric came away in his hands, and he dropped it on the concrete with a satisfying, wet thump.

Alex paused to look down at the delights he'd uncovered. The full, pale breasts that had teased him from her dress earlier in the day were on display for him at last. The creamy ivory skin was firm and flawless, the strawberry-pink tips hard and reaching out to him.

He slowly brought his palms up to each, letting her sensitive nipples graze across his rough hands in lazy circles. Gwen sighed and closed her eyes, leaning back on her hands to arch them up to him. Finally, he pressed into them, cupping each breast and letting the pad of his thumb brush the tips until Gwen whimpered. It was only then that he let himself taste them. He sucked one nipple into his mouth, then the other, teasing and tugging with his teeth and tongue until she was squirming against him and clawing gently at his back.

"Alex," she whispered, an edge of need in her voice that he'd longed to hear again after all these months without her. That was the very thing he'd wanted from her earlier.

He answered with his hand, slipping it between her thighs and stroking her through the wet fabric of her suit. He could feel the shock wave of his touch as it rocked through her body. Her hips bucked wildly against his hand, the cry escaping her lips making his erection throb painfully as it grated on the rough, wet denim of his jeans.

Pushing the suit aside, he slipped one finger inside the hot, aching entry to her body. He could feel her muscles contract around him, tightening and straining against the invasion. Slowly, he pumped into her, the pad of his thumb brushing her sensitive nub with the apex of each stroke. Gwen writhed and thrashed her feet along the surface of the water as her climax built inside her. She was a wild and passionate woman, and he'd sorely missed that while he was gone.

He watched her face with anticipation, waiting for her body to stiffen beneath him. "Say it," he whispered.

"I want you, Alex!" she cried out a second before the first wave hit.

Satisfied, he captured her mouth in a kiss. Alex swallowed the strangled cry of her orgasm, his body absorbing the violent shudders and jerks until, silent and still, Gwen collapsed beneath him.

"Now, that wasn't so hard to admit, was it?"

Gwen tried to look at him crossly, but she didn't have the energy. She was still trembling, her breath coming in short gasps, when Alex scooped her off the edge and carried her out of the pool. He stood her upright near the row of lounge chairs, reaching down to wrap the towel around her shoulders.

Once he was certain she was steady on her feet, he left her side to retrieve her bikini top and slowly made his way back. His soaked jeans hung heavily on his hips, threatening to sag to his ankles if he moved too quickly.

Alex wrapped his arm around her shoulder and guided her back to the house. He gripped his waistband to allow them to move faster through the tile kitchen, slowing once they reached the carpet that would absorb the water dripping from their bodies.

Inside her room, he shut the door behind them and

flipped the lock. When he turned back, Gwen had flung off her towel. With a bold, mischievous glint in her eye, she approached him and gave his jeans a solid tug.

As expected, they slid right down without resistance, freeing his erection to jut out to her. Gwen knelt down, letting her hot breath linger on the tip for just a moment before continuing down and helping him step out of the soggy clothing. She carried it and her swim top into the bathroom, tossing them in the sink with the bottoms she had still been wearing.

When she returned, she was completely naked. Her hair hung around her shoulders in dark, wet, blond cords. Her cheeks were still rosy from her orgasm. She stopped a few feet away from him, watching him through the damp clumps of her eyelashes. Gwen seemed almost embarrassed, although it was a little late to be shy. He'd seen her naked a dozen times and had never been disappointed.

But then, it occurred to Alex that things were different this time. The changes in her body might leave her feeling insecure. She probably wasn't as appreciative of her new curves as he was. How could she not see how beautiful she was?

Alex reached out his hand to her and pulled her toward the bed. If she couldn't see it, he'd just have to show her.

Six

Gwen let Alex guide her to the bed. He tugged back the sheets for her to slip between them, then joined her there. A chill from the pool had set in once they came into the air-conditioned house. The warmth of the blanket and Alex's body near hers felt heavenly, chasing away the gooseflesh that drew up across her skin.

The blanket also made her feel less exposed. True, her swimsuit had done little to disguise her blooming pregnancy, but somehow standing naked with Alex's eyes on her had made her extremely self-aware.

The last time they were together, she was at her all-time lowest weight after months of exercise and carb deprivation. She didn't want to look like a sausage stuffed into a pink, satin casing at the wedding. Now her body was about as different as it could be. What if it bothered him more than he thought? What if he changed his mind? It was a worry that crept into her brain without her permission. She tried to chase away the negative thoughts. Alex's desire for her was quite obvious the minute she'd tugged at his pants, and it hadn't wavered. The same firm heat pressed into her hip at that exact moment.

Gwen forced herself to relax, letting her body sink into the pillows. Alex pulled up along her side, the heat of his skin running the whole length of her body. He propped on one elbow and looked down at her. There was a softness in his expression she wasn't used to seeing. Most often there was humor or mischief or desire. The longing was still there, but it was laced with a tenderness that made her chest tight.

His fingertips brushed across her forehead to push a damp strand of hair away, then softly grazed along her jaw to her mouth. "You're so beautiful," he said.

She swallowed a denial when his thumb stroked her bottom lip and stole the words. She wanted him to kiss her again. To cover her body with his and make her forget about all her worries and anxieties, if just for tonight.

He hadn't offered her more than that. But right now, that was all she needed. Some physical contact with a man she didn't have to worry about complications with. If she had thought for a second there would be anything more to it, she wouldn't have given in. But Alex was not a guy to stick around. If she wanted more, he'd be the worst possible choice. But sex between them should be easy and gratifying. There was absolutely no reason why she should deny herself the pleasure any longer.

His mouth found hers and she opened to him once again. She relished the silky slide of his tongue, the way he could coax a low moan from the back of her throat. His lips migrated to her jaw, settling in to feast on the sensitive curve of her neck. He nipped and sucked at her skin, sending throbbing impulses through her whole body.

She was surprised how quickly she responded to him. After their encounter at the pool, she would've thought she was sated enough for one night, but she was wrong. It had simply lit a fire to dry kindling and was now building to a crackling roar of desire.

Alex's hand reached out to her beneath the blankets. His palm was a searing heat against her cool skin, blazing a trail along the curves of her body. The glide of his fingertips was electric, the sizzle warming her blood.

"Are you still cold?" he murmured against her throat.

Not when he was touching her. "No," she said, kicking at the covers.

He flung back the rest and returned to feasting on her skin. As he traveled down to her breasts, Gwen was stunned by how sensitive they'd become. Just the brush of his fingertips across her tight nipples sent a sharp throb of need to her feminine muscles, tightening them into a delicious tug of pleasure.

Alex growled low against her skin, the vibration tickling and teasing at her.

The haze of pleasure thinned for a moment when Gwen realized he was moving down her body. She tensed when his hand came to a stop resting on the swell of her stomach. Would that be too much reality for him to ignore?

Gwen held her breath; her eyes squeezed shut so she wouldn't see his reaction. It wasn't until she felt the moist heat of his kiss searing across her belly that she was able to release the air trapped in her lungs.

Alex's hand moved lower, stroking the inside of her thigh. Her muscles jumped beneath her skin with anticipation of his touch. His lips followed his fingertips, her thighs gently quivering when his warm breath brushed across her exposed core. His first taste sent a bolt of pleasure through her body that arched her back off the bed. He waited until the shock waves passed before stroking her again. Gwen held her breath, trying to swallow the cries he coaxed from her, but it was too much. He had her dancing on the edge of coming undone almost instantly.

"Alex," she whispered.

He hesitated a moment, his tongue darting out one last time before sliding back up the length of her body. Alex hovered at the entrance to her body, his golden eyes gazing deep into her own. Then he slowly entered her. She couldn't help her eyes closing as she savored the feeling she'd missed all these months with him gone.

"Damn," he groaned against her lips. The rest of his body was stone still as he hovered, buried to the hilt. His arms started shaking with the strain before he allowed himself to pull back and drive into her again.

Gwen pulled her legs up to cradle him, easily riding the waves of motion that corresponded to the swells of pleasure building inside her. She'd been so close to the edge before that it didn't take long to reach it again, but she wasn't ready to give in to it. It had been eight long months since she'd given in to her desires. Having Alex in her bed again was an unexpected fantasy she'd never thought she could indulge. This moment needed to last a lifetime in case it was their last. She wasn't about to rush to the finish line, even if every nerve in her body demanded release.

She opened her eyes, trying to memorize the lines of strain across his brow as he fought for control. Gwen wanted to remember the sound of his ragged breath and the salty taste of his skin.

It wasn't until Alex stilled that she realized he was watching her, a look of curiosity on his face. "You're thinking too much. I'm not doing a good job if you're able to focus like that."

Gwen smiled, reaching up to his face and pulling him to her lips for a kiss. "You're doing a great job," she reassured. "I'm just trying to make it last."

"The good thing about orgasms," he said with a wry grin, "is that you won't run out. You can always have another." At that, he thrust hard into her and elicited a surprised cry of pleasure from her throat. "And another."

"And another," she repeated, hooking her ankles around his hips and squeezing him until he groaned.

From then on, there were no more words. Gwen gave into the sensations, clinging to him as they drove hard toward their climax. She buried her cries in his shoulder when she came undone, the hard shudder of his own release coming soon after.

When she finally caught her breath, she looked up to find Alex hovering over her, his brow furrowed, his eyes wide with unexpected panic. "What's the matter?" Gwen asked, her voice hoarse.

His jaw dropped open in shock and he just hung there, mute, until he could gather the words. "We didn't use a condom. I forgot. I was too…" He shook his head and cursed.

Normally, Gwen would've launched into full damage-control mode. How could they forget something as crucial as that? But then she remembered she couldn't get pregnant and a good portion of the panic subsided. "That's okay," she said, brushing a strand of golden hair from his face.

"No, it isn't," he insisted. "I always wear a condom. Always."

There was a touch of alarm in his eyes that worried her. "I'm already pregnant, Alex. And it's a little late for this conversation, but I was tested for everything under the sun before the in vitro procedure. What about you?"

Her question seemed to jerk him from his thoughts. He looked down at her and nodded, clearly realizing she was right, yet still obviously concerned. "I get a full panel of testing every six months, without fail. Never so much as a false positive."

That was a relief. And at the same time a touch disturbing. How many women had he charmed into bed that he was tested so often? It was a good thing she didn't have fantasies of keeping Alex. It was an impossibility.

Fortunately, he was smart about it, so their stupidity wouldn't put both her health and the baby's in jeopardy. A nurse should know better, but apparently being in Alex's arms made her lose all her good sense.

Gwen sighed and patted his arm reassuringly. "Well, it wasn't the smartest thing, but I think it will be okay just this once." Using protection the "next time" was left unsaid. The only thing that could bring down the postorgasm buzz faster than the "oops, no condom" discussion was a clingy woman talking about the future.

Alex's jaw relaxed and he gave a short nod before leaning down to kiss her. Gwen noticed there was still a tension there, but he was trying his best to hide it. She remembered how diligent he was with birth control the last time they were together. For both of them to forget...

He eased onto his side, dropping against the mattress. His arm snaked around her and gently pulled her back to his chest.

She snuggled into him, trying not to think about the

implications of his slip and the fact that he'd positioned himself so she couldn't see his expression. He hadn't immediately rushed back to his room, so maybe she was making something out of nothing. Gwen tried to focus on just being with him, and before long, she fell asleep in the protective warmth of his arms.

It was still early morning when a beam of sunlight stretched across the bed and into Alex's face. It pulled him from the comfortable fog of sleep. His eyes fluttered open, looking around for a moment in confusion at the whitewashed furniture and blue comforter before he remembered where he was.

Gwen's bed.

Easing his head up, he saw her unruly, dark blond curls and her arm draped across his chest. She was still asleep, her breathing soft and even as she cuddled against him.

Alex needed to leave if they were going to keep last night a secret from the rest of the house. He didn't want to go. He wanted to pull up the duvet and sleep away the rest of the afternoon with her in his arms, but that was just a pipe dream. If it was daylight out, he should've returned to his room a long time ago. Will always got up early, although there was no sense in tiptoeing around him. He didn't know much about the other guests in the house, but he certainly didn't want any of them to see him dash, half-naked, to his room.

All he had were his jeans. Alex swallowed a groan when he realized they were a soaking wet heap in Gwen's bathroom sink. When he had come downstairs the night before, he was after a drink and some cake. If he'd thought for a moment he'd end up in the pool or

Gwen's bed, he would've planned accordingly. And he most certainly would've brought a condom.

The memory of the slipup slapped him in the face and made sure he was good and awake now. God, he was an idiot.

No condom. How could he forget something that important? He had never had sex without one before. He wasn't about to get snared like his father. Not once, not even one time in all these years, had he allowed himself to get so wrapped up in a woman that he could let something like that happen.

Alex wasn't quite sure why it bothered him so badly. Gwen couldn't get pregnant with his child. They both vouched for being healthy. Nothing should come back to bite either of them. What was it, then, that left him with a pool of worry in his stomach?

It was just one more thing. One more difference between Gwen and every other woman he'd ever been with. Since he'd first met her, she'd gotten through almost all of his well-fortified defenses. She probably didn't even know it, but she had. He never would've sought her out again, much less made love to her, if she hadn't gotten under his skin.

Gwen had penetrated his brain, occupying his thoughts and dreams over the last months. Making him think of nothing but having her back in his arms again. She'd pierced his physical defenses last night, getting closer to him than any other woman had. Without the barrier of latex between them, their joining had been so different. It didn't just feel different; it was almost as if it meant more than he'd ever intended.

The sound of birds chirping outside the window declared it was officially morning and distracted him from his worries. He glanced over at the nightstand and the clock sitting there. It was just after six. He definitely needed to get back to his room, jeans or no. Alex picked up Gwen's wrist and slowly eased out from beneath her. She grumbled sleepily for a moment, then curled into a ball in the warm spot he'd left behind and fell back asleep.

Alex struggled to swallow a lump in his throat as he watched her sleep. Her ash-blond hair was a tangle across the pillowcase, her pink lips still swollen from his kisses. Just the sight of her like that made his chest tighten.

Typically, the morning after was uncomfortable for him. Sunlight always brought a cold dose of reality with it. Seeing a woman sleeping or just after she'd woken up had always seemed too intimate to him. The sex… that was just sex, but the reality of a woman without her carefully crafted facade was a line he didn't like to cross. It felt like relationship territory. He preferred to leave before the veil of fantasy slipped away.

It was different with Gwen. He wasn't uncomfortable watching her like this. Not even after realizing he was playing with fire. He was overwhelmed with the urge to surprise her with breakfast in bed. He wanted to make her pancakes and kiss her maple syrup–flavored lips.

Pancakes. *What the hell was that about?* It was definitely time to go.

With a sigh, Alex ran his fingers through his messy hair and headed for the bathroom before he could do something stupid, such as cooking or tossing aside every remaining rule in his relationship book. As he suspected, his jeans were still soaked and ice cold. There was no way he could bear to slip those on against his bare skin, and he'd do nothing but drip all the way upstairs. He took the jeans and her swimsuit and moved them to hang over the bar in the shower. Hopefully they would dry better that way.

He opted to grab a towel from the rod on the wall and wrap it around his waist. Turning on the water in the sink, Alex eased down and lightly wet his hair. If he ran into anyone, he'd tell them he'd taken an early-morning dip in the pool.

Alex gave a quick glance to the bed where Gwen was silently sleeping, then crept out into the hallway. He was relieved to find the house was still dark and quiet. Six was a little early for people on vacation. When he got back to his room, he immediately slipped into the shower.

As the hot water streamed over his body and washed away her scent, his gut twisted with confusion and regret about last night. Gwen was so beautiful, so passionate. She was impossible to resist, and yet he knew he should've returned to his room instead of charging into the water and claiming her. Gwen was trying to figure out what she wanted in life. She deserved a man who would marry her and fill their home with their own children, if she decided that was what she wanted.

And that wasn't Alex.

Being here with her the last few days had roused something deep inside that wanted him to be that man for her. But that wouldn't last. Not once since hitting puberty had he had a lasting interest in a relationship. He'd seen firsthand what a hell marriage could be like. His childhood home had been a battlefield with him as one of the primary weapons. Marriage was not for him. This time, despite what he thought now, was no different. Eventually, he would feel the choking noose of commitment around his throat and he'd have to leave.

So he didn't dare offer anything he couldn't give.

He'd tempted Gwen with a few days of meaningless, mind-blowing sex, and that was all it was going to be. He wouldn't even entertain the thoughts of more in the privacy of his own mind. They were counterproductive.

By the time Alex dressed and went downstairs, Will was awake and pouring his first cup of coffee. He eyed Alex with suspicion as he settled at the breakfast bar.

"You're up early." His words were heavy with meaning as he passed a steamy mug of coffee across the counter to Alex. "Trouble sleeping?"

"Something like that," he muttered into his coffee mug, avoiding eye contact with his friend, although he knew it was pointless. Will was a newspaperman. Journalism ran in his blood. He could read between the lines and sniff out the larger story better than anyone else he'd ever met.

"What are you going to do?" Will asked softly. With his own coffee in hand, he approached the bar and leaned against it so their voices wouldn't need to carry far. Gwen's room was only feet away.

"I was thinking about going for a run," Alex answered, flatly dodging Will's real question. He was considering a jog this morning. He'd pulled on a T-shirt and jogging shorts after his shower, but it was a halfhearted effort. If he left, it would just be to escape the pull of Gwen on his thoughts. He seriously doubted even that would help at this point. She'd been the only thing on his mind since he'd decided to come on this trip.

Will shook his head but opted not to press Alex further. "Do you want company? I doubt the others will be up for a while."

"Sure, let me just absorb some of this caffeine first. What's on the agenda for today, anyway?"

"Some of us were talking about going to a couple of

wineries in the area. Several do tours and tastings this time of year."

Alex frowned, despite his general fondness for wine. "What about Emma and Gwen? Neither can drink."

Will nodded, thoughtfully sipping his coffee. "I think Emma is keen on an afternoon tanning and talking to her boyfriend on the phone. I doubt she gets five minutes of peace and solitude at home the way Pauline and George hover since the crash."

"Do you think they'll follow her to Yale?"

"No." He smiled. "But I have no doubt she'll go wild with her new freedom. Hopefully not at the expense of her grades or her reputation."

Alex grinned. They both knew Alex had had at least one semester when he'd toyed with academic probation. Economics and calculus were not nearly as interesting as playing polo and checking out the latest class of freshman girls. "What about Gwen?"

Will shrugged. "That's up to her, I suppose. She could come with us and just not drink. I think at least one of them also does olive oil and cheese tastings. And she could enjoy the tours of the gardens and vineyards."

Somehow that didn't sound like Gwen's cup of tea at all. She'd put on a brave face yesterday during the long hours of yuppie polo festivities, politely turning down the caviar and foie gras canapés and blankly staring at the horses. Following it up with a day of wine tasting was probably too much for her, especially when she couldn't benefit from getting pleasantly tipsy in the process.

Perhaps this was his chance to have some uninterrupted time with Gwen away from the others. "Maybe I'll offer to stay with her. She doesn't have a car here, so she's trapped if we all leave."

"Actually, we have the little Volvo in the garage that stays at the house. I could leave her the keys."

Alex supposed that solved the problem of Gwen's stranding, but he still didn't like the idea of her being alone all day. Emma was not likely to be good company, either. "That isn't any fun. I'll skip the wineries and take her out."

Will frowned into his coffee mug. "To do what?"

"Maybe I'll treat her to a massage."

"From you?"

"No," Alex chided. "I mean a real one at a day spa. She could get a pedicure and all that. A little feminine indulgence."

Will took a sip of his coffee, watching Alex warily. "That's very nice of you. Not exactly subtle, though."

"Can't I be nice to a pregnant woman who could use some pampering?"

"Absolutely. But don't be surprised if Adrienne smells blood in the water. And even if she doesn't get suspicious, you and I both know it's not the best idea."

"Of course it's a terrible idea," Alex agreed with a grin. It would be setting himself up for a day alone with Gwen. Sort of. It wasn't as if they'd let him in the room with her. He'd likely spend at least half the day in the waiting room reading emails on his phone. But he couldn't just walk out and leave her alone all day after the incredible night they'd spent together.

And he didn't want to, if he was honest with himself.

Maybe a day out without privacy would cool his desire for her and let him take a step back, physically, if nothing else. It might also completely implode in his face and make him feel closer to her than ever, but what was life without some risk?

Alex set down his empty mug, the caffeine finally

waking him up for the day. It was too early to make the arrangements, but he'd call as soon as he could.

"You ready for that run?"

Seven

Gwen watched curiously as everyone loaded up into a couple cars to go on what she called "the winery crawl." Even if she weren't pregnant, she would've taken a pass on this particular excursion. She was tired and really not interested in discussing vintages and bouquets. But instead of a quiet afternoon lounging and reading a book, she noticed not only Emma but also Alex beside her, waving to the cars.

"You're not going?" she asked.

Alex shook his head. "Nope."

She cast a quick glance to Emma, who had spun on her heel and whipped her phone out of her pocket before the cars had cleared the driveway. "Hey, Tommy," she said as she disappeared into the house, probably not to surface for quite some time. Gwen remembered being eighteen and completely wrapped up in a guy.

Turning back to Alex, she crossed her arms over her

chest. It hadn't been as long ago as she would like to think. The object of her reluctant attraction was wearing khaki pants and a plaid button-down shirt, his honey-colored hair falling into his eyes. As always, he was charmingly irresistible, which made her feel better for falling off the wagon. She hadn't even bothered to put her bracelet on this morning.

"Why?"

He moved in closer, standing only inches away to look down at her petite, barefooted frame. "I wanted to spend some time with you and treat you to a little indulgence."

The combination of his words and the heat of his body so close to her own made the words she had planned to say far more difficult to get past her tongue. "I hope you d-didn't pass up on the trip in the hopes we'd indulge in wild, sexual...*escapades* all day. Not with Emma roaming around the house."

Alex smiled and placed his large hands on her upper arms, exposed by her spaghetti-strap sundress. The simple touch sent a surge of awareness through her body. Memories of the night before rushed through her mind. In an instant, her breasts tightened and her sex clenched, making her wish she hadn't taken wild escapades off the table so soon.

"Actually, I have a surprise for you."

Gwen looked suspiciously at him. She wasn't good with surprises. Maybe she was just jaded, but surprises were rarely good. At least not her mother's surprises. Occasionally, Paw-Paw would surprise her with a trip into town for ice cream, or Gran would make her favorite chicken and dumplings for dinner. She could only assume Alex had planned a good surprise, but she couldn't help the flutter of nerves in her stomach.

Alex was watching her with concern. "You don't want your surprise?"

"No. I mean, yes," she corrected, "I want it. I'm just a little paranoid."

"Don't be. It will be a great day, I promise. Are you ready to leave?"

"I think shoes would be a good idea, first. The term 'barefoot and pregnant' isn't supposed to be quite this literal in this day and age."

Alex smiled. "Okay. You go get some shoes. I'll tell Emma where we're going, and we'll be off. You don't want to be late for the appointment."

They walked back into the house and Gwen headed to her room. Today she was wearing another of her flowing, tropical sundresses. While appropriate for a beach holiday, she found that they were loose enough to keep her from having to wear real maternity clothes. She'd managed to get by so far with elastic waistband scrubs and loose dresses, but eventually, she knew she would have to break down and buy a few legitimate pregnancy outfits. But she certainly wasn't going to wear them around Alex. She slipped into a pair of cute brown sandals and grabbed a sweater in case she got chilled wherever they were going.

By the time she emerged, she could hear the powerful purr of the Corvette's engine in the driveway. "We'll be back soon," she called out in vain to Emma and stepped outside.

Alex was waiting beside the car, the passenger door held open for her. He'd retracted the convertible top so they could enjoy the mild weather and ocean breeze. "Your chariot awaits, milady."

"Well, thank you, sugar," Gwen said as she eased

gently into the low bucket seat. Alex closed her door and went around to climb in on his side.

"So, where are we going exactly?" she asked as they pulled out onto the highway.

"I told you, it's a surprise. But it's a good one, I promise. Just sit back, relax and go with the flow for once."

Gwen laughed and leaned back in her seat. She couldn't argue with that. Enough of her life was dictated by schedules and appointments. And while she appreciated Will and Adrienne's efforts to make sure everyone had a great trip, there was something to be said for relaxing on vacation and taking a day as it comes. "All right. You win. I am at your mercy."

She closed her eyes and took a soothing, deep breath. Driving through the countryside with the top down was a rare treat. She barely rode in cars at all anymore, and there was nothing soothing about a cab ride through midtown. Riding in Alex's convertible reminded her of sitting in the back of her grandpa's pickup truck with the hay-scented wind whipping her hair around her face.

When she opened her eyes again, she could tell they were getting close to a town. There were more houses near the street and sidewalks lining the road. The Hamptons had its share of outrageous mansions, but her favorites were the quaint little cottages. Old whitewashed wood siding, covered porches, wild English-style gardens... These were here long before the ultrarich came and dotted the countryside with multimillion-dollar castles.

The houses eventually turned into shops, and she spied a sign for East Hampton. They drove past a gourmet grocer, a wine specialty store, a bakery and a neat little jewelry boutique. On the corner was a bistro with striped awnings and a shaded outdoor seating area with wrought-iron furniture. People were out and about, but it wasn't nearly as crowded and high-energy as yesterday's polo tournament. *Quaint* wasn't even the word for this place.

She kept waiting for him to stop and force her into a store. Alex had taken her shopping the last time they were together. He'd ushered her into Tiffany and insisted she choose something. It had felt ridiculous looking at cases filled with jewelry that cost more than a few months of her salary. And for what? It seemed a little excessive for a two-week tumble. The charm bracelet had been a choice to get him off her back. And she did love it. Actually, her wrist felt naked today without it, but she decided between the pool, the beach and the sunscreen it was best to leave it off. Besides, she couldn't wear her chastity bracelet while she was being quite unchaste.

Alex had been annoyed with her selection, especially when he'd found out what it symbolized for her. Perhaps he was trying again.

After driving for a few minutes, Alex pulled into a spot along the street and killed the engine. "We're here."

Gwen looked around in confusion. They were parked near the post office. That wasn't much of a surprise.

Alex climbed from the car and came around to open her door. She turned and swung her legs out, but her shifting center of gravity and the road-hugging chassis made it more challenging to stand than she'd expected. "This is definitely not a third-trimester car."

Alex stepped off the curb and offered two strong hands to hoist her out of the seat. His help made it much easier, and she was standing in an instant. A little too easy, actually, as the momentum sent her up and colliding against his chest. She clung to him to keep from bouncing back and falling. His hands slipped under her arms to cup her elbows and steady her and then slid up the backs of her arms to keep her held close against him.

Gwen looked up at him and swallowed hard. His golden eyes were focused intently on her. The light breeze was fluttering the honey layers of his hair. She reached up and brushed some out of his face, tucking them behind his ear, then left her palm resting against his cheek. It was still smooth from his morning shave, unlike last night when the rough stubble had tickled and tormented her bare skin.

Leaning down, he kissed her. It was a soft, gentle kiss. She could feel the tension building beneath his tight skin, but he held back. The middle of town, surrounded by people, was hardly the place to let his passion come unleashed. And yet Gwen couldn't help responding to him. She climbed onto her toes to get closer, their mouths and tongues meeting in an easy, comfortable dance.

It was amazing how quickly they had gotten to know each other's needs and wants. Last night, even after months apart, Alex remembered just how to touch her. Just how to elicit the response he sought. And now, standing in the middle of the quaint town, kissing outside the post office felt so natural. It was more like…a relationship kind of embrace.

If that unnerving thought didn't urge Gwen to pull away, Peanut's sharp kick to her rounded belly surely did. Alex yanked back in surprise, looking down at the stomach that had been pressed against him a moment before.

"What was that?" he asked.

Another hard thump followed. Gwen winced and gently rubbed the spot of the latest attack. "That was

Peanut. She's trying out for the U.S. women's national soccer team."

Gwen snatched one of his hands and pressed the palm firmly against the side of her tummy. Peanut didn't disappoint, throwing a hard kick to protest the pressing of her little baby cocoon.

Alex's eyes were wide with surprise when he looked at her belly, then back at Gwen. "Does that hurt?"

"Sometimes." She shrugged. "At first there was just this flutter. Then, a few weeks ago, she got strong enough to really make her presence known. Before long, she'll be beating the hell out of me."

"Why?"

"She's stretching and testing out her little muscles. As she gets bigger, I think it's harder for her to get comfortable. I know exactly how she feels. So…" she said, pulling away to give herself some breathing room. "Where's this surprise of yours?"

"Right this way." Alex took her by the hand and led her across the street to a two-story building with the sign Heaven-Leigh Day Spa hanging over the door.

A spa. A bubble of excitement formed in her chest at the thought. Gwen had to admit that, even if he just took her inside to buy her some overpriced shampoo, it would be a welcome indulgence. Anything more would be, well, *heaven-leigh*.

She paused when she noticed the sign on the door said it was closed. The bubble burst. So much for that. "Looks like they're closed."

"Looks can be deceiving." Alex ignored the sign, opening the door, which chimed gently, and ushering her inside.

A tall, willowy woman in white appeared from another room and approached the reception desk where they were waiting. "Good morning. I'm Leigh, the owner. You must be Miss Wright."

Gwen smiled. "Yes. Call me Gwen, please."

"Excellent. We have a full afternoon of pampering scheduled for you, Gwen."

Gwen turned to Alex in surprise. "A full afternoon?"

Alex just smiled and shrugged. "What else do you have to do today?"

"But the sign said you're closed."

"Yes," Leigh continued. "Mr. Stanton has reserved the entire spa for the day so we can give you our full, undivided attention. We have everything ready, including a prenatal massage guaranteed to make you feel like a million dollars. Are you ready to get started?"

She could hardly believe what she was hearing. An entire day spa reserved just for her. It was absolute insanity. And she was going to enjoy every minute of it. "Honey, you have no idea how ready I am."

Gwen gave Alex a quick kiss of appreciation, a wide grin of excitement lighting her face, and then she disappeared into the back for her day of pampering.

For the next few hours, Alex sat quietly in the Zen Lounge checking email and reading a travel magazine. Occasionally, Leigh would march Gwen through from one treatment room to the next. Each time, Gwen was snuggled contently into her bathrobe and looked as though she had fewer and fewer bones left in her body. He was glad. That was the whole point. He wanted to take care of the caretaker for once. A massage, salt glow, facial, manicure and pedicure were a good way to start.

She didn't care much for jewelry or flowers. She wasn't the kind to be impressed by the flash that drew other women. He didn't even recall her mentioning his money in any conversation they'd ever had. Usually it would come up. As the sole heir of a family fortune rivaling Rockefeller and Carnegie, there was always a curiosity about how much he was actually worth. Gwen honestly didn't care.

It was another reason he liked her. Another reason that set her apart from the pack.

But he knew this would be the thing that really excited Gwen. She deserved every minute of it. He would have spent three times the money he'd paid for today to see that relaxed, contented smile on her face.

When they were finally done with her, Gwen emerged from the ladies' changing room dressed, but still decidedly invertebrate. He offered her the choice of going home for a nap or having a late lunch at the bistro they'd seen earlier. She chose the bistro.

They walked through town toward the restaurant, window-shopping and taking in the sights as they went along. Neither of them were in a hurry, just enjoying their afternoon together. When they arrived at the bistro, they selected a table outside. Gwen sipped pomegranate tea in the shade, and she and Alex shared a brick-oven pizza with crispy prosciutto, figs, arugula and fat slices of homemade mozzarella.

After taking one last bite, Alex watched in amusement as Gwen leaned back in her chair and stroked her full belly. The dress had camouflaged her pregnancy most of the day, but the press of her hand against the fabric made it more obvious to anyone looking on. She looked beautiful sitting there with a smile of contentment on her face.

Actually, he wasn't sure if he'd ever seen Gwen look happier, and he was glad that he was partially responsible for it. There was a part of him that needed to make her smile. His father had always made a point of giving him anything he ever wanted growing up. That was just how he related to his son. When Alex was older, he did the same, giving expensive gifts to women instead of real affection.

With Gwen, giving her gifts was not enough. He wanted to see the joy in her eyes, not just the excitement of greed that other women had. It was important to him in a way he didn't understand and didn't want to really consider.

Glancing away, he noticed a group of older women coming down the sidewalk toward them. They'd been shopping, as evidenced by the variety of bags in their hands. One of the women, a slight little lady about Gwen's size, was watching them with the twinkle of an excited grandmother in her eye. He wasn't surprised when she stopped and leaned over to Gwen.

"How far along are you, dear?"

Gwen smiled. "Five and a half months."

"My youngest daughter is six months along. It's going to be my first granddaughter." She held up a bag slightly overflowing with what looked like pink fabric and lace. "Five grandsons so far, so I'm very excited. Do you know what you're having?"

"It's a girl."

"Little girls everywhere! How wonderful. I apologize for interrupting your lunch, but you're just glowing, and I couldn't help but stop. With such beautiful parents, I have no doubt that baby is going to be a little heartbreaker. You'd better watch out, Daddy."

Alex smiled appropriately and waved as the lady joined her group and continued down the street. Explaining the reality of their complicated situation to a little old lady on the street was unnecessary. And she was right…. They would have very attractive kids. With his golden hair and her curls. Gwen's dark eyes and his smile. It wasn't hard to picture a little boy and girl running around playing in the grass of their front yard.

When he turned back to Gwen, she was pensively stroking her stomach and staring off down the street. There was a slight frown on her face that snapped him back to reality. While he was daydreaming about blond children playing in a yard they didn't have, she seemed to have taken her thoughts down a darker path. One that focused on the fact that the baby wasn't theirs and the "daddy" was just her on-and-off, commitment-phobic lover.

That made him frown, too. What the hell was he thinking even entertaining the idea of what their children would look like? That was the kind of fantasy a smitten teenage girl would concoct while thinking about her crush. He was a grown man. One determined never to even have children. What was it about Gwen that made him think such bizarre, unproductive things?

Alex shook his head irritably and threw enough cash on the table to cover their check. "Are you ready to go?"

Gwen turned back to him, snapping out of her thoughts and nodding. The frown was gone, but he could still see the worry puckering her eyebrows beneath her sunglasses.

He wanted to say something, but he wasn't quite sure what. With the precariousness of their relationship, many things could be interpreted wrong. There were still a few days left of the trip. Saying the wrong thing now could make the rest painful at best.

Alex reached out his hand to help her from her chair. "She was right about one thing. You are glowing," he said once she got to her feet.

Gwen searched his face for a moment, then shook her head dismissively. "Of course I glow. I just had a very expensive and thorough facial and sea salt scrub."

"True, but you've had a rosy, maternal radiance this whole time. Today's treatments only made you relax." He leaned down and placed a kiss against her exposed shoulder. "And even more silky soft, if that's possible."

He took Gwen's hand and led her through the tables to the sidewalk. They walked silently back to the car and didn't speak during the drive to the house. When Alex turned into the driveway, he noticed the other cars had returned. He stopped the convertible, not wanting to end his wonderful day with Gwen on such a somber note.

"What are you doing?" she asked.

Alex shifted the car into Neutral, engaged the parking brake and turned in his seat to face her. "I hope you had a good time today."

Her dark eyes widened for a moment before the corner of her mouth turned up just slightly. She looked down into her lap as though she were embarrassed. "I did. You don't know how badly I needed a little TLC. Thank you, Alex. It was very thoughtful of you."

"You don't seem very happy now. Did that woman at the restaurant upset you?"

"No," she said. "She just made me think about things I've been trying to ignore."

"Like what?"

"Like what life is going to be like after the baby is born. After this vacation ends and you're gone again. In that woman's mind, I was just starting out on the wonderful adventure of parenthood with you by my side. The truth is that in four months, I'm going to be alone with nothing to show for the last year of my life but some oversized clothes."

Alex didn't know what to say. He wouldn't insult her intelligence by attempting to comfort her with the empty promise of his staying. The baby wasn't hers to keep. Her worries about him and what he could offer were valid. So he didn't say anything. Instead, he leaned over and wrapped his arms around Gwen, pulling her to his chest.

There was no heat in his touch. Only comfort. She accepted it, snuggling against him and burrowing her face into his neck. They sat that way for several minutes. He could feel a cool dampness sinking into the cotton of his shirt and realized she was silently crying. He didn't say anything, just held her tighter and waited for the tears to dry.

At last, Gwen spoke, her voice almost too quiet for him to hear it. "Come to my bed again, tonight."

He nodded against her, brushing a bit of her hair back to press a kiss to her forehead. "I will."

Eight

The following day included a group excursion to the beach. Their stretch of harbor property was a little too rocky, so they loaded up the Land Rover with chairs, umbrellas and coolers and left midmorning in their usual caravan of cars.

Adrienne pointed out an empty stretch of white, sandy beach, and they pulled the cars off the road to claim it. With so many people, it didn't take long to get everything unloaded. Gwen tried to help, but Alex just frowned at her and insisted she make herself comfortable in the lounge chair he'd set up for her. She didn't argue, carrying her bag over and settling in to stay out of everyone's way.

Will and Alex set up a large umbrella just behind her to shade a couple of the chairs. Except for Helena, who had a dark, Italian glow to her skin, the other women were all extremely fair and would burn even with sun-block.

As the others unpacked and set up, Alex brought Gwen a bottle of citrus-infused water and a can of SPF 75 sunscreen spray. "Be sure to drink as much water as you can and keep plenty of this on today. It's hot, and I don't want you getting dehydrated."

He had been fawning over her since they got home yesterday. Almost like a man would pamper his expectant wife. Crying in his arms had probably been a bad idea. It felt good to get it out of her system, but now he probably thought she was both emotionally and physically fragile. He'd even handled her a bit more delicately in bed last night. It was wonderfully passionate and romantic, yet she didn't remember Alex being a particularly tender lover before.

Gwen took the water and the sunscreen from him and noticed Adrienne watching them as she unpacked a few beach towels from a tote bag. "Stop fussing. It's not exactly subtle," she said.

Alex shrugged. "I'm more worried about the welfare of you and the baby than anything else, including being found out by the relationship police."

For a brief moment, the expression on his face was serious and concerned. No smirks, no winks, no grins. He was honestly worried about her. She wasn't quite sure how to respond, especially when the charming smile returned and he wandered off to help Wade and Jack unpack a few bagged chairs. He was so confusing.

After the last few days, her confusion was only getting worse. Alex was the fun guy, the exciting guy. Not the caring, relationship guy. And yet, since they'd been in the Hamptons together, that was almost how it had felt. The wild, passionate nights were paired with conscientious and thoughtful days. If Alex was any other man, Gwen might start to wonder if something more was going on between them.

But tigers didn't change their stripes.

Instead of worrying too much about something she couldn't control, she decided to do as he'd said and start rubbing in sunscreen. She could already feel the warmth on her skin that was a certain precursor to burning. Fortunately, today she'd opted for her one-piece suit so less skin was exposed. It was black and purple, and she tied a multicolored sarong low on her hips. After applying the lotion to every inch she could reach, she set the can aside and eased back into her chair with the water he'd brought her. Now that she was protected from burning, it was easier to relax and let the heat sink into her bones.

She'd spent another wonderful night with Alex. Combined with yesterday's massage, there were parts of her body she didn't even know could hurt, but she couldn't regret it. Being with Alex was a welcome distraction from reality. This trip, this place, this romance… It was all a fantastic dream she would wake up from the moment Will's car crossed back into Manhattan.

She'd tried not to let yesterday linger on her mind. She and Alex had had such a good time walking around and having lunch. His spa surprise had been a spot-on choice. She couldn't think of a single thing he could've bought her that she wanted or needed more. He really did seem to have her figured out. Or maybe he just understood women in general. What woman wouldn't appreciate a day at the spa?

Gwen had thoroughly enjoyed the tiny glimpse into what life could be like together. The sweet lady's comments at the bistro had simply snapped her out of the romantic reverie she'd drifted into. It wasn't her fault that in that moment, Gwen wanted so badly for it to be real. That they were a loving husband and wife vacationing. Expecting their first child together.

It had taken a while for Gwen to admit to herself that was part of her problem. She was falling for this fantasy they had going. It had lulled her into the idea that having a husband and family was something she wanted—something she *had*. Gwen's hand went to her stomach, stroking the curve through the stretchy black fabric of her suit. But she didn't have anything. It was not her baby. It was not his baby. She needed to keep telling herself that.

She couldn't help but glance up to where the guys were now playing Frisbee in the sand. Alex was wearing only a pair of fire-engine red swim trunks. He moved quickly, snatching the disk from the air and immediately firing it off in Wade's direction. She admired the athleticism and grace of Alex's movements as his strong muscles flexed beneath his tanned skin.

He was not hers, either. Gwen sighed and took a sip of her water.

Gwen had been thinking the strangest things over the last few days. She wasn't sure if it was the baby, being around happy married couples, hormones, or having Alex's warm presence in her bed at night, but it made her want more. For the last eight months, she hadn't been able to target what she really needed in her life. Maybe it was because she'd labeled the thing she needed the most with her mother's ugly stigma and couldn't see past it.

Love and marriage and family.

If that was what she wanted, certainly she could do it differently, right? It was such a huge leap for her, to want the one thing she'd always told herself she didn't need. But she wanted to try. If it didn't work, she could always go back to the way she'd done things before.

If she was going to start entertaining the idea of marriage and family, okay. Gwen was more open to that than she'd ever been before. But to have it, she needed to start with the basics—a man who loved her and wanted to marry her.

Yes, and all she needed to buy her own tropical island was a couple million dollars. Easy fix, right?

Gwen turned to watch Adrienne spread out a beach towel on the chair beside her and settle in with her own drink and a paperback to read. She looked adorable in her hot-pink bikini, her dark brown hair swept into a ponytail. There was no need for her to cover any of her curves with a wrap like Gwen had. She set her items on top of the small cooler that separated them and started applying sunblock to her legs.

"I thought you'd sworn off men," Adrienne said casually, slathering on the thick white cream.

"What?" Gwen looked up and followed Adrienne's line of sight to Alex. "Oh."

"When were you planning on telling me?"

Gwen gave a quick glance around to make sure no one else was within earshot. For now the coast was clear. "How did you find me out? Was it the fussing? I saw you watching us."

"Not really. That was just the latest of a hundred clues. You two are both ignorant if you think that kind of sexual attraction can be disguised. Even a ten-thousand-square-foot house on three acres is too small for people not to notice something is going on. So... Tell me what's going on."

Gwen shrugged dismissively. "Not much to tell really."

Adrienne turned to her, a curious arch to her eyebrow. "I find that hard to believe."

Her best friend was too intuitive for her own good. But short of the torture of thumbscrews, Gwen wasn't going to admit to anything more than a fun fling. After all, that was all they'd agreed to. All that it was supposed to be, regardless of how it might feel. "I'm sorry to disappoint. But you know Alex and his track record with women well enough to realize there isn't going to be more to this story than some good sex."

"Good?"

"Okay," Gwen admitted with a sly grin. "*Great* sex. He has most certainly earned his reputation with the ladies."

Adrienne smiled and started smearing the sunblock into her arms and shoulders. "How long has this great sex been going on?"

"Two days. If you don't count the two weeks after your wedding." She said the last sentence quickly, following it with a swig of water from her bottle as if she could slip the shocking news past her friend. From the look on Adrienne's face, it didn't work.

"So, what…eight months?"

"No. Eight months sounds like it's something. Eight months with a nearly seven-and-a-half-month gap in between is clearly nothing."

"But you've kept it a secret from me for that long. If it was nothing, you could've told me."

"I know." Gwen winced at the admission. "But I knew you would get spun up about it. If something went wrong, it would make things awkward, with us being friends with you and Will. It was just easier this way. I don't want this made into any more than it is."

"Great sex," Adrienne said flatly.

"Yes. I have to say I hadn't come up here intending on picking up anything with Alex. I turned him down several times. But a combination of pregnancy hormones and that damned seductive smile of his changed my agenda pretty quickly."

Adrienne nodded sympathetically. "Alex's charm is hard to ignore."

Gwen looked back out toward the water. Sabine and Emma had waded out into the waves with boogie boards. The guys were still playing Frisbee. As though he could feel her eyes on him, Alex turned to Gwen and shot her a smile before turning back to the game.

"Indeed," she agreed. Every nerve in her body had responded to him in that instant. Even after a long night of thoroughly exhausting lovemaking, she wanted more of him. And not just his body.

It was a dangerous thought, because that was all Alex could offer her. At best, she would walk away from this week with some fond memories and a fabulous day at the spa. If she let herself get too involved in this fantasy, she would walk away with a bad case of heartache. Either way, one thing she wouldn't have come next week was Alex.

Frowning, Gwen quickly scrambled into her bag for a magazine she'd brought with her. She needed a distraction. Anything to keep her brain from the train of thought it was determined to take. She'd just told Adrienne this was nothing and now, seconds later, she was sitting here thinking the exact opposite.

Flipping open the magazine, she thumbed through a few pages until she found an article on something completely unrelated to sex or love.

"Just do me a favor, though."

Adrienne's words pulled Gwen from the details of this fall's hot hairstyle trends. "What's that?"

"I know that you're not really into the long-term thing, so it might be a moot point. But don't let yourself fall in love with Alex. I've only known him a few years, but it doesn't take long to realize that behind the charm and the money is a man running from something. Plenty of women have wasted time and energy trying to chase after him only to find themselves empty-handed. I'd hate for you to be one of them."

"Of course," Gwen said, turning back to her magazine with a forced smile on her face. "I'm not stupid."

But inside, she knew the truth. If she wasn't careful, she would be on track to becoming the stupidest woman on the planet.

Alex clutched his drink in one hand and the deck railing of the ship with the other as his stomach lurched. He hated boats. Dinghies, canoes, yachts, cruise liners… It didn't matter. Even the most expensive stabilization systems and motion sickness pills couldn't keep him from getting nauseated. It was ironic, really, since his family owned a multimillion-dollar yacht and he hadn't set foot on it even once in the ten years since his parents bought it.

This boat was harder to circumvent. Will and Adrienne had chartered a dinner yacht to cruise out into the water at sunset. There was no avoiding it, especially when he saw the light of excitement in Gwen's eyes when she found out about their plans. It was a lovely, romantic idea in theory. He popped a couple Dramamine and hoped he could keep the meal down. Throwing up over the side of the railing was a definite mood killer.

So far, so good. Dinner had been an excellent New

England clambake-style spread. He could forget where he was while gorging himself on perfectly cooked seafood and spicy seasoned vegetables. Fortunately, the wind had died down. The water was relatively calm, with the reflection of the full moon dancing across it. But every now and then, they'd hit a larger wave and he'd seriously regret the chocolate lava cake they'd had for dessert.

After dinner, the ship was set to cruise around for an hour with a fireworks display before returning to the pier. The deck was decorated with colored lights and music was piped out through speakers all over the ship. Everyone seemed to be happy to talk and laugh, sipping their drinks and watching the lights from the shore twinkle in the distance. It really was a perfect night to be out sailing. If you liked that sort of thing.

Alex had quietly asked the bartender for some ginger ale in a lowball glass and moved away from the crowd not long after dessert. He found a quiet corner of the ship where he could take a moment to breathe deeply and let his dinner settle. If anything went awry, there would be no witnesses. No one knew about his issue with boats, and he preferred it to stay that way.

The wind picked up, ruffling his hair, and before he knew it, the up-and-down movement of the boat went from almost tolerable to gut-wrenching. His stomach churned and he broke out in a cold sweat.

"You've been holding that same drink for an hour," Gwen said, coming up to him.

Damn. It was bad enough to feel sick, but he certainly didn't want to be sick around Gwen. "I'm not feeling much like drinking tonight. Too much sun at the beach, I think."

Gwen watched him curiously for a moment, her eyes narrowing. "You look a little green."

"I'm fine."

"Alex, I'm a nurse, remember? You can't fool me. Are you feeling seasick?"

He gritted his teeth and gave a curt nod. Before he could say anything else, the ship rocked and the battle was over. Alex ran around the corner out of her sight and hung over the back of the ship to return his dinner to the sea. When there was nothing left, he rinsed his mouth out with ginger ale and spit it out. Feeling a hundred times better, he closed his eyes and slumped over to rest his forehead on the white metal rails.

Gwen didn't speak, but he knew by her scent the instant she sidled up beside him. Something soft and cold pressed against the back of his neck. "This wet towel should help," she said. "And suck on one of these."

Alex opened his eyes to see one of her peppermint candies in her hand. He unwrapped it and put it in his mouth. The mint was surprisingly soothing to his upset stomach. It wasn't long before he started feeling normal again.

"Feeling any better?" she asked.

"Yes. You're an excellent nurse." He attempted a grin, but his heart just wasn't in it.

Gwen gently rubbed his shoulder, then turned to grip the railing and look out into the water. "The moon is beautiful tonight."

Alex looked at her, the moonlight making the pale skin of her face glow against the dark tangle of curls that hung loose around her shoulders. Her dark burgundy satin dress was sexy and short, tying just above the waist, accentuating the swell of her pregnancy and leaving her nicely shaped calves gloriously bare. She was wearing low heels tonight so the daring, V-cut neckline of her dress brought the soft curves of her breasts a touch closer to tempt him. "You look beautiful tonight, too."

"Thank you," she said, her nose wrinkling as though she was uncomfortable with the compliment.

Alex never understood why women were always hesitant to accept compliments. Despite accusations that he was a ruthless charmer, he didn't hand them out lightly. He always meant what he said. He was a lover of women. Seeing them smile, hearing them laugh, watching them blush… He did whatever it took to coax their best from them. If that made him a charmer, it made other men lazy.

"Do you need another drink? Some club soda, maybe?"

Alex shook his head. "I already have ginger ale, thank you. Besides, you following me back here and fetching me drinks won't look good. You called me on being too obvious this morning. How subtle is the two of us disappearing to be alone on the ship?"

"It doesn't matter. We've been outed."

"Adrienne?"

She nodded. "Apparently neither of us has a future as a ninja or spy."

"So much for my retirement plans." Alex pulled the towel from his neck and tossed it into a bucket on the deck. He leaned his forearms onto the railing, bringing his height more in line with hers. "She have much to say about it?"

"Not as much as I expected, but she put in her two cents. Mainly, she advised me not to fall in love with you."

"That's wise," he agreed. "It's hard to be in love with someone who isn't into relationships."

There was a short hesitation before Gwen responded. "Is that really true?" she challenged. "That you aren't 'into' relationships? Or is it just a convenient excuse?"

Alex frowned and snorted dismissively. "And what exactly is your diagnosis, Nurse Wright?"

"It's hard to say, since I don't know much about how you were raised or what experiences you've had, good or bad. Adrienne said she gets the feeling you're running from something, and I agree. Intimacy, maybe? You've just decided you'd rather act like you're too cool to settle down, when the truth is you're trying to avoid the pain of a failed relationship."

"That's a very bold guess for someone who admits they know nothing about me."

"It feels true. You do everything you can to avoid letting a woman become important. Short or onetime encounters, buying expensive but meaningless gifts, traveling all the time, moving from one woman to the next… It just makes me wonder."

"Wonder what?"

"It makes me wonder who hurt you so badly that you refuse to even take the chance on something great happening."

Alex tried without success to swallow the lump that formed in his throat and took a sip of his drink to see if it would help. It didn't. He had never realized he was that transparent. Maybe it was only obvious to Gwen. She saw things other people didn't bother to notice. She'd just said something to him that no one else in his entire life had had the nerve or interest to ask. She was nothing if not honest, direct and sincere. He supposed she deserved the same. "I don't believe in love."

Gwen turned to him and gave a soft nod of understanding. "Sometimes, I'm not sure I do, either. What convinced you?"

"Because I've never seen it last longer than the hormone surge. By the time that wears off, odds are you've done something stupid like get married or pregnant and now you're stuck with someone you find you don't even like."

"Like your parents?"

A smile curved the corner of Alex's mouth. She was an insightful little minx. "Well, they *are* a child's closest example of how relationships work. Mine taught me they don't. They've always been miserable together, but they keep up the ruse for appearances' sake. They're rarely in the same room together. My father escaped into his work. I almost never saw him growing up, and when I did, he was buying me something. My mother used me to get what she thought she wanted, then blamed me my whole life when it backfired on her. They smile for the cameras on family holidays, but that's about it. Doesn't exactly make you want to run out and get married, does it?"

Gwen shook her head. "My parents never married. My father split before my mother was even as pregnant as I am right now. She's spent every moment since then trying to catch and keep a man. Her quest was the most important thing in her life. Even more important than her only child. Her priorities are so messed up. It just makes me more determined not to be like her. I tend to fall for the kind of guys who aren't going to stick around, so I don't bother with getting attached."

"And to think, I thought you liked me for my smile."

Gwen gave him a watery grin and turned back to focus on the ocean. "But lately I wonder if I'm missing out on something. It's like I'm the only kid in school who doesn't believe in Santa, so I'm not getting any presents. Maybe for Peanut's sake, I want to believe. I want love and happy marriages to exist because I want it for her. Is that weird?"

"No. People want better for their kids than they had. At least, they should. The problem is when people have children for the wrong reasons. Although my mother would never admit to it, my father told me when I was grown that she deliberately got pregnant with me so he would marry her. That certainly worked out well for her." Alex couldn't keep the bitter sarcasm from slipping into his voice.

"Are you worried someone would try to do that to you? Trap you with a child? I could imagine that would be a good reason to be such a condom fanatic."

Alex had been called a great many things in his life, but that was a first. "I suppose you could say that. I know it's hard for people to understand, but when your estimated worth is plastered across the pages of different newspapers and magazines, you're naturally a target. Of competitors, swindlers and gold diggers alike. I don't trust a woman to be genuine with me. They all want something from me. Except, maybe you."

Gwen turned to him with a confused look that drew her delicate eyebrows together. "I'm not sure if I should be flattered or not."

"Be flattered. It puts you above millions of other women in New York." Alex paused and listened for a moment to the music playing on the deck. "Do you hear that? They're playing our song."

Gwen wrinkled her nose. "We have a song?"

"I'm insulted," he said, pushing away from the

railing and sweeping her into his arms. "This is the song we danced to at the reception."

Alex didn't make any fancy moves to keep the seasickness from returning but held Gwen against him and gently circled around their private section of the deck. She swayed easily and comfortably in his arms to the slow, sultry music. He thought for a moment she might let their conversation lapse, then he heard her speak quietly into his lapel.

"So, is it that you don't believe in love, period, or you don't believe anyone will ever love you for who you are?"

Alex shrugged. "What does it matter? I can't change who I am. So whether it exists or not, that means no love or family for me."

"You don't want children at all, then?"

There was a touch of disappointment lining her eyes when she asked the question. It didn't surprise Alex. Gwen told him she didn't believe in love and marriage, but even since they'd been here, he'd noticed a change in her. There was a touch of sadness in her eyes when she watched Will and Adrienne together. The same sadness that was there after the woman had confused them for a married couple.

She wanted it. And not just for Peanut. Judging by the way she was looking at him, part of her entertained the idea of having it with him someday. The fair-haired babies of yesterday's fantasy popped back into his mind. Surprisingly, he'd been guilty of those thoughts as well.

Alex sighed. "It's not that, so much. The idea of having children by choice doesn't bother me. I just don't think children should be brought into a marriage without love. And I don't believe in love, or marriage, so kids are automatically out of the question."

"I suppose that's why you almost choked on your tongue when you saw me pregnant."

"Not exactly."

Gwen frowned at his response. "What does that mean?"

Alex swore he'd never voice these words out loud, but something urged him to get it off his chest. Maybe saying them would send them out to dissipate in the atmosphere instead of locking them inside to slowly poison him. "It was the opposite, really. I mean, there was this wild mix of surprise, fear and anger because I thought you'd kept it from me. But there was also a part of me…"

Gwen leaned into him, her dark eyes widening in anticipation of his words. "Yes?"

Her eagerness gave him pause. Telling Gwen how he really felt would just open the door to an opportunity that wasn't real. Even though the idea of fatherhood had intrigued him, it was a gut reaction. His ancient, caveman biology taking over. He thought better of it now. He would never marry or have children, and he hadn't changed his mind about that.

Raising her expectations was unfair. Really, everything he'd said or done to her since he'd come to the Hamptons was unfair. He should've walked away from the pool and not dragged her back into whatever it was they shared. Alex needed to put the brakes on this whole thing before he did any more damage.

A loud pop sounded in the distance and they both turned to see a shower of white sparks fall into the sea. It was followed by a burst of red, then green. The fireworks display had begun, lighting the sky and the water surrounding them with bright, colorful explosions. It was a beautiful and welcome distraction.

He watched them for a moment, then shook his head.

"Adrienne was right," he said, taking a step back from her and ending the dance. "Don't let yourself fall in love with me, Gwen."

At that, he turned and disappeared around the corner to rejoin the others.

Nine

Gwen waited almost an hour in her room that night before she realized Alex wasn't coming. She'd made the mistake of thinking that their conversation was a step forward. He was opening up, sharing his past and his feelings. But then he'd walked away and she hadn't spoken to him in the hours since then. The empty space in the bed beside her only confirmed how wrong she was. Alex hadn't just walked away from the uncomfortable conversation; he'd walked away from her.

She wasn't quite sure what was going on with him, but she could see through his suave, womanizing veneer now. He obviously chose not to let anyone, especially women, get close to him. He had his reasons. She understood that much, because she did the same thing herself.

She worked long graveyard shifts at the hospital and slept away most of her days. Gwen loved her job and her work, but it left her with little free time. She had friends, but even those people weren't allowed to get very close to her. They were as numerous and casual as Facebook friends. And just as likely to be there for her when things got tough. When she'd gotten pregnant, many had scattered.

Only Adrienne really knew and understood Gwen. They both knew what it was like to hit the rock bottom of life. She had been trying to get out more lately. Adrienne was pulling her out of her shell. Cutting men out of her life had opened up some free time to do things she hadn't before. She went to more theater, toured more museums. She'd even come to the Hamptons for a relaxing, fun vacation with a group of people who were mostly strangers.

When Alex arrived and offered her another go, she hesitated, but he was a hard man to turn down when he had his sights set on you. She'd relented, given in, succumbed to the promise of a few days of pleasure without strings. And now, here she was, alone in bed because he'd had some kind of moral dilemma. Well, forget that. He had pushed her until she'd relented, and she wasn't about to be cast off like that. They were doomed to crash and burn, but that time hadn't come just yet. He owed her two more nights.

Gwen flung back the covers and marched out of her room in the tiny tank top and shorts she wore to bed. She went straight up the stairs to his bedroom and walked in without knocking or asking permission.

Alex was sitting up in bed wearing nothing but a pair of boxers and some reading glasses low on his nose. He had a pile of pillows behind him and a file open in his lap with some kind of schematic drawings. Work stuff, she assumed. He looked up in surprise when she charged in, but he didn't move. He also didn't tell her to leave. She knew he wouldn't.

She closed the door behind her and planted her hands on her hips in irritation. "What are you doing?"

Alex pulled off his glasses and tapped the paper with them. "I'm going over the final interior design drawings of my new high-rise apartment building in New Orleans."

"Is that better than making love to me?"

His hazel gaze locked on hers and he spoke without hesitation. "Not even close."

Gwen closed the gap between them, climbing onto the bed and crawling up the length of his body. Without asking permission, she stuffed the paperwork back into the folder and flopped it with a heavy thud onto the bedside table. "Then why have I been alone in my bed for the last hour?"

"Because," he said, shaking his head, "I've changed my mind about us. I pretty much twisted your arm into having this affair, but now I'm thinking it's not such a good idea. You've got that look in your eyes. I've seen it before. So I decided to take a step back before things got too serious. I mean, Adrienne is a hopeless romantic, and even she told you to stay away from me. That can't be a good sign. I don't want you to get hurt."

Gwen listened to his argument as she straddled his hips and eased back to sit astride him. The thin cotton of her pajama shorts did little to disguise the firm length of him pressing against her. She planted one hand on the oak headboard by each side of his head as though she were leaning in to kiss him, then paused a few inches away. "Since you never even bothered to ask me what I thought about all this, I'm going to say that I think that's a load of crap."

Alex's eyes widened in surprise, his whole body stiffening, but she'd left him with no escape route unless he was willing to physically fling a pregnant woman off him. His jaw tightened as he watched her, considering his words.

She didn't wait for him to answer. It wouldn't be the truth anyway, just some canned response she wasn't interested in. "I think you're the one that's afraid of getting hurt." She pressed her palm against his bare chest, covering his heart. Gwen could feel the nervous, rapid pounding in his rib cage. "So you've made up this story about protecting me so you can feel better about running before it gets too serious."

"Gwen—"

"No. I don't want to hear it. You're not just going to put me aside like all those other women. Not tonight. You owe me two more days, and I expect you to pay up."

Alex swallowed hard, his Adam's apple traveling slowly down the length of his throat and back. He watched her for several moments, not speaking. It felt like an eternity to Gwen. She held her breath. She wasn't used to being this aggressive with a man. It could blow up in her face. But at this point, she had nothing to lose.

He sat up from the pillows, bringing his face to within an inch of hers. There was a hard glint in his eyes. Gwen couldn't tell if it was anger or the rise of a challenge. His arms slinked around her, tugging her forward with a hard jerk until she was pressed against him. His breath was warm against her skin, his mouth hovering close but not yet kissing her. It sent a scorching tingle through her body, the anticipation building in her belly.

Alex was just teasing her now. Punishing her for put-

ting him on the spot. Two could play at that game. Gwen
moved her hips in a slow circle, generating a delicious
friction as she ground into the firm heat that pressed
insistently against her. A groan escaped his lips, and he
closed his eyes when a shudder traveled through his entire body. The hands on her back fisted into tight balls
at her hips. "Oh, Gwen," he whispered, his lips brushing the curve of her jaw.

"Do you still want me to go back to my room?" she
asked, her pelvis continuing to swirl in agonizing circles.

She felt his fingertips reach under her tank top and
lift the hem. Gwen held her arms over her head to allow
him to slip the top off. He threw it to the floor, then
leaned back against the pillows. His golden gaze took
in every inch of her flesh from the full, bare breasts to
the swell of her stomach.

With a self-satisfied grin, he said, "Unfortunately,
you can't leave without your clothes."

Gwen could no longer resist the urge to kiss the smug
expression from his face. Their lips met suddenly, a
frantic emotional energy surging through the contact
that was more powerful than anything she'd ever felt
before. It was as though they were trying to devour one
another. She gave in to the sensation, letting the unbri-
dled passion overpower her.

His hands scrambled over her bare skin in a rush to
touch every inch of her as though it were the first, or
maybe the last, time. When their lips parted, she sucked
in a much-needed breath. Alex took the opportunity to
taste her breasts, the wet heat of his mouth enveloping
her aching nipples and teasing them with his tongue
and teeth until she cried out and writhed against him.

The grinding together of their most sensitive parts

sent a spike of need down her spine. The pulsating sensation urged her to do it again, but this time, not just to torture him. The warm pool of arousal in her belly grew with each passing second. She wanted Alex. Needed him unlike any other man, and she wasn't ashamed to admit it tonight.

"I want you, Alex," she whispered. She buried her fingers in his blond hair, tugging him closer.

"I want you, too," he said, his deep voice vibrating against the hard bone of her sternum.

"Then don't make me wait any longer."

Alex's mouth found hers again as his hands tugged at her shorts. They frantically shifted around on the bed until they were both free of the last restricting garments and he had quickly sheathed himself in the latex he relied so heavily upon.

Gwen leaned forward, then eased back, taking every inch of him inside her at an excruciatingly slow pace. With his arms still wrapped around her waist, she started rocking against him in a leisurely and easy rhythm that could go on for hours, both torturing and tempting their bodies with one wave of sensation after another.

But Alex couldn't take that for long. After a few slow, even strokes, he growled against her throat and lunged forward. Gwen was flipped onto her back, a gasp of surprise slipping from her lips. Hovering over her, he thrust into her without hesitation.

Their lovemaking was raw and intense, their bodies meeting at a fast and furious pace. Gwen let herself give in to the pleasure, indulging in the only part of Alex she would ever truly have. When their cries mingled in the air, she clung to him, part of her never wanting to let go and part of her knowing she already had.

* * *

Thoroughly exhausted, Alex fell asleep with Gwen curled against him. He woke up a few hours later, the world still dark outside his window. He was glad. He wasn't ready for the night to end quite yet. Tomorrow was the Fourth of July. He had no doubt the day would be jam-packed with grilling and sunshine, the night colored with red, white and blue explosions lighting the sky.

And then it would be over. Their last night at the house before returning to the city. No matter what he'd told Gwen, Alex didn't want any of this to be over quite yet.

Even if he broke his own rules and they carried on their relationship in Manhattan, things would be different. There would be work and responsibilities, not to mention the complications of the last few months of her pregnancy. This moment in time could never be duplicated. He wanted to savor it.

Alex let his hand glide from Gwen's bare hip down to splay his fingers across the soft skin of her belly. Feeling the baby kick the other day had been a surreal experience for him. A moment he'd never quite thought he'd have. He'd been filled with surprise and awe and respect for the woman in his arms. She was sacrificing so much for someone else.

He couldn't imagine what the next few months would be like for her. Although she put up a brave front, it was going to be harder than she'd originally anticipated. Alex saw the way she talked to the baby and lovingly stroked her stomach. Giving birth and handing that little girl away would be devastating. Part of him wanted to be the shoulder she cried on. To be there for her. It was a frightening thought. He'd never been the person that anyone depended on for emotional support. If money or humor couldn't defuse the situation, he was out of it.

But after spending the last few days with Gwen, he wanted to try. For her. The same part of him wanted to confide his secrets to her, share his dreams with her and start a life with her. The quiet voice in his head that wanted that baby to be theirs had grown louder with every day he spent here.

That same voice was screaming that it was tired of being an island. This baby wasn't theirs, but the next could be. They could have everything he had always been too afraid to hope for. If he could just let himself trust his heart over his brain for once.

Alex was so confused by the thoughts and feelings swirling around in his gut. Gwen had been right when she'd accused him of taking a step back out of fear. It seemed easier than dealing with how he felt about her. Love and everything that came with it was a scary proposition. But so was losing Gwen. He couldn't imagine not having her in his arms every night just as she was right now.

Just then, a hard thump pounded against his palm. He jumped, startled, and noticed Gwen did, too.

"Sorry," she murmured sleepily against her pillow. "Peanut is a bit of a night owl. Robert and Susan may never get another full night of sleep again once this little one shows up."

Alex stroked her belly to soothe both Gwen and the baby. He snuggled up against her and placed a kiss just behind her earlobe. The words he wanted to say lingered in his mouth for a moment before he had the nerve to speak. "What are you going to do, Gwen?"

He felt her stiffen slightly in his arms, and he tugged her closer to keep her from pulling away. If she was going to force him to face his fears, he was going to do the same. She was heading for a heartbreak that had nothing to do with him, for once.

"What do you mean?" she asked, her words still muffled against the pillow, although she was now fully awake.

"A couple months from now when you have to give her away," he clarified. "What are you going to do?"

"I'm going to watch the joy on Robert's and Susan's faces when they hold their little girl for the first time and know I did something wonderful for them. Then I'm going to check out of the hospital, catch a cab to the bar up the block from my apartment and have the tallest, coldest beer I can get my hands on."

"Gwen." The word was a question, a nudge, a warning and a touch of encouragement all rolled into one. They both knew that was not what he was asking or, even if it was, that her answer was just as scripted as his own had been earlier.

She sighed heavily, and there was a long silence before she finally answered. "What do you expect me to say? That it's going to break my heart to give Peanut away even though she's not mine to keep? That I'm going to cry alone in my hospital bed while everyone else is celebrating outside the nursery? That every time I pass a woman with a stroller I'm going to be reminded about how Robert and Susan have a beautiful life and family together and I've got nothing?"

Her words were like a knife to his gut, catching him off guard with the sharp pain. This was going to be rougher on her than he even imagined. He supposed there was nothing quite like giving away something you never had to remind you of that fact. Now he was sorry he'd asked. "Something like that."

"None of that really matters. I knew what I was signing up for with this. Sometimes the right thing to do is the hardest. I will have made a huge difference in someone else's life, and that has to be enough for me. When it's all said and done, I'll just go back to living my life the way I did before all of this happened—alone."

There was a sadness and resignation in her voice that he didn't like. They'd never discussed the possibility of being together past their stay in the Hamptons, but she sounded as though she knew he would be long gone by then. That when she handed over that baby to its parents, she would be handing away the only person in her life who loved and cared for her as much as she did for them.

It broke Alex's heart to hear her talk that way. In that moment, he wanted so badly to let himself love her. It would be so easy to do. If he was honest with himself, his heart was already halfway there. But he just couldn't commit to the last few steps. He couldn't open himself up to a fantasy that would crumble the moment he needed it the most.

"Maybe not completely alone," he offered. That was all he could do.

"Don't," she whispered, her voice heavy with tears he couldn't see. "Don't say things to make me feel better when you know it really isn't true. Lying here in the dark, I'm sure it sounds like the right thing to say. That it feels true in the moment. But you and I both know the truth when the light of day shines on it."

"I want—" he began, but stopped when Gwen rolled onto her back and held her finger to his lips.

"Just don't," she said. "Just go back to sleep before you say something we'll both regret."

* * *

Although she'd told him to sleep, Gwen couldn't do so herself. She'd spent the last few hours listening to Alex's soft, even breathing, but despite her exhaustion, her mind was spinning too quickly to sleep. Her last conversation with Alex half felt like a dream. The soft whispers and painful words felt fuzzy and surreal, but she knew she hadn't imagined them. Nor had she imagined Alex's suggestion that he might be there for her.

She hadn't let him promise. As much as she wanted it to be true, Gwen knew it never could be. She could see Alex struggling with taking the first steps to something more, but staying with her went against everything he knew. It was doomed to fail, even if his heart was in the right place. He couldn't help who he was. But she couldn't allow herself to fall for another man destined to leave.

It was one thing when that was what she wanted. Her whole life she'd sought out the wandering types. The more unobtainable, the more emotionally distant, the better.

She wasn't an expert in psychoanalysis, but she'd taken a few classes in college. It didn't take a PhD to see she had issues because of her mother and her pathetic, all-encompassing need to have a man. Gwen didn't want to be anything like her, so she picked men she knew wouldn't stay around, and it was easier when they inevitably left.

In that regard, Alex was the perfect man for her. And the worst if she truly wanted to break out of these bad habits and have a real chance at love and family.

Gwen rolled over in another failed attempt to get comfortable and tried to think about all the men she'd dated since high school. Had she ever loved any of them? No. She might've thought so or told people she did. But she held so much of herself back that it really wasn't possible to be truly, deeply in love with any of them. And if she was honest, she'd never felt half as much for any man as she did for Alex.

He took care of her because he knew how much she gave to others. He pestered her until she would smile. He knew just how to touch her and when, to get just the reaction they both wanted and needed. Alex understood Gwen in a way few people did. He'd gotten to her, scaled her protective walls and reached the heart she kept hidden.

She was in love with him. Damn it.

She expected a giddy rush of emotion at the realization, but it didn't come and she knew why. She'd gone out and done the one thing she knew she shouldn't do. What everyone, including Alex, told her not to do. It had taken her months to finally decide what she wanted in her life—a family and Alex. But those two things were mutually exclusive. She could never have Alex *and* a family. But for some reason she'd let him in, and what was done, was done.

Gwen loved Alex.

And he, despite his protests, felt something for her. She knew it. She could feel it in his hesitation. If he didn't care about her, he wouldn't have walked away tonight. But in her heart, she knew that regardless of how he felt, their relationship was doomed. How could she be the one to tame Alex when so many others had failed?

She wouldn't. She'd just get hurt. Dating guys who didn't stick around was one thing. Loving the guy was another matter. She'd taken a break from her merry-go-round of self-destructive relationships only to find herself in deeper than she'd ever been before.

When the first glow of daylight began to creep into his room, she sat up in bed. Alex was still soundly sleeping beside her. She realized, looking at him, that she'd never really seen him asleep before. He always woke up before she did.

A lock of dark golden hair lay across one of his eyes. The cocky, suave persona was put away while he slept. His face was relaxed, peaceful...vulnerable. That was certainly a new expression for him. While he occasionally appeared concerned or serious, she'd never once seen his guard down like this. There were flashes of it when he'd looked at her that first night and realized he'd forgotten the condom. But it had vanished in an instant.

Part of her wanted to reach out and stroke the line of his jaw and the curves of his lips, but that would wake him up and ruin it. Instead, she lay there for a few more minutes, committing that face to memory before she got up.

Finally, she slipped out of bed and collected her clothes, pulling them on and heading to her own room. Gwen paused in the doorway as she left, looking back one last time at Alex asleep in his bed. She'd meant only to go downstairs, but a part of her knew she was walking away from more than just Alex's bedroom.

With a sigh, she whispered, "Goodbye, Alex," and pulled the door shut behind her.

Ten

Gwen had nearly reached the bottom of the stairs when a bit of movement caught her eye.

Startled, she turned and found Sabine in the living room. She was wearing tight yellow workout clothes and poised on one foot on a squishy blue mat. Her arms were over her head, and the other knee was bent out to the side, the sole of her foot pressing into her thigh. She looked like some kind of neon-yellow flamingo.

"Good morning," Sabine said without stumbling from her one-legged pose.

"I'm sorry to interrupt," Gwen said sheepishly. She hadn't expected to see anyone on her way back to her room. Especially not at this hour of morning.

"You're not." Sabine smiled and brought her foot back to the floor. "I've been lazy about my yoga while I've been here, and I'm paying for it. I decided to get up before everyone to stretch. My next class back I'll be stiff as a board, and all my students will laugh at me."

Gwen paused at the bottom of the staircase. "You teach yoga? I thought you worked in Adrienne's boutique."

Sabine nodded and knelt down onto her mat. "The yoga is a part-time thing. I teach a couple evening classes and a prenatal one on Saturday mornings." She gestured toward Gwen. "You should come. When I was pregnant, my doctor recommended a prenatal yoga class, and after it, I felt good for the first time in months. After I had my son, I stuck with it, and it really helped me get back into shape."

"I'd love to give that a try. Not only to get in shape, but to help me fill some of the hours. After." When she was alone again.

Sabine nodded sympathetically. "You're doing a wonderful thing, you know? I shouldn't have said what I did the other day about how I could never do something like that. It was thoughtless of me, considering how hard it must be for you and you're doing it anyway."

Gwen shook her head dismissively. "Don't worry about it. It is more difficult than I expected and certainly not something just anyone could do. But it will be worth it."

"Right." Sabine smiled and her purple-striped ponytail swung behind her. "Would you like to try some stretches now?"

Sabine reached into her duffel bag and pulled out a second mat, this one a bright pink. She rolled it out beside her and patted it in invitation. "Just a couple for you to do at home until you can get to a class."

Gwen climbed onto the mat and worked through a set of poses with Sabine that not only made the pain in her back disappear, but stretched out all her other stiff muscles and brought a touch of sweat to her brow. When they were done, she sat back on her heels to do some deep breathing. Going through the motions had cleared her head remarkably. She never imagined something like that could help her think, but if stress and pain were clouding her thoughts, it made perfect sense.

"Can I ask you a personal question?"

"Sure," Sabine said. "I don't have many secrets."

Gwen was a bit ashamed to ask, but she needed someone to talk to about Alex, someone with some distance. She got the feeling that Sabine had some experience where doomed relationships were concerned. "What happened with your son's father?"

"We were just wrong for each other. Attraction trumped all that at first, but it didn't take long to realize it wasn't going to work between us. He was rich, I was poor. He was preoccupied with running his business. I just wanted to enjoy life. It almost killed me, but I broke it off after only a few weeks. I knew it would only get worse the longer I waited. It wasn't until much later that I realized I was already pregnant with his child."

"He didn't want the baby?"

Sabine frowned. "Oh, I'm sure he'd want the baby. That's why I never told him." She shook her head sadly. "I know it sounds like a horrible thing to do. But when I said he was a rich businessman, I also meant powerful, arrogant and controlling. I didn't want Jared to be a pawn in his empire. I refused to give Gavin the opportunity to sue me for full custody just so my son could be raised by nannies and go to boarding school. Honestly, I'm surprised I've gone this long without him showing up at my doorstep demanding his son."

Gwen couldn't help but shake her head in wonder. It

seemed like everyone had their own messes in life to clean up. "That must be stressful, knowing at any time that he could find out."

"You have no idea. But I know leaving was the right choice, so I try to focus on living my life. I'm raising Jared the best I can and making sure he feels loved and wanted. He shouldn't have to suffer because I'm a failure at relationships."

Sabine climbed to her feet and held out a hand to help Gwen up. "Love can be wonderful, but it can also be destructive. I loved Gavin. It was a fierce, passionate romance, but I loved myself too much to lose who I was to him. I couldn't sit around and wait for him to crush my spirit."

"You did the right thing," Gwen said.

"Yes. It's important not to settle," Sabine agreed. "Remember that."

Gwen nodded. It was solid advice, but it sent her mind spinning with what it meant for her after her latest revelation about loving Alex. "Thank you for the advice. And the yoga."

Sabine smiled and waved it off as Gwen disappeared toward her room. Although she eyed the bed when she shut the door, the yoga had invigorated her, and she opted for a hot shower instead.

Gwen felt ashamed for misjudging Sabine that first day. She should know better than to label someone because of their appearance. Perhaps she'd make a point to call her for lunch one day after Peanut was born. It could be one of her steps toward making some real friends and having a life outside work. And she would definitely look into that yoga class. Those poses had worked wonders on her body.

Maybe in time it would also help her with peace of

mind. A little meditation and removal of brain clutter couldn't hurt, at least. The hot water of the shower helped her body relax, but her mind was still spinning a hundred miles an hour from their conversation. She wished she could hook a vacuum to her ear and suck out all the negative thoughts.

Unfortunately, she just wasn't a "glass half-full" kind of girl. Gwen liked to think of herself as a "hope for the best, but plan for the worst" type. What did that mean for her relationship with Alex? That she hoped they'd have a good time together and her heart wouldn't be crushed when he inevitably left?

With a sigh, she rinsed her hair a final time and closed her eyes. That was ridiculous. How could a relationship be solid when she had such a large escape hatch?

It couldn't. And that was part of the problem.

Sabine was right. Gwen shouldn't settle. If she wanted a marriage and family with a great man, she could have it. If it couldn't be with Alex, she needed to accept that. But she shouldn't just sit around and wait for the day Alex left. Each minute she spent with him would make the ending that much more painful, not to mention putting off her chance to meet the right kind of guy. She needed to be proactive. To take control of her life. Right now.

Gwen was putting the last of her things in her suitcase when there was a soft tap at the door. She prayed it wasn't Alex. She wasn't quite sure what she'd say if he saw her packing to leave. It wasn't that long ago that he'd called her a chicken, and he was right. She didn't know how to deal with this.

"It's Adrienne," a voice called through the door.

"Come in." Gwen tossed her toiletry bag into the case and closed it as the door opened.

Adrienne slipped in and shut the door behind her. "You're leaving." It wasn't a question. She knew Gwen well enough to know exactly what was going on without having to ask. The story would be fully hashed out over dinner in a few weeks, when the pain wasn't so fresh and she had enough distance to talk about it.

"I have to. I'm sorry if this ruins your plans for today."

"It wouldn't matter if it did. Do you need me or Will to drive you back?"

"All the way to Manhattan? No, don't be silly. I don't want either of you to cut your vacation short on my account. But I could use a ride to the train station or maybe a jitney stop. Whatever is closer."

"Absolutely. The Hampton Jitney stops down on Main Street. You can probably book a ticket on your phone. I'll just go get my keys."

Gwen zipped her bag and turned to her best friend. Unwelcome tears had gathered in her eyes, but she refused to shed them. She wasn't about to cry while *she* left *him*. That wasn't how it worked. "Thank you."

Adrienne rushed forward and swept Gwen into a hug. "Oh, Gwen," she lamented. "I'm so sorry. I've worried about you ever since I found out what happened."

"I'm so stupid. I can't believe I let myself… I never should've…"

"Fallen in love?"

Gwen pulled away and sniffed back the tears. "With Alexander Stanton! I seriously need therapy or somethin'. I know that if I ever want a real, healthy relationship, I've gotta stop doing this to myself. So I'm leaving. I'm starting fresh. I'm going to have this baby and start living a life open to the possibilities of real love. I deserve happiness."

"Without question. And I have no doubt you'll find it. I'll meet you out front in a minute." Adrienne went out to the kitchen and left Gwen alone for a moment.

She reached over to the dresser and the silver charm bracelet still lying there. She went to slip it on, then paused. She didn't need Alex's gift to protect her anymore. She was open to love and possibilities. Just not with him. Gwen scooped the bracelet up and grabbed her suitcase off the bed.

When she met Adrienne in the living room, she had her purse and keys in hand. "Do you want to leave him a note or something?"

Gwen shook her head. "I doubt he's ever left a note for any of the women he's left. I don't know what I'd put on there anyway." Gwen held out the bracelet to Adrienne. "Could you just give him this and tell him I had to go? He's a smart enough guy to figure out the rest."

Adrienne nodded and held open the front door. They loaded the Land Rover and pulled out of the driveway.

"I've got my ticket booked for eight this morning," Gwen said as they stopped in front of the local movie theater. It was closed at this hour of the morning, and there was almost no one around.

Adrienne glanced down at her watch. "You shouldn't have too long to wait then. Do you want me to stay here with you until it comes?"

"No, I'm fine. You go back to the house and continue having a good vacation with your friends. I expect you to have some more excellent fireworks tonight."

Adrienne nodded and leaned in to give her friend another hug. "Be safe. And call me when you get back to your apartment so I won't worry."

"I will."

Gwen slipped out the car door and pulled her bag from the backseat. The morning sun had just begun shining in earnest as she rolled her suitcase over to the park bench to wait for the bus. She gave a quick wave to Adrienne as she pulled away. Once the car disappeared out of sight, she felt a weight lifted from her chest.

It was just as well she hadn't driven herself. This way, she couldn't lose her nerve and circle back to him.

Alex stood in Gwen's empty bedroom, his eyes burrowing into the cold, empty bed where he'd expected to find her sleeping. The drawers were empty, the toothbrush missing from the counter by the sink. He wasn't quite sure how to process all of this.

He'd woken up alone and thought nothing of it. Alex had slipped out of Gwen's room each night to return to his own before everyone got up. He figured she'd done the same. He'd showered, dressed and headed downstairs in anticipation of the typical Fourth of July activities. He had no reason to think anything was wrong.

Everyone but Gwen was out by the pool, so he'd gone to her room to see if she'd overslept. It was obvious now that she hadn't. She'd woken up early and gotten a head start on them all.

His mind raced through last night and everything that had happened. Gwen had seemed determined not to let Alex pull away from her. And yet today, she was gone. She'd left him without saying a word. What had happened from the time she charged into his room to the moment she'd crept out that would make her decide to go so suddenly?

A dull ache settled in his chest when he sucked

in a breath and the air still smelled like her lavender shampoo.

She'd left him.

Something about the whole thing didn't sit right with him. Maybe it was because Alex had never been left by a woman before. He was always the first to go, the first to decide that things weren't working out. He'd broken it off with his first girlfriend, Tiffany Atwell, in seventh grade after the spring formal, and it was a trend that had continued until now.

Just one more thing that set Gwen apart. For the first time, he'd been left wanting more.

He took a few steps into the room, smoothing his hand over the comforter. It was cold. She'd been gone a while. Confused, Alex sat down on the edge of the bed and stared into the bathroom where her swimsuit should be hanging.

The memory of her in that tiny navy bikini hit him in the gut like a truck. It felt as if the wind had been knocked out of him, his breath stuck in his throat. His chest tightened, the dull ache sharpening to an acute pain.

So this is what it felt like to be dumped, he thought. It sucked. No wonder he'd received so many nasty voice mails and texts over the years from his exes.

A glance at the bedside stand revealed a stray peppermint left behind the base of the lamp. He reached out for it, unwrapping the candy and putting it in his mouth. The strong, fresh bite instantly brought to mind memories of her kisses. Their first on the dance floor at the reception. The one on the pier. In the pool. His mind was suddenly driven to remember them all and savor them as his last.

Not once in his life had he ever ended a relationship

and worried later about forgetting a woman's kisses. But remembering Gwen's seemed important. Too important.

"She left early this morning."

Alex's head snapped to the doorway, where Adrienne was standing, watching him. Her arms were crossed over her chest, but she didn't seem angry. Somehow he expected that Adrienne would lay the blame at his feet for hurting Gwen and driving her away. But there was only sadness in her green eyes.

"Why? I don't understand."

"I think Gwen decided it was for the best. She knew that you two didn't have a future together, and prolonging it was just too painful for her. She's got a bad habit of falling in love with the wrong kind of guy."

"Love?" Alex perked up at Adrienne's choice of words. He hadn't expected to hear that at all. "She's in love with me?"

Her eyes widened as she stumbled for a moment to take back what she'd said. "I...that, I mean...that was just a generalization. I don't know if she loves you or not."

Will was right. He'd said once that Adrienne was a terrible liar. The truth was painted across her face. She'd let her best friend's secret slip. Alex had slowly regained the ability to breathe over the last few minutes, but suddenly the air caught in his lungs, and his heart stilled in his chest. Gwen was in love with him. In love. With him.

And yet, she was gone just the same.

Alex had heard a few women tell him that in his lifetime. Usually as part of a plea to make him reconsider staying. It never worked, because he knew their words were as authentic as their hair color.

But he wanted to hear Gwen say the words to him.
And he'd lost his chance.

"Why would she leave if she loved me?"

Adrienne walked into the room and sat down on the
bed beside Alex. "She finally decided she wants a real,
loving relationship and to start her own family. You and
I both know that you're not willing to give her the life
she wants. And she knows it, too. So as much as it hurt,
she knew she needed to leave before it just got worse."

Alex understood. But usually he was the one to see it
in the woman, and he would be the one to leave.

"She asked me to give you this." Adrienne reached
out and placed Gwen's silver charm bracelet in his hand.

He closed his fist around the cold metal. The one
thing Alex understood about being with Gwen was that
he never knew where he stood with her. She was unlike
any woman he'd ever met, and her mere existence challenged him every day. It made sense that she would be
the first to leave him feeling like crap when it was over.

"Are you going to be okay, Alex?" Adrienne looked
at him with concern in her eyes that he wasn't used to
seeing. At least, not directed at him.

"Me? Oh yeah," he assured her, although the words
sounded hollow to his ears. "You know me."

She nodded and patted his knee, but he could tell
there was a part of her that was just humoring him.
"I'm making buttermilk waffles with strawberries for
brunch, so don't stay in here too long or Will and Jack
will eat them all."

Alex pasted on one of his smiles. "I'll be out in just
a minute."

Adrienne slipped from the room, pulling the door
closed to give him some privacy with his thoughts.
It didn't take much time for him to realize he didn't

want to be alone in Gwen's room any longer. He got up quickly, heading up the stairs to return to his own private sanctuary.

Alone in his room, he felt a bit of the tightness in his chest ease up. The air in here didn't smell like her, which helped. At least until he spied the bundle of dried-up roses sitting on his dresser. When Gwen had returned them, he hadn't known what to do with the flowers, so he'd let them sit. Just as he didn't know what to do with the bracelet she no longer wanted.

Without hesitation, Alex swung his arm across the dresser top, forcefully clearing it and flinging the flowers, the charm bracelet and anything else sitting up there scattering across the floor. Now he wouldn't have to look at it and think of her.

He expected to feel better when everything crashed to the ground, but he didn't. Fortunately, he had an idea of what would help.

If Alex knew anything, it was how to bounce back after a breakup. Playing for the "dumped" team didn't change what happened next.

He'd enjoy the rest of his holiday with his friends. Drink some beers, shoot some fireworks. He would drive back to the city with the top down and soak in the warm summer sunshine. In Manhattan, he'd get a new haircut, buy a new suit and spend a few nights on the town in his favorite haunts. Maybe he'd meet a nice lady to distract him from thinking of Gwen. Perhaps he'd meet a couple ladies. Whatever it took.

Either way, life would get back to normal once he returned to the city. He could focus on work, racquetball, everything, anything, but Gwen. And before too long, she would be a distant memory, just like the others.

Eleven

"Nurse Wright?"

Gwen snapped out of her fog to see one of the doctors on rotation looking at her curiously. "I'm sorry. What did you need?"

Dr. Ellis grinned. "Still in a vacation haze, eh, Gwen?"

She forced a smile and shrugged. "Something like that."

He proceeded to rattle off a list of things she needed to do for one of the patients he'd just checked on. She pulled the woman's file and made a note of it on her chart. "Consider it done."

Pleased, he turned and headed down the hallway. Gwen watched him walk away, thinking about how Dr. Ellis had a smile that reminded her of Alex. The simple thought brought tentative tears to her eyes that she refused to shed.

By the time he'd disappeared around the corner, there was nothing left in her memory but Alex's crooked, sly grin. Unfortunately, that wouldn't help her treat Mrs. Maghee. She glanced down at her notes, relieved. She didn't remember a thing Dr. Ellis had told her, but she'd copied down every word.

Gwen sat back in her rolling office chair behind the nurses' station, disgusted. She needed to get it together. She left him. She needed to stop moping and focus. Her job was important. Her patients depended on her. She couldn't wander around in a lovesick daze.

It had been nearly two weeks since she'd returned home from the Hamptons. Life had gone back to normal. At least, as close as it could be to how life was before she'd gone on vacation. But even in her old routines, something was different.

She was different.

Gwen had always told herself that she lived and breathed her job because she loved it so much. That she didn't need love and family, because her work was so important and fulfilling. Her patients were her family. Her relationship was with the hospital.

As she looked around the sterile halls with the mint-green-and-white tile floors, it was clear the honeymoon of this marriage was over. It wasn't enough for her anymore. She wasn't about to abandon her work, but her universe wasn't going to revolve around it any longer.

When she'd made the decision to leave early and put her relationship with Alex behind her, she'd made a choice to start her life anew. At first, she'd thought packing her bags and walking out would be the hardest part. Once she'd arrived back in Manhattan, she'd realized that was just the first of many difficult steps ahead of her. She had a lifetime of bad habits to break if she wanted to be happy.

But she would do it. The one thing Gwen was determined to do was carry on. She might be the emotional equivalent of a tin man right now, but that wasn't going to stop her. Sabine was right. Gwen deserved a man who would love her and give her all the things she wanted in life, without having to settle.

The last few months carrying Peanut and the few days in the Hamptons with Alex had made it clear that what she wanted was a family of her own. She couldn't keep Alex, and she couldn't keep this baby, but she could have that and more with someone who cared enough to stick around.

Being open to love didn't make her like her mother. And every guy out there was not like her father. Or Alex. There were good men out there who would stay. Like Will. And Robert. She needed to put her issues in a box at the top of the closet and find the right kind of man for her.

A twinge of pain seized Gwen's back. She winced and tried to soothe it with her hand, but it didn't do much good. It was doubtful that even yoga would help. It really had been bothering her the last few hours. Every ten minutes or so, it would flare up something fierce. She must've slept wrong last night. She hadn't slept very well since she'd gotten home. Suddenly the sounds of the city kept her awake, when they'd never bothered her before. Or maybe it was the vacant spot in the bed beside her.

Gwen sighed and moved her hand to her belly. The back pain was a reminder that she had some time to kill—about four months—before she would be ready to put herself back on the market. She hadn't officially resumed her man-break, but if her time in the Hamptons had taught her nothing else, it was that pregnancy made relationships infinitely more complicated. It brought up all these confusing feelings that didn't help an already tricky situation.

But she was determined. She was going to see this surrogacy through and start her new life as the new Gwen. Open, terrified, but unwavering Gwen. She could do this.

"Mama Gwen, are you feeling okay? You look a little pale." The head nurse, a large and nurturing grandmother type named Wilma, approached the nurses' station, a frown lining her plump face.

Once again, Gwen pasted on a smile to cover up the pain. She wasn't about to worry Wilma with her sad tales of heartache and back pain. "I'm fine. Just a little tired. I think I got used to regular hours while I was on vacation."

"Daylight is overrated. Are you sure you're all right?"

Gwen started to nod but was interrupted by a sharp pain that radiated across her abdomen. This one put the backache to shame. She couldn't help the gasp as she clutched her stomach and looked up at Wilma with wide, confused eyes. "Maybe not. Wow, that hurts."

Wilma frowned, coming around the counter faster than one would've expected of a woman of her age and size. She knelt down in front of Gwen to examine her more closely. "Have you had a backache?"

Gwen nodded, biting her lip to keep from yelping and waking up her patients.

"Any spotting?"

"A little at my last lunch break. But that's normal, isn't it?"

"It can be. But not when you add it all together. How many weeks are you now?"

"Almost twenty-five."

Wilma frowned again. "That's about twelve weeks fewer than I'd like. I haven't worked in L and D for about twenty years, but this kind of stuff doesn't change. Mama, I hate to say this, but I think you're going into premature labor."

Alex strode into the temporary office space he leased as the headquarters for his latest building project. It was about a block away from the actual build site of the apartment high-rise, so it was both convenient and spacious for their needs. A local office supply had rented them the furniture, and a temp agency provided a receptionist for the front desk and janitorial staff.

Their temporary admin, Lisa, looked up as he came through the doors, placing a call on hold. "Good morning, Mr. Stanton. I wasn't expecting to see you this morning. Does Miss Jacobs know you're here?"

Alex chuckled softly to himself. "No, I don't believe Tabitha is expecting me." Actually, he knew she wasn't. He'd deliberately not told his project manager he was coming to New Orleans. She was competent, driven, successful... All the things he wanted in an employee. Normally, this meant he could get engaged with the fun, creative parts of starting a new real estate project, then leave her to actually execute the details. That was how he liked it.

Of course, normally, he wasn't hell-bent on getting out of Manhattan before he did something stupid he would regret. He already had enough regrets as it was; he didn't need any more. Especially where Gwen was concerned.

In the weeks since he'd left the Hamptons, he'd tried to continue on with his life as usual, but everything felt wrong somehow. The women were disinteresting, the jokes flat, the drinks bitter or tasteless. Will even beat him at racquetball for the first time. He found himself wandering through his empty penthouse without purpose. As much as he didn't want to admit it, his life didn't seem to work without Gwen in it anymore.

He kept finding himself dialing her number but unable to hit the call button. Instead he would just hang up. Gwen had left him out of self-preservation. Calling her was the worst thing he could do. Especially if he wasn't willing to offer her what she wanted.

And yet, he'd find the phone in his hand again, or ask his driver to cruise past her apartment or the hospital in the hope he'd catch a glimpse of her walking outside.

No luck, so far.

But he was playing with fire. The last time he'd needed to get Gwen out of his head, he'd flown to New Orleans and started this project. It seemed like the best course of action now as well. So he'd gotten on a plane and headed down here unannounced.

"Shall I call and let her know you're here?"

"That won't be necessary, Lisa. I'd like to surprise her."

The look on Lisa's face made it painfully obvious that she knew Tabitha very well. Surprises were not on the top of the list of things she enjoyed. Even a good surprise could piss her off because it messed with her schedule.

That just made it all the more fun.

Although he normally was not involved much past the planning stage, he still maintained an office of his own at each site. He buzzed past Lisa and headed straight for his long-abandoned desk. Flipping on the light, he set down his laptop bag, threw his coat over his chair and headed to the kitchen. He poured a cup of coffee into one of the paper cups and snatched an apple fritter from a pink bakery box on the counter.

Alex took the fritter and carried it down the hall with his coffee. Without ceremony, he walked into Tabitha's office and sat down in her guest chair to eat his breakfast.

She was busily typing at her computer, her pale red-gold hair pulled into a tight bun and her curves stuffed into one of her favorite, unflattering business suits. He could tell by her pinched expression that she knew someone was there, but she hadn't torn her eyes from the screen to see who.

The moment she did look, her expression was a jolt of pure joy he was in sore need of. He'd felt like hell since he'd left the Hamptons. Harassing his project manager was one of his small pleasures in life.

"Alex? I mean, Mr. Stanton? What are you doing here? Is there a problem?"

"Yes," he said, trying to maintain a straight face. "I am very concerned to report a severe shortage of cream-filled doughnuts in this office. It's shameful."

Tabitha's wide violet-blue eyes narrowed at him as her initial panic faded to irritation. "What are you doing here, Alex? In the last six years and seven projects I've executed for you, not once have you shown up during the build phase."

"Can't I come check on how things are going?"

Tabitha sighed and pushed an imaginary loose strand of hair behind her ear. "Of course. And everything is fine. Great. We're ahead of schedule. Under budget. We've secured contracts for over half the units already, and we're on track to being completely sold out before the last inch of drywall is painted."

Alex nodded, pleased with the progress. "You're worth every penny I pay you, Tabitha."

"I'm probably worth a few more than you pay me."

He had to admit he liked her sass. He'd date her if it wouldn't ruin their perfect work situation. Even a man with a reputation like his had boundaries. No ex-anythings of friends, no sisters of friends, no employees and no nurses. That last one was a new addition.

"Remind me to give you a raise when this project is done, then."

Tabitha opened up her calendar software, typed a note into her computer and nodded. "Done. Now, tell me why you're really here. Who is she? Is it the same woman you were down here hiding from last time?"

"I was not hiding," Alex said, setting his coffee cup forcefully on the edge of her desk.

Tabitha shrugged off his display of male aggression, picking her smartphone up off the desk as it started to buzz. Her eyes never left the small screen as she spoke to her boss. "Call it what you like. You were completely unfocused when you were here before. I assumed it was a woman."

Defeated, Alex took a bite of his fritter. "It was."

"And this time?"

"Same one."

This finally caught Tabitha's attention. Her eyebrow arched curiously at him. "Sounds serious."

"It's not. I don't *do* serious."

"Which explains why you're here with me instead of there with her."

Damn his ability to hire smart, capable women. They saw far more than he wanted them to see. "Possibly."

Tabitha sighed and pushed up from her chair. "I've got an on-site meeting with the head contractor in ten minutes. Are you going to walk down there with me?"

Alex drank the last of his coffee and tossed his napkin into her trash can. "Yes," he said with the last mouthful of apple fritter garbling his words.

She nodded and marched out the door. He followed behind Tabitha, finding her waiting impatiently at the elevator. "So how long are you going to be around?" she asked as they waited for the car to arrive at their floor.

Honestly, Alex wasn't really sure. How long did it take to get over a woman? He'd never been involved enough with one to know. But he rounded up to goad his project manager. "A couple weeks at least."

Tabitha didn't even have the decency to muffle the groan of displeasure as the elevator doors opened.

There were no more discussions once they reached the street. The central business district was busy and loud this time of day, reminding Alex of Manhattan. Part of their building design centered around heavily insulated walls and double-paned windows specifically crafted for soundproofing. You could close your eyes and convince yourself you were in the country, it was so quiet. No sirens, no honking, no neighbors' music or arguing.

The people buying his apartments wanted to be at the center of the New Orleans excitement and energy but wanted to keep the luxury and security they were accustomed to. Stanton Towers would provide all of that for an astronomical fee, and yet, he usually had waiting lists of well-off clients chomping at the bit to get into one of his facilities.

The site was currently a mess of construction. Alex was typically not involved in this phase. Cement and jackhammers were not of interest to him. Right now, the steel skeleton of the high-rise stretched nearly ten stories in the air. That was about two-thirds of its final height. A large chain-link fence enclosed the site and protected passersby from the heavy equipment and chaos surrounding the project.

Tabitha paused outside the fence and grabbed a hard hat. She handed one over to Alex, then glanced down at his shoes. "I hope those aren't expensive."

"Of course they are," he responded irritably, then realized they were about to walk through the dirt and mud to the large trailer where the site manager operated. He glanced down at Tabitha's shoes, expecting heels, and found that with her suit, she was wearing steel-toed work boots. You didn't see that every day, but she was nothing if not prepared.

"Nice look. Do you wear those shoes on the first date?" he asked as they started off to the trailer.

Tabitha frowned. "I keep these at the office for trips like this. My other shoes are tucked safely under my desk for when I get back. And for any dates that might pop up. If you ever stuck around for the dirty work, you'd have seen these already."

Alex tried to step carefully the first few feet, then realized Tabitha would leave him in her dust before too long. She was a no-nonsense woman. Probably just the kind to give him the straight answers he needed right now. The question was whether or not he wanted to hear it. "Tabitha, you're a woman," he said.

"Last time I checked," she said, drily.

"Let me ask you something about women."

"Oh, lord," she groaned, turning in her boots to face him. "I don't have time for this, Alex, so here's a quick tip. Whatever you've done, apologize and beg her to take you back."

"What makes you think I did something?"

Tabitha didn't respond, but crossed her arms over her chest and sighed heavily.

"Okay, I know I'm typically guilty of something, but this time *she* left *me*."

Alex regretted having this conversation with Tabitha immediately. Watching his uptight, driven manager crumble into a fit of hysterical laughter was too much. "You… got…*dumped?*" she asked between hard-fought breaths.

"Will you stop laughing? This is serious. She's in love with me," he blurted out.

The laughter faded and Tabitha fought to hold her composure. "Poor woman. Running was probably the right choice. But don't act like you didn't give her a reason to leave."

"She decided I was a flight risk if I found out the truth, and she left before I could."

"You *are* a flight risk. And a jerk if you're even considering chasing after her if you're not serious about this. Do you love her, Alex?"

That was the sixty-five-thousand-dollar question. He thought he didn't believe in love. That if it existed, he was immune to it. But these last few weeks without Gwen had been absolute torture. He'd lain awake at night, thinking about the time they'd spent together in that very bed. Every show on television or song on the radio somehow reminded him of her. And the worst part was this constant, dull ache in his chest that refused to go away no matter how many antacids he took.

Was that what love felt like? He had no clue. No basis for comparison. All he knew was that he'd never felt like

ANDREA LAURENCE 167

this after a relationship ended. If this was love, it was no wonder Gwen opted to leave when she had realized she loved him. Love could seriously suck when things weren't going right. He could only hope it felt better when the relationship was doing well.

"I don't know. I've never been in love before. But I can't stop thinking about her. I'm absolutely miserable."

"I hate to tell you this, but it sounds like love to me."

Alex's heart skipped a beat in his chest when Tabitha confirmed the thought that had been plaguing him for days. Love. *Love* was a big, scary word for a guy like Alex. Just saying it out loud might break him out in hives. He wasn't programmed for monogamy. He didn't even know what step to take next. "But I don't know how to fix things between us. No matter what I say, Gwen will never trust me to stay."

Tabitha glanced down at her watch, then back at Alex. "Here's your last tip, then I'm going into that trailer for my meeting, alone. This woman loves you. I have no idea why. If you love her, you need to go to her and beg her to give you a chance to prove her wrong. Offer her everything she wants and *deliver* on it."

Alex swallowed hard. Going to Gwen would mean offering everything he'd avoided his whole life: commitment, love, trust. And those things he'd never thought he wanted: marriage, children, domesticity. But he wanted it with her. If she'd give him the opportunity to try.

"You're right."

"Of course I'm right. Now, get your ass on a plane back to New York and get out of my hair. I don't want to see you again until the final walk-through before the ribbon-cutting ceremony."

Tabitha turned on her heel and disappeared, leaving

Alex to make his way back through the obstacle course of the construction site.

He took a different route, this time heading back toward his hotel instead of the office. He needed some time to process what Tabitha had said. In a matter of minutes, her take-no-prisoners attitude had cut through all the mental crap he'd been bogged down in for days. He loved Gwen. He knew that now. And if he wanted her, he had to be willing to offer her the life and the family she deserved.

But he had to do something to prove to her that he was serious. He needed to knock on her door with an engagement ring in his hands. But not just any ring. Gwen wouldn't be convinced by some vulgar and generic display of diamonds. She'd want something authentic. Something that was distinctly hers. Gwen was like no other woman, and she deserved a ring like no other. Knowing he'd put the thought into the purchase would be what made the difference for her.

Alex started on the hunt for a jewelry store. With the help of his phone, he located and rejected several shops. They all had fine products, but nothing in the store said Gwen. Looking down on his phone, he noticed there was an antiques and estate jeweler a couple blocks past the hotel. Maybe that was what he needed. A vintage piece.

By the time he reached the shop window, he'd been wandering around New Orleans for more than two hours. Waiting to catch his breath before he went inside, he admired the front display. A large and varied collection of jewelry was in the window, protected by decorative but sturdy wrought-iron bars.

After hours of fruitless searches, he was surprised to find that one of the rings called to him immediately. He leaned in to look closer. The platinum-and-gold antique

filigree setting was inset with tiny diamonds around
the thin band. In the center was a large yellow oval-cut
stone in a ring of additional tiny diamonds.

It was bright and sunny yet extremely detailed and
complicated. It was Gwen in jewel form. Curious, he
went inside the store and summoned the old man behind the counter. He unlocked the case and took the
ring with him back to the white pad where he displayed
jewelry for buyers.

"You have a good eye. It's the best piece in my whole
shop. I suppose most people don't realize what it is or
think it's citrine or some type of costume jewelry."

Alex frowned. "What is it?"

"A three-carat canary diamond. I bought it thirty-five
years ago from the estate auction of an old New Orleans
family. Their great-great-grandfather brought it here
from France in the 1760s. Rumor is it was given as a gift
to a lover of King Louis the Sixteenth, who popularized
the use of platinum in Europe. I've got bulletproof glass
and bars on the windows for a reason, sonny."

It was beautiful, rare and priceless. Alex couldn't be
sure how much of the old man's yarn was truth and how
much was fiction to justify the price, but it didn't really
matter as long as the certification paperwork held up. If
he was lucky, Gwen might not even know how valuable
a ring she was wearing. If she accepted it. And he had
no guarantee that she would. "I'll take it."

The old man's eyes widened. "Don't you want to
know how much it is?"

Alex shrugged. "It doesn't matter."

"Well," he chuckled, "okay then. I'll box this up and
get the paperwork for it together. You feel free to look
around while you wait, and see if there's anything else
you might need at an irrelevant price."

A few minutes later, Alex walked out of the store with the ring securely tucked into the breast pocket of his suit coat. He moved with more purpose now. He finally had some direction. He was going back to New York. He was going to tell Gwen that he loved her. That he wanted to marry her. Have children with her. That he wouldn't get scared and run away, and he wasn't going to let her run, either.

He could only hope that, after everything that had happened, she would believe him.

Twelve

Alex made a quick stop at his hotel. He grabbed his things, checked out and headed straight to the office. He asked Lisa to get on the phone and change his flight, and he grabbed his laptop from his desk. Thirty minutes later, he was downstairs waiting for the car to take him to the airport.

When his phone rang, he almost ignored it. He was too hyped up on love and adrenaline to let business or family drama bring him down. But he couldn't help looking to see who it was. It was Adrienne's cell phone.

Alex frowned and knew he had to answer. Adrienne never called him. Only Will. "Adrienne," he said, tentatively.

"Where are you, Alex?"

"I'm in New Orleans. But I'm getting on a flight back to LaGuardia shortly."

"Why? Did someone already call you?"

"Call me? No. About what?"

"About Gwen."

Alex's heart sank like a stone in his chest. Why would someone call him about Gwen? "What about her? Is she okay? Has something happened? Is the baby okay?"

Adrienne was silent on the phone for half a heartbeat, making Alex almost ready to leap through the receiver and shake her until she told him what was going on. "They're both fine...now."

He breathed a ragged sigh of relief, but he could tell there was more to the story. "What's happened?"

"She went into premature labor while she was at work last night. Luckily, her supervisor realized what was happening and took her downstairs. They immediately admitted her."

"Labor? What? She's only, like, six months along. Why would she have gone into labor?"

"I know. They're not sure why it happened, because she has so many weeks left and no real risk factors. That's why it's so serious. They've got her on some very strong intravenous medication to stop the contractions. They seem to have done the trick for now. But the next few months will be rough. She's going to be on mandatory bed rest. She has to take leave from work, and she won't be able to afford to keep her apartment on her reduced pay. Anything could start up the contractions again, and if her water breaks, they'll have to risk delivery no matter how far along she is."

Alex gripped his skull with his free hand. Picturing Gwen alone in a hospital bed, fearful for the baby's life, was eating him up inside. He felt helpless. "What can I do?"

"Come back. She'll kill me for doing this, but if you care at all for her, come back to New York. Be here for her. She'd never admit it, but she needs you to get through this. I lied the day she left the Hamptons, because I was trying to protect her. Gwen loves you, Alex. She's just scared of being hurt."

"I know," he said solemnly. "I love her, too."

Adrienne muttered a soft curse. "You love her? Really? The mighty Alexander Stanton has fallen?"

Alex supposed he deserved all this, but he would be the willing butt of all the jokes after he was back and he knew Gwen and the baby were safe. "Yes. I'm in love with her. That's why I was coming back to New York. I wanted to tell her that I wasn't going to let her run away from us. My flight gets in this afternoon. I'll go straight to the hospital from there."

"Call me when you get here, and I'll get you her new room number. They're moving her to a regular room this afternoon."

Alex said goodbye and hung up the phone. He couldn't get to New York fast enough. Gwen was in the hospital. Both her life and the baby's were potentially in danger. She was stable now, but what if something horrible happened and he never got to tell her how he felt? What if she lost the baby and he was a thousand miles away hiding in his work?

He couldn't bear the thought. She'd already shared with him her fears about the future and facing it alone. She certainly didn't need to go through this by herself. From now on, he wasn't going to hide from his feelings. He was going to tell her the truth as soon as he could.

No more regrets. Starting right now.

Gwen hated hospitals. It was a strange realization, given she worked in one. As a nurse, it was fine, but being a patient was the ultimate torture for any medical professional. Take your medicine. Eat your lime gelatin. Stay in bed. Listen to the medical advice of some twelve-year-old nurse who graduated from junior high while Gwen was graduating from nursing school.

Torture.

She would do whatever she had to do for Peanut's sake, but she wasn't going to be happy about it. Bed rest. Twelve to fourteen weeks of it. Absolute misery. She wanted to go home, and they promised she would be released soon, but that was little consolation. She would have enough short-term disability through work, but the reduced pay would barely cover her rent. And the doctor would not be pleased to know she lived alone in a fifth-floor walk-up she could barely afford.

That would mean either being lifted via crane into her apartment for the duration of her pregnancy or breaking down and staying with Adrienne and Will. Robert and Susan would help however they could, but they weren't in the financial position to pay her lost wages or put her up in a hotel. Their place was a slightly larger version of her own postage-stamp apartment. Letting go of her place and staying with Adrienne was the logical choice, as much as it pained her.

She hated this feeling of helplessness almost as much as she hated hospitals.

Gwen fought the urge to roll into a more comfortable position. The drugs had put a halt to the contractions, but they were taking every precaution. The doctor said it was best to lie on her left side, which was her least comfortable side, of course. It also put her back to the door of her room, so people were constantly sneaking up on her. At the very least, she wished her door would creak so she would know when someone was coming in.

"Gwen?"

At the sound of her name, Gwen jumped. Once again, someone had come in and startled her. After the sudden panic faded, a new fear crept into her mind. That voice. A man's voice.

Alex's voice.

Gwen leaned back to look over her shoulder. Alex was standing a few feet away from the bed, a small bundle of daisies in his hand. Knowing Alex, she'd figured he would show up with the largest, most expensive arrangement the hospital gift shop had to offer. The daisies were a charming, and unexpected, touch.

The doctor told her to try to avoid stressful situations, but what could she do when one walked into her hospital room? She wanted to roll back over and pretend he wasn't there, but that wasn't going to make it less stressful. Instead, she sat up and hit the button to bring the back of her bed up to a seated position. She fidgeted with smoothing out her hair and straightening her gown, but it was a lost cause.

She didn't say anything to him at first. She couldn't quite find the right words. First, there was a part of her that was embarrassed for running out without telling him goodbye. It was the coward's way out, but she never claimed to be brave when it came to relationships. Then there was the part of her pride that was wounded when he hadn't chased after her. She hadn't run with the intent of being chased, but it certainly would've been nice to know he cared enough to follow her.

There'd been no word from him since the holiday, but now he was showing up out of the blue with flowers. It made her wonder if she ever would've seen him again if she wasn't in the hospital. If not, she shouldn't read too much into his being here.

Gwen glanced down, uncomfortably, and noticed his

brown leather loafers were caked in dried mud and dirt. "Where on earth have you been?"

"New Orleans. I went to check on my high-rise, but I was coming back to see you when Adrienne called me."

A likely story. She wanted to believe that his being here had nothing to do with her condition, but it was doubtful. Adrienne had likely asked him to come, hoping it would make her feel better to see him. "There's no need to rush back here. I'm fine. Peanut is fine. We've just got to take it easy for a few months."

Alex nodded, his face unusually somber. "These are for you." He took a few steps forward to place the daisies on the table by her bed.

Gwen admired them for a moment. There were no roses or expensive lilies this time. Just a fresh bundle of white daisies with bright yellow centers. Despite her reluctance to accept his gift, they made her smile. They were her favorite flower, although there was no way he could know that. They grew wild on her grandparents' farm when she was a child. She would pick handfuls of them and her grandma would put them in a vase on the kitchen table.

"Thank you for the flowers."

Alex stood a few feet away, his posture unusually awkward. He appeared to be at quite a loss as to what to do with himself, which was odd for a man who was always in control of everything. "When Adrienne called, she mentioned you would have to take some time off work. I, uh, was thinking you might need someplace to stay for a few months. You know that my place has more than enough room. I'd have someone come in to cook for you. You wouldn't have to worry about bills or stairs or anything until the baby arrived safely."

Gwen's gaze narrowed at him. Part of her had hoped

he was here to make some romantic gesture, but she never once believed he was actually here to offer that same old song and dance again. "Did Adrienne ask you to do this?"

His gold eyes widened at the sudden venom in her voice. "What? No. She just told me you were on bed rest. I thought that—"

"You thought what, Alex? That you could just waltz in here like my knight in shining armor and I would be grateful for any scraps you threw my way? Don't you think next week's fling will wonder why there's a grumpy pregnant woman hiding away in your apartment like Mr. Rochester's crazy wife in *Jane Eyre?*"

He swallowed hard before he spoke. "That's not at all what I was thinking. I was just offering what I could to make your situation less stressful. I'm certain I've already caused you enough stress as it is. I'm sorry that you felt you had no other choice but to leave. I tried to call you over a dozen times after you left."

Gwen couldn't take her cell phone with her to work, but she was good about checking for voice mail or missed calls. "I didn't get any messages from you."

"That's because I never hit Send. I worried that you were right. That leaving was the best thing for you. I didn't want to drag you back into it if you wanted so desperately to be rid of me. So I decided to go to New Orleans and focus on work and let you get over me, if that's what you wanted."

Gwen only wished he was that easy to get over. The reality had been much tougher, even though she had been the one to leave. "But you said you were coming to see me, even before Adrienne called."

"Yes." He cleared his throat. "I was coming to tell you that I…"

Alex hesitated and she watched a touch of color drain from his face. His pupils were fully dilated, a touch of moisture breaking out across his brow.

"Are you about to pass out?" she asked. "Do I need to hit the call button for the nurse? I can't get up to catch you if you—"

"I love you, Gwen." Alex spit the words out as quickly as he could. It almost made her wonder if she'd heard him wrong. He could just as easily have said, "I loathe blue gin," although that would have been random and out of context.

"What did you say?" she asked. If he'd said what she thought he'd said, she wanted to hear it again. Louder and slower. Even if it made him squirm. Especially if it did.

Alex walked over to the bed and eased down beside her. He gently scooped up her hand, careful not to disturb her IV, and held it. "I…love you. You took my heart with you when you left, and I've had nothing but an aching hole in my chest these last few weeks. I'm stupid and stubborn, and it took me way too long to figure all this out. But I want to spend the rest of my life with you. I want to get married and have children of our own. I want to wake up every morning with you in my arms."

She'd always worried that Alex was too smooth for his own good and she would never be able to tell when he really meant what he said. But there was no doubt in her mind that he spoke the absolute truth to her now. There was a painful sincerity in the tone of his voice with no hint of his usual charming mischievousness. Alex was serious. And Gwen was dumbstruck. She couldn't even form the words that she loved him, too. All she could do was reach out to brush his honey-colored hair from his eyes. She let her hand linger on his cheek, his eyes closing as he leaned into her touch.

"When Adrienne called and said you were in the hospital with complications, there was this horrible moment where I thought I might've lost you forever. Or that something had happened to Peanut. I know she's not our child, but she's as close as I've ever come, and it would hurt just as badly to lose her. And to watch you go through that, knowing there was nothing I could do to help, would've broken my heart."

"I was so scared, Alex."

He leaned in to hug her, and the tears she'd been holding back since she was admitted to the hospital came rushing all at once. At first, she'd been too concerned to waste time crying, and then she hadn't had more than a few moments alone, with Adrienne, Robert and Susan hovering over her. Now, in Alex's arms, the dam broke.

"All I could keep thinking was that I'd messed up. And how crushed Robert and Susan would be if something happened to their little girl. I'd tried to do everything right. I just had one job—to keep their baby safe—and somehow, I'd failed."

"You didn't do anything wrong, Gwen," he whispered into her hair before sitting back to look her in the eye. "Sometimes these things happen. You're lucky you work at a hospital and had people around you who could help. It could've been so much worse. But everything is fine now. You and Peanut are safe. The doctors are going to keep a close eye on you. And like it or not, you're coming to live with me at least until she's born, if not for the rest of your life."

Gwen pulled back, the irritation on her face poorly disguised. "Now, what makes you think that telling me you love me gives you any more right to boss me around than before?"

"You're right," he conceded. "You're a grown woman who makes her own decisions. But I would very much like you to come stay with me. My apartment has felt cold and lonely since I got home. The memories of the weeks we'd spent there together were like ghosts, haunting me. I'd like us to make some new memories there. Unless you'd rather stay with Will and Adrienne...." He smiled.

At that, Gwen knew her argument was lost. It was one thing to be forced into staying with someone because they felt you couldn't take care of yourself. It was another entirely when they loved you and wanted to keep you safe and healthy. And she wanted to be with Alex. Just not as a burden. Her soft groan of defeat was enough encouragement for him.

"You're going to have the most comfortable and luxurious bed rest any pregnant woman has ever had. I'm not taking any chances with your health and welfare. The whole flight back here, I worried that I'd almost lost my chance. That because I was afraid to chase after you, you might never know how much I loved you."

"I knew," she whispered, a small smile curling her lips. "I was just waiting for you to get with the program."

Alex returned her smile. "I wish you would've told me that and saved me the last few weeks of angst."

"You wouldn't have listened. You needed to figure it out for yourself."

He nodded. "You're probably right. Does this mean that you'll agree to come stay at my place until the baby is born and possibly never move out?"

"Yes. I don't care if I ever see my miserable little apartment again."

"And you forgive me for letting a woman as great as you almost slip through my fingers?"

"Yes."

"And does it mean that you still love me, too? A little birdie told me that you did, but I want to hear it from the source."

"Yes. I do love you."

His hazel gaze searched her face for a moment, absorbing her answer before he spoke again. "Then I have one last question. And I hope that the answer to it will be yes, as well."

Gwen's breath caught in her throat. Just a minute earlier he'd mentioned marriage and children, but those were abstract plans for the future from a man who had just started wading into the commitment pool. If he was about to say what it sounded like he was going to say, some very concrete plans were about to be put in place.

Alex reached into his coat pocket and pulled out a small red box. "Will you, Miss Gwen Wright, do me the honor of being my wife?"

The top opened to a most unexpected find. The ring had a large yellow stone, surrounded by tiny diamonds and set into an intricate two-tone band with more tiny diamonds inset. It was beautiful. And unique. It had an antique feel about it, which made her think it was probably very old. Maybe a family heirloom. She would've been happy with any ring he gave her, but she appreciated him making the effort to give her something different.

Gwen knew in that moment that he really did love her and had for even longer than he knew. He'd paid attention to her, noticed the details, knew what she liked, put

her needs first, bought her things to make her happy...
It had just taken him this long to realize all those things
were the actions of a man in love.

Tears filled her eyes again, but at last, they were
happy tears. He wanted to marry her. Alex Stanton—
the man who made her laugh, made her smile, made her
feel like the sexiest woman on earth—was going to settle down with her. A nobody from Tennessee who had
wondered, not two days earlier, if she might be lonely
her whole life. "Yes."

Alex grinned wide and leaned in to gently embrace
her again. Gwen closed her eyes and relished the feel
of being in his arms—the warm scent of his skin and
cologne mingling, the heat of his body scalding her
through the thin cotton of her hospital gown. When he
pulled away, it was only to slip the ring on her finger
and kiss her properly.

On her long, lonely bus ride back to the city, Gwen
had searched her mind for their last kiss. It had been
nothing but a quick peck before they'd fallen asleep
in his room. It pained her to know that might be the
last kiss she ever shared with Alex. Now, with his lips
against hers and their futures intertwined, she no longer needed to worry. They would have many kisses to
fill her memory for years to come.

She never wanted to let him out of her arms' reach
again. And soon, she wouldn't have to.

"Now, I hate to go, but there's so much for me to
do before you're discharged. I'm going to go back to
my place and get it ready for you. If you give me your
keys, I'll have movers boxing up everything you own
before the end of the day. I'll handle everything, including talking to your landlord. I also have to make a very

important trip to my insurance agent to get that ring properly protected."

Gwen looked down at her engagement ring in a moment of confusion. It was beautiful, but was an insurance policy really necessary? Then it hit her. She examined it more closely and shook her head. "I suppose this isn't a really nice golden topaz, is it?"

Alex grinned and shook his head. "Would it make you feel better if I told you it was?"

Gwen shook her head and gazed at her ring again in amazement. A giant canary diamond. So typically Alex.

"Before I go, is there anything else I can do for you?"

"Loving me is enough." She smiled, then Peanut kicked at her. Gwen felt the relief wash over her, feeling the baby move again after the last twenty-four hours. Everything was going to be okay. She knew it now.

"But, if you don't mind smuggling in a hot fudge sundae…"

Epilogue

"I'm really starting to hate this car."

Alex frowned as he reached down to help Gwen out of the convertible. She was no longer pregnant, but only a couple weeks out from delivery, she was still too sore to climb out of the low bucket seats of his Corvette without help.

"We're getting married and having children. I am throwing away my little black book and putting my salacious ways behind me. But I draw the line at getting rid of this car. I will buy you a more sensible car of your own, if you insist."

Gwen eased up and planted a kiss on his pouty mouth. "I would never ask you to get rid of your baby. Maybe we could just put some monster truck wheels on it." She patted his shoulder playfully and the light sparkled off her engagement ring. The yellow oval diamond was dazzling in its antique setting, hit by the

sunlight as it peeked through the bare branches and falling autumn leaves.

Alex took her hand and led her to the fellowship
hall of the Trinity Wall Street Episcopal Church, where
they were holding the belated baby shower. "I feel like
I should've brought a gift," Gwen said, as they slipped
through the heavy oak doors.

"I think you brought the baby, honey."

Gwen laughed and shook her head. "I still should've
picked up something."

The hall was decorated in white and pink for a combined welcome celebration and baby shower. When
Gwen was hospitalized, Robert and Susan had decided
to hold out on having a shower. Now that Abigail was
a healthy, happy, fifteen-day-old girl, party time had
arrived.

The hall was filled with round tables, each alternating with pink or white tablecloths and centerpieces with
bottles or candles. A spread of catered food lined one
long table and ended in an adorable three-tiered diaper
cake that had "Welcome Abby" in alphabet blocks along
the bottom. Beside it was a large sheet cake with "Con-
gratulations!" written on it in pink icing.

"Gwen!" Susan shouted from across the hall.

The crowd of people milling around all stopped to
look in her direction. She had no doubt that they all
knew who she was. Susan had been touting her as some
sort of sacred vessel to anyone who would listen. It made
Gwen a little uncomfortable, but one look into Susan's
excited face melted it all away.

Susan came through the crowd with a white bundle
in her arms. Abby was dressed in a pale pink and lace
gown that had been in Susan's family for generations.
Through the last few weeks of Gwen's bed rest, Susan

had spent a lot of time with her. They'd chatted for hours about her plans for the nursery, her excitement about motherhood and details of Gwen's upcoming wedding. One day, Susan had brought the gown with her so Gwen could see it.

Gwen gently reached across the baby to hug Susan and smiled down at the tiny ivory-and-pink face of the most beautiful baby girl in the world. Despite the excitement, she was out cold in her mother's arms.

"Would you like to hold her? I feel bad that you haven't gotten to see her since you were discharged."

"Susan, she's your baby, not mine. You don't have to share custody with me."

Gwen stroked her finger along Abby's fat little cheek and whispered, "Hello, my Peanut." The baby stirred slightly at the sound of her voice, smiling sweetly in her sleep.

"What about you, Alex? You can get a little practice in for all those babies you'll be having soon."

Alex's eyes grew wide with panic, but before he could argue, the tiny infant was thrust into his uncertain arms. Gwen watched with amusement as he looked down at the baby as if she might sprout another head or start leaking something on him. But then, after a few moments, his expression softened and he watched Abby with a sense of newfound wonder.

Gwen felt the tiny prickle of tears as he gently swayed with her and hoped that one day soon, she would see him holding their own child just like this. "You're a natural."

"I've got a surprise for you," Susan said, pulling her away from the touching sight.

"For me? Why?"

"Robert and I talked about it, and we thought this would be a wonderful way to say thank-you."

Robert came over to them with a copy of the freshly issued birth certificate in his hands. After the adoption was finalized, it had to be redone with Susan's name as the legal mother. Gwen looked at it and was surprised to find the name *Abigail Gwendolyn Thatcher* written there.

"I thought you were naming her Abigail Rose?"

"We were, but we thought naming her after you would make it more meaningful. We always want Abby to know how special she is and how a wonderful person sacrificed so much to give her to us."

Now the tears were rolling in earnest. Gwen embraced Susan and then gave a hug to the reluctant Robert.

"They're crying again," he said to Alex. Apparently he had gotten his fill of crying women at the hospital the day Abby was born.

Alex shrugged. "They do that. As the father to a daughter, I suggest you get prepared. Here," he said, holding out Abby. "Hand one of them the baby. That will distract them."

Robert gave Abby over to Susan, who immediately stopped crying and started smiling again at the sight of her little girl.

Alex came up beside Gwen and wrapped his arm around her waist. "I never knew your name was Gwendolyn," he admitted.

"That's okay," she said with a smile as she stood on her toes to give him a kiss. "We've got our whole lives to learn everything we need to know about each other."

Alex gave her a sly grin and bent down to kiss her again. "I'm looking forward to every minute of it."

* * * * *

LET'S TALK
Romance

For exclusive extracts, competitions
and special offers, find us online:

- facebook.com/millsandboon
- @MillsandBoon
- @MillsandBoonUK

Get in touch on 01413 063232